LOVE'S DREAM

Chastity's mind was far from her room as her tired body relaxed in the warm water of her bath. Her dreams were of a man with the lightest blue eyes in the handsomest, tan face that she had ever seen, so she did not hear the door to her room gently open, nor did she see the man standing over her still form as she restesd in the tub.

But when sh felt a splash of water hit her face, her green eyes flew open with fright. The fear was instantly replaced by a smile of pure pleasure as she saw before her the same eyes and face that had been plaguing her dreams.

"Ah, my little lady, you looked so beautiful lying back with your eyes shut and that wondrous look on your face. Tell me what you were dreaming of, my sweet?" Deke's tender voice filled her ears, as he bent down to the rim of the tub.

Chastity shook her head, too embarrasseds to tell him of her thoughts.

Deke's strong arms lifted her from the water; then he sat down and brought her gently down upon his lap. "Let us partake of your dreams, only this time they shall not be dreams and you shall not dream them alone." His words were whispered against her soft pink lips, before his mouth gathered them to his own. . . .

HISTORICAL ROMANCE IN THE MAKING!

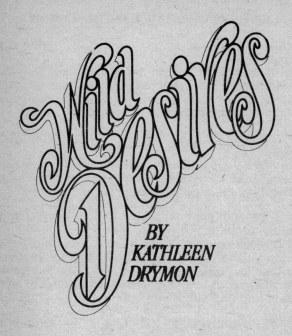

Wild Desires

BY
KATHLEEN DRYMON

ZEBRA BOOKS
KENSINGTON PUBLISHING CORP.

ZEBRA BOOKS

are published by

KENSINGTON PUBLISHING CORP.
475 Park Avenue South
New York, N.Y. 10016

Printed in the United States of America

With all my love and thanks to Ronnie, Kim, Bubby, and Kellie.

Christine
(1708)

Chapter One

Copper-gold tresses flowed freely and without any hindrance down to the young girl's trim waist. The young woman-girl sat primly upon a worn sofa. Her dark violet-blue eyes looked up from the chipped teacup she held in her smooth white hand. "Once more then, Mother." Her finely chiseled features showed a bit of irritation as she looked across the small space of the room, to the frail gray-haired woman sitting on the only other piece of furniture that graced the room. "Please may I have a bit more tea?" The teacup she extended had held at one time a brief design of flowers on its side, but with extensive use and age the well-valued object was now chipped and the lilies worn from view.

The scene within the small room seemed somewhat out of place. The two women, one a young beauty, behaving with all the grace and refinement that any well-brought-up young lady of that day should proclaim, the other, obviously a worn and tattered creature of low degree, also acted the part of lady enjoying her afternoon tea.

"May I be excused now, Mother?" Dark brows rose archingly, as the girl half rose from the old sofa. Her thoughts were already outside the small though well-scrubbed, plain, dank room.

The eyes that rose to the young girl's seemed as old and tired as time itself. The young girl's mother sighed loudly then forced a smile on her thin lips. "Yes, yes child, you have done fine for today. I feel a bit tired. I think I shall lie down for a time. Do not be too late, dear." The old woman rose wearily from the chair and brought her hand to her head as though in pain.

"We shall have our soup early this evening. It is getting colder nights now and without any heat it is better to be abed instead of stomping about in the cold."

The young girl noticed as though it were a revelation that her mother was getting older. She sat and watched her mother as she left the room and entered another.

Red-gold locks glowed down her slender back as the girl left the front door of the hovel that she called her home. Though her dress was patched and mended she walked with an air of genteel breeding and refinement that none about her could match. What was it that someone had once said? "That Tate girl walks as though she is royalty and owns the world."

"Christine, Christine." The call came from a male voice across the street. "Where ye be off to? I were aiming to come and visit with ye for a spell." The dirty, unkempt young man who ran across the street and walked at a pace with the young girl continued, "I dinna want to knock at yer door for fear yer mum would answer. It's glad I was when I sees ye step out of the door."

"Aye, me mum's not too pleased to see ye come about, Bobby." The girl's manner seemed to change once she left her mother's house. Her carriage remained straight and regal, but her voice seemed to instantly pick up the lisp of the inhabitants of the street, and her violet-blue eyes seemed to harden with an almost flint-like glint.

"Where be ye bound for, gal? I'll walk with ye if ye like?" Like that of all street youths, the young man's glance constantly swung about, never knowing when an opportunity would turn up in his favor.

The streets of London were jammed at this bustling time of day. Venders shouted the price of their wares, old women walking back and forth across the streets shouted out for old rags, for anything anyone wanted to part with for a modest price. Fruit peddlers pushed their carts and called out, "Fresh fruit, fresh fruit for sale," to the people passing by.

Christine's deep blue eyes took it all in as though viewing the scene for the very first time, when in fact she had been born on these streets and had used them as her playground as a child.

Her mother had not been able to feed herself and her child and also to pay someone to keep an eye on her daughter while she worked every day of the week for the gentry at sewing, cooking, or cleaning. Her mother was not above doing the most menial chores to insure that her daughter would have a loaf of bread for her supper. And while her mother worked her fingers to the bone, Christine ran wild with the other street children during the day, returning home to a house and mother completely different from that outside world.

Every day Christine went through the same ordeal with her mother, playacting at a make-believe tea party, showing her mother her stitching and always talking in refined speech while inside their small home. Her mother had learned well from the swells she worked for, and all this she taught her daughter, swearing that one day her beautiful little girl with the long red-gold curls and deep violet eyes would be a fine lady, with fancy gowns to adorn that perfect form, golden shoes to fit snugly against her tiny feet, and fine, beautiful carriages to carry her about the London streets.

Christine had been brought up in this manner of daily changing from rough ragamuffin to a refined lady, and to her it was as easily done as changing from one tattered gown into another. She was indeed a fine actress she told herself time and again.

"What was that, Bobby?" she asked looking to her companion, being pulled from her thoughts by the sound of his voice.

"I was telling ye that I spied an old hag this morning selling some scraggely chickens. Perhaps we'll see her about. She be wearing an old torn-up black gown."

"Ah, that would be just the thing for Mum's soup this evening," she murmured. Since her mother had lost her job two months ago, they had barely had enough to eat to keep them alive. Usually herb soup was the main meal of the day. It would be an extra treat for her mother if she were to bring home some meat to add to that thin broth. "I think me mum may be coming down with the ache; she don't seem to be herself these past few days, and a chicken may just be the thing she be needing," she told the boy at her side.

They turned down one street and rounded another, their eyes searching out all movement.

As they went about a corner, Bobby hissed in her ear. "There she be, Christine." He nodded his head in the direction of an old, stooped-over gray-haired woman with two chickens in small pens that rested in a small pushcart.

"You stall and I'll fetch," he whispered and walked quickly away from Christine, whistling a jaunty tune, with his hands crammed into his pockets.

Christine waited until Bobby was only a few steps past the old hag then approached the two birds. "What ye be asking for these scrawny creatures?" she questioned, looking the old woman over and feeling

12

no shame or remorse for the act she was about to commit.

"Be ye got any coins about ye?" the old woman asked, her eyes taking on a greedy luster.

Christine stepped toward the old woman, a step or two from the desirable birds. "Of course I have the coins. Name ye price, old woman." At that moment Christine put her hand to her head and started as though to faint against the frail old hag.

"For the love of the lamb, what be ailing ye, gal?" The old woman reached out a gnarled hand to steady the young woman.

With the old woman's attention drawn away from the cart and her prized hens, Bobby made a run straight at the cart, passing at a full trot and grabbing a chicken, clutched and screaming under his arm.

Christine, seeing Bobby whiz by, recovered quickly from her ailment; and as a caterwauling voice shouted for the authorities to come quickly, she ran down one street and up another, where she found Bobby laughing gaily and swinging the hen about in the air as though it were a prize won in a tournament of honor.

Christine's own laughter filled the streets, tinkling off the walls of the nearby buildings. This was life to her: to take what you wanted with the thrill of a merry chase and to clutch your prize aloft in your hand; this daring of fate filled her whole body with an unholy exhilaration.

Losing herself to the gay abandon she felt within, Christine swung her arms about wildly, laughing and shouting to the people they passed; kicking out at the trash strewn about the street and alleys, she felt alive and free.

In no time they found themselves at the front steps to Christine's house. Bobby took hold of her arm as she started up to the door. "Meet me tonight, Christine." His voice was urgent as though his very life depended upon her answer. "Sneak out and I'll be a'waiting for ye here by the sideway. I be dreaming about ye and wanting to hold ye something fierce, Christine." His hope was deeply reflected in his dark brown eyes.

Christine knew exactly what this young man she had known from childhood wanted, and she did not show the slightest anger as she looked at his soot-smeared face. Most of the girls she had known while growing up had already given their bodies away at a much younger age than she. Some even made a modest living by selling themselves daily. But this was not for her. She would not easily be misled by a pair of lovesick eyes. She was made of tougher stuff than anyone imagined, and she knew that for a woman in her circumstances there was only one thing of value that she possessed, and it would indeed take a fortune for her willingly to give herself up.

"Nay Bobby, I cannot do it. Me mum would skin me sure if she caught me sneaking out to meet a boy." She shook her head and he knew by her set expression his answer once again was no.

"I got to be going now if I want this chicken ready for the soup by the time me mum wakes from her nap." Quickly and without awaiting his reply, girl and chicken disappeared behind the door.

The rattling breathing filled both rooms of the shack the Tates called home. Its vibrations sounded off the walls and filled Christine's very soul with a black dread.

"Here, Mother, try to take a bit more of the soup." Tenderly the girl lifted her mother's graying head from the pillow lying on the pallet near one of the dingy board walls.

The older woman's eyes were glazed and her body was a raging hot fever. Her frail chest heaved up and down, gasping for breath.

Christine after her exhilarating venture with Bobby had gone straight out the back door and plucked, decapitated, and gutted her chicken. When she had gone back into the house she had not heard her mother moving about, so she had put the fowl on to boil. She intended to let her mother rest until the meal was completed. Fleetingly she wished for a few coins with which to purchase a loaf of bread. But coins were scarce in this household and she scolded herself severely about her wishful thinking.

The chicken, having been boiled until it tenderly fell from the bone, was then put into the pot of herb soup, left over from the night before. Its aroma filled the two rooms, causing Christine's stomach to growl with impatience.

"Mother," she softly called, entering the other room and kneeling down upon the pallet. As soon as she looked upon the woman there her heart gave a mighty lurch. She could tell something was definitely wrong. Her mother's face was flushed a deep red and the noise coming from her throat was horrible to the ears.

"Mother, wake up." Christine gently nudged her mother's shoulder, hoping that upon waking the older woman would once more be her old self.

But this was not to be the way of things. Her mother slowly opened her eyes, and a soft smile played upon her lips for a very few seconds as she saw her daughter squatting beside her. All too quickly though her heavy lids shut back over her tired eyes.

"I shall bring you some soup, Mother," Christine whispered, fighting her tears back. "I found a chicken and added to it. It shall make you better in no time,"

15

She said this last part more to reassure herself, for her mother was delirious and beyond hearing anything she might have to say.

This night was to prove the longest of Christine's life. Tenderly she cared for her mother. She wrapped her in everything she could lay her hands upon, the only two thin blankets they owned and every piece of clothing she could find. If only they had wood and a warm fire blazing in the cold, damp room, she thought. If she could keep her mother warm perhaps she would have a fighting chance.

But though she tried all the long night to spoon warm broth between her mother's lips and to sponge her fevered brow with cool, soothing water, by the light of day, her efforts had proved futile.

During the night her mother had acquired a racking cough, one which bent her body double in a convulsive manner and left her barely breathing.

Large tears slid down Christine's cheeks and wet her gown. What was she to do, her mind screamed over and over.

If she could find a doctor and get some medicine perhaps her mother would survive. But doctors and medicine cost money and she did not possess a single farthing to her name. The few coins her mother had been able to hoard over the years had been spent over the last few months.

Christine herself had volunteered to find employment but her mother had forbidden it. She would not have her daughter emptying chamber pots and scrubbing until her hands were bloddy raw. But now as Christine looked down at the haggard form, bent double the pallet she wished for the thousandth time that she had disobeyed her mother this one time in her life. A few coins were all that came between her mother's life and her death.

Coming to a decision, Christine rose to her feet. "I'll be right back, Mother," she told the figure beneath the covers. "I am going to find you a doctor."

The streets were full of people busily going about their business, no one noticing the young girl with the beautiful copper hair and the tormented look. No one truly cared; everyone had his own troubles and woes.

Christine deftly made her way through the London streets until she found herself in the better section of town.

Now mostly businessmen and gowned and be-jeweled ladies walked about or were seen in the windows of their fine carriages.

Christine bided her time, waiting for the right opportunity to present itself. But her fate seemed to have been plotted for her long ago by the stars. She saw an elderly gentleman with powdered wig, cane, and the very richest clothing Christine had ever seen, step out of a carriage and enter a small stop, which, on its window, boasted about having the richest tobacco and the finest cigars within. Christine stood patiently beside the building and awaited her victim, plotting over and over in her mind how best to make her score.

Her wait was drawn to an abrupt halt as the elderly gentleman stepped through the door only a few minutes following his entrance.

Christine swiftly pulled herself away from the building and started to walk directly toward the man. Coming abreast of him she acted as though she were losing her footing and fell straight against her intended mark.

"Excuse me," she exclaimed, as she felt his arms encircle her to steady her balance.

"Quite all right, my dear. I am only glad to be here

to catch your fall." He gave her a kindly smile as he steadied her.

Perhaps Christine would have felt some form of compassion for this grandfatherly man if circumstances had been different, but all she could think about was finding the money for a doctor for her dying mother. So as the play upon the street unfolded, Christine was too-far gone into her part to back out.

Swiftly and with nimble fingers she touched upon the gentleman's wallet inside his waistcoat. But as her hand slowly lowered, her arm was grabbed in an unyielding grip.

"So you think to fall upon an elderly gentleman and relieve him of his valuables, do you girl?" The old man's voice had changed from that of a kindly grandfather to one of iron hardness.

Christine saw her mistake at once and tried to pull free and run. But she had completely underestimated her victim. He might be old but he was by all means as sharp and quick as any young man she had ever met. "I do not know what you are talking about," she replied in the haughtiest voice she could manage. "Release me at once, sir, or I shall be forced to call out for the authorities." She could only hope he would let his guard down for a minute so she could flee.

"Hand it to me, miss." With Christine glaring at him as though he were a madman, he gave her arm a tremendous jerk, half wrenching it from the socket.

A small crowd had formed about the couple and someone had run off shouting that he would find the authorities and bring them.

Christine's arm ached unbearably and her face felt flame red as she brought her hand up with the gentleman's bulging wallet. "I was but trying to get the coins to see that a doctor would tend my mother, sir. She is so sick and she is needing medicine."

The crowd seemed to hiss in one single breath as they saw the young, beautiful girl pull her hand up with the gentleman's wallet.

Someone yelled that the authorities were on their way; and a fat, pock-faced woman shouted that they should teach the little twit a proper lesson and one she would not soon be forgetting.

Christine was beginning to become frantic. She could not let this man hand her over to an officer; who then would care for her dear, sick mother? "Please let me loose," she begged the elderly man.

But before his answer came, her other arm was seized firmly, and as soon as the elderly gentleman released her, that arm also was recaptured.

Her heart beat a rapid tatoo; she felt faint and flushed at the same time as her eyes met those of her captors.

"Well, missy, ye done made one too many mistakes this here fine day," the tall, stern-looking officer admonished her harshly. "Ye shall regret this day for a long time coming, I swear ye will," he added, pulling her along after him.

"Please," Christine wept. "I did not mean to do anything wrong, it was all a mistake."

"Aye, it be a mistake and a bad one at that." The other officer, shorter and squatter than his companion, leered at her. "But ye best stay quiet and keep yer begging for the magistrate; me and Freddie here has got our orders and our duty, and one way or the other we always carry it out.

Christine was taken down a street where at the end a small horse-drawn cart awaited. She was helped into the back and her hands were tied to the side panels.

The cart smelled of horse dung and food refuse. And indeed Christine found herself sitting in the middle of filth-strewn straw, as she rode down the

London streets.

She soon found out the reason for the filth in the back of the prison cart. Children and some adults alike ran after the cart as it passed them by, shouting and throwing trash, rocks, or anything at all their hands could touch upon at the pitiful creature in the back. Any kind of excitement was seized upon to break the monotony of their humdrum lives.

Chapter Two

Newgate. The very name of the dreaded prison filled decent people with a shuddering fear. The interior was dark, damp, and dreary. The walls stank of the filth and human excrement within. Long, dark corridors led to huge cell doors, which slammed shut with a resounding clang; keys grated harshly in the locks, and the moans and cries of the inhabitants filled the foul air.

Christine felt nothing. She was numb, frozen to the bone, her mind filled with a tormenting fear as she looked about at the other occupants of the cell she was shoved into.

Against one wall sat two women, their faces huge, toothless grins as they saw the young beauty thrown into their midst. "Come over here, dearie," the dirtiest called out in a cackling voice.

Christine ignored their crude remarks, went to the opposite wall, and gingerly sat, her back straight, her arms wrapped about her knees, trying to find a small measure of warmth.

"It'll do ye no good luv; ain't nothing can warm ye

in this hole." A young girl who appeared to be no older than Christine plopped herself down and started to braid her knotted, straw-filled hair. "I been here now I think all about two months and I tell ye true the only way to keep yerself passably warm is to bury down in this filthy straw." She threw a small handful of the stinking stuff up into the air.

Christine shuddered visibly, as she viewed the straw the girl was speaking of.

"You say you have been here almost two months?" Because of her trauma she forgot her manner of speech for a moment.

"Ye be talking alful fine fer a gal in a ragged dress and in this rotten place," the girl said suspiciously. "If ye care anything at all about yer hide ye had better not let those two over there hear yer fancy tongue."

"I thank ye kindly fer that piece of information." Christine instantly stepped back into her street language. "What be yer name? I'm called Christine and I canna tell ye how glad I am to have someone to be talking with."

The girl sitting next to her wore a big smile as she heard the other's voice change from that of a fancy lady to the gutter talk of the London streets. "I be called Cora, me mum she never told me my last. She always told me it be doing me no good to know who the yokel was that sired me, and I never did give it much thought. Yer own name is pretty sounding to the ears. Christine; I be liking the sounds of that. I don't recall ever knowing a Christine before now; I think ye and I will become good friends."

Christine smiled fondly at this curly dark-haired minx. "I shall be truly glad t' have ye as me friend, Cora, I doubt if I could take this horrible place without someone to talk with."

"Oh, we should'na be here too much longer. I hear

21

tell that tomorrow the prisoners in this cell will start to go before the magistrate. What did the sorry louts nab ye fer anyway?" she asked, her finger deftly catching a flea between them and squeezing until it was dead.

For a moment Christine sat mesmerized, watching the girl pursue the bugs, then she related the story behind her sorry circumstances. Great tears gathered in Christine's blue eyes as she told of her mother's illness and of how no one would be there to tend to her needs.

Cora herself had tears in her green eyes as she listened. Her own tale was somewhat the same. She had been working in a small bookstore dusting and cleaning. The whole time of her employment her boss had done nothing but eye her; and whenever she was to get near him, having to pass him as she went between the aisles of books, his hands reached for her overly abundant form. She denied his every attempt, until one afternoon with rain pelting the sidewalks he had quietly locked his shop up early while she was still inside.

She laughed as though at a great joke at the story. The old man more than surprised her with his strength, and more quickly than she could think what to do he had relieved her of her gown, tossed her onto a goose-down mattress in the back of the shop, and raped her. It was not the first time a man had used her body but the others had been of her own choosing. Immediately after he fell off her body and his loud gulping snores filled her ears. She then robbed him of his watch and all the money in the register. What she had not counted on was the old man's sharp ears. As soon as he heard the little bell ring over his shop door, at her leaving, he had jumped from the mattress and soon found watch and money gone. He had wasted no time in calling the authorities, making up a lie about

22

one of his girls sneaking into his shop while it was closed, and then telling them her address.

That evening, as she lay sleeping in a tiny room with six brothers and sisters, she had been pulled from her bed, and, with her mother's wailing filling her ears, she had been dragged and tossed into the prison cart.

"This all happened over two months ago," she sighed. But with any luck it wouldn't be much longer before she found out what her sentence would be.

After listening quietly to the story Christine tried to tell Cora how sorry she was that she had been forced to stay locked in this pigsty for over two months and still did not know what her fate was to be.

But Cora, Christine was soon to learn, was not one to take pity. Her rich laughter filled the large cell, sounding odd and out of place in that dismal atmosphere. "Don't ye be wasting ye pity on me, gal. It truly ain't so bad, at least ye get yer gruel every day here. Where at home with six other children fer me mum to try to feed, I can tell ye about many a time I had to go to sleep with me own gut making such a racket it would wake me up. I figure I can't be much worse here than there."

Christine could not truly understand the girl's reasoning. But no matter, she herself was overjoyed to have a friendly young woman to confide in.

The next morning Christine was rudely startled from sleep in her makeshift bed by a large, burly guard, pounding on the cell door. "Get yerselves up, sluts, and make yerselves presentable. The magistrate's ready to hear ye cry yer innocence. He, he, he," he laughed through his blackened teeth. "Yeah, ye sluts can be a-crying all ye likes but it won't be a-making no never mind to the old magistrate, fer today ye fine ladies, ye be going in front of Sir Tom Sly."

"Eat this slop now before I be getting back." Still laughing, he left their cell and went on to another.

Cora grasped Christine's hand firmly, and to answer the girl's questioning look Cora whispered as she brushed the clinging straw from her hair and dress. "They call old Judge Tom the hanging magistrate. He be known fer sentencing a body to hang fer the simplest crime, just to be seeing the crowd gather around the poor bloke."

Christine's breath caught and she felt her throat constrict and her knees knocked loudly throughout the room. If the hanging judge was known to be so hard on prisoners who had committed a small offense, what would be the outcome of her punishment when she stood before him and he was told that she had stolen a gentleman's wallet.

Cora patted her arm in a gentle manner. "Perk up luv, I doubt your crime be any worse than any of the rest of ours." She swept her arms about the room indicating all the other occupants. "We all be in the same boat, and like I be a-thinking, that if what I been told is right, most likely we all will be a'sailing for the colonies before a fortnight!"

"The colonies," Christine gasped aloud. She had grown up on the street, fighting for herself and surviving with the poor, but she had also grown up sheltered from the harsher aspects of life, and right now she was learning, with all the horrors about her, just how sheltered and protected her life with her mother had been.

The guards had said he would return in about an hour for the women; and all, after finishing their morning mush and green brackish water, tried to primp and make themselves more presentable. Running their fingers through their hair and

24

smoothing their tattered gowns was the best they could do. But their long enclosed imprisonment had left its mark on most of these grimy creatures. Their skin had a yellow tinge, from bad water and enclosed quarters; their hair was matted in clumps and looked to be alive with crawling vermin; and above all the stench of the women about her, who had not been able to bathe since their imprisonment, was so over-whelming that no matter how hard the women tried they could not make themselves appealing.

The gavel banged clearly, resounding dully throughout the large courtroom. "If you have no more defense than what you have just presented to the courtroom then I shall without any further delay pro-nounce sentence upon you." The strong, dominating voice filled Christine's ears as she stood before a long table behind which sat three gowned and bewigged gentlemen, each appearing in similar dress and manner except for the one in the center.

Sir Thomas Sly stared at the young girl quaking before him, and his tall, skinny frame shivered with the power he felt in his hands. He held complete sway over whether this girl lived or died, and no matter how many poor souls had stood before him with that same quaking fear staring starkly out of their eyes, he always knew the same feeling of total and complete power when he looked upon them. He knew deep down inside that this was the only joy that kept his body breathing and his mind wishing to see the next day.

"I sentence you, Christine Tate, to not more than or less than twenty years of servitude in the colonies of the Americas."

The doom of his voice circled around her and filled Christine's body with a shocking numbness. She felt her knees buckle and her body fall.

She came to later in the same cell she had shared the night before with Cora.

She looked about and found Cora sitting against the damp stone wall, her features totally absorbed in her thoughts, and if Christine could read expressions at all, she knew that the other girl's thoughts had to be as black as the word doom itself.

Feeling eyes lightly appraising her, Cora turned to Christine, masking her feelings as though she were a born actress. "So ye finally came to yer senses. Fer a while I thought perhaps the shock had been too much fer ye and ye'd never be yerself again." Her pale, lightly freckled face grinned as though the previous afternoon had been nothing more than some grand lark they had undertaken.

Christine was much more serious as she looked at the girl. "What-what did you?" She could not finish, her voice cracked with her unshed tears.

"There, there luv. Don't be taking on so. You and me we be going to have us some high adventures. Just ye wait, gal, you and me we'll stay a team." Tears started to fall from her hardened face.

Christine went to her and wrapped her arms about Cora's shaking body.

"It ain't meself I be a-weeping like a babe fer. But that me mum ain't going to be a a-knowing what happened to me. But then I guess she mightent really care; she be having so many younguns to be a-worrying about. She might have already given up worrying on me."

"Hush, hush." Christine soothed her, patting the dark hair and pulling the girl against her chest. "You have me and we'll stay a pair."

The two stayed huddled together, comforting and soothing one another as though they were lost children in an alien land. Christine found that her friend Cora's sentence was the same as her own except for the number of years. Since Christine's victim had been a gentleman she had gotten twenty years of indentureship, but Cora's sentence had been ten years less for she had robbed a lowly storekeeper, who amounted to hardly more than she herself.

Christine's thoughts had been constantly of her ailing mother; and as she thought of the long years ahead of her and away from England—for she had been told that the ship taking the prisoners to the colonies would leave within the week—great diamond-like tears coursed down her cheeks from her haunted violet eyes; and the thought fleetingly crossed her mind that she might never again see that tender, old face or hear her mother's sweet voice again.

They were awakened before dawn, and herded together into one long line, emptying most of the cells of Newgate of its prisoners. Down the long, damp corridors they were marched out into the fresh London air. Christine took long gulps of it, trying to fill her lungs with freedom, though her arms and legs were shackled to the woman in front of her and to Cora in back of her.

The long line of filthy, upkempt prisoners was marched to waiting carts, loaded within, and driven to the London docks. This took place in the dark hours of the morning so as not to affect the sensibilities of the populace.

Once at the docks Christine, along with the others, was herded aboard a large merchant ship that had on many previous occasions been used for other human cargo, under different circumstances. It was a slave ship, whose captain had spent most of his time running from the African coast to the Caribbean

Islands, transporting his cargo of men and women.

As Christine's cart was pulled to a stop on the docks, in front of the ship they were to board, and she was pulled to her feet, a soft voice in the shadows of a side building called out to her. It was Bobby's voice, she held no doubt.

She peered in the direction of the voice and whispered in an urgent voice. "Bobby, be that ye?"

"Aye," came his reply.

The guard had made his way to the front of her line, so she felt a small amount of freedom to talk.

"Tell me of me mum, Bobby. How is her cold? Does she seem to be getting any better at all?"

Her answer came cold and hollow, for the youth answering her direct question did not know how to coat his words to come out soothing to the ears. "I dinna want to tell ye, Christine, but yer mum died the same day ye were pinched by the officers. I found out ye had been caught and went directly to her, but when I entered the house I felt that something was the matter, and when I entered the other room she looked to be sleeping peaceful like but she were dead."

Tears silently rolled down Christine's face. Her heart seemed to be in a tightening vise. A deep and warm part of her heart was gone, and now the only thing to take its place was imprisonment and drudgery.

"I went to yer trial, sneaked in I did, and I heard yer sentence. I seen ye go into a dead faint with the magistrate's words. Perhaps it were fer the best yer mum be lying in the ground and not knowing what be happening to ye." His logic was unsettling but in his own subtle way he was trying his best to be the friend she had always known him to be.

Before any more was said Christine's hands were jerked by the chain and she was pulled along as

28

though in a daze, with the rest of the prisoners.

If not for Cora, Christine thought, she would have tried to put an early end to her wretched life.

The conditions of the ship were worse than those at Newgate. The prisoners were fed only once a day and were given only half a cup of water each. There was no fresh air and the stench was even worse than in the prison. They were kept locked in the bowels of the ship. The only good thing the vile captain had done was to separate males from females, claiming that to leave them together would only cause fights and confusion.

As the days went by and they were pulled farther and farther out to sea, Christine realized how lucky she was to have Cora for a friend. She herself had never been on any kind of ship before and surprisingly she at once found her sea legs. But as the waves lapped against the sides of the great ship, the tiny, cramped quarters the women shared resounded with the moans and cries of women lying on the floor and rolling back and forth from sea sickness. Christine found herself hardy and able.

Cora proved herself invaluable from the outset of the journey. Each morning every prisoner was given a share of gruel that was to last through the long day. As soon as the ship's mate who brought down the large caldron had climbed back up the ladder and closed the hatch, Cora emptied her bowl of the pale-looking, gritty concoction into Christine's and made her rounds about the hull. Anyone who could not defend her meal was fair game to her way of thinking, and did without the meal for the day. The same was true for the water; Cora in her tough manner always managed an extra cup or two a day for herself and Christine.

Christine hardened herself to try to survive from day

29

to day. Fever and sickness were ever-present on the ship, but the two girls remained in a passable state of health thanks to Cora's quick wits. In both their minds lurked the ever-present threat of contracting something from one of the other women.

Already halfway through their journey several women had died, the ship's mate, having found the cold bodies on his morning rounds with food, had hauled the bodies up the ladder, leaving no doubt in the other prisoners' minds about where they were being taken. They were food for the sharks that constantly followed behind the ship, waiting for anything that was dumped overboard.

Christine shuddered each time another body was taken above, and prayed that she and Cora would both be spared.

"Land ho." The shout carried across the expanse of water and down into the bowels of the ship.

The activity above deck was rampant and that below was no less busy and boisterous. Those who had survived the trip felt a sense of jubilation that one part of their journey was finally over.

Christine clutched Cora's arm happily. "We've made it," she whispered in a voice of sheer wonder. "Did ye ever have a doubt luv?" Cora gayly shouted, taking Christine around the waist and dancing a jig about her.

"Oh I had my doubts, I'll tell ye sure." Christine laughed, joining in the light frolic.

The other women were the same, some laughing, dancing, and shouting. Others, large tears glistening in their eyes, realized that the airless, cramped trip was finally over.

Debarking from the ship was much like getting aboard, except this was done during broad daylight, and it seemed to Christine that most of the populace of New Orleans had turned out for the event.

The ragged, grimy line of stragglers marched down the main street of New Orleans. None were healthy; all had a pale, yellowish pallor, and bones were prominent on all of their bodies. But they, for the most part, felt good for they had endured the long and arduous trip.

The inhabitants of New Orleans had been told of the arrival of a ship with its hull full of indentured servants that morning. Shopkeepers and planters and poor people alike had turned out for the event. They stood along the sidewalks, and all kept an eye out for a person of special talent or strength who would be of value to them.

The prisoners were led down a street at the end of which rose a large stockade. Big bold letters printed over its gate read: Simmons, Live Auction, Five O'clock Sunday Afternoon.

Christine, like all the others, was led through the stockade. Her shackles were released, and she was shoved into a roofless pen. To the prisoners' surprise they were not the only inhabitants of their new prison.

The women again were separated but soon they found that their color was of no concern. Blacks shared the same pens with whites.

Neither Christine nor Cora had ever seen a black person before and stared on in horror at the few women who already were within the walls confines.

One of the white women came up to Cora and Christine as they stood staring at a large, ponderous black woman nursing her child at her breast; and she said that she had, indeed, seen a person of this color once in England. He had been called a blackamoor and had been dressed in silk and satin; he also had worn a thick pure gold necklace, and attached to it had been a long gold chain at the other end of which was a fancy-gowned woman.

But these creatures in this stockade had no such luxury as silk, satin, or gold chains to adorn their necks. They barely had rags to cover their frames, and their large black eyes held a fear so great that no hanging of their heads could hide it. Even to the women from the prison ship they kept their eyes downcast and their talk always respectful. They lived only to serve a master, and Christine fleetingly wondered if she and the other women about her in time would be reduced to this same state.

Then and there Christine hardened her heart to any kind of softer emotion. If she was no better than chattel then she would give only as much as she received. She would steel herself to be auctioned to the highest bidder as though she were an animal. She would endure, and she would bear up, she swore. But no matter what, she would never bend completely.

Three long, hot and sweaty days slowly crawled by; and then on a steamy Sunday morning Christine with all the other women in the compound was herded into a different pen, where they were brought one at a time to stand on a large wooden platform before a crowd of onlookers, while a big-mouthed, potbellied man proclaimed the virtues of each person brought out.

Christine never before had felt so foul and insignificant as she did at the moment the fat man, sitting atop a high stool, started shouting to the group of people as she was brought forward.

A wooden gavel slammed against hard wood as a murmur raged over the dust-strewn crowd when the copper-haired young woman was brought out.

" 'Tis the best of the lot, gentlemen." His voice

cracked like a whip. "Her teeth are sound and her back is strong; bid on her, gentlemen, and purchase yourself a bargain." There seemed a sly undertone in the auctioneer's voice. "She's got twenty years to learn how to be anything ya could want. Maybe make a fine housekeeper to some lucky plantation house."

The murmurs and whispers started up once again as the auctioneer paused.

"She looks a mite puny to me," a voice shouted from the front of the crowd.

Christine felt her face turn a flame color. How could these dreadful people put another human being through so humiliating an exhibition? Never once did it cross their minds as they directed their cruel fun at her and looked her over like some animal that, if fate had been different, any one of them could have been standing up there in her place.

"How about a little feeling the merchandise?" a surly voice shouted. "If I aim to spend good money for a servant I like to know what I'm paying for."

"Two hundred dollars," a gentleman called from the back of the group, causing the funmaking to come to a halt.

Christine's breath held and caught. It was finally happening, she thought. She was finally being sold to the highest bidder.

"Three hundred," called the auctioneer, ignoring the gentleman's bid.

The bidding lasted for quite some time. It seemed two gentlemen were interested in trying to obtain the red-haired girl who stood frightened and filthy up on the platform. One of them Christine could easily see from where she stood. He looked to be in his early thirties, tall, slim, and elegant. The other she could barely make out. He sported a top hat, and from as far as Christine could see, seemed to be quite elderly.

Finally after an overwhelmingly long time the bidding came to a stop at the unheard-of price of eleven hundred and fifty dollars.

Christine could not believe that a human being would offer that amount of money for another human being. She had never heard of so large an amount of money being so easily passed about, and especially not for someone like herself. She had not been able to tell which of the two gentlemen had purchased her indenture papers, for neither had moved or showed any interest in claiming his property.

Strong hands helped her from the platform and ushered her back to one of the pens.

Cora passed her with a tight smile, she being the next to face Christine's earlier humiliation.

Christine's face and neck were damp with sweat when she was locked back in the pen. What would be her fate? Her thoughts were a mixture of fright and anticipation. What would it be like to have a master such as the young, virile gentleman who had stood before her and made his bid. She did not let herself dwell on being placed in the hands of the older man.

It was just before dusk when a short, almost tiny black man came to the gate of the stockade and talked to the guard. Without preamble Christine's name and the names of at least three of the black women were called. Christine saw the fright written in the black women's eyes. They huddled together in a small group and had to be prodded out of the gate by the guard, who placed chains upon their wrists.

When it came time for Christine's arms to be manacled, she shook her head fiercely, keeping her hands tightly clasped behind her back. "I can go on my own." She spoke in the haughtiest manner she had learned.

The guard's hand raised a cruel-looking whip, as though ready to strike. But before a single blow could be struck the small, wiry black man grabbed the guard's wrist. "Do not touch de missy. Master Blackthorn not like getting anything but what he already done seen. You be making one little Tiny mark on de master's property an' you a'gonna be a-paying a large price."

Christine saw the fear come to the man's eyes at the mere mention of this small man's master's name, and she wondered what kind of man would be holding her fate in his hands.

"Follow me, missy," the man told Christine simply as he took hold of the chain binding the three black women and started off down the dusty road.

Christine hurried behind, not letting the small group out of her sight. She was too frightened to attempt an escape; where would she go—even if she could build up the nerve to try?

In only a few minutes a wagon was in sight, upon which sat a dark form, smoking a long, tapered cigar. One leg crossed over the other, he waited at his leisure.

The three women were helped aboard and then the small black man held out a hand to Christine. "Watch yer step, missy," he spoke in a kindly tone.

The man upon the seat turned at the sound of his servant's voice.

At first glance Christine realized that her daydreaming of that afternoon had been incorrect. Her master was not to be the young, pleasant-looking man but the elderly gentleman who had sported the elegant top hat. He also carried a cane and his clothes were perfectly tailored. His features were expressionless as his dark eyes raked over his new possession.

Christine did not have a chance to think about the

power of those dark eyes, for she was quickly handed into the back of the wagon, and within seconds the tiny man was shouting for the horses to, "Giddy-up" as his long whip crackled overhead.

The ride seemed endless, the night black, moonless, and quiet. Christine lay her head down upon the sweatest-smelling hay she had ever known.

Her sleep was dreamless, but all too quickly she was pulled from her slumber by the wagon coming to a jerking stop. The small black man jumped down from the seat and went to the back to help the women out.

The dark, mysterious gentleman, who now owned Christine's papers, slowly walked up the front walkway to the veranda of a huge stone mansion.

"You gals there, come on over here and let me unlock those chains on you alls arms," the small black man said, seeming to be in charge of the new servants. "You gals go on over to that there big wood building." His bony fingers pointed in the direction of a large structure that had a lantern burning in its window. "You all ask for Lil and she'll give you all something to eat and show you where to sleep for the night.

As the women started to shuffle off in the direction he had indicated, he turned his large black eyes onto Christine. "You follow me, missy; we go on behind the big house and to the kitchen, and Miss Tam she'll fix you right up."

Christine followed meekly behind the sprightly old man to the back of the stone house.

As soon as they turned the corner of the mansion Christine felt her stomach starting to growl, from the wafted aroma of good-smelling food coming through the screen door.

"Miss Tam?" the small black man called from outside, not daring to enter until given permission.

"That be you Joel? What for you be out there in

the dark? The master he done come home; why you ain't in there fixing him a good hot toddy and lighting him one of those fine cigars he be liking so well?" The woman talking stood at a huge wood-burning stove stirring pots and directing two young black girls as they turned a spit of meat over an open fire in a corner of the large room.

"Miss Tam, the master told me to bring this new girl to you," the old man called Joel said, stepping past the screen door and pulling Christine behind him.

Until this moment the negress called Miss Tam had not turned or broken stride with her cooking, but at Joel's words her dark black head turned to see what he had brought her.

Her look was one of complete disbelief. "You must be mad, boy!" She sounded outraged, as she lay her spoon on a side table and motioned for one of the girls in the corner to tend to the bubbling pots on the stove.

"What you be about bringing a white girl to my kitchen? Master Blackthorn could'na sent her to this old hot place."

"Master Blackthorn said for you t' see she get's something t' eat and some proper clothes. If I was you, Miss Tam, I'd be a-boiling plenty of good hot water. This here child seems to be crawling alive with lice and fleas."

"I reckon Master Blackthorn be a-knowing what he a-doing, but I tell you this, Joel, it's been near on to forty years since there be a white lady living here at Iva Rose. I don't be a-knowing how things a-going to work out with her being a servant. Seems to me to be asking for nothing but trouble. I never could abide with these white people a-being sent here and treated like they be black slaves. Just don't seem right to this old black lady."

"I don't know Miss Tam, I truly don't know. But Master Blackthorn done bought her papers and now she belongs to the master just like everybody else here at Iva Rose."

"Well, I guess you had better go tend to the master before he be getting his temper up. Just let the girl sit over there," she said indicating a long wooden table against one stone wall, "until I finish with the master's dinner.

As she sat all alone at the long table, Christine wished that Cora had been brought along with her. She wondered what had happened to the other girl, for she had not seen her again after they had passed on her way to the auction block, and she had no idea who could have purchased Cora's papers. She would have to find out somehow, for Cora was her only friend in this foreign country and a dearer friend she could never ask for.

"How old you be child?" She was pulled from her thoughts by Miss Tam's questioning.

"Eighteen, mam." Christine had decided in the stockade that day that she would use her best manners, and perhaps she would gain a better place in her servitude.

Miss Tam looked sharply at this ragged form, sitting at her table. It was plain the child had been properly brought up. She idly wondered what could have brought her to this sorry state. To be a white woman and to be sold like a common black was a terrible experience.

"What you be called, honey?"

"Christine, mam," she answered dutifully.

"That be right pretty, honey. Now step on out of those rags you got on and step into this here tub." The black woman poured hot steaming buckets of water into the wood tub in the center of the kitchen floor.

Without shame or thought Christine obeyed, stepping lightly out of her gown, her pale skin gleaming in the firelight reflected from the hearth.

"Why you be beautiful under all of this here dirt and grime, Miss Christine." Miss Tam sounded surprised as she stepped back from her job of scrubbing and rinsing the girl in the tub.

She had so far gone through two tubs of water, trying to rid the girl of the filth and living creatures upon her body, and now finally after over an hour of scrubbing she could see some headway being made.

Christine's copper hair glowed like a rich cloak of fire, curling down her back; her white creamy complexion glowed pink and healthy from Miss Tam's scrubbing, and her blue eyes twinkled merrily as she listened to the older black woman rushing about the kitchen.

"Wait until the master be a-seeing you, gal. He sure won't be a-recognizing you for the dirty, ragged child he done bought off the auction block."

Christine had listened, hanging on to each word Miss Tam said. It seemed that the woman had been here at Iva Rose since she had been a young girl. She talked little of the master of this large plantation, saying only that there was no mistress and there had never been one. Master Blackthorn, from what Christine could make out, must have a very bad temper at times, for all of the servants tried to anticipate his every wish, even before he himself knew what he wanted.

"Here raise yourself up, honey." A large, soft towel circled Christine's body, burying her in its luxury.

"Sit yourself down here by the hearth while I go and try to find something for you to wear." Miss Tam sat her charge down on a low stool.

Christine had about dozed off before Miss Tam returned with a simple cotton gown thrown over one arm and a pair of dark pumps in the other.

"Here's you a chemise, honey. It mght be a bit mended but it's the best I could do and you be a-needing something to sleep in tonight."

Christine did not answer but smiled fondly at the black woman. She already knew that whatever Miss Tam did would be in her best interest. The slim, angular dark woman seemed to be kindness itself. And already there seemed to be a close bond being formed between them.

Miss Tam showed her to a small cot in an empty room, off from the house servants' quarters. As soon as Christine's head hit the soft down pillow she was immediately asleep.

Chapter Three

Dawn broke early at Iva Rose, the soft golden sun shone down upon the dew-soaked velvet lawns about the old stone mansion, making it look like sparkling diamonds glittering brightly. The green ivy clinging to the stones on the front veranda, and the roses, blooming open and fresh sent a clean, pleasant smell into the air. The fields were planted in neat rows of white fleecy cotton spreading as far as the eye could see. Off in the distance the chanting song of the slaves toiling in the fields could be heard, falling gently and pleasantly upon the ears.

Christine, stretching and yawning, awoke to the beautiful morning. Rising she slowly made her way to the window and the sight that filled her eyes left her breathless and staring.

Beautiful, was so inadequate a word she thought. Never before had she seen anything like this place in which she now resided.

If only things were different, the thought fleetingly crossed her mind. If only she simply lived here and were not another servant bought with the purpose of maintaining the house.

A knock sounded at the door, and before Christine could answer, Miss Tam entered, carrying a large tray of delicious-smelling food. Christine had already found that the food at Iva Rose was the best she had ever eaten, and at the prospect of the good-smelling repast on the tray, her mouth began to water. "Oh, Miss Tam, you did not have to bring this in here. I could have come to the kitchen."

Miss Tam smiled fondly at the beautiful young girl before her. She seemed even more delicate and lovely in the light of day. Her fragile, high cheekbones added a highborn quality to her tender beauty. "It be no trouble Miss Christine. You be a-needing at least one day to rest up and I like to have a lady to be a-waiting on."

Christine's tinkling laughter filled the tiny room. She had never been waited on before, though she had to admit she did rather enjoy all the pampering Miss Tam had showered upon her. She still could not forget who she was and why she was here. "You shall spoil me terribly, Miss Tam, and you know what they say about a spoiled servant?" Christine's laughter was contagious and the usually stern Miss Tam's face broke into a huge grin.

"Sit yourself down over here and eat this breakfast while I brush out all these curls." She ran her black fingers through the burnt-gold tresses, marveling at the sheer beauty of such hair. Never had she seen any-thing to match it.

Christine obeyed willingly setting her fork to the fried ham, the heaping plate of potatoes, eggs, and biscuits set before her.

All this first day Miss Tam barely let Christine lift a finger. She was allowed to sit on a high stool near the stove and watch while food was prepared for lunch and dinner, but nothing else.

"You be having plenty of time to be put to work in this old house," Miss Tam told her. "You just rest yourself up for a day or two and then we be setting you to work."

Christine met the two black girls that Miss Tam had help out in the kitchen. The short, plump girl with a calico bandana wrapped about her kinky hair was called Mandy, and the other, almost an exact replica of the first, was called Dell. Christine tried all that first day to make friends with the two young girls, but they were shy and had never before talked with a white woman, having been born and raised here on Iva Rose. They giggled and hung their heads every time she looked in their direction, so finally she stopped trying and kept her conversation for Miss Tam, who more than made up for anyone else's company. The older woman was a world of information.

At dinner time Miss Tam made Christine go to her room and run the brush through her hair.

"Now you take this bowl of greens and this platter of shrimp and wild rice out to the table."

When a look of fright crossed Christine's features, Miss Tam smiled fondly and patted her shoulder. "You be just fine child. Just take these, set them where the master can reach them, then hurry on back out here to me."

Christine swallowed hard, trying to brace herself for the ordeal ahead. She had not as yet met the master of Iva Rose face to face, and now she wished she could put it off until another day, but by the set look on Miss Tam's face she knew it could not be put off.

She took the bowls, and with one last pat on her shoulder was through the door leading from the kitchen into the dining room.

Her hands were shaking badly when she reached the mahogany table and saw the distinguished elderly gentleman sitting at one end and sipping a glass of wine while waiting patiently for his meal to be served.

His green eyes appraised her, not showing any emotion as he set his wine glass down.

"Your name is Christine, is it not? His voice was commanding, used to giving orders and expecting no arguments.

Christine cleared her throat, as she set down the bowls in front of him. She had not been expected to talk to him but now she had no choice in the matter. "Yes, sir, my name is Christine Tate."

Dark brows rose archingly at the clear even tones of her feminine voice. "Christine, he murmured and went back to his wine.

Christine thinking herself excused started toward the door.

"Christine," the gentleman said softly.

She whirled about. "Yes, sir?"

"I like the sounds of it rolling on my tongue, quite pretty." He said this leaning back in his chair in a manner of reflection.

Christine stood frozen, not knowing whether he required an answer or if she should just turn and fly.

Some of her fear must have shown on her face for the next words out of his mouth filled her with relief. "You may go back to Miss Tam now, Christine."

No more had to be said; Christine turned on her heels and fled, leaving a frowning master of Iva Rose.

"What can I help do, Miss Tam?" Christine had awakened early and, dressed in the same patched cotton dress, had rushed out to the kitchen to help Miss Tam. Her one day of inactivity was enough for her; today she would begin her duties.

Miss Tam shook her head. "I don't be knowing, Miss Christine. Master Blackthorn he done go to town and say he be back in a few days and he not wishing for you to be doing too much."

"Why would he say something like that?" she wondered aloud.

"I don't be knowing, honey, but he say you to do no more than a bit of sewing. Can you sew, child?" she asked as an afterthought. "Though I don't be a-knowing what you could sew. The girls in the cabins out back sew for their own families; the only sewing to be done in this old house is that of master Blackthorn's mending."

"Why yes, of course I can sew," Christine answered absently, wondering why if her papers had been purchased for the purpose of indenture, her new master did not wish for her to work to reimburse him for the price he'd had to pay. These people in America were a strange breed, she thought. Even the slaves treated her like royalty and she was actually no better than they. Her life had been turned upside down since her arrival at Iva Rose; she neither knew her place nor how best to act around the people in this strange house. And now, having been told that she was not to do any more than sew a few stitches, she was completely baffled.

"Here's you some breakfast, honey; sit yourself down and I'll fix a pot of tea. Delly you gal, go on out back and call one of them yard boys to come and carry in some buckets of water," she added, rushing from one end of the kitchen to the other.

Christine sat down and thoughtfully nibbled at the meal before her. Things seemed so strange and to be going at such a fast pace, she hardly knew how to put them in their right perspective. "Miss Tam, I cannot possibly go day after day without a thing to do," she complained, while sipping at her tea. "Perhaps I could find some material and fashion myself a gown."

Miss Tam sighed audibly. "Why sure, child, as soon as you finish we'll go on out to the storage shed and find what you be a-needing to fix youself something real nice." This had been easier than she had thought. When Master Blackthorn had told her to watch out for the girl and not let her do anything more than that which the master had left orders for, she truly had thought she would be having some trouble but now things would be fine. She would get her needle, thread, and materials and with the girl keeping to herself everything would run smoothly.

Four boring and dreary days passed by before the master of Iva Rose returned to his domain.

Christine had been in the library, curled up in a chair and reading when she was pulled from her romantic dreams of love and intrigue in a French court, by the clearing of a male throat.

Jumping straight to her feet and clutching the book behind her back, Christine looked at the gentleman, standing in the doorway, as though she were as guilty as a common thief.

Edward Blackthorn had just arrived at Iva Rose, and as it was his usual routine on returning after a time away, he went straight to the library to pour himself a goblet of brandy and to relax with a good cigar. His shock was apparent as he reviewed the young woman, with feet tucked up under her dress, curled in one of the overstuffed leather chairs in his private room. She seemed in another world, so immersed was she with her story. He found himself becoming surprised at every turn by this red-haired beauty. First she served his meal to him and when questioned talked as though she was quality itself, and now he found his indentured servant in his library reading from his finer books. There was more to this woman than met the eye, and he promised himself he would know the whole of the story.

"I-I am sorry," she stammered, setting the book back on the shelf and starting to hurry from the room.

"Stay," his powerful voice commanded in that rich tone she had heard the night she had served him his dinner.

Christine's eyes were blue pools of fright as her hands clutched the folds of her gown in order to quiet their trembling. "Yes, sir," she murmured.

"Please, have a seat," he ordered, going to the sideboard and pouring himself a drink, after which he sat behind his desk. His dark eyes studied her from the tips of her shoes to the top of her beautiful curls. Ah, why he had ever brought her papers in the beginning was still a mystery to him; but the minute he had seen the ragged, unkempt beauty standing on the auction block, he had been pulled, as though without any will of his own, to bid on her; and when the bidding had become a bit steep, his pride had made him bid all the higher. He was a man used to gaining that which he set out for, and no matter how expensive this woman, he would have met the price.

Christine herself sat as had been bid her and silently studied this man. He was even older than she had first thought. His once-fine dark hair was streaked with gray that all but completely covered the darker color. Deep-lined wrinkles ravaged the skin about the light green eyes, and deep lines furrowed about his once-sensual full lips. Though his age she could not determine, his manner and superior bearing seemed to fill the very air about him. His dress was perfect: light fawn-colored jacket and pants, dark brown waistcoat with gold-leaf design, and black leather knee-boots so shiny one could see his own reflection mirrored in their sheen.

"Tell me a bit about your past, Christine." The man's voice was commanding, bringing Christine from her thoughts.

"I-I, there is not too much to tell," she answered, truly feeling frightened. She had no idea what he wished to hear. She was sure he did not wish to hear of her life of strife and deprivation in the London streets.

"Tell me of your family and the circumstances of your imprisonment." He studied her carefully, noticing her flushed cheeks and shaky composure.

Christine's years of playacting at being a member of the gentry all came back to her in a rush. All of her mother's stories of the rich and her expectation that one day she would see her daughter riding in a fine, fancy carriage burst into Christine's mind and as though through no will of her own, tiny glittering tears squeezed through her deep blue eyes and her new identity took over. "It was my mother, sir," she said softly, taking the hem of her gown and dabbing at her eyes.

Edward Blackthorn, feeling his heart skip at her tears, pulled a satin handkerchief from his jacket pocket, made his way to this pitiful creature's side, and, kneeling, slowly gave it to her.

He waited patiently for her sobbing to quiet and for her to begin again with her tale.

"You see, sir, my dear mother took ill. Let me start at the beginning. My mother and myself lived about two days' ride outside London. My father had been a gentleman of means, owning a sizable estate and having quite a few tenants bringing the rents. Well, my father died from a congestion of the lungs some ten years ago and my mother overtook the running of his finances." At this point Christine having truly gotten into her part, once again dabbed at her eyes and waited for the gentleman's gentle probing.

"Yes, I am sorry, sir," she responded to his gentle look.

"Christine continue, there is nothing to be sorry for." His look of gentle concern was something new to him and genuine.

Christine was as observant as a cat and knew that she had the master of Iva Rose in the palm of her hand at this moment.

She bent slightly toward him, her frailty and vulnerability making him feel more manly then he had in years.

"My mother tried her best to keep things together but it seemed like she was doomed from the start," Christine said softly, continuing with the story she believed he wished to hear. "My father it seemed was quite far in debt, but mother tried to pay the bills and work the estate. After a few years though it became apparent that it was a futile affair. She was forced to sell the furniture, things which had belonged in the family for generations were all but given away and then the estate itself had to be sold. We moved to London and lived on the small amount which came from the sale of our family home." Once more she sniffed aloud.

"One day our worst fears were realized; we were without funds and with everything else going wrong my mother became ill. So ill was she that I feared that

48

if I did not find a doctor and get her some medicine she would not live out another day." Tears streamed down her cheeks at this part of her story. She must be the most convincing now, she told herself, glancing sideways at the sympathetic man kneeling at her side.

"I did not know what to do or where to go," she continued sobbing lightly. "My mother lay so ill. I left the house hoping to find some help and I must have gone a small bit crazy with my desperation. I could think of nothing to do and when I saw a gentleman pass by on the street I tried to take his wallet. Oh," she wailed. "I know I did wrong. It was as though another person had taken possession of me."

Edward Blackthorn patted the young girl's hand; sympathy was a new feeling for him, but it was obvious that this beautiful girl sobbing out her pitiful story had been dealt a rather shabby hand by both fate and the magistrates of London. Imagine their sentencing a young girl of quality, as she was obviously every inch as highborn as could be wanted, to a life of strife and servitude.

"Do not say any more, my dear," he murmured, raising and going to the sideboard to refill his goblet. "Put the whole unpleasant episode from you. You are among friends now."

Relief and gratitude were plainly written upon Christine's features as she looked toward this man who held her fate. He had believed her story, thought that she was highborn and that her faimly had fallen on hard times. Her whole life would be changed after this afternoon, though she did not know it.

"Do you know of your mother?" he gently questioned.

Her head sadly went from side to side. She could speak of the truth on this one instance. "The morning we set sail on the prison ship from London, a friend of

49

mine risked being imprisoned himself to bring me the news that my dear, sweet mother had passed away the very same day I was taken to Newgate."

Edward Blackthorn truly felt sorry for this young woman. "I am sorry my dear, and I promise there shall be no more questions of this type. Perhaps you would like to lie down for a while. I shall send Miss Tam to you in a bit."

Christine knew when she was being excused and rose from her seat. "Thank you," she murmured softly, reaching the library door.

"Perhaps you would like to take along the book you were reading." He smiled, something he thought he had not done for some time.

"Thank you," Christine replied, "but for now I think I would rather rest and put some cool compresses to my eyes."

"Very well, my dear, as you wish." Edward Blackthorn watched her form leaving the room and heading down the hall toward her own chambers. What was he to do with the girl? he questioned himself harshly. Her story seemed sound to him, and though he had bought her papers in good faith, he knew he would never allow those soft white hands of hers to do any menial labor. But what would he do with her? She seemed to have some sort of hold upon him that he had never known the feel of before; and he, he admonished himself, was old enough to be the girl's father.

Christine awoke to Miss Tam, humming and puttering about in her small room.

"Why child, you finally waking yourself? I thought for a time that I would have to hum a little louder." Her face broke out in a huge grin.

"Did you need me for something?" Christine rose from the small cot.

"No. No, honey, I just be bringing you in this here gown and telling you the master be wishing for you to join him for dinner."

Christina looked at the lovely yellow silk and taffeta creation that Miss Tam stood lovingly caressing, and gasped aloud, jumping to her feet. "It is for me?" Her eyes were round saucers.

"Master Blackthorn done bring this here gown home from New Orleans just for you, Miss Christine, and I tell you, honey, I just can't wait to see you in it."

Christine felt as though she were walking into a dream as she was bathed, perfumed, and gowned by Miss Tam. Her hair was pulled atop her head but small curls cascaded down the nape of her neck and dangled at her temples.

Truly she could not believe her eyes as Miss Tam ran from the room and in a few seconds returned carrying a mirror. She barely recognized the woman staring back at her, so beautiful and different did she look.

"Why you be just a vision, child," Miss Tam exclaimed, patting one last strand of hair into place.

Christine could not reply, so entranced was she with the vision in the mirror. If only her mother were alive to see her daughter now. This was exactly what her mother had wanted for her daughter, a beautiful gown, a grand house, and a man of power and position. Perhaps she did not have the latter two yet, but before she was done she had no doubt she would have all her mother had ever wished for her.

The dress seemed to hold a form of power over her. She felt confident and in full charge of her destiny as she left her chambers and smiled graciously at Edward Blackthorn, who awaited her presence in the dining room.

He seemed almost to gape at her as she walked into

51

the room. The gown was the perfect color to complement her fair beauty, as he knew it would be when he had passed Madame Dupree's dress shop window and seen the creation hanging within. He had wasted no time but gone straight in; and after arguing for the better part of an hour with the tiny woman who owned the shop, she insisting the gown was to belong to another and he throwing his influence and money about. He had left the shop with a large package under his arm.

As he helped Christine into her chair he caught a glance of bosom and the delicate scent of her perfume filled his nostrils; he knew that without reservation he would willingly once again spend another afternoon haggling over a gown for her.

Christine's soft smile lightly touched upon the master of Iva Rose as she viewed his slight flush when he took his seat at the head of the long table.

"Thank you for the gown, Mr. Blackthorn," she commenced the conversation, feeling in complete control of the situation. "It is quite beautiful."

"You most surely are welcome, Christine. You do me great honor by wearing it and having dinner with me this evening." Her very smile filled him with an exhilaration he had not felt in years. "Perhaps you would also do me the honor of calling me Edward. You must know by now that my interest in you is not that of employer to servant."

Christine smiled at him, a knowing smile, though she was far from realizing exactly what this strange, gentle man wanted their relationship to be. "Very well then, Edward it shall be."

The mere mention of his name by those soft pink lips made him feel eighteen once again. The power this woman had over him seemed to rage through his veins.

By bringing in the first course of the meal, Dell and Mandy interrupted the exciting spell that was cast about the room.

The two conversed lightly throughout the remainder of the meal. At the finish of the delicious repast, Christine retired to her bed chamber and Edward to his study.

Two glorious and carefree months swept by, and to Christine it seemed the past had never existed or had indeed been some bad dream. Newgate, the prison ship, and even the small clapboard home she had shared with her mother seemed now to hold no reality for the woman who lived at Iva Rose. Her gowns were of the finest material; her chambers had been moved from the small downstairs room, with one single cot, to a large, scrumptious chamber on the second floor of the stone mansion, with every appointment she could have ever possibly imagined.

Edward Blackthorn had proved more than a gentleman. He was kind and considerate, her every whim granted. He seemed to enjoy pampering this luscious beauty who lived under his protection. He tried to anticipate her every wish, often being over-zealous in his dedication.

Often Christine found it a bit boring, being petted and pampered day in and day out. At times she wished she could kick off her slippers and shout and laugh aloud, but never did the feeling persist. All she had to do on these occasions was to think back to the days of herb soup, patched dresses, and freezing cold with no way to warm herself, and all thoughts of acting in any such a manner flew out the window.

The only thing from her past that nagged at her was her remembrance of Cora. Still she had not heard about the girl. She had asked Edward one evening as she sat across from him in the parlor, sipping sherry and reclining against the settee, if he by chance had observed who had purchased the papers of the girl who had followed her that day at the auction.

This was the first time that Edward Blackthorn had treated this young beauty any way but fondly. "I have no idea what could have possibly happened to anyone else at that auction." His tone was haughty, almost arrogant, and Christine knew without asking that she had made a mistake by asking about Cora. He would never lower his Blackthorn pride by trying to find out what had become of a filthy beggar such as Cora. That was the last time Christine had asked about the other girl but Cora was constantly in her thoughts.

Edward, as the master of Iva Rose had insisted his bond servant call him, taught Christine how to ride a horse and even ordered several riding habits to be made for her in New Orleans. At first Christine had tried to pretend that she could sit a horse, but it was obvious she had not had any previous experience in riding and Edward seemed to enjoy the small project of teaching her.

Christine had been afraid that he might think it odd, her not being able to ride, when she had told him she had been raised on a country estate. But he did not seem to think it strange, or at least he did not mention any mistrust, so she was able to breathe easily and enjoy her daily outings on her mount.

However Christine was truly held in a form of limbo. She did not really understand Edward Blackthorn's intent toward her. There seemed to be some kind of underplay in his devotion. At times she caught him unaware, his light green eyes holding her with almost a burning desire, one that was so out of place in the kindly old man that she thrust the thought from her mind, putting it down to her own imagination.

All too soon though Christine was to learn of Edward's thoughts. Dinner that evening was as usual, in the formal dining room, with light conversation, good food and wine. Afterward Edward led Christine to the small, informal parlor, for a glass of sherry.

Christine felt something different in Edward's manner that evening. His eyes held a certain light, which she had not seen before, and when they met Christine's blue pools he seemed to stare intently, as though trying to pull a string of secrets from their depths. His fingers lightly brushed against her shoulders, lingering overly long, as he seated her at dinner. This was the first such touch that Christine had received from the master of Iva Rose, and she felt herself trembling with nervous anticipation for the close of the evening.

"You look exceptionally lovely this evening, my dear," Edward drawled, his old eyes lingering on the abundant display of creamy bosom, revealed at the top of her gown. "That mint-green color suits you quite well." His voice was deep and very appreciative.

"Thank you Edward," Christine murmured, feeling a bit uncomfortable as she sipped at her wine and felt his eyes on her breasts.

Edward leaned back and took a deep draught of sherry. "Tell me Christine, what do you think of Iva Rose? Since your arrival over two months ago you have not told me how you feel about my home. You seem to be getting along well but I would like to hear from your own lips what you feel."

Christine's look was questioning as she listened. "Why, Edward, I love Iva Rose. I find I do not truly know my place, but as you treat me as a favored guest and have lavished so much upon me I find that I have never truly been happier."

The room was held for several minutes in an electrifying quiet before Edward finally spoke again.

"Your place you say? Ah, that is exactly what I wished to speak with you about."

Christine looked to the elderly man.

"I bought your papers, and at the time had thought of you as a servant; but after hearing your history and getting to know you somewhat over these past months, I find the idea of you doing any kind of labor preposterous. I have thought of nothing else, Christine, for the past few days except how to phrase my next question." He paused here, watching for her reaction. "I shall continue, I find myself at a complete loss except to come directly out and ask you to become my wife."

Christine was beyond being dumbfounded; she sat all but paralyzed. Had she heard this old, wrinkled man correctly? He had actually asked her, Christine Tate, the daughter of a man she had never known and a woman who had worked out her life's blood on the streets of London, to marry him? But, of course, he had no idea about her mother and father and her horrible life growing up a poor, ragged creature of the streets. He thought her a woman cheated of her inheritance and cast by fate into the hands of the dishonorable. She had certainly played her part well, not slipping one time in her dealings with the master of Iva Rose. And she had won; all she had to do was say yes to this man, and all of her mother's hopes for her as a child would come true.

Edward took her quiet for reluctance. "I know you must think me quite a bit older than yourself, but I assure you I shall not be lacking in any of my husbandly functions."

Christine's face turned scarlet; she had not even for a moment thought of the things that men and women do in the marriage bed. Would she be able to endure having that old, parched skin next to her own? But did she really have any other choice? she questioned herself. This old man owned her for twenty years. Twenty years was a very long time. He would most likely be dead by that time, and what would become of her in the meantime? If she consented to his wishes she would never again be anyone's servant; she would be free except for being tied to that old, frail body sitting across from her.

Edward Blackthorn sat watching the emotions racing across her smooth, creamy features. He held no doubt of her eventual answer. After thinking of advantages, there could be only one answer, yes.

"What would your friends think? You marrying your bond servant?" Her voice was hardly above a whisper.

"You know me by now, Christine. I do not ask or care what others may think. Many men before me I am sure have married their servants, and I am sure none have had the goodness of your gentle birth, nor have any been as beautiful. Do not stress yourself with worrying about others. If you consent to marry me none will dare to question."

Christine did not need any more time to think over her decision, her future would be secure, she would be the mistress of Iva Rose.

The wedding was held at Iva Rose three weeks after Edward's proposal that evening in the parlor.

Christine awoke earlier than usual, lying still under the coverlet and letting the full force of the day and its meaning flow over her mind.

It was impossible to back out of her agreement with Edward at this late date she told herself, feeling light flutterings in her stomach. "Lord," she breathed. She prayed she would not become ill and ruin the day.

For a minute she held her eyes tightly shut, thoughts going through her mind of the events that would be taking place that very evening there in that very room.

Though Christine had been raised in an unusual manner and had needed to harden herself on many accounts, she still was like most young women of her own age in the manner of her heart and love.

What would it be like to have an old man's hands caressing her high, full breasts? And for those same hands to roam even further over her body? A cold shudder coursed over her and she buried more deeply under the covers.

For a fleeting second a familiar dream filled her mind. She had dreamt it on more than one occasion until it had become a pleasant and sensual experience that could be pulled to mind anytime Christine wished. And as she lay abed on the day that marked such a drastic turning point in her life, she pulled this dream to the forefront of her mind.

Her whole body seemed to fill with a hazy, sensual languorous feeling. She lay in a large bed of soft satin, her golden-fire curls fanning across the pillows, her luscious, tempting body clothed in a clinging, revealing gown of silk; and there at the foot of the bed stood a browned, muscular, virile young man. Never in these dreams did Christine see the man's face clearly, but his voice seemed to vibrate through ever fiber of her being; he whispered huskily words of love and devotion in her ear as his body, lowered to the bed over her own, drove her on to a frenzy of passion.

She held no restraints over herself as his body touched her own. She seemed to hold no modesty as her hands roamed over his muscular haunches, lingering on the broad expanse of chest, her breath catching as her hands grew bolder and moved lower.

The man himself seemed to possess an animalistic nature; his pulsating and throbbing body was a machine of love; not seeming to care for anything but Christine's alluring body.

His lips burned a fiery path over her forehead, over her deep blue eyes, and across her creamy skin until they found the sweet pink lips that provoked and tempted. His hands traced a scalding path over her most intimate parts as her body writhed with untold passion. Strong, lean fingers played a fine tune of sweet, sensual music across her breasts, bringing them to rosy peaks of throbbing wantonness; then lower those fingers played, tantalizing and probing, leaving Christine panting and gasping for breath.

As this bronzed and virile anonymous man rose up and over Christine's body and slowly spread her shapely thighs, she felt shudder after shudder of desire run through her; but as quickly as he came to her mind he vanished, leaving her lacking and wanting.

Only in her dreams had she known those feelings of such desire course over her body, and now the thought invaded these dreams that she would be married today; this indeed was her wedding day. Whatever could have possessed her? What kind of woman, on the morn of her wedding, behaved in such a horrible manner, she berated herself.

Edward was perhaps not as young as the man of her dream or as well set up, but he was kind of heart and concerned for her well-being. Perhaps she would never know how her dream might end, for never in those dreams had the man ever reached his goal, Christine always came awake before the finish. But though in Edward's arms she might never know that consuming, fiery passion, she would be secure and safe; she would not have to be afraid that at any minute her bubble would burst, and she would once again be thrown to the cruel world outside. She would not have to worry about her next meal or to worry about clothing to cover her body. She would have a wealthy husband after this day.

Even with these thoughts of reality boldly going through her mind, again images of her young, virile seducer-dream-man flirted daringly before her minds' inner vision.

"Oh dreams, oh dreams," she felt like weeping. Would this be her reality, an old man's body in bed next to her own at night, and her dream-man secretly tucked away in a hidden recess of her mind, awaiting the times when she could no longer remain unsatisfied and he came rushing to mind?

Only a few of Edward Blackthorn's friends were invited to the wedding and these were business associates and their wives.

Miss Tam outdid herself with the wedding dinner and in seeing that everything was in order on such short notice.

Christine entered the large formal parlor on the arm of Edward's attorney, James Courtly. A startling hush came over the guests as this vision in white lace floated in. Edward stood at the opposite end of the room with a broad grin on his face.

He had sent an urgent message to the same dress shop, the morning after Christine's consent to wed him, for Madame Dupree to design and sew the most beautiful wedding gown she could. He had also written that there would be a large bonus if the gown was done on time and was up to his expectations. He made a mental note now as Christine swept into the room, the most beautiful woman he had ever seen; Madame Dupree would, indeed, receive a very large bonus from him.

Her hair had been piled atop her head; tiny curls

glittered from the pearl hairpins in their centers. Miss Tam had lightly painted blue eye shadow above each eyelid, and rouge lightly dusted her cheeks. Her eyes had a sparkle that took in everything, and Edward, his heart beating at a rapid pace, tried to calm himself.

The ceremony was hurriedly gone through, Christine remaining cool with almost an icelike bearing.

She had prepared herself for this day and for the whispers spread about the room by Edward's friends, some most shocked to see the elder man marry a young girl such as she, others beyond shock that he would dare to marry a simple bond servant. But nothing would prevent Christine now from taking hold of her own destiny. Let them talk behind her back and whisper behind their fans, she couldn't care less what anyone of them would think; she would be mistress of Iva Rose.

The afternoon went by in a whirl for the newly married couple. Friends were entertained, gifts were opened, and toasts were offered. All too quickly though for Christine, night came, and try as she did to fortify herself with abundant glasses of champagne, still she was not prepared to make her way to the bridal chambers when the time came.

Miss Tam had spent hours that afternoon decorating the chambers all in white, curtains, carpet, and even the white satin counterpane draped across the large fourposter bed. There were white and pink flowers, in a variety of different-sized vases, placed about the room. Christine's thoughts as she glanced around had no relationship to the joy and expectation a young bride was suppose to feel; the room brutally reminded her of the evening ahead.

Her nerves seemed completely shattered from the long, drawn-out day that lay behind her and from having to keep a becoming smile plastered on her face for Edward's guests, and for her new husband.

She gulped down a small glass of champagne quickly and poured another. Thank God, Edward had left her to prepare for the evening ahead, on her own. He had remained downstairs, lingering with his guests, his old rheumy eyes following her as she glided up the stairs.

She knew her reprieve would be short-lived, but as Mandy, who had been elevated from the kitchen to be lady's maid to her mistress, prepared a brass tub of steaming water, Christine tried to get a better grip on herself.

Finally she was Mrs. Edward Blackthorn, mistress of this vast planation, Iva Rose; and all she now had to do to seal the agreement was to bed the old master.

Christine found she could not stop her shivering; even as she relaxed against the rim of the tub, letting the heat of the water cover her to her chin, her teeth rattled and she could not seem to quiet her fear.

"Mandy, pour me another glass of champagne." Perhaps if she drank more she could numb her mind and find the strength to endure.

Many girls before, she was sure, had gone through this same ordeal. She reminded herself of the young prostitutes along the London streets, shouting out to any man, young or old, who passed their way. They endured for their lives depended on it, and she herself must follow their example; she would harden her heart and seduce the master of Iva Rose the best she knew how.

He truly was not all that bad, she reminded herself. He was always kind and concerned over her well-being, and since she had told him that evening that she would become his bride, he had shown her even greater affection. The only thing that truly placed so cold a dread over the whole affair was the matter of his age. But she was a great actress, she reminded herself, and she had played many roles throughout her young life; now she would pretend to play another part, although this one would be for her future, a future of position and wealth if she was good enough.

Mandy returned quickly with a glass bearing the sparkling liquid and a large, fleecy towel.

Christine's nightgown was of the sheerest material, pale yellow and clinging to every curve of her voluptuous body. Long slits ran up the sides to the swell of her bosom and were held together by tiny yellow ribbons. A matching robe was placed over all, and then Mandy saw her slightly wobbly mistress into the small chair in front of the dressing table, and proceeded to take the pearl hairpins from Christine's curls, brushing the copper mass until it glistened like sparkling fire in the dim candlelight.

"Oh, Miss Christine mam, you be the prettiest bride there ever be," Mandy exclaimed, stepping back and viewing her handiwork.

"Thank you Mandy," Christine murmured softly, as she looked on at the woman staring out at her from the mirror.

Could this possibly be Christine Tate looking back at her? She felt distant from herself, as though she were watching through a hazy glass window a woman who looked and acted as she.

Her body relaxed with these thoughts. If she could go through the rest of the night with this strange detached feeling within, she would congratulate herself in the morning for being truly a great actress.

Her thoughts were so deep and so wrapped about herself that she did not hear the chamber door open, hear her new husband enter, or hear Mandy's leave-taking.

Edward Blackthorn stood quietly entranced with

the vision sitting across the room. The sheer beauty of this woman seemed to ravage his body of his very breath. She was a goddess, a woman truly beyond human reach, one whose beauty would surpass and even overwhelm that of any mere mortal on earth.

Christine must have heard some small sound of his harsh breathing, for she whirled about on her chair and faced the man who now claimed to be her husband.

Edward smiled nervously, as he pulled the door to and started toward her. He did not speak until he stood directly in front of Christine. "You are truly lovely." His voice was full of worship as his eyes slowly devoured her own.

Christine's heart seemed to still, but the champagne and wine she had imbibed during the afternoon had done their job well. Her mind was held in a blue haze, everything in her vision seeming to soften, including her new husband's elderly features.

A small, wavering smile came to her soft pink lips, and she slowly extended her hand for Edward to help her to her feet. "You are overly kind with your compliments, my lord," She shocked herself as much as her husband with the seductiveness of her sultry voice.

Edward, for a fleeting minute, held the thought of wishing that he could once again be a young, virile man of twenty-one. But quickly the thought passed as her incredible beauty wrapped about him and entwined itself fully through his mind and soul.

This was why he had never married before, he told himself. Never could he have found a bride so desireable and so beautiful as he now possessed. And though it had taken him over sixty years he finally held the one woman in all the world with whom he wished to share his name and bed.

There was no backing out now for Christine, the die

had been cast that fateful day she had said yes to Edward Blackthorn's proposal. And now, as she felt his lips placing soft, tiny kisses upon her forehead, Christine shut her eyes tightly and tried to imagine that she truly cared for this kindly man who held her tightly in his arms.

Edward's senses were filled with this beauty who now belonged to him, and slowly he drew her robe from about her full, soft body. His breath caught for a full minute as he viewed the sweet, sensual curves that were laid bare to his vision, with only the thin, sheer material covering her.

"Ah Christine, you have driven me mad with the want of you. In all my years I have never seen beauty such as yours." His voice was low and husky and filled with deep emotion, as he drew her to the large four-poster bed.

Christine sensed her earlier nervousness return as she felt his hands reach down and draw the gown over her head.

His breathing was audible and seemed to fill the room with its vibrations as he looked down at her white creamy satin skin and rose taut nipples rising and falling daringly with each breath she drew.

To Christine everything seemed to be happening in slow motion. She watched, as though a ghost of herself, the passing events.

As though in a dream Christine found herself lying flat on her back on the satin counterpane and watching as Edward, as quickly as possible, shed his clothing.

Christine was surprised as she viewed his body objectively. His figure was in fine shape, from horseback riding and the excercize that daily he experienced in the running of his plantation; she was a bit shocked at his figure for a man of his years. Though his muscles and skin tone were not as tight as a young man's, he did not have the usual paunch and flab of a man of his years.

Christine's breath caught in anticipation as Edward rose above her, spreading her thighs and softly probing the valley between.

Soft, sweet words of endearment came from his lips, and his tongue gently teased the tips of her breasts.

Christine lost herself in the sensations burning hotly and rushing fiercely through her veins. For a fleeting moment she thought of she had been simpleminded as to dread this man's making her his. She had nothing to fear as far as Edward Blackthorn was concerned.

Quickly those fearful thoughts vanished as Edward, rising above her and looking deep into her violet-blue eyes, made a gentle but persistent push into her body.

A small moan of pain filled the room and her husband's ears as Christine's virginity was broken through.

Edward's own face registered shock. He had never questioned his new wife on the matter of her virtue but took for granted that she certainly would not be a virgin, after her rough life of imprisonment and the horrors inflicted upon her.

His heart swelled with a tender love for this woman as he viewed the tears silently making a path down her cheeks.

"You hurt me, Edward," she wept, sounding more like a tiny child than a beautiful, sensuous woman; she could not believe that her kind and understanding husband would ever do anything to bring such pain to her as he had just willingly done.

"Oh, my dear," Edward said softly, stilling his body atop hers. "Never again shall I ever bring you any pain. You are dearer to my heart than my own very soul."

Christine looked up into his weather-beaten face, hearing the truth of his words, and in those few seconds she felt herself changing. His features softened to her vision, and her hardened, cold heart seemed to crack and find in its center a warm, tender spot for this gentleman who was now her husband.

She raised a small white hand and laid it tenderly against his cheek; slowly she outlined the weathered lines about his lips and eyes. His truly was the face of kindness and gentleness, she told herself.

Edward felt true jubilation at this gentle caress from his wife and tightly he clasped her to him. His eyes brimming with unshed tears, he swore to himself that he would never regret his decision to marrying this woman; she would make him a fine wife and he would never find a more fitting mistress for Iva Rose.

Chapter Four

For over fifty years Iva Rose had lain dormant, existing only because of a will far greater than that of the ancient, cold stone walls that marked its boundaries; the sheer strength and endurance of the masters of this fertile land, had forced it to thrive and lie placid. Now after these long years a new and strangely exhilarating pulse seemed to beat throughout the extensive grounds and in the interior of Iva Rose. At last there was a mistress, perhaps one without the breeding and background that the long-dead Blackthorns would have wished in one who sat regally over their domain but still a mistress.

Instead of the soft-spoken words that had previously

been whispered inside the stone mansion, now laughter and a genuine feeling for life seemed to thrive within.

Christine herself seemed to be quite a capable mistress for Iva Rose; and Edward Blackthorn found in her more than just a wife; he also found a woman who could read and write, one to whom he could come home and tell his problems or his good fortune. Rarely did she share his bed but on the nights they spent together he knew he would never go lacking or disappointed. He had waited until late in life but he found that the wait had been well worth it.

Edward seemed to feel his youth returning everytime he glanced in the direction of his young wife. He scheduled his days about her, including her in all he did. Whether it was riding about and seeing to his plantation or business matters brought to him by James Courtly, Christine was always present, and Edward found her more than just a pretty ornament; she had a sound business mind, and many of her suggestions about running Iva Rose and other matters were taken into consideration.

Christine now lived everyday as she had been taught by her mother; she was dressed in the most fashionable and expensive gowns that could be found, she was draped with jewels, both family heirlooms and priceless pieces that Edward continually brought home from business trips to New Orleans. There was nothing she lacked that money could buy; her every whim was satisfied. The only thing missing in her life could not be bought; she had no close friends. Oh, of course, there were the usual friends of Edward's who made it a point to invite her to outings and parties, but she knew these invitations were only sent because of Edward's importance and wealth. If he had been a poorer plantation holder who had dared society and married his bond servant, she knew with a certainty that the pair of them would have been shunned by decent society and treated as outcasts.

Christine felt a coldness go through the marrow of her bones every time she was around those women who pretended to be her friends, for under their fine surface she could sense their withdrawal and actual dislike for the beautiful young woman who had come from a prison ship, been sold on an auction block, then with a stroke of luck that none of them could comprehend had trapped and seduced one of the richest men of New Orleans into marriage.

Like a dutiful wife who did not want to worry her husband, Christine kept all these feelings harbored unto herself. She truly knew that Edward would be hurt to know that so many of the people he had always held as friends could be so cruel as to question his judgment about whom to wed, and that they whispered behind his back about affairs that to him would have seemed none of their business. Christine once again found her acting ability a blessing as she smiled graciously to one lady or another, but beneath her beautiful features was a cold heart screaming for vengeance.

Her one true friend had been Cora, she reminded herself almost daily. She had begged Edward after their marriage to try to find the girl so she could have her for her own personal maid. He had promised to try to determine her whereabouts, but so far he had been unable to garner any information. Perhaps, she told herself, Edward would have better luck this week in New Orleans. She would not be going along on this trip; she had been feeling rather poorly these last few days, the heat perhaps or some slight ailment. Miss Tam had suggested lightly that morning, as she placed her tray of tea and rolls upon a small table next to her bed and at first Christine had shuddered and had to look away, that perhaps she had picked up a flu from one of their guests the week before. Perhaps that was it she told herself as she reclined against the satin counterpane across her bed. But whatever, it should not last much longer, then perhaps she herself could ask about for the dark-haired, freckled-faced girl who had been sold on the auction block the same day as she.

"Aha, this is where you are hiding." Edward entered her room, his face in a big grin and all concern. "Miss Tam told me this morning that you still did not feel too well. Is there anything I can do for you, my dear?"

Christine found that the face before her was the dearest she had ever known. She held out a slender white arm to him and gently smiled. "Sit with me, Edward. I do not feel so badly now and would greatly appreciate your company."

These few words were like a life raft thrown to a drowning man and quickly he did as bid. "You still look a little pale, perhaps I should not go and leave you for the week. I could postpone this trip until you can accompany me."

"Oh no, Edward, I will be fine and Miss Tam is here with me. I do not wish to be a burden and truly I feel better. I think I need only rest for a few days."

His light green eyes seemed to penetrate deeply into her own violet depths, trying to see the truth of her words. Finally a light smile replaced the frown that had clouded his features. "You are right as usual my dear, I only lose all sense of reason as far as you are concerned. But to be on the safe side I shall leave Joel here at Iva Rose, and if you feel the least bit worse you have only to tell Miss Tam, and she shall have Joel leave at once and get word to me at our house in New

Orleans."

"Edward, Edward, what would I do without you?" Christine murmured, softly placing a light kiss upon the weathered forehead.

"I hope it shall be a time before you find that out, my pet. You have brought joy and happiness into this house and into my heart. You have done what no other has been able to do, and I would move heaven and earth to see that you stay well. To postpone a trip is a light concern compared to leaving you ill."

"Perhaps you think me sicker than I truly am. I do but feel a slight bit under the weather and I shall not hear any more of your postponing your trip. Every time your wife has an ailment you shall not be able to tell your business associates that they shall have to proceed without you." Her small delicate face broke out in a grin.

Edward's deep throaty laughter filled the bed chamber. "You with your lovely looks, you are a witch." His lips took hers in a tender embrace.

Christine did, in fact, at the onset of evening feel better. It seemed strange but she mostly felt ill in the mornings and by evening was feeling well and rather hungry. "Witch you say, my lord? I shall have you know there has never been a witch in my family, at least none that I have ever heard about." Her own laughter fell in with his, and before long she found herself entangled in her husband's arms. Their love as on nights previous was not the passionate, throbbing sensation of a younger couple but rather that of gentleness for one another, closeness, and sharing. Christine had not known any other lover so she was satisfied with the feelings that Edward brought to her.

Early the next morning Christine stood on the stone steps leading to Iva Rose and waved good-bye to her husband. She stood watching until he and his great black horse were out of sight then made her way back to her bedchamber. Again this morning she sensed her stomach turning and felt a bit faint. She had tried to appear well and fit in front of Edward, for she knew if he thought her ill he would not go into New Orleans. She had no wish to disturb his usual routine; she had already turned his life about and changed everything from his clothing drawers to the place where he usually kept his favorite pipe.

She smiled as she thought of these changes she had made. He had not wanted to seem upset by her changing things about but instead had looked here and there trying to find the simplest of items. She had told him time and again only to ask and she would get him anything he wished, but more than once she had found him not wishing to disturb her but instead looking in drawers and cabinets with no results.

Ah, indeed she had been lucky that fateful day in New Orleans, standing there in front of that crowd, on an auction block. Her lucky star must have been shining down upon her for Edward Blackthorn to have noticed her at all.

"Are you all right, Miss Christine?" Mandy entered the room and, as she went about her duties of straightening up and putting the room to order, questioned her.

"I am afraid my illness is back upon me, Mandy," Christine replied, climbing back into the large, four-poster. "I cannot understand it, I feel so queazy and nauseous."

Mandy gave a knowing smile. "My mammy she felt the same way two years back when she was taken with my little brother, Miss Christine. But I don't be as knowing if'n you being a white lady if you be in a like fix."

Christine could not quite make out the words and

questioned her with a penetrating glance. "What on earth do you mean, Mandy? Taken with your little brother?" She shook her head.

Mandy grinned broadly. "Why, Miss Christine, I be meaning that she was a-carrying young Jeremiah in her belly."

Christine stiffened as though turned to stone. She had not even thought of that; could she possibly be pregnant with Edward's child? She had thought him too old to father a child. But did she know that for a fact? Were not her symptoms the same as other women's when they were with child?

Edward would be proud and jubilant if she were to bear his child, she knew, but would she herself want a babe? She had never thought to bring a child into the world; she truly had never thought she had the mother instinct that most women possessed.

Mandy once more brought her from her thoughts by asking if there was anything else she could be doing.

Three days whirled by in a blue haze for Christine. Miss Tam agreed with Mandy that her mistress's symptoms were those of most pregnant women.

Instead of the happiness most women feel at such a time, Christine felt rather cold and let down inside. But she was determined that if this should prove to be what was the matter with her she would do her best to please her husband and be a good mother to the babe.

The day seemed warmer than the others and try as she would, Christine could not find a cool spot in the stone mansion. Sweat trickled between her breasts and lightly glistened on her upper lip, as she fanned herself on the front veranda.

Mandy brought out a cool glass of lemonade, and as she placed the tray upon a table she straightened, and shading her eyes she looked down the oak-lined lane leading to the main road.

"I think we be a-having a visitor, Miss Christine."

"Oh, really? I wonder who it could be. I do not recall anyone being invited to Iva Rose. Perhaps it is only Mr. Downs, the overseer, coming to report some minor infraction or problem in the fields." She seemed to be talking more to herself than to her black maid, for of a sudden she felt a cold dread come over her heart.

The man came at a full gallop, riding a light brown, foam-flecked horse, which looked ready to drop from exhaustion. "Mrs. Blackthorn?" the man questioned.

After Christine's nod, the man leaped from his mount and started to the steps.

Just then Miss Tam arrived at the front door because Mandy had rushed to the kitchen to tell her of a visitor. She thought that perhaps whoever it was would care to sit down to supper, but one look at this strange man's face and she knew this was no social visit but one of grave importance.

Christine rose from her chair, feeling faint.

"I am afraid, mam, that I have been given the unfortunate duty of bringing you bad news."

"Edward!" Christine shouted, grabbing the back of the chair in order not to fall.

The young man saw in an instant the state in which the woman before him was and rushed to her side.

Miss Tam also was out the door and at her mistress's side.

"I shall be all right," Christine murmured, as she was helped to sit once again in the wicker chair.

"I am sorry, Mrs. Blackthorn."

"You said you have some kind of news?" Christine questioned, afater taking a sip of the lemonade.

"I was sent by Mr. Courtly, mam. I'm afraid it concerns your husband." The young man did not know how to continue.

Christine felt a steel vise encircle her heart and pull tight. "Tell me please," she whispered, her hand clutching at her throat.

"I know no way to cushion the blow, Mrs. Blackthorn. Your husband was found this morning along a side street in New Orleans. It appeared he had had either a heart attack or a stroke during the night."

Great tears slid from Christine's violet eyes down her cheeks. She felt numb; her whole world seemed to be shattering around her, and she was powerless to do anything about it.

Miss Tam also seemed to be in shock and stood staring at the young man who had brought the message of doom.

"If there had been any way, mam, that I could have made it easier I would, indeed, have tried, but Mr. Courtly requested that you please come to New Orleans as quickly as possible and claim the body."

These words seemed so cold and harsh to Christine. The body? Those words were meant for her husband, Edward. She had to go and claim Edward's body? Is that what this young man was saying?

Miss Tam pulled herself from her stupor. "Thank you sir; my mistress shall be in New Orleans as soon as possible. You may take this message to Mr. Courtly if you would be so kind."

The young man nodded his head in understanding. "I surely will, and Mrs. Blackthorn, I am awful sorry."

Christine did not hear his words or his leaving. She was led slowly into the house by Miss Tam's strong arms and placed in her large bed.

Joel was sent for and told to go to Mr. Courtly to

help with the invitations to the funeral, for their mistress was too ill to attend to the affair herself.

The funeral was held two days later. A light drizzle pelted the guests who had come this one last time to pay their respects to a dear friend.

Most of the people who attended had been invited by Mr. Courtly, having been told that Mrs. Blackthorn was ill and taking the death of her husband badly. Some whispered behind their fans, and others did not even have the decency to whisper; they did not believe the young bride of such an old and sometimes hard-to-get-along-with gentleman, such as Edward Blackthorn had been, could truly be so upset by his demise that she could not bring herself to send out her own invitations.

Left to Christine though, none of these vile friends of Edward's would have been there that day. She would have preferred to grieve alone for the man she had learned to love and respect, as she had no other.

Those so-called friends, she thought, were there merely out of curiousity about what would be happening at Iva Rose. Mr. Courtly had brought out Edward's will and after the funeral was going to read aloud, to the few people who were mentioned within, the contents of the papers. Christine herself had no idea of the contents of the will. When she placed a lone red rose atop her husband's casket, as it was lowered into its grave, a cold hatred came upon her. She had loved this man in her own fashion and these people did not even care. They only sought out their own interests. What was she to them but a criminal, come off a prison ship and sold as a mere slave. They cared nothing for her or her feelings. A trembling sob escaped her as she was drawn from her husband's graveside by Mr. Courtly.

"You mustn't stay out here any longer, Mrs. Black-thorn. You'll catch your death in this foul weather." He grasped her elbow and drew her after him, up the path leading back to the stone mansion.

Christine did not realize she had been standing at her husband's graveside all by herself. All the guests and most of the slaves had already left to seek shelter from the steady downpour. She noticed now as she and Mr. Courtly left that they were the last to depart. Soon the slaves would cover Edward's casket with cold dark earth, and only his dear memories would live on in her mind forever.

The only gentlemen whom Mr. Courtly had asked into the den along with Christine and himself were a Samuel F. Lenox and a Terrance Altman. The first owned a small number of shares in Edward Black-thorn's shipping line, and the latter had been Edward's lifelong friend and a captain of one of his ships.

"Gentlemen, and you also Mrs. Blackthorn, if you will allow me to play host while we are here in the library, please kindly take a seat." Mr. Courtly pointed to three chairs facing Edward's large, impos-ing desk.

"Edward's will is frankly quite simple. Mr. Black-thorn left all his possessions and wealth to his beloved wife, Christine Blackthorn."

Tears glistened on Christine's lashes as these words reached her ears.

"His exact words to me were that he had found late in life the love he had always looked for, and that his wife did, indeed, care for him and not for what she could gain." Mr. Courtly smiled kindly at Christine. "I must admit I questioned Edward on the wisdom of this new will he had me draw up for him less than six months ago, but after the conversation we had I was convinced that what he had done was truly the best way."

Christine knew from these words the extent of Edward's love for her; to have convinced a man who thought her a scheming money grabber that she was entitled to all he owned, was a great feat.

"I doubt you know the extent of your late husband's holdings and his wealth, Mrs. Blackthorn. Besides Iva Rose your husband owned two other plantations, one in Virginia and one in Georgia. He also owns property on Martinique, an island in the Caribbean. It shall be, of course, up to you, whether you wish to sell or to go on as Edward had and draw off the revenues.

"Also there is the shipping line, consisting of over twenty ships, which is where you gentlemen come in." Mr. Courtly paused here as he looked to the two men.

"You Mr. Lenox, Edward had great faith in. He sold you shares in his shipping line at a time when you were in need; true he did not dispense of too many shares but enough that he worried. He requested that you consider selling back these shares for a handsome price."

Samuel Lenox's face held a small grin; he was sure to make a good deal of money, even though he knew his few shares could hardly matter one way or another.

"And now for you, Mr. Altman." Here Mr. Courtly let out a long sigh. "Edward loved you as a brother; he told me this once, you know. He said you two had grown old together and had seen much of the world together. He leaves you two of his finer ships with the condition that you sail for Mrs. Blackthorn as long as you remain a captain and in charge of a vessel."

Terrance Altman opened his mouth to speak but seemed to be struck dumb. Tears slid down his browned cheeks.

Christine did not in the least begrudge the man these ships; in fact knowing the love Edward held for him made her want to shower even more gifts upon him.

"I am afraid, Mrs. Blackthorn, that under such quick notice I have not as yet been able to complete a sheet on the precise amount of the funds, jewels, and other valuables, including properties and the town house in New Orleans. It shall take a while but I can assure you that you are quite a wealthy woman and shall have no financial worries whatsoever."

Christine did not know how to respond. Was she supposed to feel some kind of joy in knowing that her Edward had left her all he had owned? She would rather he were sitting here beside her now, instead of these strange men. "Thank you," she murmured, not knowing what else was expected of her.

"Will you be staying out here at Iva Rose, Mrs. Blackthorn?" Mr. Courtly asked.

"As far as I know, Mr. Courtly, I shall send word to you if I decide to come to New Orleans."

"Fine, fine, then I think that shall be all. If anything comes up that you should know of I shall not hesitate but come straight away to you here at Iva Rose. You may rest assured that I shall keep your best interest at heart."

"I know you will, Mr. Courtly, I am sure Edward told you about my ability to sort out business matters rather quickly. I am no mincing, pouting female, Mr. Courtly, and you shall do well to keep this in mind." She wanted this man who would be handling all her affairs to know right off that she would not broach any setbacks in her finances.

Mr. Courtly smiled fondly at the lovely young woman sitting across from him. "Indeed, Edward told me of your unusual abilities and quick mind. I am afraid he seemed not to be able to talk of much else but you and of all of your virtues. You may rest easily, child, I shall have only your best interest at heart in all my dealings."

Christine smiled fondly at the older man and rose from her chair. "I am sure we shall get along quite well then, Mr. Courtly."

"I am sure we will," came the lawyer's reply.

The guests who had attended Edward Blackthorn's funeral were seen to the door by a stern-featured Christine. Now that she knew she owned all about her, she was not about to put on any kind of act of friendship to these people who had always treated her coldly. The only ones to receive more than a slight nod of the head from her were Mr. Courtly and Mr. Altman.

As the days swept by Christine, always wearing her widow's black weeds, remained at Iva Rose, coming to grips with her morning sickness and her protruding stomach. Mandy and Miss Tam had been right in their belief that her discomfort was a bit more lasting than a few day's flu.

Not long after Edward's funeral Christine sent for a doctor, knowing deep down what her "ailment" was but needing to have it confirmed by a medical man.

After a slight examination the squat, gray-haired doctor smiled fondly at the mistress of Iva Rose, rubbed his forefinger through his mustache, and nodded his head. "You are indeed pregnant, madam. My congratulations."

Hearing the words aloud and knowing there was no turning time back to set the situation aright, Christine thanked the kindly man, paid him the small price he asked; and after his leaving, retired to her bed, not to see anyone but Mandy for over a week.

During this time she searched her mind and soul; she did not wish to have a child, but she also knew that she would, if only to insure an heir for Iva Rose; she at least owed Edward that one thing. After all he had given her, she could endure a few more months to bring his seed into the world.

Stepping from her room that day was a new Christine Blackthorn; gone was the young woman, so full of life. What remained was a hard-shelled woman of authority and power.

She sent for James Courtly when she became so large she could no longer hide her burden behind her skirts. She wanted to insure the future of the child she carried in case something might happen to her.

She also had another situation about which she wished to talk with him. The girl Cora, she wanted her found, and she was willing to spend any amount of money in order to do this. In the short time she had known the girl, she had formed such an attachment that she could not forget her. The girl was truly the only reason that Christine herself was alive; without Cora she knew she would never have withstood all the tortures of prison and the foul prison ship. Perhaps if she could find her; she would once again have someone to confide in and to care about.

James Courtly was a man of quickness and fortitude; not more than two weeks passed since he had left Iva Rose before he was once more standing on the front veranda.

Christine was surprised at his speed, but she knew that Edward had treasured this lawyer highly, and now she saw for herself one of the reasons; he was not one to sit mildly by and await things in their own good time; he accomplished what he set out to do and he did it as quickly as possible.

"Come into the parlor, Mr. Courtly; we can talk

there and Miss Tam will bring us tea and cakes. She does make the most wonderful treats now that I am in this condition." Christine laughed lightly and she saw the flush overtake his face, as his eyes moved to her protruding stomach. She knew this old gentleman was not used to women speaking their minds, especially about parts of the body, but she found herself genuinely pleased with herself for being able to bring a gentleman such as this to such uncomfortableness.

"Aha," Mr. Courtly cleared his throat as he entered the parlor and took a chair. "Perhaps we should get right to the subject at hand, Mrs. Blackthorn."

"Indeed do," Christine smiled. "I am quite anxious to hear what you have been able to find out."

"Well to begin with I had my investigators start from the last place you had seen the young woman, at the auction."

Christine sat on the edge of her seat, her pulse hardly beating as she listened to his words.

"She was, indeed, sold after yourself as you had thought. I found out who purchased her papers and all I could of the young woman at this time."

He caught his breath here as Mandy brought in a tray of tea and cakes.

"Continue," Christine said in a strained voice, ignoring the girl as Mandy turned about and left the room, leaving the door slightly ajar.

"Well, as far as I have been able to find out, the young man who bought her papers also had placed several bids on your own. His name is Justan Carrington. He owns a plantation quite a way from New Orleans and also a small house in town."

"And what of Cora?" Christine asked anxiously.

"It seems this Mr. Carrington also rents a small, though I am told comfortable, house on the outskirts of town, where if all my reports are correct the young lady in question now lives."

"You mean he confines her in his house as a kept woman?" Christine was shocked, though she did not quite know why. It was a common practice of wealthy men to keep mistresses. It had never occurred to her, though, that Cora would be living in such a situation; she rather thought the young girl would be slaving over a big tub of steaming water, washing out some plantation owner's clothing. But now she found that, not living the life of a servant, Cora might not want Christine's help, nor desire to leave the arrangement in which she now found herself. If the gentleman Mr. Courtly had mentioned, who owned Cora's papers, was the same who had bid against Edward, she herself remembered his good looks well. Perhaps she should just leave the situation as it stood and not interfere, she thought, as Mr. Courtly sipped at his tea.

"I will be more than happy to approach this Mr. Carrington on the subject of procuring this young woman's papers for you," Mr. Courtly gallantly offered.

"No, no." Christine waved away his offer with a flick of her wrist. "I think perhaps I should go myself and talk with Cora before approaching the gentleman."

Mr. Courtly looked toward this young determined woman with complete shock. Things were not done in this fashion; a decent woman such as Mrs. Blackthorn did not simply go into a notorious part of town and knock on the door of a woman of Cora's occupation; if not thinking of her own reputation she at least should think of the unborn child.

"Now, Mrs. Blackthorn, I do not think that to be a wise decision. If you stop and think a minute I am sure you will agree."

Christine felt a small flash of anger, and her violet

eyes registered a challenging glare. "You dare to tell me what is wise, Mr. Courtly?" Her brow rose archingly.

"Why, I but thought you would see the sense of prevailing upon my services in this matter. I can assure you I have bought and sold many human properties for your husband in the past and also for a wide range of other gentlemen."

"I have not the slightest care for all that nonsense, Mr. Courtly. If you will be good enough to give me the address of this house that Mr. Carrington rents I will be most grateful." Christine's voice could not hide its icy tone, nor could she hide her agitation at his tone of voice as she reached out a shaky hand to take the sheet of paper he held out for her.

"As you wish, Mrs. Blackthorn; I only hope you do not come to regret your brash decision once you have stepped upon this path you insist on treading. The neighborhood this young woman lives in is not the safest in New Orleans."

Christine gave the man a small smile. "I assure you, Mr. Courtly, nothing could surprise me. I have seen the worst in life and I shall see this thing through without your help or any other's."

Mr. Courtly felt his indignation rise and hastily left his employer's home, refusing her offer of dinner, by saying he had a previous appointment.

The next day Christine, Mandy, and Joel left Iva Rose and headed for New Orleans. Christine had no idea how long she would be staying so she had packed for a lengthy stay at her town house.

It was early afternoon when Joel pulled the team of horses to a halt in front of a large residence. Christine felt a quick and piercing stab of loneliness for Edward as she gazed out her carriage window.

Edward had loved this house and this town almost as much as he had loved Iva Rose. She thought back to the first day he had brought her into town and to this house. A small smile glided across her pink lips as she remembered the animation and happiness that Edward had shown that day.

As soon as the carriage had been pulled to a halt, Edward had grabbed Christine's hand and pulled her from her seat. "You shall love it here, Christine, I promise," were his words as he hurried her up the walk and through the large oak door.

And Christine did, indeed, love the house and had fully enchanted her husband as she had gone from room to room exclaiming her joy at all before her eyes.

The town house was furnished expensively and expertly; most of the downstairs was done in white and gold. The foyer was white marble with gold-leaf design; and the parlor, as Christine stepped through the portal, nearly took her breath away. The carpet was lush and thick, the furniture the most brilliant white with tiny pinstripes of gold interwoven through sofa and chairs. On one whole wall there was a white-marble fireplace, and scattered about the room were a variety of tables and shelves holding small white porcelain figurines.

At first Christine had thought the room so perfect that she dare not move about too much for fear of disturbing something.

But as Edward followed behind her and swept boldly into the room and swung his arms about, she seemed to relax somewhat and let her breath out.

Edward had told her many times to change anything she did not like, but Christine had found that everything in the town house was perfect to her taste; not a thing did her hands replace or move in a different order.

As Joel pulled the carriage door open, small paths of tears could be seen wetting his mistress's face. He knew her thoughts well, for this was also for him the first time of coming to this house without his master. He stood patiently, his face averted so as not to embarrass his mistress.

"Thank you, Joel," Christine softly spoke, her words of thanks, as much for his kindness and understanding as for his services.

Christine felt exhausted, completely drained as she entered the front door of the brownstone house. Quickly, barely glancing about her at the beautiful elegance of the rooms, Christine made her way up the stairs and to the bedchamber she had at one time shared with her husband.

Sitting down slowly on the soft down bed, she looked about the familiar room and thought for a minute that she would not be able to take any more of life's pressures.

As Mandy entered the room disturbing the quiet and as she made to fill the large tub with steaming water, Christine scolded herself harshly; life had to continue. Edward was gone from her and there was nothing she could do to change that fact. What was to be was to be and no matter what happened, it could not be changed.

Later that afternoon, after a leisurely bath and a soothing massage, Christine called Joel to her and explained to the old black man her wish that he go to the address Mr. Courtly had told her was that of her friend, Cora. She told Joel not to mention her name but to explain that his mistress would like a few minutes' time with the lady of the house tomorrow afternoon, if it would be convenient at two o'clock.

She did not wish Joel to mention her name because she wanted to see for herself the surprise written on Cora's face as she, Christine Tate, the girl Cora had met in the depths of Newgate prison, pulled up in front of her house in her elegant carriage and descended from that same vehicle in all her finery. She had, aboard the prison ship one night, told her best friend how she had been brought up and how her mother had promised her all through her younger years that she would be a fine lady one day. She could remember Cora's and her own gay laughter that evening, as rats ran over their bare feet and their own stench wafted about their nostrils, while they banished thoughts of the impossibility of such an event ever happening to a girl who had been sentenced to be a servant. The only future they had to look forward to in those days was one of torment and servitude. Cora certainly would be shocked by Christine's change in fortune, she thought, smiling at the anticipation of seeing her friend's face.

Joel, used to taking orders, reacted only with a rise of his dark brows when given the address by his mistress. He recognized the street name at once, being familiar with all the streets of New Orleans from having been Edward Blackthorn's driver. The street was close to the waterfront district. In most of this section the poorer classes of prostitutes were housed by their protectors, while the majority of the girls living along the waterfront area were on their own and shouted out their many virtues from windows or street corners to any passing stranger. But knowing all this, Joel remained quiet. He had been raised to follow orders and that was exactly what he would do.

A short time later he reported back to his mistress that the lady of the house had said she would, indeed, be pleased to receive a visitor tomorrow afternoon.

Christine felt a surge of nervous anticipation all that morning; she could barely wait to see her friend. Even if the girl did not wish to leave the situation in which she now found herself, perhaps the two of them could visit, even go shopping together; they could again become good friends. Christine realized how dearly she missed Cora as the time for her to leave approached.

The street was even more repulsive than Mr. Courtly had led Christine to believe. But she truly was not daunted; she had grown up in much worse conditions. These streets brought back vividly a life in the past that she would as soon have forgotten but one from which she would not turn her head.

The small pink-brick house to which Joel pulled up seemed a bit out of place there on that filthy street. There was a small yard with roses growing in the garden, and a white fence circled its exterior.

Christine was helped down from the carriage and walked up the stone steps to the front door. She was not prepared for what was to meet her eyes. As the oak door was pulled open, directly following her light knock, she automatically stepped back in alarm.

There stood Cora, or what remained of the girl she had once known. Her black curly hair now was dyed in a reddish tint, her face was painted a ghostly white, and dark circles smudged her eyes.

"Cora," Christine gasped aloud, as her blue eyes took all in.

Cora herself stood as though stunned. "Christine, is it truly you?" She blinked her dark eyes not believing who was standing before her.

Christine could not reply; her violet eyes filled with tears for the girl. How could she have altered so in the short period that they had been parted?

"Come in Christine." Cora swept her purple skirts aside to allow her company to pass through the door. "I have forgotten my manners in all my confusion at seeing you here before me."

At first the two were uncomfortable, neither speaking a word as Cora led Christine into a small sitting room and showed her to a chair.

"You seem to have done rather well for yourself," Cora broke the quiet, noticing Christine's black satins and silks. She also noticed the bulge in her middle but thought not to say anything until the other broached the subject.

Cora's voice had changed over the months; its quality was not that of the gutter as before, but it seemed harder, perhaps too hard.

"Tell me of yourself, Cora," Christine said ignoring Cora's remark.

A cold fright seemed to fill the girl's eyes, and she answered in a guarded voice. "Oh I ain't complaining none, mind you. I guess I got it as good as any around hereabouts. At least I have only one man at a time coming to see me and he pays for the things I'm in need of."

Christine could tell there was more that Cora wished to say, but for some reason she did not dare.

"Cora it is me, Christine. You can tell me."

Christine's eyes penetrated deeply into those before her. She was determined to find out exactly what was going on in this cozy little pink house and especially how Cora felt about her situation.

"I already told you; it's not too bad and it could be a lot worse."

Christine relaxed against her chair; perhaps she was using the wrong approach. She talked of old times aboard the prison ship, reminding Cora of the close friendship they had shared.

Large tears silently slid down Cora's freckled cheeks. Only one time before had Christine seen this hard woman cry, and that was when she had been sentenced and she was afraid her mother would not know what had happened to her.

Suddenly as naturally as laughing and crying, the two girls found themselves clinging to one another as they had long ago in Newgate prison.

"Oh Christine, it has been so terrible; I've tried to take the pain and humiliation that Justan inflicts upon me, but every day I pray he is killed or maimed so he cannot come back at night to this house."

"He made me dye my hair this awful color and paint my face until I look half-dead. I even thought that when the man yesterday brought the message of his mistress coming today, I thought it was another of Justan's cruel jokes. I thought you were his wife. He has told me so many times how he tells her all about me and what goes on in this vile house," Cora sobbed. Once starting her tale, she seemed not able to stop.

Christine let her talk it all out, her rage at the man, Justan Carrington, beginning to boil to the surface. How could a man treat a woman so? And a white woman at that. Why she did not go to the authorities was a wonder to Christine, but later when she asked this question Cora answered that Justan had told her that if she left the house he would have her put in a bordello under lock and key.

Christine had never thought to see Cora afraid of anything, but she now saw plain, raw fear in the other's eyes.

"You must leave, Christine, you cannot be here when Justan arrives. He would be furious; he has such a temper." Cora's eyes were wide and she wrung her hands together upon her lap.

"I shall do no such thing," Christine stated bluntly.

"I am not afraid of this Justan Carrington. My status in life has changed somewhat Cora, and I no longer quake and shudder at the mere sound of a man's voice."

Cora looked on in awe. This was definitely a new Christine; she had certainly changed in the past several months. No longer was she the docile young woman who needed someone to protect her. Their roles in life seemed to have been reversed.

"Do you wish to leave this house and this man you speak of, Cora?" Christine questioned, already knowing her answer but wishing to hear the other say the words.

"I would do anything to get away from him. But how? If I run away the authorities would be sure to find me and bring me back, and then things would even be worse than they now are." The frightened girl paced back and forth, going to the front window pane every now and then and looking down the street.

"You do not have to run away, Cora. I shall simply purchase your papers from this Mr. Carrington," Christine stated, seeming to find no fault with her reasoning.

"You will what?" Cora's dark eyes stared hard at her old friend.

"I said I shall purchase your indentured papers," came the reply again.

Cora was completely dumbfounded. What did she mean, by buying her papers? It would cost a small fortune for her to do this thing, and even if she had the money who was to say that Justan Carrington would let her go? It was true though of late that he had been threatening to sell her to a whorehouse on the waterfront. He had been complaining more and more lately that she was becoming too expensive and he did seem rather bored.

"Listen to me, Cora. I have let this go long enough without telling you what has happened to me since last I saw you." Christine drew the other girl down on the settee next to her.

"I am rich," she said simply at first, letting the words fill Cora's mind with their meaning. "The man who bought my papers that Sunday morning at the auction was the kindest man I have ever met. He changed my whole life; he made me his wife and the mistress of his plantation, Iva Rose. He turned my whole world around, then only a few short months ago he had a heart attack and died, leaving me all he owned."

"Blimey," Cora stuttered. "You aren't fooling old Cora now are you, Christine? Your story sounds as though it comes straight out of some fairy tale book or something of the like."

Christine's tinkling laughter filled the tiny room. This sounded more like the old Cora, full of life and all excited.

"I am telling you the God's truth, Cora." Christine hugged the girl tightly to her. "I have all the money needed to buy your papers and to take care of you and myself."

Cora thought herself dreaming and pinched herself until a large, red welt rose on her arm. How could fortune turn so in one's favor in such a short time, she asked herself.

"Hurry, Cora, I want to be away from here before this Justan Carrington arrives. Pack a small bag, only what you shall be needing for this night. Tomorrow we shall go and have you fitted for a whole new wardrobe." She smiled, setting Cora into action.

"We shall leave a note here on this side table for Mr. Carrington; I shall tell him your whereabouts and request that he make his presence known at my house as soon as possible. I am sure we shall be able to sit down and reach an understandable agreement."

"I'm ready." Cora stepped out of the bedroom even sooner than Christine had time to finish her short note. The girl looked radiant and full of zest, standing there holding a bandanna—containing the few possessions she wished to take along with her. A huge grin spread across her face.

"Let us hurry." Christine grabbed her by the arm and pulled her out the front door and down the steps to the waiting carriage. "Do not look back, Cora," she laughed aloud. "Never look back."

The interview with Justan Carrington was not as pleasant as Christine would have wished nor would have imagined. She found the man completely without scruples and a total cad.

He had at first threatened her with the authorities, laughing and sneering that she would once again be back on the auction block if she did not watch her step.

Christine, at this, had gone into a dark rage, shouting that she would have him arrested for the foul abuse he had inflicted upon a white woman, and screaming that if it took every cent that Edward had left her she would see to it that he would be ruined and lose all he owned.

At these angry threats, Justain Carrington turned a bit paler and sat upon a chair. "You do play a hard hand, Mrs. Blackthorn. It is too bad that Edward outbid me that day, for I would have loved taming you to do my will."

"You can count yourself lucky, Mr. Carrington. You would have found the task most unpleasant, I can assure you," she haughtily struck back at him.

"Ah, I do doubt that, my lady," he added as a final jibe.

"Your price, Mr. Carrington, if you do not mind? I

have not the time to sit and talk with the likes of you."
The man was absolutely the lowest form of humanity,
she told herself.

"You certainly do play the lady well, don't you?" he
said, leaning back and sipping the brandy that had
been served him earlier. "I remember another day
that you were not so fine and arrogant."

"If you shall not name your price, sir, I shall have
my servant show you out and you can take up this discussion with my attorney, Mr. James Courtly." Christine was truly angry now and did not intend to waste
any more of her time with his kind.

"All right, I see you must have your way in this," he
sighed. "I paid a high price for the slut and have
taught her quite a bit. I want double what I paid for
her, not a penny less."

"Done then." Christine rose from her seat. "You
shall have a check tomorrow morning at the little pink
house. There is a piece of paper there on the sideboard; write down your price and then leave my
house." With this she turned and walked from the
room, leaving the servants to show her visitor out.

Lord, how she felt sorry for Cora, having to endure
a man such as he for the time she had. And to think
that at the auction that day she had wished for him,
not Edward, to bid the winning price for her. She
sighed aloud as she went up the stairs and into her
room. Her body was in need of a hot soaking and as
usual Mandy was there to see to her needs.

Chapter Five

"What on earth are you up to now?" Christine waddled into the front parlor and watched as Cora sat with her feet curled up in a chair, puffing on some kind of contraption she had placed upon a low table.

Cora looked up with a grin. "Hurry, Christine. It just arrived today. I saw it in that magazine you had lying about in your chambers so I ordered one. Try it for yourself." She handed her a long tubelike thing that had a hole at the end.

"Pray tell me what it is?" Christine still could not figure out what the girl had.

"Why it is called a hookah. It is a Turkish water pipe, and for centuries men have been using them; and I for one do not see why we women should miss out on such fun."

Christine could neither believe her eyes nor her ears. "A Turkish water pipe?" she questioned. "Why Cora, you do not smoke." She could not restrain her laughter any longer and clutched her bulging belly with her mirth.

"Laugh all you like, Christine." Cora grinned. "But I'll bet you that once you try it you will not be able to put it down. This tobacco has the mildest taste."

"Oh, you are a card. I do not know what I would do without you." Christine said this jokingly but, in fact, she knew these words for the truth. She did not know what she would do without Cora. She was to have her child any day now, and the thought of not having this fun-loving soul beside her would be pure misery. Cora kept her spirits up at all times, and was someone in whom she could confide and to whom she could tell all her deepest secrets. She was a true friend.

She had offered the woman the funds to go back to England or to buy herself a house in New Orleans, but Cora had refused, saying that she would much rather stay with Christine if she did not mind. Mind? She had been ecstatic, she would not have to be alone again.

"Are you sure you won't try it?" Cora questioned as Christine sat gingerly on the edge of the chair.

"Perhaps after the baby is born." Christine smiled, not knowing if she would ever dare to approach the strange-looking device that Cora was now puffing smoke through.

"You see the smoke is cooled in this small vase containing water, so it does not burn your throat. It really is most pleasant."

Christine smiled. "After the babe," she again replied; she was not in the best of spirits today. She felt some slight nagging cramps in her lower back. Perhaps this would be the day for the child to make its way into the world.

Cora noticed her pensive mood and asked lightly, "Is it the babe? Should I send for the doctor?"

"Not just yet. I hear the first can take hours and I'd rather not be put to bed quite so soon."

Fear came over Cora's features. "You are all right, Christine? I would not want anything to happen to you."

"I truly am fine, go on with your pipe. I find the sight rather interesting."

"Interesting you say, a woman sitting and smoking a pipe? I wish you were the bulk of the men in New Orleans, and on seeing this sight they would only reply that it was interesting." Cora's voice had grown husky with her sally, as she tried to enliven her companion's spirits.

Christine knew that Cora had no use for the men of New Orleans after the cruel treatment that she had been put through by Justan Carrington. She herself found it hard to trust men to any extent. They were forever trying to force a woman into her place, which of course was fully set by men. But lucky for her she found herself in a somewhat better position than most women of that day and time; she could pay her own way and make her own decisions, without having to depend on any man, thanks to Edward.

"Oh fiddle, Cora, since when do you give a single fig over what anyone thinks of what you do?" Christine smiled.

"You're right, I don't."

Christine's smile turned into a slight frown and her hand went to her middle. "Perhaps you should get the doctor, Cora." A wrenching pain seared her abdomen and bent her double.

"Christine!" Forgotten was the water pipe as Cora jumped to her feet and ran across the room. "Joel, Joel," she screamed as she clutched Christine to her.

Hurried footsteps could be heard running down the hall. "What be the matter in here?" Mandy called, entering the room, her vision filling with her mistress bent over in pain and her friend Cora holding tightly to her.

"Hurry, Mandy. Call Joel and have him fetch the doctor. It is time for Miss Christine to have her baby. Then come back here and help me get her up the stairs and into her bed." Cora was in full command of the situation now.

Joel was gone in a matter of seconds, and Mandy rushed back into the parlor and helped Cora half carry Christine up to her bed chamber and place her under the covers.

The doctor came over an hour later, and he, Cora, and Mandy helped Christine all during the long night.

Her labor was hard and long, bringing scream after scream from her parched, dry lips.

But in the early hours of the morning, with the dawn light just starting to stream through the French windows in Christine's chambers, a loud wail, that of a baby, could be heard resounding throughout the room.

The tiny heir of Iva Rose, and all that Edward Blackthorn had worked so hard for all of his life, was given the name Chastity Blackthorn. Christine had picked this name very carefully, wanting hers and Edward's child to have a name that would reflect upon her life, and the name of purity was the one that held the most meaning for her at that time.

Indeed, the child was that, as pure and good as any new infant and with the beauty of its mother tempered by the resemblance to its father. Everyone who saw her at first sight was pulled and held by her special beauty, remarking that never had they seen an infant so lovely.

Christine's pride in the child was boundless, but still she felt the pull of the weight of having a tiny life to tend. She truly had no wish to be nursemaid to an infant, and she did not care who thought what of her; she would provide for the child, of course, and she would see that Chastity was taken good care of and had all the love that she needed. She was just not the one to give that special love and care that a child required.

At first she hesitated about broaching the subject with anyone; she knew that people would think it unnatural of a mother not to want to nurture her own offspring, but finally one day she burst out weeping and told all to Cora.

Cora sat with an understanding smile upon her features. "You thought I would think ill of you, didn't you, Christine? Listen to me. I know better than anyone that you love that little girl lying in the room next to this. I understand exactly how you feel, I would feel the same. We grew up hard and fast on the streets of London, and now all of a sudden you have a tiny life thrown into your arms whether you wish it or not."

Christine's tears dried immediately.

"There is nothing wrong with not tending the child yourself. The gentry have always had servants raise their children. There is no need of your being any different. You have plenty of servants who would love the chance to take care of that little darling." Cora patted Christine's folded hands.

"You are right." She looked with amazement written on her face. "Why should I be worrying about what anyone will think. If I do what I think right for the child, that is all that matters. And Miss Tam would dearly love the chance to care for her, I know."

Cora smiled fondly at her dear friend; she had not seen Christine so animated since before the child had been born. "As soon as you're able to get up and about we'll go out to Iva Rose and show little Chastity her new home."

Miss Tam's face split into a wide grin as she held the tiny baby in her arms and cooed her to sleep. "You done just fine, Miss Christine. I do be wishing the master could have seen this tiny bit of fluff. I don't be a-thinking I ever did see a youngun as pretty," the old black woman said in wonder, looking at the infant in her arms.

"I am glad you like her, Miss Tam," Christine said, sitting down at the kitchen table and munching on an apple.

99

"Why, like her? Why, I be loving this here youngun, sure enough."

"I shall be needing your help, Miss Tam," Christine said slowly. "I find I am not exactly the motherly type." She had no idea how this stern black woman would take this news, but after a moment she found she could relax.

"Why, Miss Christine, you ain't needing to tend to this here little thing. You white ladies are more delicate than us with our babies. Why me and that little old girl Dell shall take fine care of this little lady."

"Thank you, Miss Tam." Christine stood up and placed a light kiss upon her dark forehead.

Cora was amazed at Iva Rose. Never had she seen such a place and so many servants. The lawns were so beautiful they could take one's breath away. And all one had to do was ask and anything one could wish for would be granted, if possible.

Still, though, she missed the busy life of the city, the hustle and bustle, the pushing and shoving of walking the streets on shopping day. She also missed the theater, since she and Christine had started attending occasionally, upon learning that Edward had had his own theater box. This life excited Cora far more than that of a country matron. So when Christine told her two weeks after their arrival that she was ready to go back to New Orleans, Cora was more than willing to accompany her.

Christine's life after the birth of her daughter was changed forever. She would now spend one week out of each month at Iva Rose, visiting her daughter, seeing how she was growing and learning, and making sure that all was well. The other weeks of the month she and Cora spent in New Orleans, going to parties, to the theater, and living a life of complete independence.

Christine found that she did not have to try too hard to put her daughter completely out of her mind, except when she visited Iva Rose.

Her inner thoughts were mostly filled with her dead husband's vision, how she had learned to love and depend on Edward Blackthorn; she knew she would never be able to do the same again with another man.

Her nighttime dreams though, after the birth of her daughter, were not plaguing ones of her husband, but instead her dreams were fiery and passion-filled as they had been long ago before she had become Edward's bride. Her stranger-lover was once again brought from the dark recesses of her mind to offer her some slight remote feeling of release.

Chastity
(1729)

Chapter Six

Long honey-gold curls glistened down to a tiny, hand-encircled waist. Emerald-green eyes stared out from under silky, long lashes. The young girl's complexion was creamy smooth, touched with the dew of the sun, bringing a golden tawniness to the surface. Her smile as she sat and posed for her portrait was that of the purest innocence.

"Ah mademoiselle, just one minute longer and we shall rest for the remainder of the day," the artist, tall, lean, and sporting a straight black mustache, coaxed the young woman. Never had he been commissioned to paint a lovelier creature than the one sitting before him, and he swore that this would be one of his best works.

For the past month he had spent his time at Iva Rose, having this vibrant beauty all to himself each afternoon. His shyness prevented him from letting his true feelings show in front of her, but at only her slightest breath he could feel his masculinity swell, and feel his face turn a deep red, while he hoped that she, with her frail purity, would not notice his predicament. He lived daily for the nights now, and for the dreams, in which he could imagine his arms encircling her luscious body. This woman was the epitome of all his hopes and dreams. But she was also beyond his simple reach, and he realized this daily, as he looked into her beautiful face and saw nothing there for him but tolerance, not even for him but for his profession.

A small dark cloud covered the sun, obscuring its bright rays and causing Chastity to let out a small sigh. Her back was aching from the long hours of sitting in the same spot, and the high lace collar of her gown was beginning to scratch her unbearably; and if all this was not truly enough, her wide-brimmed lace hat felt as though it were drooping from the heat. How on earth this young man could stand half the day in this sweltering weather and not even sweat was a mystery to her. She herself felt like melting, and she at least had the pleasure of sitting under a large oak tree, a portion of its high branches bringing her a small measure of comfort.

Why her mother had insisted she have her picture painted in the middle of the summer instead of waiting until the weather was somewhat cooler was a wonder to her. But then she reminded herself that most everything her mother did was of some curiosity to her.

"Miss Blackthorn, if you will only keep your face tilted to that same angle we shall finish soon. The sun is fading fast and my light is already vanishing," the young artist said abstractedly, his hands flying over his canvas.

Her only answer was the same wistful smile he had seen for the past few weeks. Chastity's mind was miles away from this charming young man. She was thinking of her mother, at least the woman who claimed to be her mother, the woman she did not truly know in the least. The only time she saw Christine Blackthorn was on her monthly visits to Iva Rose, and these stays were somewhat hurried and strained, neither mother nor the daughter seemed able to find a line of communication that could open the gap that had formed years before. There was a coldness, almost an icy withdrawal wedged between the two.

These one-week-a-month visits of her mother's were almost too much of an ordeal anymore for Chastity, more than she even liked to admit to herself; after all the woman was her mother, she reminded herself often enough. It was as though her life was not her own but was ruled by this woman on her visits. She bought Chastity's clothing; never had the girl enjoyed a choice in either the cut of the material or the style that she wore. She had had the finest tutors that money could buy brought out to Iva Rose to live until their pupil had learned all they could teach her. Her mother had seen to all for her, she had to admit, except for the one thing that she had always wanted most, a friend, someone to love and with whom she could share her secrets. The only company she had was that of the servants or an occasional employee her mother sent to teach Chastity something new, or such as this Mr. Robert Pursell, sent to do an odd job for her mother.

"Just another moment, almost through, almost through," the young man kept mumbling to himself and rushing about behind his easel.

Finally, after what seemed like an endless amount of time had gone by, Chastity was able to stretch her limbs once again. Lord, she would be glad when this affair was finished. Mr. Pursell claimed that only one more sitting would be needed and the portrait would be finished in time for her mother to view it on her next visit, which was only two days hence.

"Your dinner be a-waiting for you, child." Miss Tam, older in years but still full of life and zest, met Chastity at the door.

"Oh, Miss Tam, I am afraid I am exhausted. Could you send a tray up to my room and ask that girl Dabs if she would bring some hot water up? I am in need of a long, soothing bath." She had removed her hat and was fanning herself hurriedly with it.

Miss Tam saw at once how tired and hot her young mistress was and gave her a loving smile. "You gets yourself on up to your room, honey, and Dabs'll be right on up."

Chastity caught herself before losing her manners completely. "Oh Mr. Pursell, I do hope you will forgive me." Her deep green eyes beseeched him with such winsomeness he felt himself losing reason and falling into their depth.

"Of course, of course," he stammered, causing Miss Tam to chuckle lightly to herself. He could see she was utterly exhausted and thought that perhaps he was pushing her a bit too harshly with the sittings, but the last time her mother had been to Iva Rose she had made it abundantly clear that she wished for him to be completed by her next return. His heart went out to Chastity but there was no help for it; the only thing he could offer was that tomorrow would be the last day. He felt a small pain in the bottom of his heart at the thought that it would probably be one of his last days in the presence of this lovely young beauty also.

"It is indeed quite breathless, Mr. Pursell," Christine Blackthorn complimented the grave young man standing beside her chair, as she studied the portrait set up before her. "Surely you must have worked quite hard to bring my daughter to such a degree of realness on a piece of canvas." Christine was truly amazed; she had been told that this young man was the best artist to be found in America, and now sitting before her was her proof; she could not have been more pleased. The girl in the portrait was exactly as Christine saw her daughter each time she made her visits to Iva Rose. Her beauty was astounding, even more lovely than she herself had been at that age. There was an

108

innocence about Chastity that shone from her eyes and through every pore of her skin; and this young man had captured that innocence and haunted look to perfection.

"I had hoped you would be pleased, Mrs. Blackthorn. Your daughter was the perfect subject." His tone was wistful, and Christine thought for a moment that she had detected a bit more in his manner of speaking. If she did not know her daughter and her icy resolve so well and had not gone into this young man's background with a fine-tooth comb, she might have been troubled about what had taken place in her absence. Even knowing the young couple as well as she did, she had placed all her faith in Miss Tam, who was not one to go about the house without knowing every move that went on inside its walls; and she had already been assured that everything had been quite proper and mannerly in her absence.

"You shall be quite handsomely paid for this work, Mr. Pursell. The only regret I have is in telling you that you shall no longer be needed here at Iva Rose." Just in case the young man had any ideas or designs on her daughter, she would at once squelch any such thoughts. She had better plans for Edward Blackthorn's daughter than to waste her on a mere artist.

"I had thought as much, Mrs. Blackthorn, and have already packed my bags. I have only to tell Miss Chastity good-bye and I shall be on my way."

"I hope you have somewhere to go?" Christine asked; she did not want to be known for throwing a young man out into the street after using his services.

"Oh, yes, madam, I have already been commissioned to do another portrait. I shall no longer be in New Orleans but in Richmond, but I hear the countryside is quite lovely, and I do have a wish to see all I am able to while I am still a young man."

Christine nodded her head, already dismissing the man from her thoughts while she once again gave her full attention to the portrait in front of her.

Mr. Pursell, knowing when he was no longer required, left the room in search of Miss Chastity.

Chastity was sitting on the front veranda, reading a book of poetry, so absorbed that she did not hear the front door open, nor did she notice the young man standing and watching her with a look of pure desire on his features.

When she had awakened that morning Dabs had brought her breakfast up on a tray and had also brought the news that her mother was downstairs and closed up in the small parlor with Mr. Pursell. She had not wished to disturb the couple so she had brought her book out to the veranda and had lost herself in its pages.

Robert Pursell stood allowing his eyes their fill of the beauty he was about to leave. He would never again feel about a woman as he did about this one, and what tore even more at his heart was that she did not even know that he existed. He was a mere employee of her mother's and accounted for nothing as far as she knew.

Mr. Pursell was clearly correct in his assumption that Chastity did not know he existed other than as the artist who had been hired by her mother to paint her portrait. But she would neither have noticed him if he had been bold instead of shy, or handsome instead of having those lean, bookish looks. Chastity was not like most young girls at the age of eighteen; she did not dream of a fine knight riding up on a large mount and taking her to some faraway haven; she thought only of everyday pastimes and of her reading and stitching. She had never gone to a party or a ball and had never danced to a waltz; oh, she knew the finer steps to all the dances; that was included in her studies, but she had never been in a young man's arms and swung around as though floating upon a cloud, across a dance floor. So truly she had no thoughts or ideas whatsoever on the havoc that was tormenting this young man's very soul.

Some small movement on Robert Pursell's part brought Chastity's eyes from her book to look up into his face. She at first saw a look on his features that completely baffled her, but he was quick to hide his thoughts, and with face turning a deep red, a look of his she had indeed seen a number of times, he cleared his throat and started to speak.

"I have come to say my good-byes, Miss Chastity, and to wish you every happiness." He did not know what he should say. He only knew he could not say those words which were so near his heart.

"Are you leaving Iva Rose so soon then, Mr. Pursell?" she questioned, closing her book, to give him her full attention.

"Yes, yes, my work is done here and your mother was quite pleased with the results of this past month."

"I am glad to hear that." Chastity smiled, bringing a ray of sunshine to his heart. "I am sure you would not care, as I would not, to endure that ordeal again if she had not been pleased with your work. I am afraid another month as this past, sitting out in the hot sun everyday would have completely unnerved me and you both." Her light laughter filled his ears.

"I assure you not," he dared to venture. "Another month as this past would only seem like heaven to me."

"I know you do jest, Mr. Pursell, and I thank you for those kind words," she laughed, thinking his words only said in gallantry.

"I doubt we will ever see each other again, Miss

Blackthorn, so I only wish to say that you have brought great joy into my heart in this short time of knowing you."

Chastity's laughter died in her throat. There was something in his voice that rang with the simple truth, not mere words of flattery to fill her ears. "Why thank you, Mr. Pursell," she murmured, looking for the first time directly at this young man. It was too bad that she had not realized before this day what a truly nice and gentle person he was. She might have had a true friend in this Mr. Pursell. "I too shall miss your company."

"Well, I had best get my things together and be on my way," he smiled, taking her hand from her lap and kissing the back in a gallant manner, defying his own fear and shyness at one time.

Chastity sat dumbfounded after his leave-taking. Could she have been so blind this past month and not have noticed that the young man had been enamored of her? she questioned herself. But no, she would have known such a thing as that. It was only his good-bye that had bothered her, and the fact that he was the first young man to kiss her hand in that manner. A soft smile played on her features as she sat reflecting on what had just transpired between her and the artist.

"Just leave the tea here, Miss Tam. I shall pour. Chastity and I have a few things to talk about," Christine told the black woman. She sat before the portrait as she had all the morning.

Chastity had dressed carefully for this interview with her mother, choosing a pink satin gown, with a high neckline and puffed sleeves; she had never worn the creation before but her mother had brought it as a gift on her last visit to Iva Rose.

112

Christine wore her customary black. She had adopted wearing the color after Edward's death, some eighteen years before. She felt comfortable and at ease with the somber hue and felt herself a dominating step above others when she met them. Her manner was cool and haughty to all, even to her own daughter, the only exception being Cora. Their friendship had endured through all the years; they had both remained living in the townhouse in New Orleans. They ventured out hardly ever nowadays, Christine's visits to Iva Rose being her main outings, and Cora's going to the theater once a week.

"Tell me how you have been, my dear." Christine surprised her daughter with her first words, as she poured the tea.

"Why quite well, mother," Chastity answered regarding her mother with a new interest. She knew her mother could be quite sly when she wanted. She had heard the servants talking when they had not thought her around, and occasionally tutors had let slip what they thought of a mother who acted like a man, giving out orders, smoking a pipe, and always wearing dreary black. All these stories had never affected Chastity before, but now she sensed something new in her mother's voice when she asked after her welfare.

"Quite well you say?" Christine sat back in her chair and repeated the words her daughter had said as though reflecting on their meaning. "You do not find it a bit lonely here with only servants to tend you? You have never before told me how you feel about staying here while I stay in New Orleans."

Chastity was indeed shocked; what could this conversation be leading to? she pondered. Her mother had never asked questions of this nature before. Always their interviews were short, a few inquiries about her studies, whether she needed any new clothing, whether she still rode her horse, and she was shortly dismissed.

"I have never given the matter much thought, Mother," she answered.

Christine's fine brow rose a degree. "You say you have not given the matter much thought? Surely you must have thought that you would not forever stay to yourself here in the country?" Could the child be that naive? she asked herself.

"Honestly I have never thought." And truthfully she had not; she had always done as others had told her without question, and, of course, she had always thought that she would stay forever at Iva Rose.

"Well, my dear daughter, you do surprise me." Christine felt somewhat uneasy with this young girl. Cora had admonished her time and again for treating her own daughter in so cold a manner, but truthfully she did not seem able to treat the girl any other way. Each time she looked at her she had to remind herself that she had borne the child, that she was, indeed, the girl's mother. It seemed to her that it had all been some bad dream and she had been left with a stranger for a daughter.

"I have been studying the portrait that Mr. Pursell has finished." Christine tried deliberately to soften her voice. "I had not realized how much you have grown; why you are a young lady now, Chastity."

Chastity felt her face flush at these kind words from her mother.

"I am afraid I have been quite derelict in my duty toward you."

Chastity felt a strange foreboding fill her body. What could she possibly mean—derelict in her duty?

"I have thought the matter over very carefully, dear, and I think that you should come to New Orleans with me; we shall introduce you to all the right people and perhaps even have a ball in your honor. Your Aunt Cora will be quite pleased to have you under her wing and to show you about town."

Chastity felt her mouth gaping. Was she hearing correctly? Had her mother said that she was to go to town to live and that she would be going to parties?

"You have nothing to say on the matter, child?" Christine could hardly believe anyone coming from her body could be that weak and complacent; it must be the Blackthorn blood she reasoned. "Come now, you must have something to say? Are you not excited about the idea one little bit?"

"I am sorry if I do not seem to appreciate what you are telling me, Mother; it is only that I do not know if I wish to move from Iva Rose."

"What do you mean you do not know if you wish it? I am your mother and you are my responsibility; you are of an age now where I feel that you should have more for company than only black servants."

Chastity, as ever, did not argue; she simply hung her head and did as told, only her heart and mind rebelling at her mother's words.

"We shall leave in two days. Make sure Dabs packs everything you shall be needing, and tell the girl that she also shall come with us; it will save me from having to find a new servant to tend you." With this Chastity was dismissed.

Chastity's chambers were her sanctuary. She wept, she stormed, and she railed against the cruel woman who had come to Iva Rose and ruined her whole young life. She swore that she would not find any kind of happiness in the new home to which she was being taken. She would die before she found any kind of happiness away from the only home she had ever known, and away from especially Miss Tam; she would miss her dearly; the old black woman had been more of a mother to her than her own. Miss Tam had changed her diapers as a baby and comforted her as she grew into young womanhood; now some strange woman whom she barely knew had come into her life and told her that she would be pulled from all she loved, and her whole world would be changed.

Dabs took the news with a large, toothy grin, eager and ready to be away from Iva Rose and into the big town. She had a cousin there whom she hardly ever saw, except on certain holidays when some slaves were permitted to visit relations. Then old Saddie had been able to get a pass from her mistress and to visit her family, who still lived on at Iva Rose. She had filled Dabs's head on more than one occasion with the sights and sounds of the busy New Orleans streets. She told of events that Dabs could hardly dare believe, so unusual were the sounds of those stories.

Chastity felt herself restraining the urge to pinch the thin black girl into silence. Her rushing about the room, packing and singing, was enough to drive her to distraction. A few minutes later after no letup, Chastity ordered the girl from the room, threatening to leave her at Iva Rose if she did not do as she was told immediately.

Now alone, Chastity could sink into self-pity without anyone to tell her nay. She knew she would do as her mother wished; willing or not, she would behave as she always had — and that was to do as she was told.

New Orleans was teeming with life and adventure for a young girl of eighteen if she only reached out and took what was being offered. But for the past several weeks the only thing that Chastity had done was work on some needlepoint and begin a new romantic novel.

Christine had stormed at her for the first few weeks to get out and meet people, to go to the theater with Cora, or to go out shopping for a new dress or hat. She herself had offered to accompany her daughter to do the latter. But Chastity felt hemmed in by the crowds in the street and out of place with any of Cora's or her mother's friends, so she refused to leave the house, preferring to stay in her rooms.

It was Cora's idea to hold a ball so that all New Orleans could view the beauty housed under their roof. Christine agreed heartily with the idea, hoping that her daughter would be able to meet some young people her own age and perhaps open up somewhat.

Chastity met this idea with her usual cool attitude. There was neither joy nor despair on her face at the news of the ball. She had already learned that no matter what she said things would go as her mother or Aunt Cora wished.

Christine had brought with her from Iva Rose the portrait of Chastity. She had ordered it hung over the mantel in the parlor, and whenever Chastity entered the room, her eyes were automatically drawn to the woman in the painting. She knew it to be herself, so exact a replica that even the eyes held the same deep emotions as she saw daily in her mirror. But what mystified her most was that she could stand and objectively appraise herself as she looked up at the picture. There was truly something unusual about her; she had thought this more than once before. It was as though she were untouchable, not of this earth. Her white dress and hat held a ghostlike quality, and her bright green eyes seemed to be focused in another land, not seeing anything about her. This was how she knew she truly felt deep down inside, so far down that neither her mother nor anyone else could sense her feelings; she was different and did not wish to see all the bad and ugly about her.

Cora found her the day before the ball standing in the parlor and looking up into the portrait. She was reminded for a moment of a lost little girl trying to find out who she was. "You grew into a fine beauty," she said lightly, coming up behind Chastity and putting her arm about her waist.

Chastity at first jumped in surprise but then as quickly relaxed against the arm about her. She loved her Aunt Cora, and had even on occasion remembered wishing that it had been she and not Christine who had the right to call her daughter. She smiled fondly at the older woman. "I come here often and look at the portrait; it seems to hold some strange power over me," she said jokingly.

Cora saw the truth in the girl's words and did not smile. She also had seen the deep, saddened beauty in the picture, so much like that of the real girl. She had hoped that with Christine bringing her daughter to live with her, the two of them would have gotten to know each other and become friends. But this was not to be; Christine was too used to giving orders and not letting people get too close to her, and her daughter, the complete opposite of her domineering mother, was not up to the hard fight it would take to win her mother's respect.

"You know your mother truly loves you?" Cora said, not knowing what this girl thought about anything; she kept everything confined so deeply that not a shred of her thoughts ever escaped.

"Certainly, Aunt Cora," was the simple answer. Sometimes Cora wished she could shake first the mother, then the child, until she could rattle some sense into their brains.

"Are you in the least excited about the ball tomorrow evening? Your mother is going to a lot of trouble and expense for you, Chastity. She has not invited any guests into this house in the last ten years, and now I hear there have been over two hundred invitations sent out. Knowing your mother as I do I am sure all will be here."

"I am not unappreciative, Aunt Cora. I only do not wish to have such a fuss made on my account. I could have as easily stayed at Iva Rose and around the things I was used to." She finally had told someone, in part, how she was feeling.

"But child, you must try to understand; your mother thought ill of herself for not noticing that you were becoming a young woman without the benefit of women to see after you. She could no longer leave you to the care of the servants and to yourself. You need help in molding yourself into the young woman you shall have to be to one day handle the Blackthorn estate."

"I know, I have heard it all before from my mother," Chastity answered, her tone turning cool.

Cora let the subject drop, knowing that it was not her place to try to break through the icy reserve that Chastity had built up over the years, besides which she doubted that she could, in any way, puncture the girl's exterior in the slightest. "Let us talk about the dress you shall be wearing. I caught a glimpse of it yesterday when that girl from the dress shop brought the box up to your room. Do you want to show it to me or shall it be a surprise?"

Chastity smiled. "Of course it is no surprise, and you of all people can come to my room to see it at any time. I was going to ask you if you would mind coming to my room tomorrow evening before the first guests arrive, and putting the final touches to my coiffure. You always do your own hair so divinely." Chastity hated hurting the older woman and had not meant to be so cold earlier, so she tried in this way to make it up to her.

Cora's smile filled her vision. "I would be happy to help with anything you wish, Chastity. And then I shall see your gown. Well, I had better leave you to yourself for now, dear; I still have to help with the selection of the wines for tomorrow evening." She turned and started to the door.

"Thank you Aunt Cora," Chastity called after her.

Chastity's gown was a shimmering white satin, its neckline so low that the tips of her swelling bosom were all but showing. On first glance at herself, she had put her hands up against her breasts; never had she owned a gown anything like that. Her mother had ordered the material and had told the dressmaker the design she wished; Chastity, as in most everything else, had had little to say about the affair. It had taken her some time and Dabs's reassurances that this, indeed, was the style, and that lots of the ladies in New Orleans wore gowns cut even lower than this, before she could relax somewhat and finish her toilet.

Her honey-gold hair was piled atop her head, and Dabs had taken the good part of the afternoon arranging her ringlets; tiny emerald stones peeked from each curl, and soft tiny curls dangled at each temple. Chastity hardly used any makeup, her own golden complexion being the perfect color; the only cosmetic added was that of a light green coloring to the lids of her sparkling eyes.

She stood breathless, staring at the mirror before her. Never had she viewed herself as she did now. The person looking back at her was no longer the girl she had always known, but some woman with a beauty she had never seen.

"Why, Missy, you be just plain beautiful," Dabs

repeated for the dozenth time that day, but Chastity no longer told her to hush, for she saw the truth of the words.

And when Cora entered the room that evening to see if she could help Chastity with her toilet, the young woman was once again reassured.

"My God, girl, you are simply a vision," Cora gasped as she looked Chastity up and down. "Wait until your mother gets a look at you. I can hardly wait to see her reaction. I can hardly believe my own."

Chastity felt her cheeks flaming from the generous compliments.

"You shall have half the men of New Orleans at your feet this very night, and the other half shall only linger to avoid being seen by their wives or girl friends." Cora laughed. "I am so glad Christine brought you out from that country life. You shall add something that has been missing for a long time in our lives."

"Thank you, Aunt Cora," Chastity whispered.

"Come now, love." Cora grabbed her by the hand. "Let us go down and show your mother what a truly lovely child she has. Some of the guests have already started arriving, and we can see the looks upon their faces when they see your winsome beauty." Cora was so excited she did not notice Chastity's withdrawal. She could not imagine anyone this lovely not wanting to show off her beauty.

Music filled Chastity's ears as she and Cora descended the stairway. Eyes of various descriptions followed them as they made their way across the dance floor to the side of Christine Blackthorn. All questioned whether this beauty walking along with Cora could be Christine's daughter who, rumor had it, had remained cloistered at the plantation, Iva Rose, until recently.

Christine was amazed as she looked at the couple coming toward her. She had been talking to Mabel Compton, the wife of the owner of a large plantation bordering the Blackthorn land, when she stopped in midsentence and all but gaped at her own daughter and her best friend.

Cora wore a grin from ear to ear as she sidestepped people right and left in order to bring Chastity to her mother.

"Here she is, Christine. I hope we are not too late." Cora placed Chastity's cold hand in her mother's.

"Thank you, Cora," were the only words that Christine could get out at that moment. Her eyes were reviewing the beautiful creature who was her daughter.

"Perhaps you would like to introduce her about, Christine. I am sure she does not know a soul." Cora tried her best to ease her friend's dismay.

"Yes, yes, of course." Christine pulled herself together and squeezed Chastity's hand lightly. "Come child, and let me introduce you to New Orleans, or to be more exact let me introduce New Orleans to my daughter."

Chastity smiled for the first time that she could remember, at her mother. "Fine Mother, I will be delighted to meet your friends." Chastity had made up her mind while coming down the stairs that, as long as she had to be forced into attending this ball in her honor, at least she could act as though she were having a good time and not disappoint her mother any more than she already had. And who knew, perhaps something good would come to the two of them because of this affair.

Christine led her daughter about, introducing her to her guests, and telling her what the social status of each was in New Orleans. To Chastity, her mother was somewhat of a snob. She seemed to look down her nose at most of her guests, and she did not pretend otherwise. Chastity did not know of Christine's past so she saw no other reason for her mother's behavior.

Chastity could hardly remember a single name. All of them seemed to run together as she was led about the room. Her mother did not appear to have missed a single person, Chastity thought as they finally stopped to rest and sip a cool glass of champagne.

Couples had already started to swirl across the floor in a brilliance of colors, when a young man of some height and handsome good looks approached Chastity while she was still in the company of her mother.

"Good evening ladies. I wonder, Mrs. Blackthorn, if I may beg the hand of your daughter for this dance?" The young man asked politely, showing particular deference to the elder Blackthorn woman.

"Why of course, Mr. Carlin, you young people go right along and enjoy yourself." She handed her daughter over to the young man.

Chastity felt her face flush. She had never danced with a man and she felt that she would commit some horrible misdeed.

"I came as quickly as I dared."

Chastity looked to the young man as he started twirling her across the floor; her look showed that she failed to understand.

"I meant only that I came before any of the other gallant young men could claim you for the first dance." His laughter reached her ears, as he danced her across the floor.

Chastity found that she did, indeed, have the ability to dance well. Her tutor had been an excellent teacher, she soon learned, for after this first young man she was swept into arm after arm.

She was breathless and half panting by the middle

123

of the evening, and as another gentleman came to ask for her hand, she herself begged for a breather and a glass of champagne.

Soon she found herself the center of all male attention, as she stood to one side of the dance floor and drank deeply from the champagne glass that had appeared, as if by magic, in her hand.

"Would you care for a refill?" a red-haired young man, with a spattering of freckles asked as she brought the glass down empty from her lips.

"No thank you," Chastity replied, hardly believing that all this attention was meant for her.

She was circled by a small group of men, asking her to dance, some questioning her about her calendar for the coming weeks. She had always been shy, but she found that she had either changed somewhat or the champagne had already gone straight to her head, for she found herself laughing and answering them one after another.

She was talking to the young man who had first approached her and asked her to dance when she glanced across the room, her emerald eyes seeming to have a will of their own. The sight that filled them almost stopped her in midsentence; there standing as though he owned the world and everything within it was the most handsome man she had ever seen.

He was a good head taller than anyone around him, and his shoulders were wide and sturdy as though he had been a wood cutter. His hair was jet-black, curling at the nape of his neck, and a stray lock hung loosely over one dark, straight brow. She could not detect the color of his eyes from this distance, but they seemed light, a striking contrast to his dark, tanned face.

The man was talking to a striking woman, who seemed to hang on his every word. He appeared to

Chastity to be somewhat bored with their conversation, for a lazy smile played about his soft, sensual-looking lips.

Who could this man be, she questioned herself, not daring to ask about a gentleman. What would people think of her if she was to ask about a complete stranger, and one to whom she had not even been introduced?

She had no more time to think about the gentleman across the room, for she again was swept across the dance floor. And between her concentration on her steps and the gay conversation of her partners, thoughts of the stranger completely disappeared from her mind.

Sometime later her mother again approached her, taking her arm and begging her companions for her daughter's release for just a short period. She wanted Chastity to meet some people who had arrived a little late, one of them being James Courtly, their attorney. She wanted her daughter to know about some of their business matters and to meet the gentleman who had proved invaluable to Christine over the years. She wanted her daughter to know that if something was to happen to her she would have a true confidant in Mr. Courtly.

"James," Christine greeted the portly, elderly gentleman. "I want you to meet my daughter, Chastity."

"This is a pleasure, Miss Blackthorn." He held a beefy hand out to Chastity.

"Mr. Courtly is our attorney, dear, and a valuable friend."

"It is a pleasure to meet you, sir," Chastity responded, with a sweet smile for the older man.

"Indeed, my dear, indeed." Mr. Courtly vigorously pumped her hand. "I have been waiting a long time to meet you. Your father and I were good friends and I hope I can say the same for your mother."

Chastity's smile never left her face as the man talked on and on about the past and of business matters.

As she and her mother were about to leave, Mr. Courtly cleared his throat. "Here is the young man I told you about earlier, Christine. The one I invited to your party. I wish for the two of you to become acquainted. You may find you have some interests along the same lines. He also has holdings in the Caribbean, in fact, on the same island as your small cane plantation, on Martinique."

Christine smiled graciously at the tall, good-looking gentleman who now stood before her.

"Deke, this is Mrs. Blackthorn and her lovely daughter, Chastity. Ladies this is Mr. Deke Saxon."

"It is a pleasure, ladies." The young man made a gallant half bow in Christine's direction, then turned and looked into Chastity's lovely face. His breath caught for a minute as he looked into the emerald eyes before him.

Chastity also was held as though in a trance as she looked up into the features above her. This was the same face that earlier she had been studying. She had not even dared hope that she would be able to meet this man, let alone talk with him and hear that deep masculine voice, that sounded from the base of his chest.

"Perhaps later, Mr. Saxon, we can talk about business." Christine pulled them from their study of each other. "Mr. Courtly has told me about you, that you may be in need of some cargo to take on your next trip home. Perhaps I will be able to oblige you."

"That will be fine, Mrs. Blackthorn," the man said, his mind still throbbing with thoughts of the woman's daughter. Harshly he scolded himself. "Yes, anytime you say will be fine with me. James here also has told me a great deal about you and about your shipping line. Perhaps we can arrive at a satisfactory arrangement between us."

Christine's smile told all that she approved heartily of this young man. He would go far in this world, she thought to herself. "Come, dear," she said to Chastity. "There are still several other people I wish you to meet." She politely left the men gathered about her and her daughter.

Chastity's mind was in a turmoil as her mother led her about, from one small group to another. Never had she felt as she did in the presence of this Deke Saxon. There was something stronger than her will and all too compelling about the way he looked deeply into her eyes.

Once again she was twirled across the floor, when her mother had finished with her, but after her meeting with the tall strange man she did not hear or notice much about the young men who held her close on the dance floor. Her green eyes seemed to search out every corner for that gentleman. Hearing a deep-throated laugh she swung about in her partner's arms, hoping to catch another glimpse of him.

But she did not see Deke Saxon again that evening or any other. She did not have the courage to ask, but she had overheard a young woman talking about this handsome man, who had, after leaving her mother's library, headed straight to the door and out into the night.

A few days later her mother mentioned the man again. Chastity tried to appear not eager to hear about him, but her ears were strained, listening to every word. It seemed the man did come from Martinique and had left two days after her ball with the hull of his ship full of goods from her mother's warehouse. One thing Christine did add to the information Chastity was trying hard to accumulate about the handsome gentleman, and this information she could well have done without, was that he had a bride waiting for him on the island of Martinique.

Chastity's world seemed to crumble about her at these words. Married, married, the hated words vibrated again and again in her mind. She should have known by the way he had not even asked her for a dance that he had another woman. How could she let that strange man to whom she had not even spoken affect her in this manner? What could have come over her?

No matter how Chastity berated herself, still she could not get the image of those light blue eyes, set in a dark-tan masculine face, from her every thought.

The day after the ball, invitations started to arrive for Chastity to attend all manner of affairs. At first she went along and even allowed young men to call on her, entertaining them in the parlor, and trying her hand at light flirtation; but after hearing her mother say that Deke Saxon had a wife waiting for him, Chastity seemed to wilt, to lose all her enthusiasm for fun and gaiety.

At first her mother thought that the ball had been just the thing to bring Chastity out and around young people; and it seemed for a short while to have worked, but as time went by, the girl seemed to withdraw into herself even more than in the past. Christine noticed daily that there were fewer invitations, and Chastity's number of admirers seemed to be dwindling to nothing; but for the life of her, Christine was at a loss to know the reason for her daughter's depressed mood.

She talked it over with Cora at great length, trying to find a reason for Chastity's behavior. Neither could come up with a clue, and as the days went by the girl seemed to grow even colder.

Finally, a few months later, after Christine had thought the girl would drive her insane with her moping about, Christine hit on an idea with which Cora surprisingly agreed. She would send Chastity to Europe for a season and see if that would improve her spirits.

Dabs would accompany her and they would leave on a Blackthorn ship. Terrance Altman's eldest son, Thomas, would captain the vessel and see that Chastity arrived safely at her destination. Edward Blackthorn had owned a town house in London and even a small estate outside, so the girl would have a house; and servants still were retained at the home so there would be no need to worry about hiring help. She could simply sail to London; Mr. Courtly would send word to his agent in Europe to find a suitable woman for a companion, and perhaps the girl would try to have a good time. The Lord knew, Christine thought to herself, the poor girl deserved a good time after years of doing nothing but locking herself in a plantation.

Chastity greeted the news without a flicker of emotion. She seemed far older than her years to Christine, as the girl simply nodded her head while her mother explained her plans for her. She seemed not to have any life within her shell of a body. What could be the matter with her, Christine wondered as she sat and watched her daughter's face for any kind of reaction, with none forthcoming. Well, perhaps the English air would perk her up some, for it seemed nothing she tried to do in New Orleans was going to help the girl.

The ship, named the *Carry Queen*, was as sleek and trim to the eye as any on the seas. It was a cool, crisp morning when Christine and Cora stood on the dock and waved good-bye.

Chastity had stood by the rail until she could no longer see her mother and aunt and then had gone to her cabin and lain down to rest her bursting head. She often seemed too quiet nowadays and frequently had to lie down with a headache.

The next few days were uneventful; dinner was served each evening in the captain's cabin, with only Chastity, the captain, and the first mate attending. After two evenings of their company, Chastity sent Dabs to make her excuses and to ask for a tray.

Neither Chastity nor Dabs had ever been aboard ship before, but they found that they both were lively mates upon the water. Chastity truly loved the *Carry Queen* and spent most of her time at the rail looking out at the never-ending blue-green water. She loved it best when the wind was blowing and filling the sails full, and light sprays of the soft salt water showered her, as her long hair blew in all directions. To be always on this tranquil swell of water would be a dream come true. She knew now why men went to sea, staying until the years would not allow them to go anymore. She had heard that her own father had been a good sailor and captain of his own vessel. She decided it must be in her blood, for she dearly loved the feel of the rocking ship.

The captain of the *Carry Queen* let Miss Blackthorn wander the ship at will, trying to cater to her every desire. He tried to stay out of her way as much as possible, for he, even in his later years, knew that a young woman of her uncommon beauty would be too tempting a tidbit with whom to pander. His men had been ordered at the beginning of the trip to show the women no disrespect or discourtesy in any way. They were told to watch their language and to be sure that neither of the women was above deck when they had to answer nature's call. They had all willingly agreed, being told that the slightest infraction on any of their parts would result in a flogging of one hundred lashes with the cat-o'-nine-tails. All complied, most turning their heads if either of the women appeared, none wanting to risk the slightest mistake in his manners.

Bad weather was the fear of every ship upon the sea, and the *Carry Queen* was to have its share through the years; later it would be remarked that the *Carry Queen* had been a gallant ship during any kind of weather, and the sailors who walked upon her decks would tell their children and grandchildren of the valiant fight they had made to save the Blackthorn ship in the worst storm they had ever seen.

Rising from her bed, Chastity could feel something wrong in the very air she breathed. It was as though the air was charged with high tension. She quickly dressed and woke Dabs; the black girl was also feeling the strange emotion, her black eyes large circles of fear.

"Dabs, hurry and dress," Chastity instructed. "I am going to above to see what is happening."

"Oh, Miss Chastity, please don't be a-going up there by yourself. I be done in a minute. Don't be a-leaving me here all alone." Large tears slid down the girl's cheeks.

Chastity felt irritated at the girl and rebuked her sternly. "Do not be a baby, Dabs. I shall only be gone long enough to see what is happening. I shall be back before you even finish dressing." With this, Chastity went out the door, leaving a terrified Dabs behind.

Going up to the companionway Chastity felt a light film of perspiration on her forehead and upper lip. The heat was so intense for this time of the morning, that it about took Chastity's breath as she reached the deck. The sky was pitch-black, encircling the *Carry Queen* as though it were the cloak of night. Everywhere that Chastity glanced, men were scurrying about, trying to secure the ship. A rope was stretched over the deck in case one were to need a guideline during the storm ahead, and the men were battening down all loose cargo.

The captain caught a glimpse of his passenger and rushed to her at once. "Miss Blackthorn, please go back to your cabin. This is no place for a lady."

"What is the matter, Mr. Altman?" Chastity gasped, already knowing but needing to have her fears confirmed.

"I'm afraid we're in for a bit of bad weather, miss," came the distracted answer as the captain shouted orders to the first mate.

"Do you think the storm shall be a bad one?" Chastity ventured.

"I'm afraid by the looks of the weather and the feel of the air, it indeed may be quite bad. Mr. Anderson, be sure to secure that crate over there. If that's all, miss, I suggest you go below where you will be safe." He turned and walked away, expecting her to do as he had bid her.

The wind had started to stir lightly and Chastity could feel the change in the air. She hoped the storm would not be too bad; she had never before been on a ship let alone in a bad storm at sea. She had better get back to her cabin and check on Dabs; the girl looked as though she would not be able to bear up by herself.

The storm was not, as hoped, small but a towering rage, bringing destruction and death in its wake. It lasted for over two days; great bolts of flashing lightning spiraled through the sky, thunder roared overhead until everyone aboard the *Carry Queen* shuddered with every sound.

Most of the two days Chastity sat upon her bed holding Dabs close against herself, as the black girl cried and called out to God to save her from the fate that seemed so close at hand.

They had been ordered not to leave their cabin at the onset of the rains, and Chastity had to admit that for nothing would she want to step foot out the door.

At times the ship had dipped and rolled, causing the two women to be almost thrown from the bed. They clung more tightly to each other with each pitch of the ship. The *Carry Queen* at one point had made such a shuddering sound that Chastity had thought they were sinking and had jumped to the floor, only to be thrown against one wall, hitting her head against a table. Dabs had bravely rushed to her and helped her back onto the bed, and the two of them had waited fearfully for the water to start rushing into their cabin.

As the ship straightened itself and the girls realized that they were not sinking, a great feeling of relief came over them. They were safe for a short time longer, Chastity told herself, for she now had no doubt that the *Carry Queen* would not make it out of the storm. The storm had tormented them too long and no ship could endure the treatment it was receiving.

On the second afternoon a cabin boy brought the two women a tray with hard rolls and a pot of tea on a plate. "I'm sorry, mams, but this is all there is; the cook took a bad fall and the captain thinks he done broke his leg."

Chastity dared not ask the questions that were swimming in her mind. She could feel and hear the storm outside the cabin doors raging with fury. "Thank you," she stammered, not rising from the bed, so the youth set the tray upon the coverlet, gave the ladies a wan and tired smile, and was out of the room.

"We's going to die, Miss Chastity, we's going to drown, and them there sharks that swim these waters are a-going to eat us up," Dabs wailed after the boy had left the room.

"Hush Dabs, and eat one of these." She tossed the girl one of the hard rolls; and, indeed, the rolls felt days old, although after not having a thing for almost two full days, they found the tea and rolls tasted delicious.

Chastity also thought they would not make it through the storm, but she knew there was no sense in bemoaning the fact. What was to be would be and there was not a single thing that she or anyone else could do. This was how she had felt about things most of her life, and she put this storm down to just one more situation over which she had no control.

The next morning the storm ended; its finish was as quick as its beginning; without any warning the winds slowed, the sky cleared, and the rains slackened to a light drizzle.

Chastity felt the storm's letup by the quieting of the ship and the gentle smoothness of the roll of the *Carry Queen*. As quickly as possible she left the cabin to investigate the extent of the damages to the vessel.

She was met on deck by Captain Altman, who seemed to be in a slight daze. "Captain? How did the *Carry Queen* fare?" she asked, noticing his nervous irritation.

"Miss Blackthorn, you should have stayed to your cabin until sent for. You shall not find things too pleasing to your eyes above ship, I'm afraid."

"Is there anything I can do?"

"I'm afraid not, there doesn't seem to be anything

anyone can do."

Chastity looked to the captain, not understanding his meaning. "The storm, sir, it is finished, is it not?"

"Yes, yes, I did not mean to worry you, Miss, but you shall have to be told sooner or later, the *Carry Queen* is taking on water and is sinking."

The words went through Chastity as would a piercing knife. "Sinking?" she asked stupidly.

"I'm afraid so, Miss Blackthorn. And what makes it worse is I have several injured men and have only one lifeboat that was not tossed overboard during the storm." He saw the stark fright standing out on the young woman's features, and tried to reassure her. "Have no fear, madam, you and your servant shall be safe from any harm." He was too weary to say any more and looked about at the destruction lying at every angle aboard his ship. Lightning had struck the main mast, leaving it lying haphazardly across the deck. Wood and debris were strewn about, and the day before lightning had struck the deck, catching the wood afire and leaving a blackened pit in the flooring. All this they could have survived, but the turning and pitching about by the angry waves had done the real damage. The hull was taking on water faster than they could pump it out; Captain Altman knew now that it would be only a matter of hours before they would have to abandon ship, and all try to survive in the small lifeboat or by hanging on to the sides, those who could not fit within.

Several of his men had been severely injured; and many others were this minute laid up in their cots, bleeding from gaping wounds or unconscious from severe blows to the head from flying debris.

Never in all his years on the sea had he seen a ship's crew so harmed with the ship still afloat. Barely ten of his men had made it through the two days unscathed, he included in this number. Even the ship's doctor had been killed and washed overboard. Now he had even further trials before him; he let out a tremendous sigh. How could he see that his men and the two women made it safely to shore? They had been so blown off course, he was not exactly sure of their position; all his instruments had been damaged by the storm, leaving him only to guess at their position.

"Sir!" the first mate shouted, running up on deck. "I'm afraid we will not have much time as we had hoped for. The water is coming in now quite a bit faster." The first mate had broken his arm when a piece of wood had fallen on him and knocked him to the deck. His arm now was tied in a makeshift sling, securing the broken limb and alleviating some of the pain. "I've ordered the men from the bottom of the ship and had them begin to get the injured men ready to board the lifeboat. I only hope we have enough room, sir."

"Aye, we can only hope." The captain seemed deflated, almost lifeless. "Do not forget the women, Mr. Anderson. Be sure to leave room for them before anyone else."

"Yes, sir." Mr. Anderson saluted with his good arm, always so trim and correct, even in the face of disaster.

Chastity and Dabs were ushered up on deck by a young man sent by the first mate. They were told not to pack any of their belongings for there would be no room for any extra weight. So quickly Chastity stuffed her few jewels into her blouse, grabbed Dabs's hand and started to the deck.

The deck near the lifeboat was littered with moaning men. All the medical supplies had been washed overboard along with the man who knew how to administer them, so the wounded were writhing in pain or numbly staring and holding their injuries.

Chastity's heart went out to these poor creatures; but she did not know any way in which she could help, and when she ventured to ask the young man who had brought them up on deck, he told her not to worry herself.

Just as a sailor was about to hand Chastity and Dabs into the small lifeboat, the cabin boy who had been watching from the highest portion of the ship, called out in a loud voice, "Sail ho."

All eyes turned in the direction toward which he had aimed his glass.

"Can you make out who she is, boy?" the captain shouted up to the youth.

"No, sir, she is still too far but she is heading straight to us."

Relief filled the captain's features. As long as it was not a pack of roving pirates they would be safe.

Chastity had rushed to the rail; shielding her eyes from the glare of the sun, she stared out to sea until she finally could make out in the far distance a tiny speck, which after a time became a sail and then the features of a ship.

"The name of the ship, sir, is the *Sea Wind*," the boy finally shouted down to the waiting captain.

"Aye, the *Sea Wind* be it?" the captain said in a level, reassuring tone.

Once the other boat was in easy-seeing distance she seemed to swoop down upon the *Carry Queen* in a matter of minutes.

The other ship looked about the same size as the *Carry Queen,* and as she came alongside, a young man in dark trousers and jacket leaned over the rail and shouted to Captain Altman. "We saw the tilt of your ship, sir, from some distance. Can we be of any assistance?"

"Aye," came his reply. "Some of my men have been injured and more have lost their lives. We were caught in the storm. I also have two passengers aboard, women sir. I would appreciate it if you could accommodate my crew and passengers to the nearest port," the captain shouted back.

"It will be a pleasure, sir. Our captain is in his cabin studying some charts, but he bid me welcome you aboard the *Sea Wind.*"

The next few minutes went by so fast for Chastity that she hardly could recall later what actually did happen. Men were jumping aboard the *Carry Queen* from the *Sea Wind* and carrying the injured aboard the other ship. She now did not have to do without her clothes, for strong able men transferred her trunks to the other ship. Then she herself was lifted in a pair of strong arms and carried aboard the *Sea Wind,* Dabs following in her stead.

After all were aboard the *Sea Wind* the captain introduced his passenger to the young man who had stood over the rail. "This is Miss Chastity Blackthorn, sir. I would like to see that she be treated with the utmost courtesy and appointed appropriate accommodations."

The young man looked Chastity over with some interest. He had heard about the Blackthorn lass, and true to all he had been told the woman was by far, even with her hair in disarray and her gown all wrinkled, the most beautiful woman he had ever seen. "It is a pleasure, mam." He bent over her extended hand. "I am the first mate of the *Sea Wind,* Jamie Scott. My captain should be here shortly and then we shall see to finding you and your girl here a cabin."

Chastity smiled sweetly; she rather liked this young man, who seemed quite polite and well-mannered..

"Here comes the captain now," Jamie Scott said

loudly and looked in the direction from which a tall, dark-tanned giant of a man was coming.

Chastity felt her breath falter for a moment and thought she would faint. It couldn't be, she told herself; the man before her could not be the same who had attended her ball, and left an undeniable mark upon her soul. But it was the same man and she found herself staring without will into the lightest blue eyes she had ever seen.

Deke Saxon also was left dumbfounded; he had been told that a ship had been sighted and that she looked to be in trouble. He had left his first mate to handle the affair, as he had charts that had to be gone over, and his mood of late had not been too favorable. He had not thought the affair to be too hard to handle. They would take the crew of the ship to their home port, which was only a few days hence, and their captain could see to their passage home. But now, as he stood before the group surrounding his first mate, he felt himself drowning in the sheerest green eyes and remembering another time he had looked into that same beautiful face.

Jamie Scott was truly puzzled by his captain; he had never seen him act in this manner before. Staring at the woman seemed so out of character for the captain that Jamie was tempted for a second to lay hold to his arm and ask if he were feeling ill.

But before he had to do anything that drastic Deke Saxon shook himself with some will power and bowed to the young woman. "Miss Blackthorn," he spoke directly to the woman, ignoring even the other captain.

"Mr. Saxon," Chastity answered in a tiny voice.

Captain Altman cleared his throat, not knowing the meaning of this interplay. "I see you know my passenger, Captain?"

"Aye, I know the lady," came the reply, but Deke's eyes never once left Chastity's face.

Chastity felt her cheeks starting to burn a deep red from this man's close perusal of her.

Captain Saxon must have sensed her discomfort for he suddenly turned and looked to Captain Altman. "You are welcome aboard my ship, sir; our doctor shall tend your wounded and there shall be food readied soon for you all. I am afraid though that we may be somewhat crowded; you sir, shall have to bunk with Mr. Scott here and the ladies can take my cabin. The rest of your men shall have to make do where they are able." His talk was quick and to the point; he seemed not to have the time for light chatter. "If you would care to follow me to my cabin, I shall pour us a drink and toast the fortune that brought my ship to your rescue." He meant these words sincerely, for the *Carry Queen* had all but gone underwater, and the thought went through his mind that if Chastity Blackthorn had been out long in the tiny boat they had been about to board she might not have survived. The very thought nearly brought him to his knees. This woman was of a rare quality.

Chastity was asked to join the gentlemen. The captain's cabin was quite handsome. Its interior was done with dark wood panelling; a small bunk was placed along one wall; a huge desk, littered with papers and books rested against the opposite. A thick blue carpet was on the floor, and in the center of the room two comfortable-looking chairs sat facing each other; between them a small table had been placed holding a tray with a decanter of dark red wine and four crystal goblets. Everything was pretty much in order, but as Chastity looked about the room she noticed it held a definite masculine feel to it, which she told herself was exactly what she would have expected of a room housing a man such as this Captain Deke Saxon.

"Would you care to sit, Miss Blackthorn?" Deke asked, taking her elbow and leading her to one of the chairs in the middle of the room. She had no choice and he stood behind her chair, making her feel quite nervous and self-conscious.

Light toasts were offered by Captain Altman, and the first mate and captain of the *Sea Wind*. The wine was delicious and Chastity felt herself beginning to relax for the first time in the last few days.

"Were do you intend on making port, Captain Saxon?" Terrance Altman asked.

"We are only a few days from my own home port, so we shall go directly there, to Martinique." His strong voice seemed to beat into Chastity's very soul.

She had caught the name Martinique and sat puzzled. Did not the Blackthorns own a plantation of some sort on that island? She would have to question this Deke Saxon and find out if he knew of its whereabouts.

"Well, Captain," Captain Altman was saying, "I thank you for all you have done for me and my crew, but now I think I should be going to make sure they are all comfortable. I feel quite responsible for what happened to them and shall try to make up in any way I can for all that has occurred."

"Do not blame yourself too harshly. The storm was not your fault and I am sure you did all that could have been done," Deke Saxon assured the older man. "I can understand your feelings though. I would feel the same, so go tend your men the best you can. I shall see Miss Blackthorn comfortably settled."

Captain Altman looked guiltily toward Chastity, who now after three glasses of wine could barely keep her eyes open. He had completely forgotten the girl was in his charge. "I thank you, Captain. I shall come back shortly to make sure that all is in good order." With this he left the room, going in search of his men.

Deke Saxon took the chair opposite Chastity's, the one the captain had just vacated. "Mr. Scott, perhaps you would care to assist some men with Miss Blackthorn's trunks. You can bring them in here and find room for them. Then you can see that the crew of the *Carry Queen* are fed and comfortable."

"Yes, sir," the young man answered and left the room.

The silence that filled the cabin with the departure of young Jamie Scott was clearly felt.

Chastity sat, her hands folded primly in her lap and her eyes watching those hands as though expecting them to perform some curious feat.

Deke also was at a loss, his hand clutched a goblet, but his eyes were not watching what that hand was doing but rather watching the young woman opposite him. "I hope you shall find this cabin satisfactory, Miss Blackthorn," Deke said, breaking the quiet.

"I am sure I will Mr. Saxon," Chastity answered, hardly above a whisper.

"I may find it necessary to use my desk during the day but I promise you I shall try not to bother you."

A small smile came to Chastity's lips. "You shall not bother me, Mr. Saxon."

Deke sat spellbound; never had he seen such natural beauty. She was above all he had ever seen.

A small yawn escaped her lips. "Oh, excuse me," she murmured, covering her mouth with one slender hand.

"You are tired," This was more of a statement than a question. "I shall leave you so you can rest. I had forgotten that you were caught in the storm. It must have been frightful for you." His voice was soft and tender, bringing out hidden emotions that he had not

142

expressed in a long time.

Chastity's smile stayed upon her lips. "I am afraid you are right. I can barely keep my eyes open. I am sorry to be a bother but I have not truly slept in over two days." Another yawn escaped her.

Deke's laughter filled the cabin. "Get yourself to bed, Miss Blackthorn. I will stop by later after you have refreshed yourself." He rose and started to the door.

"Thank you, Mr. Saxon."

"There is no need for thanking me." These simple words held meaning for the couple. There truly was no need for thanking where they were concerned. Something beyond all that was forming between the two.

Right before twilight Deke Saxon once more entered his cabin. He brought with him a tray for his passenger. Her maid was still busy helping his doctor care for the crew of the *Carry Queen,* so Deke had made the offer of bringing Miss Blackthorn her dinner.

Chastity was still asleep, her one slim arm thrown out from beneath the covers and her face turned toward the wall.

Deke set the tray down upon the table and softly made his way to the side of the bunk. He harshly scolded himself for what he was doing but something stronger than his will drove him now.

She was beautiful even in her slumber, he thought as he stood over her watching her sleeping form. She had taken off her gown and slept only in her chemise, with a light blanket thrown across her. Her skin appeared so soft and creamy he had to restrain himself from reaching down to feel its velvety texture. Her bosom rose and fell with each breath, and his own breathing grew ragged as he stared down at her. He pulled himself away. What had possessed him, he raged at himself as he took himself over and sat in one of the overstuffed chairs. How could he prey on a girl-woman such as she? Was he getting so depraved in his years that he would resort to such a low trick? Something was wrong here, he warned himself. The girl seemed to stir feelings within him that he had never known existed; the image of her sleeping form plagued his mind and soul. He could not leave the room and be away from her.

Chastity finally stirred, as though sensing someone's presence. Her head turned from the wall and her green eyes sought out what had awakened her from her sleep. There sitting in a chair was Deke Saxon; her mind filled with the image of him and she felt her breathing quicken. What strange power did this man hold over her? she questioned herself. With only a mere look from him she felt herself go to pieces.

Deke felt her eyes on him. "So you have awakened?" He smiled, his straight white teeth showing with his grin. "I shall light a candle; it is getting a bit dark in here. I brought you a tray for your supper. I thought you might be hungry." He seemed to rattle on, even to his own ears as he struck flint to light the candle on the table.

"Why, thank you." Chastity started to rise, then realized that she was not dressed.

Deke saw her predicament and rushed to his own wardrobe. He poked around then drew out a dressing robe of a dark blue satin. "If you would care to wear this until you can get your own from your chest, I would deem it an honor."

Chastity's smile filled his vision. "Thank you." She held out her hand for the robe, still clutching with one hand the blanket to her chest.

As he walked to the bunk and came within hand's reach of the woman upon his bed, green eyes met blue, caught, and held for a full minute. He felt as he would a staggering blow, this unseen thing that was lying between them.

Chastity broke eye contact first, her face turning red as she reached out and took the robe from his hand.

He walked to his desk, his mind in a turmoil, showing the woman upon his bed his back and providing a chance for her to cover herself before he lost all control completely and let this animal instinct that was coursing through his veins take over. He kept telling himself to leave the woman, to get out of his cabin before it was too late, but he shunned this advice and he stayed, not able to leave, tempting fate and his own reason.

He heard her moving about the cabin before he turned in her direction. The sight that filled his eyes brought a glowing light to their depths. The dressing robe was at least three sizes too large for the tiny woman, but never had it seemed so filled to him. The clinging satin material showed off every angle of her body, bringing her breasts to soft tempting peaks, and outlining her legs and hips clearly. She had rolled the sleeves up several times, and the hem dragged across the carpet but her rare beauty outshone every flaw.

Chastity felt his eyes upon her and blushed a delicate pink. "I am afraid your robe is a bit large," she stammered shyly.

"It has never been more perfect," he ·breathed, going to sit across from her.

Silence greeted the room after these soft-spoken words.

Chastity questioned herself severely as she started to eat her dinner. What on earth was she doing alone and wearing nothing but her chemise and a robe, with a man who was married? It was as though she were losing her mind. Never in her life had she acted in such a manner. The man must have bewitching powers that were working to ensnare her. But still she was powerless to alter in any way the course of events; though she knew what was right she could not change her heart.

Neither talked while she ate, but both knew the other's thoughts; it was as though an electric current were being charged between the two, and the heat from this invisible charge was intensifying.

As she put her plate on the tray, Deke smiled. "I hope you enjoyed it, Chastity."

This was the first man ever to call her by her given name, and from his lips it sounded like a satin caress. "Thank you, yes," she murmured softly.

"I shall leave you now to get your rest," he said, gathering the tray, his eyes automatically resting on hers.

Chastity's thoughts flew for the briefest of minutes. She did not know why, but she could imagine herself running her fingers through the dark curls lying at the nape of his neck; and caressing his strong jaw. She could almost feel her fingers tracing the outline of the thin scar that stood out next to his mouth. She had never wanted to be near a man before, let alone to touch one in the manner she had just imagined.

Deke, sensing some of her confusion, rose from his chair. "I hope you rest easily, Chastity."

She sat staring after him as he left. What was wrong with her? she questioned herself. Whenever she was around that man she simply lost all control and reason.

Dabs entered the room shortly after Deke's departure. The black girl, as always, took Chastity's mind off her own problems. She told her mistress all about the ship, how she had helped the doctor tend the wounded, and then had helped to serve them their meals. She seemed quite pleased with herself and did not notice Chastity's solemn mood.

The next morning Chastity and Dabs were awakened by a light knock at the cabin door.

Dabs jumped from the pallet she had made on the floor, next to her mistress's cot, and Chastity sat upon the small bed and shrugged her arms into the robe she had worn the night before.

Dabs opened the door to receive a young boy, of about twelve or thirteen years, carrying a tray laden with delicious-smelling food. "Captain Saxon told me to bring your breakfast to you, mam." His manner was cool and aloof.

Chastity eyed the boy, thinking what a good-looking lad he would be if only he would wipe the frown from his face. "Thank you, you may set it there on that small table between the two chairs."

This he did and before leaving added, "The captain also said to ask you if it would be all right for him to use his desk for a while this afternoon."

"Of course, tell Mr. Saxon that he can use his cabin anytime." Chastity smiled, trying to be friendly to the boy.

Her effort was wasted; the boy simply turned his back on her and left the room.

"What a strange boy," Chastity said aloud, as she sat down and started to fill her plate.

"He sure enough is, Miss Chastity. He could kind of give you the creeps, I be thinking," Dabs said rolling her eyes up into her head.

"Do not be silly, Dabs; he is only a child. He must have had a hard life to act the way he does, but I cer-

147

tainly would not say that there is anything wrong with him."

Dabs did not answer, but finished eating what was on her plate. She kept her own thoughts about people, and there was no sense in telling her mistress for she would only scold her for her terrible thoughts. Sometimes she thought her mistress too good for this earth; she never saw any bad in anything. "I think I be going back to see if I be needed by that doctor man to help tend them hurt men." She liked seeing to the injured men's needs; in fact she pretty much liked men in general. She liked the way their eyes roamed over her full body, and all the pretty talk they were always telling her.

"All right Dabs," Chastity said nervously. She had hoped that the black girl would stay with her in the cabin, but since she wanted to help with the sick, Chastity could not very well tell her no. She would again be alone with Deke Saxon; the thought started her heart racing.

Deke Saxon was in a black mood as he made his way to his cabin. He had spent a sleepless night on deck, prowling about, his mind in a confusion that had about left him senseless.

His knock upon the door brought Chastity out of her seat, and she almost dropped the book she had started to read. "Come in," she called nervously. He tried not to look in her direction, going at once to his desk and sitting behind it.

"My apology for this intrusion," he said.

"Of course not, it is your room," came her reply, which hardly reached his ears. Damn, he thought, the woman had the sweetest voice he had ever heard. Shaking his head roughly to clear it, he opened a ledger, took paper and pen out, and tried to get some work done.

Chastity sat back on the chair and once more opened her book. She felt a bit hurt at his abrupt manner, though for the life of her she could not truly point out why.

A small amount of time passed, and Chastity was so engrossed in the book before her that she did not feel the light blue eyes upon her. Deke had finally closed his ledgers, realizing that there was no way he could accomplish anything with the smell of this woman's perfume filling his nostrils, and the thought of her fragile beauty so plainly in his mind. Giving in to his needs, he leaned back in his chair and tried to satisfy his body by merely watching her.

Clearly to his way of thinking this would not be enough; never before had any woman brought him to such strained peaks of inadequacy. He felt the need to take her in his arms and to show her what kind of man he was, to teach her the art of loving.

As his mind wandered, his conscience reminded him that he already had a wife, one with whom he perhaps did not share many things, but one who clearly shared his name. For a time he thought about his Nicole on Martinique. She had not been his choice for a wife but had been that of his father. Their marriage had been arranged by their two families, neither partner truly loving the other. Nicole clearly was not the loving type; she was cold and neat, not given to any kind of humor or display of affection. They had been married for over ten years and still they had nothing to show for their time together. She did not wish for children, saying that a child growing inside her belly would ruin her figure forever, and besides children made too much mess and fuss. That was why, Deke reflected, he had taken the cabin boy, Christopher, in and all but legally adopted the lad. He wished for children, for someone to whom he could leave, when he was gone to his grave, what he had accomplished. He had even allowed Christopher to take his last name. The boy's own past was so sordid that he would not tell a soul his true last name. But Deke had been proud the day that young Christopher had asked if it would be all right if he used the name Saxon instead of his own. From that day Deke had taken the boy under his wing.

He had taken him to live at his home, even though Nicole had complained and shrilled at him that he would live to regret taking in a waif such as the boy. He had clothed him and taught him to sail a ship and to become a strong young man. The boy would make him proud one day, he thought; and Christopher would be all he would ever have close enough to call his son.

He came back to reality, his eyes still directed at the lovely creature sitting across the room. If somehow things had been different and his Nicole had been something like this girl, he would have forever been the happiest man alive. For this girl was innocent of wrong doing; she did not know the meaning of being cruel and uncaring. She was the type of woman whom all men deep in their hearts secretly want to make their own. And as he realized that, he, least of all men, had any right to her, let alone to allow the thoughts that had been plaguing him since the night of the ball when he had first set eyes on her. He wanted to shout to the sky the unfairness of it all. He wanted to beat his head against a wall and weep out all of his frustrations.

Chastity closed the book, leaned her head back against the chair and sighed her pleasure with the pages she had just finished. She was young and had only just felt the first opening of her tender heart, this was a book about other young girls who were tasting the first fruits of love.

Deke's thoughts of his wife, and all other black pre-occupations, fled his mind as he stood and slowly made his way to her side. "Thank you for allowing me this time in your room."

"You are welcome." Her heart seemed to be beating so fast she thought it would burst from the confines of her gown. "Do you have a moment to talk?" she ventured, surprising even herself at her ability to say such a thing.

"Of course," Deke responded, sitting in the chair across from her.

"You say you are going to Martinique?" With the nodding of his head, she ventured even further. "Would you know the whereabouts of the Blackthorn plantation? I was told that we owned land and a house on the island. No one ever talked much about it and I doubt my mother ever went there herself; she may have when I was younger, I am not sure."

"Your mother has never visited our island, Chastity, and I, indeed, know where your plantation is. It lies on the other side of the island from my own. I would be glad to show you how to get there, and to see you settled in until you can get passage home." Deke was glad to be of any service to her.

Chastity's face lit up. "I am so happy that you can help me. I do not know what I would do without you."

His face suddenly turned serious. "You need but to ask and I shall do whatever is in my power to help you."

At that moment there sounded a knock outside the door and the cabin boy, Christopher, entered. "Captain sir, you are needed on deck. Mr. Scott asked me to fetch you."

"Thank you, Christopher. Have you met our passenger yet?" Chastity could see the affection in Deke

Saxon's face for the boy.

"No, sir, not formally," came the clipped reply.

Chastity could sense a certain hostility in the youth's voice.

"Let me introduce you then. Miss Blackthorn this is my cabin boy, Christopher Brice Saxon. Christopher this is Miss Chastity Blackthorn."

Chastity could not believe her ears. Had he called the boy Saxon; was he introducing her to his son? Her confusion was plain upon her features.

"I see you are wondering about the last name." Deke smiled. "This boy is my adopted son."

The first smile Chastity had seen the boy wear appeared for a fraction of a minute then disappeared as quickly. "It is a pleasure to meet you, Christopher."

"You also, mam." The boy stood stiffly, as though ill at ease in her presence.

"You may go now, Christopher. Tell Mr. Scott that I shall be there directly."

"Yes, sir."

When the boy had left the room Deke turned to Chastity. "You will have to forgive the boy; he finds women hard to trust. His past has not been an easy one."

Chastity's tender heart went out to the boy who had been adopted by this kind man. "I did not take offense at the boy, Mr. Saxon."

"Good. Sometimes he must be reminded of his manners. Well," he sighed, rising to his feet, "I must be about my ship. Perhaps you would care to share dinner this evening with me?" He held his breath awaiting her answer.

Chastity knew she was doing wrong; this man had a wife with whom he probably was in love. But for the life of her she could not help herself. "That would be very nice." She hung her head shyly.

Deke smiled softly. This woman was amazing, one minute the shy innocence, the next talkative and questioning. "Until this evening." He bowed out the door.

Chastity spent the rest of the afternoon straightening out the cabin and going through her trunks of clothes, trying to find something suitable to wear for dinner. She tried not to dwell on the approaching evening. Each time she brought to mind the man across from whom she would be sitting, she felt cold chills course over her entire body.

What would be the harm in dining with the captain, especially after the kind way he had been treating her since having rescued her from a sure death aboard the *Carry Queen*. But trying to reason with herself was no good. There was a part of her mind that screamed out that she was doing wrong. She was not a wanton who did as any man asked; and this one, especially; he was married and she knew already that she could not trust herself where he was concerned. But no matter what turbulent storms raced through her troubled thoughts, she could not change the fact that she would, indeed, be entertaining the captain of the *Sea Wind* in her cabin this evening.

She had hoped that Dabs would be in the room when the captain arrived, but the girl had returned to the cabin and asked her mistress's permission to dine with the doctor and a few of the less-injured men.

She had seemed so radiant and happy that Chastity could not bring herself to tell her no. And, honestly, Chastity felt a surge of joy at the girl's request. She did not have a choice now; she would be all alone with this man who had changed her feelings completely.

Dabs stayed only a short while then went back to the injured men, claiming they were in need of her care.

Chastity paced about the cabin for a time then proceeded to dress. She would have to do for herself this evening, as Dabs had already left. She should have told the girl to check back with her in case she needed her to arrange her hair. Well, she would just have to do her best, she told herself, as she slipped her wine-velvet gown over her head.

Its color was rich and becoming to her skin tone, bringing out the lustrous highlights of her honey-colored hair. The only real trouble Chastity encountered was in trying to hook the buttons at her back and in tying the ribbons at the side of the gown. The rest seemed rather easy. She brushed her hair until it fairly shone, a glistening color, its length reaching to the waist of her gown. She never wore her hair down; always Dabs had brushed it up and about her face, but tonight without Dabs's help Chastity left the mass hanging with only a ribbon, matching the color of her gown, to catch it back from her face. The only jewelry she would wear this evening were tiny diamond earrings. She stood back and looked hard and critically at the mirror. She looked well enough she thought, at last, patting a stray strand of hair into submission.

The cabin boy, Christopher was the first to arrive bearing a large bottle of champagne, which had been cooled all that day in the hull. He told her in a rather stilted tone that his captain would be along shortly and left the room.

Chastity did not have long to ponder over the youth, for directly following his leave-taking the door again was knocked upon and opened, admitting two men laden with two large trays of delicious-smelling food.

The captain was the next to arrive, and Chastity

could barely keep her eyes from his dashing figure as he entered the room. She had thought the first night she had met him that he had to be the most handsome man she had ever seen, and tonight again the thought came to her.

He wore a dark blue jacket and matching pants and a waistcoat of the lightest blue satin, shot through with a silver-leaf design. His shirt was snow-white silk with ruffles upon ruffles at the throat and cuffs, these ruffles detracting not at all from the masculine allure with which he seemed to vibrate. His high boots were of a shining black leather, glistening with recent polish. His garments all fit to perfection, showing off his muscular, highly masculine body to its fullest.

"You are beautiful," was his soft-spoken greeting, as he walked into the room and looked Chastity over from her soft loose hair to the tiny red slippers peeping from beneath her gown.

Chastity felt her blush. "Thank you, Mr. Saxon."

Deke smiled softly, taking one of her tiny hands into his big, calloused one. "Are you hungry?" He still smiled down at her.

"Yes." Chastity found herself smiling back.

"Let us sit down then for I am famished. I did not find the time for lunch today." He started filling their glasses with the champagne.

Chastity took the cool liquid and sipped at it slowly while he began to fill both their plates.

"We should consider ourselves lucky; being this close to home, the cook is not afraid to prepare anything in the larder. I am hard put for a good meal when we are far out to sea. I think the good man thinks to starve me into returning to port."

Chastity's light laughter filled his ears as he handed her a plate.

"You have a beautiful laugh. It is not often that I

155

hear a woman laugh." His thoughts seemed to be away from this room so Chastity did not answer.

The rest of the dinner was mostly completed in silence, his only questions being if she would care for more of the champagne or something else to eat. She refused more food but found the champagne delicious; more often than not she held out her glass for a refill.

She felt relaxed and quite carefree at the completion of the meal. "I do hope you do not think ill of me, Mr. Saxon." At his confused look she continued. "For entertaining you here and alone without even my maid present. But she did not want to stay; she much prefers the company of the doctor and the injured men." She smiled to herself as she finished; she seemed to be running on but she did not care too much. It must be the champagne, she told herself.

Deke chuckled lightly. "I could never think ill of you Chastity, and I see nothing wrong in the two of us having a light supper together." He knew he was not quite telling her the truth. He knew what he was doing was wrong; but at the moment, as he sat watching this enchanting creature before him, he did not care.

"Oh good, then," she exclaimed. "I shall tell you the truth. I have never before entertained a gentleman; you are the very first."

Deke Saxon knew that the champagne had loosened her tongue, and he found her utterly charming in her slightly intoxicated state. "I am quite proud then, Chastity. For a woman as lovely as you, I would think you would have found all manner of gentlemen trying to win your favor." He said this jokingly but truthfully found himself wanting to know about any other men in her life.

"Oh no," she laughed, sipping at her wine. "That is why my mother sent me away." At his stony look she continued. "She thought that perhaps the English air would do me some good and that I would be able to get closer to people." She realized for a moment that she was telling this man things she would never have told any other person and somehow she did not care. She had been so lonely for so long and this handsome man was the one to whom she wished to talk.

"Ah, then you were on your way to Europe. I had not even thought to ask about your destination before. Do you think you will continue on or return to New Orleans?"

"I do not know." She frowned; she had not really thought about the matter until now. "Perhaps I shall decide to stay on your island." Her eyes caught his.

"I would like that," he said softly, reaching over and taking one of her hands in his own. "I think you will find Martinique quite beautiful."

Chastity did not feel the slightest bit shy now, and she looked on as he sat rubbing the back of her hand with his own. Her senses throbbed at the feel of him—from that one simple touch.

Deke felt the same strong feeling come over him and was powerless to resist. "Chastity, I had better leave you now." He abruptly stood up and dropped her hand.

"Must you?" Chastity's innocence was clear, as she also stood.

"Oh Lord," he moaned aloud. "You do not know what you do to me, do you?" He looked into her eyes, so green and clear that they reminded him of a time long ago when he had gone to Ireland. Her eyes were the same color as a green Irish sea.

Chastity watched his features change from those of a smiling charmer to those of a tortured man. She did not know what had happened but she knew she was to blame. "I am sorry." She almost wept the words; she

157

had no desire to hurt this man for whom she was beginning to feel so much.

"It is not you who should be sorry." He bent his head and took the soft pink lips that had been tempting him so severely. His move was gentle, not wanting to hurt in any way.

Chastity felt her mouth being taken by his and felt her heart race at a tremendous speed.

It seemed as though an eternity had passed before Deke finally pulled himself from the haven he had found.

Chastity at his release almost fell; she was so shaken from that one kiss. She had never been kissed before; never had any other man taken her lips in that tender manner.

"I am sorry." Deke steadied her on her feet, taking her shoulders and looking into her dear, sweet face. God how he wanted this innocent woman standing before him. He had traveled the world over, but nowhere had he ever met a woman about whom he had cared more.

"Do not say that." She reached her hand up and lightly traced the small scar she had seen the day before. How she had dreamed of doing that. She smiled secretly to herself. She would also like to touch his dark hair but she thought better of it.

Deke reached up and grasped her hand; bringing it to his lips, he lightly kissed each pearl-like fingertip. "I must go Chastity. I can not stay any longer." He pulled away, with superhuman strength.

Chastity stood holding to the back of the chair. "I know," was all she could say as he left the room.

She sat back in her chair and gulped down the rest of her drink. What had she done? She had kissed Deke Saxon and she had enjoyed it. She could find no shame in herself for what had transpired between

158

them. She even found herself smiling at the thought of her fingers traveling over his strong jawline.

She rose from the chair and started to undress, half falling over as she tried to unhook the buttons at the back of her gown. She giggled aloud when she became entangled in her gown and her petticoats, landing on the bunk with nothing on but her chemise.

She did not hear the door open but jerked her head up when she heard strong male laughter. A smile broke her lips as she saw Deke Saxon standing in the doorway, watching her trying to undress. She told herself that a decent woman would be outraged but she found that with him she could only laugh at herself.

"I came back because I had to talk with you." He came to the side of the bunk and leaned down so as to look into her face.

She smiled trustingly up at him.

Deke Saxon was not one to take advantage of a woman and especially one about whom he cared as much as he did Chastity Blackthorn. Tenderly he reached over and took the blanket, bringing it up to cover her body. "Perhaps I should come back tomorrow and then we can talk."

But Chastity would not hear of it. "Oh, do not leave me again. You may talk to me now; I can understand you." A loud hiccup escaped her and she threw her hand over her mouth.

Deke smiled fondly down at her. "You are delightful, Chastity. I came to tell you something that I wished for you to know." His tone was serious and brought her back to her senses somewhat.

With her look of inquiry, he proceeded. "I know of only one way to tell you this. You have completely captured my heart Chastity." Seeing her tender smile, he continued. "I would like to say more but I have not the right. You see I have a wife." He thought that she

159

would scream or rave; when she did neither he was utterly surprised.

"I know, Mr. Saxon. My mother told me long ago."

"You knew and still you let me into your room?"

"I know it was wrong of me." She seemed completely sobered now. "I did not mean any harm in it. And to tell the truth I could not help myself. Each time I told myself that I was doing wrong, something I cannot explain would come over me and tell me I wanted to be near you and to hear your gentle voice speaking my name."

Deke's smile lit her heart. "You then have been plagued by the same bug as I, my lady." He sat beside her now on the bunk, resting one arm about her. It was amazing that she felt the same all-consuming power drawing her to him that he had felt each time he had looked into her beautiful face.

Chastity rested her head against his chest, feeling for the first time in her entire life at peace. Her eyes shut and she slept.

Deke held her throughout the night, she under the blanket and he on the outer side.

Later Dabs entered the room, made up her pallet, and went to sleep, not caring what her mistress was about.

The next morning the captain of the *Sea Wind* awoke to the first dawn light. He stretched out upon his bunk, and at the soft pressure of a body next to his own he remembered where he was.

His light blue eyes slowly opened, savoring the sight before him. Chastity lay asleep, curled up to his body, one slim, white hand lying across his chest, the other snuggled up under her chin. She looked like a sleeping child to him and a tender smile played about his lips. How he would like to wake up to that beautiful face every morning. If only he were free to make this woman his own. Reaching over he softly placed a light kiss upon her pouting lips and rose from her side. He stood for the briefest of moments looking down upon the sleeping form on his bunk. A soft moan escaped his lips. There was something about this woman that made it impossible for him to resist her, and come what may he knew as he stood there watching her that he would never let her go from him. He left the room quietly as not to wake Chastity or her servant, his mood thoughtful and reflective.

Dabs lay against her pallet, one eye barely opened, watching the movements of the captain. A huge grin spread across her face as he left. Her mistress may have been good and all purity, but not for long, she told herself. No one in her right mind would be able to resist a man as good-looking and well set-up as their captain.

"Land Ho." The call went through the ship, making all available men look off into the distance to the spot of green that jutted out into the ocean.

Chastity also heard the call and she felt her heart skip a tiny beat. Martinique would be out there in the distance—and also Deke's wife. She had not talked again with Deke Saxon since that night in her cabin. The only interchange between the two had been polite words of greeting, or on occasion, Chastity would catch him regarding her with such a tender look her heart would melt and she would want to rush into his arms and taste those lips that she had felt upon her own for only a few short minutes. But she and he seemed now to be holding a silent agreement to practice restraint, and she knew that she could not be the one to break the barrier down.

Patting the last few stray curls under her wide-brimmed hat, she left the cabin to find Dabs. The girl had become impossible, forever running off on the excuse of tending the injured men. You would think that a doctor would be able to tend a handful of men without the aid of Dabs. She certainly would be glad to get off this ship and get the girl on her regular routine again. She had been dressing herself and arranging her own hair now since boarding the *Sea Wind* and she missed the girl's attentions.

As she reached the deck she met Captain Saxon. His slow, lazy smile swept over her form, telling her more than words that he thought her beautiful. She returned his smile and walked in his direction. "Are we near land, Mr. Saxon?"

"Aye, Chastity. It should not be long now and you shall see Martinique. I hope you will not be disappointed." His eyes devoured her, his mind reviewing what he wished, in reality, he could do.

Chastity had lost all her shyness with him since the evening they had shared dinner and he had spent the night holding her tightly in his arms. Neither had talked about that evening but it was never far from their minds. "I am sure I will not be disappointed, Mr. Saxon." She smiled up at him.

Each time she favored him with one of her smiles his very breath seemed to stop in his chest. "Chastity, can you not find it in your heart to call me Deke?" he asked softly, so no other would chance to hear his words.

She looked upon him with questioning eyes. "Deke," she said the name so sweetly soft it reminded him of a butterfly touch.

At that moment Captain Altman came up to the couple. "Ah, Miss Blackthorn. I hope you have been comfortable? I have found myself rather negligent of you these past few days, but my men needed special care and I was rather strapped for time." He actually had not been all that busy that he could not have visited her at least once a day, but to him women were rather a nuisance, and beautiful ones even more so than the others. As long as she had gotten along without his assistance the better for him, he thought.

"Oh no, Captain, there is no reason to apologize." Chastity smiled brightly at him. "Captain Saxon was good enough to see to all my needs."

Deke smiled wickedly at Chastity, knowing that she was teasing the other captain.

What was going on here? Captain Altman asked himself. What did the girl mean by the statement that Captain Saxon had seen to all her needs? And what was that smile from Captain Saxon to mean? Could something have happened between the two of them? Mrs. Blackthorn would have his hide if something foul had happened to her daughter. "See here now," he stammered, turning beet-red in the face.

Chastity's look was one of genuine concern for the elder man; he seemed to be having some sort of stroke.

Deke Saxon knew Captain Altman's thoughts, and his deep laughter issued over the deck of the ship. "All was proper, Captain Altman; I assure you that I would never let any harm befall Miss Blackthorn while she is in my care."

Captain Altman relaxed somewhat, his color returning to a more normal hue. But still he did not trust this other man. He seemed a bit too handsome and carefree to suit him. He would be glad to get this young woman back into the hands of her mother, and as soon as he could arrange for passage he would have her aboard a ship and headed back to New Orleans. "Miss Blackthorn, as soon as we reach the island I shall make the necessary accommodations at an inn for you and your servant. I do not know how long we shall have to wait for a ship to take us back to New Orleans, but let us hope it shall not be too long." He looked from the young woman to the man standing beside her. Something was definitely wrong here.

"Captain Altman, that will not be necessary. My maid and I shall not be staying at the inn. We shall be going straight on to the Blackthorn plantation on the island. Mr. Saxon here has been good enough to agree to take me to it."

"But, Miss Blackthorn, do you think this a wise decision? You know nothing about this island." The captain would be hard put to explain this to his employer if something should happen to the head-strong young miss.

"But Captain, what shall there be to know? I am sure the island is quite lovely, and there is a strong and sturdy house on the plantation. My own father spent some time there in his youth." She had been pushed around all of her life, and now she wished a taste of freedom, and she was not about to let this elderly, pot-bellied, sea-going man change her mind.

Captain Altman saw her determination and knew there would be no changing her mind. "Well, if you feel that strongly about it, I suppose there shall be no harm in a short stay. I shall keep a daily contact with you though and shall send word the minute I can find a ship going in the direction of New Orleans."

Chastity's smile was noncommittal; she would see what time brought her. Perhaps she would decide not to return with Captain Altman; she would just have to wait and see.

Deke felt a small pride begin to grow in his chest for this woman; he had not thought her capable of standing up to Captain Altman but she had done a fine job as far as he could see. The poor man still looked a bit under the weather.

164

"There she is, Captain." Jamie Scott came up to the group and looked out to sea.

And there, as Chastity faced the rail, she saw before her rising out of the green-blue depths of the ocean, mystically an island, its green, lush, hilly jungles, and white sand beaches looking mysteriously out of place surrounded by the vast blue depths of the sea around her.

"Aye, Mr. Scott, we're home once more." Captain Saxon's voice seemed to hold a touch of sorrow in its depth. The first mate look sharply at the man, though he could not blame Deke Saxon for dreading the homecoming that he usually received; he also would dread having to come back time and again to a woman such as his captain had married. Oh, Mrs. Saxon had never been sharp-spoken or quick with him, but he could sense the type of woman she was in a minute, and he for one would not want too much to do with the ice lady, as they called her in Fort-de-France.

"It is beautiful," Chastity breathed as the ship sailed closer to the island.

Deke smiled down at her, finding it hard to be displeased when this woman was about him.

"Aye she is that," Captain Altman replied, taking in the same view as Chastity. "I have been to the island only a few other times, but I find each time I come to the Caribbean Islands something to carry home in my memory."

On the shoreline they now could see buildings of every description, and shapes moving about that had to be people. Chastity looked excitedly toward the shore.

Other ships were in the harbor and she guessed the island to be busy with trade. Her own plantation was said to produce sugar cane, but she had no idea how much they harvested in a year, or even if, after all these years, the plantation was still functioning. But soon enough, she would know all about the Blackthorn plantation.

The capital of the island, Fort-de-France, was a thriving town. The port had ships coming and going, mostly French ships bringing cargo from abroad and loading the bowels of their ships full of the products of the island. The community was mostly of French descent, and as the *Sea Wind* came into the harbor, Chastity saw women prancing about in the latest styles, and gentlemen in fancy-cut outfits going about business. She also saw that the island was populated with slave labor, for everywhere she ventured to look she saw black men and women, as though back in New Orleans, tending to their masters' bidding. She had never thought much on the matter of slavery. She considered it necessary, for she had been brought up on a thriving plantation, and without their black people they could not have survived.

The *Sea Wind* weighed anchor a short way from the harbor. They would have to wait for space to bring their ship close enough to unload their cargo, but a small lifeboat was lowered and awaited the pleasure of those ready to go ashore.

Dabs had found Chastity, and the two women waited by the rail until it was their turn to be lowered into the small boat. Leaving his ship in the hands of Mr. Scott and his crew, Captain Saxon took the boy, Christopher, along with him in the lifeboat. Captain Altman and the ladies were the only other passengers to board the small boat, besides the two men who would row them ashore.

The two men used sure strokes and soon the small boat reached land. Deke took Chastity's hand and helped her out of the boat first. He left Dabs to the help of Captain Altman, and Christopher jumped from the small craft to stand at the captain's side.

Chastity looked all about her, taking in all the sights.

Deke Saxon called Christopher to his side and told him to go to his house and tell his wife that he would be late getting home; he had business to which he must tend.

Christopher knew what this business was but did as Captain Saxon asked him. Deke was more than a father to the youth. Christopher worshiped the older man, trying to be like him in all things, except for one, women. Christopher could not abide them, and the more he was around them the stronger this feeling of dislike became. Nicole Saxon was the type of woman around whom Christopher had been all of his young life, and the women in his past had treated him harshly. Not that Nicole was cruel to him; on the contrary she was nothing to him. She treated him as though he did not exist, looking through him when they were in the same room and speaking around him when she had words to speak. Christopher knew that she resented the fact that Deke had taken him under his wing, but to be near Deke Saxon was worth any kind of abuse to the young boy.

After sending Christopher on his way with his message, Deke turned to Chastity. "Stay here with Captain Altman for just a moment, Miss Blackthorn, and I shall go fetch a carriage." He left, not awaiting any answer.

Chastity stood along with Captain Altman under a small enclosure, watching the traffic along the harbor street, and fanning herself hurriedly with the small ivory fan she had brought with her. It certainly was warm there on the island, Chastity remarked, as she felt herself sweltering under the lavish gown she had donned.

Deke was gone only a short time and returned with a small buggy, driven by a lanky black man. Chastity was glad to get inside the vehicle, and be on their way, grateful for the small breeze.

Dabs rode up front with the driver, not minding in the least sitting on the uncomfortable seat. She thought the black man good-looking in a skinny sort of way and, favoring him with a smile, received a large toothy grin in return. "Watch your step, missy," he called, helping her up by the hand and settling her down next to him on the plank seat. "You sure enough be a pretty little thing." He snapped the whip over the horse's head and the carriage pulled to a start.

"We shall go by the hotel first," Deke stated. "Perhaps you also would care to stay the day here at Fort-de-France, Miss Blackthorn? It is a few hours ride to your plantation. You may not feel up to it, just coming off a ship."

Chastity looked across to the gentlemen on the seat facing her. "I am sure Mr. Altman here," she smiled into the good man's face, "will be most anxious to get settled, Mr. Saxon, but I would much prefer to go on to the Blackthorn plantation. I, too, would like to get settled as quickly as possible, and I desire to see where I shall be living." Her smile turned to a frown as she realized that he might have other business to tend to instead of showing her the plantation. "Mr. Saxon, I did not think; if you have other matters to attend I will stay on at the inn. I was only considering myself."

Deke's eyes filled with a special light as he looked across at her. Ah, what a beauty she was. Her thoughts always gentle and of other people. "No, Miss Blackthorn, my afternoon is free. Mr. Scott shall see to my ship." He smiled softly at her, their eyes meeting and holding for the briefest of seconds.

Mr. Altman did not like the way these two young

people talked to each other nor the way their eyes seemed to linger when looking at each other. Perhaps he should accompany them to the plantation, but he was tired and wanted nothing more than a warm bath and a soft bed. He must be getting old. He was not used to sleeping on a hanging cot as he had been made to on the *Sea Wind*. He was a captain and used to the comforts that the title afforded him. To hell with worrying about this young lady, he thought tiredly. She was not a child but a woman, and she was not going to listen to anything he might say to her anyway, so there was no need for him to worry over her.

The carriage pulled up in front of a small, two-story white-washed building, where Mr. Altman alighted and made his way to the door. Once again the whip snapped sharply over the team of horses, and the carriage renewed its journey over the dusty roads.

Inside the carriage all was quiet but each occupant felt the other's presence sharply. Chastity tried to concentrate on the scenery outside her window, but she found herself hard put to block out of her mind thoughts of the man sitting across from her.

Now that they were alone within the carriage, Deke did not restrain his light blue eyes; he let them roam freely over Chastity, taking in all her beauty at his leisure.

The ride, indeed, was a long and tiring one. The carriage was jostled over rocky roads and wound around lush tropical mountains. Chastity found herself growing tired as the sun hung high in the sky and beat a tremendous heat down upon the vehicle.

Deke caught her nodding and rose from his seat. He took a place next to her, reaching up and pulling her head against his strong, broad shoulder. "Go to sleep my lady. It shall be a time yet," he whispered against her soft rose-scented hair.

Chastity obliged him fully, not arguing. She shut her eyes and was immediately drawn into a soft, deep slumber.

To Deke, time appeared to stand still as he held this woman in his arms. His breathing seemed to grow ragged and his heart filled with a slow, sweet pain. He knew he was torturing himself by being near her but he was powerless to resist. He would be taking her to her home, knowing that he should not return, but he would; he knew this without doubt. He would return and return, and each time he would see her his very soul would be in torment, knowing that he had no right to touch her, to love her, to protect her—and most of all, no right to claim her as his own. He felt slow, stinging tears fill his eyes, tears he had not shed since he was a small boy; but for this woman whom he now held and barely knew, he could weep. For without her he knew he would forever be empty. Like an old lost man, set out in a tiny raft upon the sea, he would forever be adrift without this creature beside him.

His thoughts turned to his wife, waiting at home for him and his features became a black scowl. He could see her in his mind as he would step inside the door for his homecoming. She would be cold and erect, holding one powdered white cheek out for him to lightly peck, as though he were an old man of eighty. Her voice would be harsh and demanding, asking after his trip, not truly caring one way or another as long as he came home to her and did not make her a widow. She could not stand pity or talk from other people, and if he were not to come home she would be the talk of Fort-de-France.

Chastity stirred; uncomfortable from the position she had been in during the past hours, and Deke pulled her a bit closer against his own body. She felt so soft and vulnerable to him, as though she trusted him implicitly as she snuggled her head deep into his jacket.

Another hour had passed before the black driver pulled the carriage down the dirt road that led to the Blackthorn plantation.

Deke awoke Chastity, tenderly calling her name. "You're almost home, Chastity; open your eyes so you can get your first view of where you shall be living."

Chastity pulled herself upright. Realizing where her head had been lying, she found herself not able to make an apology for she truly was not sorry. She liked the comfort that this tall, rugged man gave her. She smiled sweetly up into his face. "You have been my pillow?" she asked instead.

"I have indeed, madam," came his soft reply. "Never have I had a head more to my liking upon my shoulder than that of the past few hours."

Chastity did not reply except for the soft smile upon her lips.

"This is the lane leading to your house," Deke informed her, trying to restore some order to his rumpled clothing.

"It is lovely." She looked out the window, turning her head in various directions. The lane was shaded by trees, and along the side of the road beautiful tropical plants were bursting with heavily-scented flowers. Her breath caught as the carriage pulled through a group of trees, and there sitting all to itself was a large frame house. A beautifully tended green lawn ran up from the drive, and ended in a profusion of multicolored tropical flowers that encircled the large airy-looking two-story house.

Chastity felt joy at its highest peak as she was helped by Deke down from the carriage and she started up the huge stone steps that wound from the lawn to the front porch. "Deke, is it not beautiful?" she asked, thinking that her own father had viewed this very same sight. When he came through that same lane and saw the sheer beauty of this tropical paradise, what had he thought? she wondered. She knew without thinking what he must have thought—that he had to possess this lovely place and so he had bought it.

Deke's thoughts were on other matters. She had called him Deke once again, and the name had gone through him like an arrow to the heart, striking its target. His happiness was in viewing the total joy in her lovely face. He took her tiny hand in his own and squeezed it for an answer.

As they reached the front veranda, a tall, regal-looking brown-colored woman of indeterminate age, stepped through the front door and out into the bright sunshine. "Can I be helping you?" she questioned in a regal voice that suited a woman of her bearing.

Deke took Chastity's elbow and helped her up the steps to the veranda. "I think you can," he said. "This young lady is Chastity Blackthorn. She has come to stay here for a time."

The woman looked Chastity over with a critical eye. "Chastity Blackthorn, you say?" She looked to Deke, and at the nod of his head she continued on. "We were told that the old master died some years ago. The Blackthorn's agent stops by regular and checks over the plantation, but he has never mentioned that the old master had a daughter."

"Edward Blackthorn was my father," Chastity said softly.

Something in the young girl's tone struck the older woman and she went to her and took one of her hands. "You are welcome here, child. Your father was a kind master and everyone here loved him, though it was a long time ago."

Chastity's face lit up with thankfulness, and Deke squeezed her other hand, as the tall black woman led them into the house.

Light, airy furniture was placed sparsely throughout the rooms of the lower floor; the pieces were made of a wood that Chastity surmised to be native to the island. Large windows had been placed at every angle of the house to catch any breeze. It was exactly as Chastity would have imagined it to be from the outside, and her face revealed that she was not in the slightest displeased with a single thing.

After seeing that Chastity was happy and that she would be welcomed in her home, Deke told her that he would have to be on his way. It would be dark as it was when he reached his own home, and he could well imagine his wife' angry words if he were too much later.

At the thought of his leaving, Chastity felt a stab of loneliness strike at her heart, but she reminded herself harshly that he had already done more than she should have expected. She could not expect him to respond to her slightest call. "Thank you Deke, for all you have done for me." She lightly placed one tiny hand on the arm of his coat, her eyes speaking the tender words she did not dare utter.

Deke Saxon's very soul seemed to be pulled from his body as he looked down into those liquid green eyes before him. He wanted to reach down, take those soft pink lips, and to tell this beautiful woman everything that was raging within his heart. But instead he merely let one hand lightly caress her fragile jaw line, turned his back on her, and left the house, ordering the driver of the carriage back the way they had come.

Chastity stood at the door with her eyes shut, still

feeling that hand lightly brush her face.

The woman, whose name Chastity had learned was Ellie, called out to her from the sitting room, bringing her from her thoughts of Deke Saxon.

"Would you be caring for some fruit juice, missy?"

Chastity did not truly care for anything to drink. There was only one thing that her body craved, and that was the man who had just left her house. But she went into the sitting room, smiled at the woman, and drank the juice handed her.

Dabs had been sent up to Chastity's bed chamber to air the coverlet and arrange the room to her mistress's taste. She had brought only one light bag of clothing with her. Deke had told her that he would have a couple of his men bring her trunks out the following day. The black girl did not have too much to do, so a short time later she went downstairs, and Ellie at once took the black girl in hand.

"You be tending the missy and nothing else in this here house. I got one girl that helps in the kitchen and one that helps with the housework so you be needing to take care of your mistress and stay to yourself."

The housekeeper spoke bluntly, and to the point. She wanted no troubles in her house with no black girl from America.

Overhearing this exchange, Chastity laughed lightly to herself; it would do Dabs good to be set back upon her heels. The girl had become impossible lately, but by the sound of Ellie's stern, no-nonsense voice that would be coming to a halt soon.

It was already past dinner time, but Ellie insisted that Chastity dine on a light repast before retiring for the night. She fixed the girl cold meat with delicious-smelling bread and a large bowl of fruit on the side. Chastity was to find that each meal consisted of a variety of fruit from the island; her beverage was usually from one of these fruits. She ate in the dining room feeling somewhat lonely all by herself in the large room, then went to find her way to her room.

She found her bedchamber, like the rest of the house, large and roomy, with light-colored rugs scattered across the wooden floor, and large windows opened wide to catch the night breeze. The bed was the only thing so far in the house that she had found that was not made of the island wood. It was a large brass bed, spread with a satin coverlet that was embroidered with exotic birds. She reached over and felt the inviting bed and smiled a slow, tranquil smile; this would be heaven to sleep upon, she thought, as she watched her hand sink into the downy mattress.

A few minutes later Dabs entered, carrying two large buckets of hot water and mumbling under her breath about bossy black women who thought themselves better than those around them.

Chastity knew the girl was steaming about Ellie, but she refrained from saying anything as the girl prepared her bath water.

After a long, soothing bath Chastity donned a short, light pink dressing gown of the thinnest, sheerest material. She would have to find herself more gowns in this mode. She imagined the nights on this island could be miserably hot.

Dabs brushed her hair until it hung long and silky about her waist, then left her mistress and made her way to her own quarters at the back of the house. She resented not being able to sleep near her mistress, but at least that mean old Ellie had not sent her from the house. She found her room near the kitchen; it was not much bigger than a cubbyhole, she thought, as she pulled her cotton dress over her head.

Chastity laid her small frame on the large brass bed and felt herself sink into its soft folds. She smiled contentedly to herself as she shut her eyes. She felt at peace there on Martinique; perhaps this was where she would find true happiness. As she drifted off into slumber Deke Saxon's kind and gentle face came to her mind and a small, soft moan escaped her pink lips.

The man of Chastity's dreams was not lying peacefully content in the folds of his bed, but rather was locked up in his study with a bottle of good, strong rum.

Deke cursed aloud to the empty room then took another long drink from the dram of liquid. He had dared to hope that mayhap this time his homecoming would be different, but it seemed as though Nicole over the years had acquired a blatant taste for being nasty, and the minute he had walked into the house she had started shouting at him and sneering in his face about the little trollop he had brought back with him on this trip.

How she had found out so quickly about Chastity Blackthorn was a mystery to him. He knew Christopher would never have told her; she treated the boy even worse than she treated him. It must have been one of her French cronies, who were forever hanging about the house. He sighed, taking another pull of the liquor.

How he had ever held on as long as he had was a wonder to him; the woman he had married was harsh and totally uncaring. He had tried to explain to her the situation with Chastity, not wishing for any nasty gossip to start about the innocent girl because of his wife. She had not listened though; as soon as he had started telling her about the ship being sunk and their rescuing the crew and passengers, she had laughed cruelly, saying she supposed he had fallen all over himself with his willingness to give the little whore his bed.

Deke had tried to hold his temper, knowing that, in part, what she was saying was the truth. But as she raged on and on about his infidelity something snapped within his mind.

How dare this frigid bitch stand before him, as though she were the queen of pure virtue, and act as though he made it a habit to jump upon any woman who came his way. He had heard rumors about her and her French pet, Randolph, but he couldn't care less what this woman did as long as she did not do it before his very eyes, so that he would be forced to defend his honor.

But when she acted as though the mere mention of the word bed would send her into a fit of the vapors, and then demanded that he stay true to her, it was galling, demeaning to his own manhood.

As she strutted before him, prancing in her fine rage, Deke could see in his mind his large hands taking that slim white throat and squeezing until she breathed no more. He shook his head to clear his vision, his own face turning a bright red.

"You!" he shouted at her, bringing her own angry words to a halt. "You, who claim to be so virtuous and deny your own husband any access to your bed, but as rumor has it, sneak about with your French dandy, dare to stand before me and shout that you are being played falsely by a mere girl who is of the purest innocence?"

Nicole Saxon knew when she had gone too far. Never had she riled her husband into such a temper. Her white, chalky face turned even lighter as she viewed the fire storming within his blue eyes. She had made a mistake in accusing him so soon. She should have waited and found out more about this woman whom Randolph had run to tell to her about, the minute he had seen them at the harbor.

Deke saw the fear enter her dark eyes, and a twisted grin came over his own features. He rather liked the look of fear on her face. He had finally told her that he was wise to her and her French friend, He could well imagine the fearful thoughts running through her evil mind. He would show her that he would not be screamed at or charged with her vile accusations any longer. He took a step in her direction, his fist clenching and opening with his anger.

Nicole knew when to retreat and this was the time. She turned and fled up the stairs; reaching her bed-chamber door she hurriedly shut and locked the portal.

Deke watched her escape and his deep, harsh laughter filled the lower portion of the house. Did the bitch really think that he would waste his energy hitting her? She was not worth the effort, he told himself, heading to his study and a bottle.

He had drunk as much as he could hold and still walk when he left his study and started up the stairs to his own chambers. It was late into the evening and the house was dark and stifling. He turned about on the stairs and made his way out the front door of the house. He would go to the stables and saddle his horse, if the damned bitch hadn't sold the steed while he was gone, he thought drunkenly.

Atop his large black stallion, he gulped in deep, cold breaths of air as he raced through the night. He had sobered somewhat by the time he looked about. He must have been riding for some time, for he saw the house that he had left earlier in the day, the Blackthorn plantation.

Even in his drunken state, his subconscious had known where to lead him. Chastity was there, sleeping peacefully in one of those upstairs rooms.

He dismounted and made his way to the back of the house. If he could just find her room, he would but stay for a minute. His body was craving just one look at her, one glance to make sure that she was real and not some figment of his imagination.

A large, old tree grew up against the back side of the house, its huge leafy limbs reaching up and over to the roof. He could not believe his luck. He would climb up and into a window. One of the rooms upstairs had to be hers, and she would be the only one sleeping on the top floor, so there would be no chance of his stepping into someone else's room.

Deke shimmied up the tree as lithely as a young boy. The tree shaded the window of one of the bedchambers upstairs and this window was open wide. He easily swung his body through the window and stood, straining his eyes in the dark and trying to get his bearings.

It took a minute for his light eyes to adjust to the dark and when they did his breath caught and held. There lying on the bed was a form; he silently walked toward the bed.

Having been hot during the night, Chastity had thrown the covers down about her ankles and her short nightgown had ridden up her thighs.

His breath came in short, sharp gasps. God she was beautiful, he thought as he let his eyes take in her form from head to foot. Her long, honeycomb hair fanned across the pillow; tiny damp curls rested against her cheeks.

With a will of its own, Deke's hand reached out and gently touched one of those curls; as he bent over her, her rose-scented perfume filled his nostrils, bringing his senses to a giddy unreality.

Chastity's small form shifted in her sleep somewhat,

and her lips moved softly, whispering his name.

Deke Saxon thought his heart would burst from within his chest. Could it be that she was at this minute thinking about him in her tender dreams?

Chastity's eyes opened slowly; and, thinking herself still dreaming about the man who stood before her, she held out her arms and clasped them about his neck, bringing those strong, possessive lips down upon her own.

She truly awoke with a start when she felt strong arms wrap around her and Deke's body lying next to hers. His lips took hers in a kiss so consuming that she thought he would pull the very substance of her being from within her body. She tried to push him from her, but he was too strong, and a part of her cried for him to keep hold of her and not to ever let her go.

Deke could not believe it when Chastity had surprised him and wrapped her sleek arms about his neck, drawing him down upon the bed with her. He knew in an instant though, that she had not been awake and had no idea of what she was truly doing. When she tried to release herself from his grip, he could not bear to let her go. Perhaps it was still some of the rum he had drunk earlier, but he could not stand the thought of letting her go now that he held her in his arms. "You are beautiful," he breathed as he placed light kisses upon her forehead, eyes and lips.

"Deke you mustn't," Chastity cried as he freed her lips, not wanting him to stop but not daring to let him continue.

"I know, I know," the words were torn from deep in his chest, as he tightly drew her against him.

"What are you doing here?" Chastity questioned, when she could catch her breath.

"I could not bear to be away from you." The truth rang in every syllable as his eyes looked deeply into hers, and he brought one hand up and gently placed his fingertips against her lips.

Chastity could not believe her ears. "But what of your wife?" she softly asked, staring into those blue depths before her and all but losing herself in their tender appraisal of her.

"She means nothing to me, Chastity. You may not find this too easy to believe, but she has never meant anything to me. You are all that matters in my heart. I feel that all my life before meeting you was void, held in a black abyss, having no meaning until that night I first laid eyes upon your beautiful face."

His words touched sorely upon her heart. She was amazed that he would think she would not believe every word he told her, for she had those same powerful feelings within her own heart. "I believe you," she whispered lightly, her words hardly reaching his ears.

Deke's lips once more took Chastity's in a passionate embrace. "I love you, Chastity. For now and for all time."

"And I love you also," came the reply that it seemed to him he had been waiting years to hear.

His large, strong hands moved down her arms caressing the silky substance of her skin and marvelling at his good fortune.

Chastity's moan was one of pleasure, as his hands roamed freely over her body and his lips devoured her own.

With the sure hands of a practiced lover, Deke eased the gown covering his beloved's body over her head.

Her breath caught audibly as she saw the naked desire and love reflected deeply in his blue eyes. She had never learned a great deal about the things that men and women did in their beds, but now as she sensed this feeling of white-hot fire coursing through

181

every portion of her body, her skin quivered with the desire to know more.

"Your body is beautiful," he whispered, his fiery lips making a scorching path from her feet to her forehead. Not a place did his passionate mouth leave unattended, searching out and probing the secret valleys of her luscious body.

Chastity could never have imagined the feelings that were now coursing over her body. Her very flesh seemed to be acutely aware of this man's every touch, every caress. She moaned in sweet agony as his gentle hand slid between her thighs and tenderly caressed the treasure within.

Deke undressed himself, his hands and lips never leaving Chastity's body; his own desire for this woman beneath him so all-consuming and devastating that he thought he would burst within if he did not make her his.

As he rose above her, his manhood proud, fierce, and throbbing for release, and he looked into her frightened eyes, he knew that he loved her beyond all reason, far beyond all that he had ever known, not for just this moment but for all the years ahead. "I love you," he said softly, his manhood finding the desired jewel of her body. "I shall never leave you, you are mine, and I shall make you as one with me." His words were so tender and so heartfelt that shining tears glistened in his eyes.

As Deke had risen above Chastity, his body naked and throbbing with passion, she had felt a stab of fear, fear of the unknown, for she truly was an innocent and did not fully know what he was about. But as his eyes looked into hers and tender words of promised love filled her ears, she no longer feared what would happen to her; her love for him banished all fright as though it had never been.

Deke saw the fear leave her green eyes and a tender smile filled her vision. "I shall try not to hurt you." He knew this would be the first time she had ever lain with a man, and his thoughts were filled with trying not to hurt her in any way. As he slowly penetrated her willing body, her moan from the sharp pain of losing her virginity sounded heart-rending to his ears.

His motion stopped, and his lips tenderly kissed the silent tears sliding down her cheeks. "I shall not hurt you again, love. It shall only get better now," he soothed, his own heart breaking with her pain.

Chastity had never thought to find a love as wonderful as he, and her tears now were from his tender words, as much as the pain she had felt by his entry. "I love you," she whispered, wrapping her arms about his neck and bringing his lips down upon her own in a fiery kiss.

"Oh, love, love," he sighed, as his lips were released, his heart seeming to burst with joy from her words of love.

Chastity now felt no pain, but as his body kept up a steady, rhythmic motion she felt a delicious sensation of languorous rapture starting to grow at the depths of her belly.

Deke's only thoughts were of pleasing this woman who now filled his heart. Her soft, yielding body was like a temple of love to him, quenching his thirst with its heady liquid and setting his very soul afire with its passion's taste. Never in all his years of sampling of other women, had he been so swept up in such earth-shattering pleasure as he was now feeling.

Chastity also was pulled beyond herself into a form of nonreality, where nothing in the world seemed to matter except this man atop her, and the exquisite, tormenting pleasure that he was bringing her. As her own inexperienced body started, of its own will, to move in the same pulsating and trembling motion as Deke's, she began to feel a glorious sensation, as if she were starting to dissolve in the center of her being. For the first time she knew true pleasure. She clasped her own body tightly about that of her lover, and from her soft, tempting lips his name escaped.

Deke could see sweet pleasure coursing through his lover's body, and he himself lost all reason, his climax matching hers with its earth-shattering effect.

Quiet filled the bedchamber, as they both were brought to a slow, seductive pleasure. "You are wonderful and I love you beyond understanding." His tender voice filled her ears as she lay trying to catch her breath, her heart beating a rapid tattoo.

Chastity's eyes bore her love plainly. "I love you also, Deke, but I do not know how we can go on. We should never have done this thing." Now that they were quiet and lying next to each other, some reason was starting to return to Chastity's mind.

Deke's tender voice seemed to harden for the slightest of minutes. "Do not do this to my love for you, Chastity. I cannot change and I shall not leave you. You are mine now more than any wife could ever be. We shall find a way; do not worry. I shall not let any harm befall you."

No matter what was to come of this folly, Chastity was completely at this man's mercy. She loved him more than life, and nothing could ever change that all-consuming feeling. Without another word she took his lips and drew them to her own, once again feeling the fire of his touch. Their love-making lasted early into the morning hours, each not seeming able to get enough of the other. Finally though, with the dawn light streaming in through the large windows, they slept, locked tightly in each other's arms, as though they were tiny children trusting the outside world.

Chapter Seven

Martinique was more than just a beautiful island, abundant with tropical flowers and singing birds. To Chastity the island was a refuge, a place that she had been looking for all of her life. She was the ruler of her own future, the only person in charge of what was to happen to her. And she shared this idle existence with her lover. Though she knew she was sharing him with another woman, the times he came to her, and spent holding her tightly in the circle of his arms, were worth all the tears of loneliness when he was not near, and all the pain of not knowing when he would return.

Each day seemed to draw the couple closer to each other, their very souls seeming to twine and become one. Days when Deke could leave Fort-de-France and his business were spent horseback riding on Chastity's property, taking a picnic lunch, while Ellie packed for the handsome couple.

Laughter filled their hearts as they left the house in search of a secret spot to call their own. And, on one such day, Deke did, indeed, find the spot that they had been looking for. They had been riding for over an hour when Deke turned off on a path that they had never noticed before. This path wound about a small, lush tree-covered mountain, the undergrowth so thick that, if one were to get off the path he certainly would be lost.

As their mounts reached the end of the path, they both sat as though stunned, not believing what was spread before their eyes. There was a small pond, glistening in the sun's bright rays as though shimmering sparks were cast about its depth. About the pond's edges, lush green grass grew so thickly that whoever walked upon its surface sank in its very softness.

Chastity jumped from her mare and shouted out her pleasure. "Oh, Deke, it is wonderful." She twirled about, her arms outstretched.

Deke smiled down at the tiny woman whom he had grown to love more than life itself. "Aye, my love, it is that." His thoughts were more on her than on the beautiful scenery before him. He jumped from his steed, grabbed up the blanket tied to the saddle, and spread it next to the pond. "Come over here, sweet," he called to her, his mind's eye appraising the delights of her body.

Chastity's tender smile filled his vision as he lay back upon the cover. She slowly pulled out the pins that held her hair in place, and the luxuriant mass silently fell to her waist. "You are wicked, you know?"

Husky, triumphant laughter resounded about the pond. "Only where you are concerned, Chastity. You drive my mind from every other coherent thought except the pleasure that lie beneath your gown." He reached up quickly and pulled her into his arms.

Chastity's tinkling laughter followed his own. "You are indeed a rogue, Mr. Saxon." She lightly ran her fingers through the thick, matted hair on his chest, having easy access through his opened shirt.

"And you, my little love, enjoy every minute of it, do you not?" His lips ran a tormenting path of kisses from the top of her gown to the soft indentation near her ear, as his hands undid the tiny gold buttons running the length of her dress.

Her full, rich bosom burst from its confines, and

Deke's lips greedily latched on to this temptation, his tongue licking her pink, taut nipples into submission.

His love play was glorious, as though his own body played a sweet tune of ecstacy upon her willing body. Afterward, he pulled her to her feet and carried her into the pond of warm water, submerging her to her neck, his strong hands holding her in an easy grip.

"Can you swim, love?" His eyes were full of laughter as he dipped her in and out of the water.

Chastity jumped from his arms, causing his laughter to turn to fear. "Like a fish, my darling, like a fish." She laughed, swimming in long, sure strokes to the other side of the pond.

Deke, sensing the mood of her play, in moments was cutting across the water after her, her small body no competition for his larger, stronger frame.

Chastity stroked the water frantically, seeing him coming up behind her as though she were barely moving.

With one sure grab, he caught her bare foot and pulled her under, tightly clasping her fighting body to his own.

Her head came up from beneath the water sputtering and spewing out water. "You beast," she gasped, trying to catch her breath.

His laughter drowned out her words. "You played me false, madam. I thought you could not swim and that I would have the pleasure of teaching you a few strokes."

"I know full well the manner of strokes you have a wish to teach me." Her voice held a wicked tinge to its silky depths.

"Ah, you lusty woman," he mocked, his handsome face holding a leering grin, as he scooped her up and carried her onto the bank. "You think I only wish your body?" His hands once again began to stroke and

187

plunder, bringing soft moans of pleasure from her throat. "Tell me, my love, who is the one who seems to be taking advantage of who?" His question was a soft caress to her ears and was quickly lulled by the sensations coursing over Chastity's body.

Afterwards, as they lay in each other's arms, Chastity disrupted the quiet. "I thought I would go into Fort-de-France for a few days." After Deke's questioning look she continued. "Captain Altman sent word this morning with one of his men, that he has booked passage."

Deke's dark brow furrowed in a deep frown. "Do you wish to leave Martinique, Chastity?" They had not as yet talked about her staying on the island or going back to New Orleans. On his part it was because he feared her answer; if she were to wish to leave, he knew that he would either have to follow her or, with her gone, he would be lost to any kind of feeling.

Chastity traced the thin scar beside his mouth with her finger and tried to wipe away the pain she saw on his brow. "I love you," she finally said softly. "I would never wish to be apart from you. The time that we do not spend together is like a pain that I cannot bear. I shall never leave Martinique as long as you are here." She had never before expressed her feelings so fully to this man.

His strong arms clasped her tightly to him as though for all time. "You shall not be sorry," he whispered softly in her hair. I shall leave Nicole, perhaps now she will give me a divorce."

"No, no." Chastity placed her fingertips against his lips. "Do not say those words; she shall not let you go and we both know this. Do not torment yourself as well as me with these hopes." Small tears brushed against her cheeks.

They had not talked about Nicole before this day.

Both knew that the other woman would not think of a divorce; she was a proud French woman, and to divorce would bring not only bring dishonor upon her family, but shame upon herself. Chastity knew that Nicole had not a care for her husband, but to bring his affair out in public for all of Martinique to know that she, Nicole Saxon, could not keep her husband, would be unthinkable.

"I am content to have you with me when I can," Chastity said, wishing to relieve some of the tension from their conversation.

Deke kissed her lips; it was not a light kiss but one that spoke more than his voice could convey, it sealed the love he held for her, it promised all to her, it carried them into a world where only they existed.

That same evening Chastity sat down and wrote to her mother and her Aunt Cora. The letter to her mother was long, begging her forgiveness for not coming back to New Orleans with Captain Altman. She left out her association with Deke Saxon but told her mother instead of the peace and true pleasure she had found on the island of Martinique. She told her of the beauty and the lushness of the place, eloquently expounding upon the Blackthorn plantation.

She found herself feeling no remorse for staying on the island, nor did she feel any homesickness over not being with her mother or in New Orleans. She had never been that close to her mother, and her home had always been Iva Rose. If she did, in fact, miss anyone it was Miss Tam, but on Martinique she had Ellie, who reminded her in many ways of her dear Miss Tam.

Her letter to Cora was longer, telling the woman of their storm at sea and a little about their rescue. She did not tell Cora about Deke either, thinking that if the two women knew they might in fact, insist on her coming home. She told Cora about the various sights on Martinique and of her plans to stay in Fort-de-France for a few days. If she did miss either of the two women, she supposed that Cora was the one she missed the most. The two of them had grown close during her stay at the town house in New Orleans. Cora seemed to understand her more than her own mother; perhaps it was because she did not have the worries her mother had. But no matter she loved her Aunt Cora dearly.

With her letters tucked away at the bottom of her reticule, Chastity finished her packing. She would not be needing to take too many gowns with her, for she planned on finding a good dressmaker and having some lighter dresses made up before she returned to the plantation. Most of her gowns were of a heavier material than what was needed for the climate of the island. It would be a small pleasure she thought to treat herself to something new. She in fact, would look forward to picking out her own clothing.

It took her way into the evening before she finished and lay down upon the soft, comforting bed in her room.

The next morning Ellie had one of the field hands come up to the main house and hitch up the carriage, which had not been driven in years.

The man's name was Jake; he was a large black man, with a straight face and ready to do whatever he was told. "You be watching your manners now boy. When the mistress comes out and you take her on in to the city," Ellie warned, her old black finger pointed at the young black man.

"Yes, mam. Yes mam. I be doing just what the missus tell me, Miss Ellie. I watch what I be doing, I promise." He thought himself for better off than the rest of the blacks out in the fields, chopping cane. He had all but thrown up his hands and shouted with joy when Miss Ellie had gone to his mama's shack and told her that the missus was in need of a driver to take her into Fort-de-France. She had told his mama that she thought Jake would be the boy to watch out after the Missus. When his mama had told him the news after he had come in from the fields the day before, his huge chest had swelled with pride. To be picked to do a job for the mistress of the plantation was an honor, indeed, and all the other black people on the plantation knew it.

Chastity stood outside the main house, ready to be on her way. "I shall only be gone a few days, Ellie, and I shall pick up the supplies that we shall be needing."

"Yes, mam." Ellie smiled, handing up one of her mistress's bags to Jake up on the carriage.

"Dabs, you had better hurry," Chastity called toward the house, as she climbed into the carriage, with the help of Jake's strong hands. She thought to give the girl one more chance and take her along to Fort-de-France. But this would be absolutely the last time she would be taking her anywhere if the girl did not mind herself, and she had told Dabs those exact words only the day before. She would not put up with her acting as she had aboard the *Sea Wind* again.

Dabs came running up to the carriage from the back of the house, her features all smiles as she reached her hand up for Jake to help her up to the seat of the carriage.

Jake was a little unsure of his ability in driving the carriage; the only similar experience he had had was in taking the team of mules to the neighboring plantation once a month.

Chastity was jerked almost off her seat with the first lunge of the vehicle. After a few minutes though, the carriage seemed to steady itself into a rhythmic pace, Jake calling every now and then to the horses in a gentle tone.

The interior of the vehicle was much more comforting than the one she had ridden to reach the plantation the first day. The seats were more cushioned and its general appearance was much more pleasant. But still the ride was long and arduous, and by late afternoon when Jake brought the team of horses down the main street of Fort-de-France, Chastity felt as though every bone in her body were ready to drop, as he pulled in front of the inn to which she had directed him at the start of their trip. This was one trip she would not be making too often, she told herself as she was handed down from the carriage and wearily went into the cool shade inside the building. The heat, she reasoned, took so much out of you, even riding in a closed vehicle that perhaps with lighter clothing she would make out much better.

She found, when she went into the inn and talked with the proprietor, that Deke had earlier that same day made her arrangements for one of the best rooms in the inn. She would be staying in the same building as Captain Altman, but she certainly did not feel like having any kind of appointment with that good man today. So she left a message with the proprietor to send word to Mr. Altman, saying that she was in Fort-de-France, and asking if it would be possible for the two of them to meet tomorrow morning sometime.

She was then shown to her room. Carrying a large bag, Dabs followed behind her mistress, and Jake brought up the rear with the rest of Chastity's belongings.

Chastity ordered bath water the minute she saw her

room and the large brass tub sitting behind a bathing screen.

Dabs hurriedly did her mistress's bidding, this time knowing that any slackness on her part would keep her home in the future.

Chastity lay back on the bed, waiting for the girl to finish preparing her bath. Dear, sweet Deke, she thought, recalling his handsome face. He had seen to all her needs, and had left a message that he would be stopping by that evening to take her to dinner.

She could still feel the proprietor's sharp eyes upon her as he had handed her the sealed note. Everyone on Martinique knew who Deke Saxon was, and also knew the woman to whom he was married.

The man did not wish any trouble in his establishment, but he knew that to refuse Captain Saxon a room for his lady would bring more trouble down upon his head than he would receive if he simply did as told.

Dabs finished the water and quickly helped her mistress undress, hoping that she would not be needed any longer. She had her own tryst to keep; that big, strong buck, Jake, had given her the eye all the way from the plantation, and he had whispered in her ear to find him later in the barn. Now if all went well, her mistress would be dismissing her and she would see what kind of man that Jake really was.

Chastity leaned back against the rim of the tub, luxuriating in the soothing warmth. "You can go and find your own room, Dabs. Tell the man downstairs that your mistress does not want you too far away. I shall be in need of you later." Chastity closed her eyes and almost immediately was in a dream-sleep state.

Dabs hurried from the room, her face one large grin. She would quickly talk to the owner of the building, then hurry to the barn. She would have to be quick, for she did not want to anger the mistress again.

Chastity's mind was far from her room as her tired body relaxed in the warm water. Her dreams were of a man with the lightest blue eyes in the handsomest, tan face that she had ever seen, so she did not hear the door to her room gently open, nor did she see the man standing over her still form as she rested in the tub.

She did of a sudden feel a splash of water hit her face, and her green eyes flew open with fright. The fear was instantly replaced by a smile of pure pleasure as she saw before her the same eyes and darling face that had been plaguing her dreams.

"Ah, my little lady, you looked so beautiful lying back with your eyes shut and that wondrous look on your face. Tell me what you were dreaming of, my sweet?" Deke's tender voice filled her ears, as he bent down to the rim of the tub.

Chastity shook her head, too embarrassed to tell him of her thoughts. "You are mistaken, I was but sleeping. Do you not knock before you enter a lady's room?" she ligthly chided.

"So you refuse to tell me, do you? You think to change the subject, I will not hear of it. Tell me of your dreams, my lady; were they of a lover perhaps? And did he do this?" His lips took hers in a possessive, and consuming kiss.

Chastity's breathing grew ragged, and the tops of her breast, poking out of the water rose and fell shallowy as his lips claimed her own. When he released her she brought her hands up against those same rose-tipped breasts, trying to shield them from the penetrating gaze of Deke's love-filled eyes.

"You surprise me, Chastity." He gently took hold of the hands that tried to block the view he wished to enjoy. "After all of this time that we have shared

194

together, you still blush as though you were a young virgin, and still you try to hide your beauty from my sight." He rose from the side of the tub and turned.

Chastity thought that he would leave her to her privacy, but he quickly put a stop to all ideas of that nature. He strode easily to the door and locked the latch with a soft clicking noise.

"What are you about?" Her voice held a tremor of desire in its depths.

"Why I intend to share your bath, my lady." He casually made his way to the side of the tub and started to pull off his boots, then his trousers and shirt.

As he stood before her in all his splendid nakedness, Chastity felt her senses racing.

Deke's strong arms lifted her from the water; then he sat down and brought her gently down upon his lap. "Let us partake of more of your dreams, only this time they shall not be dreams and you shall not dream them alone." His words were whispered against her soft pink lips, before his mouth gathered them to his own.

The rest of the afternoon was spent in making love and splashing about in the brass tub. After they had toweled themselves dry and lain back against the covers of the bed, Chastity gasped aloud when she viewed the mess the room was in. "You, sir, have turned my chambers upside down; my girl shall be shocked and think ill of me for this water upon the floor."

Deke's laughter filled the room, as he gathered his love up into his arms. "Do not worry, my sweet; we shall stay locked up in your room until it all dries; then no one will know how you love to splash in your bath."

Chastity's smile filled his vision like a ray of sun,

and her sleek arms wrapped about his neck. "You make me forget myself and all reason, Deke Saxon." Her lips reached up and took his own.

It was far later in the evening when the two descended the stairs, hand in hand, their eyes holding only love and tenderness for one another, to leave the inn for dinner.

Chastity need not have bothered herself with worry over what her girl would think of her. By the time the black girl found her way back to her mistress's room the water on the floor had, indeed, dried itself. Dabs had spent her time finding out what kind of man Jake was, and what she had found she could not bear to leave. Never had she met another like her Jake; he was all man, big, strong, and virile. And as she emptied the tub of water and put her mistress's room to rights, she grinned to herself. It would be a long time, indeed, before she would grow tired of that man. Her hands busily went about her business, but she wished to get back to the barn and spend the rest of the night in that big black man's arms.

Captain Altman's mind was sharp, and he had heard the rumors going about the island concerning his employer's daughter and the captain of the *Sea Wind*. His penetrating glare was now focused on this woman who had been plaguing his thoughts since his arrival on this accursed island, and stonily he listened to her words.

"If you will just give my mother this note." Chastity's long, tapered fingers held out the note she had penned before leaving the plantation. "It explains my reasons for not continuing back to New Orleans, Captain Altman. I shall be deeply in your debt if you will do this small favor for me."

The girl since her arrival on the island had grown more sure of herself. He thought the matter over carefully before accepting the letter that she extended to him. It was going to be hard enough to explain to Mrs. Blackthorn about the loss of one of her ships; must he also explain the loss of her only child? This woman before him though, he reasoned, would one day, herself, be the head of the Blackthorn shipping line. One could never tell how long a person would be upon this earth, and if for some chance, something were to happen to the mother, he would surely want to be on the good side of the daughter. He could take the letter, and let it explain all; if questioned by Mrs. Blackthorn he would tell her all he knew except about Deke Saxon. She would surely have his hide if she knew what he had left her daughter there on the island with a married man.

He took the letter from Chastity's hand. "I will be proud to do you this small service, mam. And I hope you shall be happy here on the island. I am sorry I did not get the chance to visit you out at your plantation, but my men told me about it and brought word to me daily on how you were faring."

Chastity smiled wanly. This man's men had become a nuisance out at her plantation, coming each day to find out about her for their captain. "It was kind of you, Captain Altman, to take such an interest in my welfare."

"Think nothing about it, my girl; it was the least I could do."

"I do have another letter." She pulled the one to her Aunt Cora from her reticule and handed it to the captain. "I hope you will not mind also giving this to my mother?"

"Of course not, of course not." The captain smiled, wondering if this was all the girl thought him, some

197

lacky to do her bidding.

"Your ship sails tomorrow so I doubt that I shall see you again, captain." Chastity stood and held out her hand. "I am sorry I have to rush, but I have an appointment with a dressmaker and I do not wish to keep her waiting."

"Yes, yes. You mustn't keep her waiting." He gallantly took her hand to his lips. Damn, he thought, the girl was a beauty. "I hope that I shall see you again, Miss Blackthorn."

"I am sure you shall, captain." Chastity withdrew her hand and turned from the man to head out the door of the restaurant and down the street in the direction of the dressmaker's. She did not wish to be late. Knowing that she wished to have some gowns made up while she was in Fort-de-France, Deke had set up this appointment for her. In fact she hurried so that she almost ran into a short, elderly gray-haired man.

The mere thought of Deke caused goose bumps up and down her arms. After they had dined the evening before, in a small cafe, he had returned to her room at the inn and had not left until the early hours of the morning. How she loved that man who had stormed into her life, she thought as she reached Madam Nadine's small, cluttered dress shop.

Madame rushed to her side the minute Chastity opened the door, and a small tinkling bell sounded overhead. "Enter, enter, you must be the woman sent by Monsieur Saxon?" With the nod of Chastity's head the dressmaker took her by the arm and led her to the back of the room, her conversation going on and on as though she had known Chastity for years. "Sit here, madame and I shall get the swatches of material. Deke, you do not mind my use of his given name? Of course you do not. Monsieur Deke told me something of what you have in mind, some gowns of a lighter material than those you now have?" Her long fingers took up the hem of Chastity's gown and felt the material.

"Yes, yes." She shook her head as though in horror. "You must have something new at once. You will surely melt in this material." Then she left Chastity's side for a few minutes.

The tiny blonde woman reminded Chastity of a whirlwind. She was in constant motion. Why on earth Deke had picked this woman to be her dressmaker was a sheer mystery to her.

She had not time to think long. Madame Nadine swirled back into the room her arms full of swatches of material.

"I am sure you shall find something you like in these." She laid the swatches about on the floor in front of Chastity then sat on the floor. "Perhaps you would care to join me?" She smiled up at the girl on the chair, as she dusted at the floor next to herself.

Chastity did as bid, thinking the woman a bit strange. The material though was beautiful in more colors than Chastity had ever imagined, and the feel of some was so light to the fingers that she could imagine herself with the shimmering materials draped about her.

"Perhaps this one." Madame held up a sheer, mint-green satin. "You would look gorgeous in this, and Monsieur Deke, he will be struck dumbfounded, no?" She laughed, holding up one piece of material then another.

Chastity felt her cheeks flame at this woman's frank manner. How presumptuous of her to speak in such a familiar tone when they had only just met, and to talk about Deke as though she knew all about their affair. But the woman did not seem to notice her slight insults, so Chastity was forced to believe that this was truly her regular manner, and she was not just saying those things to offend.

The two women sat for over an hour going through the swatches, and Chastity found herself bent over with laughter. This woman was amazing; she truly was a character. Madame Nadine knew a bit about everything that went on in Fort-de-France, and she knew even more about the people. Most of the wealthy women of Martinique frequented her small shop, and more often women of a slightly different character employed her dressmaking talents. What she did not find out from the good women of the island, she did hear from those of ill repute.

She even told Chastity about Mrs. Deke Saxon being a regular customer. At first Chastity felt a small catch of embarrassment, for she knew that Madame Nadine knew what was going on with her and Deke, but as the woman said "Mrs. Saxon," she made a long, sour-looking face and muttered something about a French bitch.

"The woman is an unfeeling, cold-blooded baggage," she stormed as she gathered up the swatches and went into the back room, leaving Chastity with those words to keep her company.

"She parades herself about Fort-de-France as though she were the royal queen, and I tell you the work I must do on her gowns. Her waist is impossible. I have to push and tug, and each time she leaves I remind her to leave the pastries alone, but do you think she listens to me? No, on her next return she is even larger." Madame Nadine had returned with her arms loaded with sketches of gowns for Chastity to choose from; her conversation about Mrs. Saxon continued as though she had never paused.

"This here one, my dear, is the one I was telling you

about. See how the sleeves are only more straps, and the bosom, oh la la. That green satin will be just the thing; do you not think so?"

The woman was a genious, Chastity had to admit. The sketch was beautiful and the material would be just perfect. "You are right, madame." Chastity was engrossed in the booklet of sketches before her.

"I usually do not make mistakes as far as gowns are concerned." Madame smiled. "When I was but a small girl I only wished to sew and to feel the touch of soft material through my fingers. My mother used to scold me for my foolishness, but always one day I knew I would have my own shop and sew fine gowns for wealthy ladies."

Chastity wished that the woman would say a bit more about Deke's wife, but Madame Nadine seemed to be on another track now. She talked about some of her other clients and about gowns she had sewn for them, but she did not return to that one subject Chastity most wanted to hear about.

Most of the day was gone before Chastity left the small shop, promising to return in two days' time for her fitting. She had not thought to be gone so long, but after finding the gowns she wished to be sewn and fitting the right material to each, she had been stood on a small stool and her measurements had been taken by Madame Nadine.

Chastity was exhausted when she finally reached her room at the inn. Dabs was no where to be found, so Chastity did not bother to undress or to bathe but lay herself across the bed and instantly fell into sleep. Her morning with Mr. Altman and her afternoon with Madame Nadine had truly left their marks upon her weary body.

She was awakened by the gentle lips of a tender

lover. Her eyes slowly opened and her arms wound about the neck of the man who was lying on the bed next to her. "I did not expect you so early," she murmured, snuggling her body next to that of the man she loved.

"It is not early, my lady." His lips roamed freely over her face. "It is already past the dinner hour. I had a bit of work to attend to and had even supposed you to be worried, but instead I find you peacefully asleep here upon your bed."

Chastity jumped from his arms and off of the bed. "I am sorry Deke, I had no idea that it was so late. I hope you did not wait dinner for me? I wonder where Dabs could be. Wait until I get her; she should have awakened me hours ago." Chastity looked about the room her eyes falling upon the clock sitting on the mantel.

Deke leaned back on the bed, resting his arms beneath his head as he watched this lovely woman strut about the room in a small rage. "Come here love. We can have dinner sent up to your room. Perhaps your girl did us a favor by not waking you." A gleam of pure lust filled his eyes and Chastity's own desire flamed as she understood his meaning.

Quickly she was out of her gown and into his waiting arms. Their love play was long, languorous and sweet, devouring in its intensity, as though there were to be no tomorrow, only that minute in which their bodies twined together and filled one another with the delights of their love.

Chastity giggled loudly as Deke rolled her over and over the large bed; she felt carefree and adored by this large man as his body pursued hers over the bed. "Ah wench, you do try me beyond all endurance." His voice was husky and full of amusement as his hands roamed over Chastity's belly and down her silky thighs.

As his hands gently caressed Chastity's womanhood, all thoughts of light love play fled her mind. A soft, passion-filled groan came from deep within her throat and filled Deke's ears, causing his own thoughts to soar.

His lips nibbled softly along her swanlike neck and moved lower to her bosom. Teasingly, his fiery tongue made tiny circles around her pink, taut nipples, wanting to bring her to an aching wantonness.

Chastity was beyond caring or comprehending; all that registered within her mind was this man atop her, and the feelings that he had evoked deep within her body.

Deke's movements were slow, gentle, and languorous as he moved up and down with a rhythm of sheer sensual pleasure upon Chastity's body. He played the song of love to its fullest, striking a cord deep within that drove Chastity to a shattering climax, leaving her unable to move and barely able to breathe because of the feelings of delight that coursed over and over her body.

Deke looked down into his love's face with an expression of tender adoration, and after a few minutes he also was pulled into an uncontrollable climax.

As they lay in the aftermath of their loving, Deke wrapped his arms about Chastity and pulled her tightly to him. "I have waited to tell you this sweet, but I can no longer hold it at bay."

Chastity's eyes were green questioning orbs.

"My ship sails with the morning tide."

His statement was to the point and seemed to Chastity as cold as death.

He sensed her uncertainty as he looked down at her. His strong hand outlined that lovely face as though he would never again see it. "I did not mean to hurt you.

I love you."

Chastity looked deep into the eyes above her and found that all her trust lay within that strong, handsome face. "I love you also, and shall wait for you." Her words were mere whispers in the night.

"Ah, love, truly I have found what heaven is really like here in your arms. You shall not have too long a wait. I shall not be gone long, only a few weeks."

"Where are you bound for? You had me worried with your serious voice, Deke. Do not scare me again." Tears shone from her eyes and her hand clutched and unclutched his muscular arm, as though she would never turn him loose.

"We but go to a neighboring island. We shall pick up cargo and sell what we have on board. I did not mean to scare you; it is only that any time I am not near you tears at my heart, and this shall be the longest we have been separated."

Chastity laughed lightly, relaxing now against him. "It shall go by quickly; you know what is said, 'absense makes the heart grow fonder.' I can wait a few weeks, Deke. It shall not be easy, but it is preferable to what I had at first thought."

"What did you think, my love?" he asked, looking deep into her eyes.

"When you said your ship was to sail and that you would be leaving, I thought that perhaps you had grown tired of me. I would not blame you." She brought her fingers across his lips to silence the words he was ready to speak. "I know how it must eat at you to have to cheat on your wife, knowing that everyone must surely know about you and me." Tears now were flowing without letup, tears for the scare she had received only moments ago, and tears for the life she was forced to live for the man she loved.

"Oh, my love, my love." Deke's hand brushed at the

salty tears and his lips kissed away all the hurt on her delicate features. "I can not help the way I feel for you, as I can not help having the wife I already have. If possible I would abandon all for you, but I know that you love me for the type of man I am and to do that would be to forsake that love. One day I hope I shall be able to make you my wife, for you deserve only the best. If I were any kind of man I would get out of your life forever." His lips sought hers in a passionate hold. "But, God help me, you are like a fever to my blood. If I were to put you from me I would be a dead man. My life would hold no more meaning than if I were a senseless wanderer."

Chastity's tears now were for his words; she knew that each one had come from a heart that was being torn between his desire to do what was right and his desire to hold that which he loved.

They made love then, knowing this would be their last night together for several weeks. They did not think about the dinner that they had missed, or about the girl who had not come to awaken her mistress. They thought only of each other.

Deke's lips seared Chastity's skin where they touched, and his hands were like a fiery brand on her soft, pliant skin.

He spoke sweet words of love and endearment. He worshiped her luscious body as though he could not get enough of her, as though he wished to have her image imprinted forever on his mind.

Chastity herself was no less enthusiastic. Deke's every movement caused vibrations deep within her that made her moan and writhe with undeniable pleasure. Her senses fired and soared, making only this man atop her real in her passionate world of unreality. Savoring his every heated touch, Chastity met his every thrust with one of her own and wrapped her legs tightly about his waist, accepting all of him, and delighting in her wild abandon.

As though the center of her being had become a throbbing, pulsating, roaring volcano Chastity felt the depth of her stomach bursting with brilliant embers of glowing liquid. She clung to Deke's back as though he were her one link with this world and with eternity.

Deke looked down into Chastity's emerald eyes which were shining with unshed tears, and he knew that never had there been a stronger feeling of love in his heart for this woman. "You are my heart, my soul, and my very life," he whispered softly against her ear, then he, too, was brought to a climax whose peaks were higher than any he had ever known.

Afterward, they lay panting and damp from sweat, neither willing to let go of the other. They clung to one another, as though this, indeed, would be the last time for the two of them to relish those soul-shattering feelings.

No words were said; each savored the feel and touch of the other, and shortly they were again pulled into a world wherein only their desires and passions could endure.

Deke left early in the morning, not bothering to light a candle or to wake the woman whom he had held throughout the night. He tenderly placed a kiss upon her soft lips then stared down at her for a few short minutes. She looked like a lovely child, snuggled up to his pillow, her eyes softly closed in her slumber. With the power stronger than that of which he thought himself capable, he left the side of the bed and walked away. Her image would accompany him through the long days ahead.

Chastity, upon awakening, reached out to touch the man with whom she had shared the night in such joyous rapture, but only his pillow filled her arms. His scent of cologne, and fine tobacco still lingered on it.

A lone tear slid down her cheek as she realized that he was gone and had left her only the memories of a shared night. She pulled the pillow closer to her, feeling somewhat reassured by his lingering scent. He would return to her, she thought, and once again fell into sleep.

The next day Chastity felt more like her old self; she had stayed in her room all the day before, having sent Dabs to fetch her meals and to run a few small errands. The girl had shown up that morning with a look of shame and hanging her head. She had claimed that she had been so tired she had fallen asleep that afternoon when Chastity had first missed her, and that she had slept the rest of the night. Chastity had let the girl go with only a light reprimand, not feeling the strength to really punish the girl as she could have for her disobedience.

This morning, though Chastity had told Dabs not to venture from her room. She had said that upon her return from Madame Nadine's Dabs had best be where she should be, or she would send her back to the plantation that very day. The other girl had shook her head, swearing she would do exactly as bid, as Chastity left the room to go for her fitting.

The tinkling of the bell above the door brought a hurrying Madame Nadine, smiling with pleasure, to her door. "You are just in time. We have only just this morning finished cutting and basting a few of your gowns. We need only have you try them on to be certain the fit is sure, and then we can sew them up."

Chastity smiled. Madame Nadine had been true to her word, and must work her girls, as relentlessly as she ran herself.

"Step behind this screen, take off that gown, and I

shall have Sal bring out the first creation." She pointed to a dressing screen next to several bolts of cloth in a corner of the room.

Chastity did as bid. As she was unhooking the tiny buttons in the front of her gown the familiar tinkling of the bell atop the door sounded, and she heard the clatter of Madame Nadine's shoes hurrying toward her customer.

"Oh, madame, surely we did not have an appointment today?" Chastity could hear the worry in the friendly little woman's voice.

"Of course not, Madame Nadine. I have never known you to forget anything, least of all an appointment." The other woman's voice seemed frigid, even to Chastity behind the dressing screen. "I simply came by to see if you had received that new bolt of cloth you told me about last month when I was here."

"Um, I am not so sure about the one you are meaning, Mrs. Saxon. Perhaps it would be better if you were to come back another time, I am rather rushed today, a big order you know?" Never, in all the years Madame Nadine had owned her own shop, had the wife of a patron and his mistress been in the same room. Small beads of sweat glistened across her upper lip.

Nicole Saxon looked about, sensing the dressmaker's nervousness. "You must know the one I am talking about, Madame Nadine, the light mint-green satin. The one you raved so about the last time I was here."

Madame Nadine knew in an instant what the woman was talking about, but the mint-green was impossible for this woman, her coloring was way off; it would be overpowering with her jet-black hair and powdered face. And besides, she had already made Miss Blackthorn a gown from the material; in fact, one of the very gowns she was to try on today was of that satin. What was so to do? Thank God, the young woman behind the screen was remaining quietly hid. "Perhaps with an appointment we shall be able to come up with something more suitable to your coloring, Madame Saxon."

But the woman standing before her was more than a worthy adversary and would not be put off. "I insist on seeing the mint, Madame Nadine." Her back was ramrod straight. Who did this woman, who depended for her livelihood on people like herself, think she was? Nicole Saxon knew what she wanted, she wanted the mint satin, and she would have no other.

"I am sorry, Madame Saxon, but I shall have to ask you to leave. You see I am busy as I have told you and I have another lady coming at any moment." Madame Nadine's temper began to show in her voice. This woman in past years had never been one of her favorites and now she was become quite a nuisance.

Nicole Saxon's look was one of pure venom as she glared at the dressmaker. "You dare to order me from your shop?" She had never before, in all her life, been ordered from any establishment, and now she was being insulted by this wisp of a woman whom she could buy ten times over. But she left in a huff; she could not say too much to Madame Nadine because she was truly the only dressmaker in all of Fort-de-France. All the others were nothing compared to her. And if she were to be banned completely from having her gowns made by the woman she had no idea where she would then find anything suitable for herself. She would take her troubles to Randolph. Perhaps he could advise her since her own husband had left the morning before. Her temper flared even higher at the thought of Deke. The bastard had not even bothered to say good-bye to her. Since that night when he had returned from sea, he had barely had a civil word to say to her. Not that she minded; in fact, she rather liked his leaving her to herself. He had even taken lodging in a small inn, claiming his work was keeping him so often away from home, he might as well rent a room to sleep in while he was in town.

She had not argued with him; she liked being left to herself, with Randolph visiting whenever he was able. She was never bored. There were always friends about, though she questioned those friendships, wondering if she were not as wealthy and free with her food and wine whether they would still consider her their friend. Her thoughts were cut short as she stopped before the inn that housed her lover.

At the dress shop a frantic Madame Nadine tried to calm a shaky Chastity. She brought out a small decanter of wine and two glasses. "Perhaps you would care to join me?" she asked Chastity as she looked behind the screen to find Chastity sitting on a stool, her gown halfway unbuttoned and her entire body shaking.

"Yes, yes," the girl mumbled, still not believing that of all the women in Fort-de-France Mrs. Saxon, Deke's wife, had come into the dress shop. Only a few moments sooner and the two women would have been face to face. Would the other woman have known who she was? Would she know that she was the woman who had enjoyed her husband's caresses and gentle kisses the night before his departure on his ship? How on earth had she gotten herself into such a fix? Could she spend the rest of her life hiding behind closed doors or, like today, hiding behind dressing screens? Was this the life she wished for herself?

The rest of the morning went by in a hazy rush for Chastity. Madame Nadine apologized again and again for the unfortunate incident, swearing that this

210

was the first time such a thing had ever happened, and she would have done anything to insure that it could not have happened.

"How on earth was I to know that the ice lady would be coming by my shop today of all days." She wrung her hands, as she watched some of the color return to Chastity's face.

Chastity assured Madame that she was fine and that of course she did not blame her in the least. But she realized that the sooner she could leave the shop and get back to her own room the better she would feel. She felt her head throb as she went through the motions of trying on the gowns.

Madame Nadine could not get the incident out of her mind and begged Chastity not to let Deke Saxon find out what had happened. It could ruin her business she repeated over and over. If her clients did not feel safe coming into her shop, they would find someplace else to have their gowns made up.

Chastity absentmindedly nodded her head. Of course she would not tell her lover that she had all but confronted his wife. How could she tell anyone of the surge of sheer mortification she had felt as she had heard Madame Nadine say the name Madame Saxon?

As soon as possible she left the dress shop, promising to return in two days for her gowns. She would be more than glad to have the gowns and to return to her plantation; she had a lot to think about. She now was not so sure about her future. Could she go on as she had, thinking not of tomorrow but only of today?

Two days later in the heat of the afternoon she was once more in her carriage, with Jake driving the team, and Dabs sitting on the outer seat keeping him company.

She tried to shut her eyes and sleep, not wishing to burden her mind with terrible thoughts. That morning, picking up her gowns, she had once more been reminded of the horrible experience she had endured only two days earlier in the same shop. She had promised Madame that she would return to her dress shop. She had been affected by her near mishap more than it appeared.

It was dusk when the carriage pulled into the familiar lane leading to her plantation house. She felt at peace as she viewed the front veranda. In this one place where harm would not catch her, she was safe and secure. Ellie would chase away any evil being lying in wait for her.

Chapter Eight

For the next few days things went smoothly for Chastity. She pushed from her mind thoughts of all of the events that had happened in Fort-de-France, even scolding herself whenever she was wont to think about Deke Saxon. She knew that she was going to have to sort things out concerning herself and the man with whom she was in love, but she did not want to think about it now, so she pushed those thoughts to the back of her mind, thinking that, before his return to the island, she would have plenty of time to make up her mind about her future.

She rode daily about the plantation, trying to avoid all the places that she and Deke had already discovered. She would ride down to the beach that adjoined a small section of her property and she would swim, enjoying the warm rays of the sun which beat down on her naked body. She held no fear on her own property while she went about on these adventures, for who was there to harm her? She felt as safe as a child in her mother's arms.

Dabs, since returning from Fort-de-France, had become sulky and lazier than usual. She was forever claiming that she was sick in the mornings and in the afternoons she would plead that the heat was too much for her to bear. Chastity had thoughts of questioning Ellie about replacing the girl, but she felt some loyalty toward her, since they had both come from Iva Rose.

Several mornings after their return, Dabs came to her weeping out her story. The girl was pregnant. She had been caught and was not sure who the father was. It could either be the doctor aboard the *Sea Wind* or the driver, Jake, the first being the more likely for she and Jake had spent little time together, and she admitted that she had felt unwell for the past several weeks.

Chastity was appalled. How could the girl get herself into such a fix? But upon reflection she knew quite well how. Still, her case was different; she loved the man she had bedded; this black girl, weeping before her, had no feelings other than those of the moment for the men with whom she had shared her body. Nonetheless Dabs problem brought home as sharply as a knife wound Chastity's own position. She could no longer put off her problems, and the sooner she faced her choices and came to some kind of decision the better off she would be. She was truly overwhelmed by these thoughts and could not really give the girl her full attention. She told Dabs not to worry, that things would work themselves out. After all, hardly any of the black women were married when they bore their children; why should Dabs be any different? It perhaps would inconvenience Chastity somewhat as the girl began to grow large with her burden, but she could always find someone to replace her. Dabs was not the kind who was irreplaceable.

Dabs left her mistress's room still wiping at her eyes. She should have told her mistress sooner about her condition, she told herself. But Miss Chastity had not been in too good a mood lately. She seemed jittery and tense since they had returned from Fort-de-France. It was as though something had happened during their stay in the town. Perhaps she and Captain Saxon had gotten into a fight, the girl speculated.

But Chastity's thoughts were far from any fight that she and Deke might have had. Her mind was consumed with thoughts of their loving. There was something so unreal about their love that the merest thought of it could start her breath to deepen and her flesh to crawl, craving his touch. How could she possibly stop loving him? How could she control those feelings of wanting him to hold her and to kiss her lips, to feel his body tightly pressed against her own? She seemed possessed by some kind of monster whose only thoughts and cravings were for Deke Saxon. And how on earth she was supposed to supress these feelings was a mystery to her. But deep in her heart she knew that to keep on with her affair with a man who already had a wife was only to lay her heart bare to an angry wound. She had been taught that what she was doing was a sin; one did not love another woman's husband, under any circumstances.

"Dear God," she cried aloud to the empty room. How was she to stop loving her very reason for living? How could she go back to the way it had been before she had met this man? To leave this beautiful island

and return to her mother's home, was this to be her future, never again to love or be loved? She knew well that no other man in all the world could make her feel as Deke had.

She threw herself upon the bed, her tears flowing and her mind in raging torment. What was she to do? How could she endure for long without him?

Deke Saxon's thoughts were far from those plaguing Chastity Blackthorn. He had awakened that same morning to Christoper's gentle knocking at his cabin door, the signal that the boy was bringing in his breakfast. And on this morning, as on all others, his thoughts were aflame for the woman he loved. He had tried to hurry his trip so he could once again be at her side. He did not like leaving her so long without his protection, but he knew that he could not idly sit back on the island either. He had to run his ship and his crew, and there were people on Martinique who depended upon him. But his thoughts were constantly of Chastity. It would only be two more weeks and he would again be at her side.

These nights at sea had been the worst. As he stood his watch, in the early hours of the morning, when not striding from one end of the deck to the other, he would lay his head on the deck of the *Sea Wind,* and his light blue eyes would linger on the star-filled sky. Chastity's very scent would seem to float to him in the wind. He was bewitched, he told himself on those dreamy nights. He was bewitched and he could do nothing to correct it. But truly he did not wish to. Chastity was his very breath now. He could never go on as before their meeting. And one day he would claim her as his own, he swore to himself; she would be his wife in every way.

"Miss Chastity, Miss Chastity, you be having a

visitor. Where you be a-wanting me to put him till you ready to receive him?" Dabs hurried into her mistress's room, her tone rather excited. It was a rare thing to be having company way out there, so far from Fort-de-France. And the man who had come calling, Dabs thought with a small flutter to her heart, was very good-looking in a rather roguish way. What on earth he wanted with her mistress was a complete mystery to her.

Chastity looked up from her dressing table, with some surprise. "Is it Mr. Saxon?" She felt herself feeling all but faint with the thought that Deke had returned and was now, this very moment, downstairs waiting for her.

After Dabs shook her head no, Chastity asked, "Who is it then, Dabs? We were not expecting any callers." She patted the last piece of hair in her coiffure.

"No, mam, it sure ain't Captain Saxon. This here gentleman didn't say his name but he sure ain't the captain." The girl was still excited and some of her excitement came through in her voice.

"Well, show the gentleman into the parlor, Dabs; do not keep him standing in the foyer. And see if he would care for some refreshments. If he came all the way from Fort-de-France he more than likely would care for a cool glass of something to drink. I have only to change my slippers and I shall be right down."

Dabs nodded, assuring her mistress that she would take care of the guest.

As Chastity entered the parlor she took in every detail about the stranger who stood next to the hearth and stared up at the painting over the mantel.

He was tall and slender; his dark black hair was worn shoulder length and pulled back in a ribbon. He seemed at ease with his surroundings, one slender

216

hand resting on the mantel, the other holding a tall glass of liquid. At first glance Chastity felt something sinister about this man; perhaps it was the twisted grin on his lips as he looked up at the portrait, or it could have been the fact that he was dressed completely in black, except for his starched and ruffled white shirt.

As though sensing that he was being looked over, the man turned and gazed directly in Chastity's direction, his cold black eyes sending tiny pinpricks of fear running the length of her back.

His bow seemed more mocking than polite, and his face remained holding the same twisted grin. "You must be Miss Blackthorn? I have heard of your rare beauty but truly I did not think it possible until now that one could be so lovely."

Even his voice seemed threating to Chastity, and for a moment she thought of turning from the room and fleeing. Quickly, though, common sense returned. What was the matter with her. She had not even met this stranger and she was thinking evil thoughts of him. "Why, yes, I am." Her voice was not as warm as the voice in which she usually greeted a guest but this man did not seem to notice. "May I help you with something?"

"Indeed," came his reply. "I have been told that you would perhaps be interested in selling your property here on Martinique."

"I sell?" Chastity asked, shocked by the question.

"Let me introduce myself, Miss Blackthorn, and then we can talk over some business. My name is Randolph Beauclair. I have a house in Fort-de-France and that is where I heard about your wish to sell this lovely place." He looked about him as though he were an interested buyer.

"I can not imagine who would have given you this information, Mr. Beauclair, but I am afraid that you have wasted your time coming out here."

"Oh, you do jest? I did have my hopes on a place like this, way out and all to itself. Perhaps if I tell you who advised me you would remember mentioning the matter?"

"I am afraid not, sir. I can not sell this plantation or any other. It belongs to my mother, as my father bought it years ago. I am only staying here for a time."

"Why then I have surely been misled. I shall go right to my source of information as soon as I return to Fort-de-France. She will be quite upset, I assure you, at hearing this bit of news."

There seemed some hing of malice in the man's tone. He seemed to want desperately to tell her who his informer was. As Chastity sat across from him on the settee she tried to see into his slick mind. What could be this strange man's game? Who in Fort-de-France would tell him that she wished to sell the plantation?

Randolph Beauclair sipped deeply of his drink. This woman was quite lovely and would prove a more likely challenge than he had been led to believe. It would give Nicole what she deserved, for telling him that this woman was nothing more than a mousy spinster, if he were also to bring the young woman under the power of his charms. He felt his features smile at the thought.

Chastity considered his twisted smile. There was something evil and unnatural about this man.

"The woman who told me of your wish to sell your plantation was Mrs. Saxon, I think you know her husband?" His words came out slowly and silkily.

Chastity froze in her seat. She now knew his game. Nicole Saxon had sent him to try to get her off Martinique. "Yes, I do know Mr. Saxon. He rescued the ship I was on as we were sinking at sea." She would

218

not let this man know how he was effecting her. She certainly would not give Deke's wife the satisfaction of knowing that she was afraid of her. What had Madame Nadine called her, the ice lady; well now Chastity knew why she was called this hateful name. It was a rather cold and calculating thing to do, to send this man to persuade her to sell her property.

"Ah, yes, I heard of your near mishap at sea. I have also heard of other rumors but I would not speculate on their validity." His features were hawk-like now; he seemed to be waiting for his prey to make a futile mistake so he could swoop down and devour it whole.

Chastity knew what he was hinting at, and she felt her face turn to flame. How dare this complete stranger say these things to her. She rose to her feet, her breathing harsh with anger. "I shall have to ask you to leave, Mr. Beauclair. I do not like your manner nor your insinuations."

Randolph Beauclair also rose but his expression did not change. "Now come my *petite,* you do not wish for me to leave. You think this Deke Saxon quite the man, do you? Well, I can tell you, this is not so. Just ask his own wife who is the better man."

Chastity could not believe her ears. This man was actually standing there and telling her that he was a better man than Deke. Did he think that she would perhaps prefer him to her love? Was he truly that inflated with himself? Her outrage was beyond anything she had ever felt before. "You dare to think yourself better than Deke Saxon?" she finally got out.

"Aye my *petite,* let me but hold you in my arms for a few minutes and you shall also know the truth of my words." Randolph Beauclair did, indeed, think himself the better lover. Nicole had often told him how unsatisfying and clumsy her husband had been. She also showered praise upon Randolph, claiming to

219

much prefer his trained and experienced hands. What she had failed to admit was that she had not shared a bed with her husband enough to know about his love-making. She only wanted to keep Randolph for herself, so she had made up those lies to boost his male ego.

Chastity's mouth flew open at his assertion that he was the better man. "Leave my house at once," she shouted, not caring who heard what was happening in the parlor. "You would not have a chance against Deke Saxon. He is more man than you could ever be. He could snap you up in an instant and spit you out. How dare you come to my house and try to take advantage of me; Deke will kill you." She completely lost control, not caring now that she was admitting that she loved Deke Saxon. She cared only that this man knew how she despised him.

Randolph's evil, twisted grin turned to one of pure hate as he looked upon this woman. How dare she say these things to him? He knew what Deke Saxon was, and this girl standing before him in all her fine outrage was nothing more than a trollop, dressed like a grand lady. "You will regret your hasty decision, madame. You and I could have had a good thing. I could have shown you delights you could not imagine." He started to the door.

All of a sudden this hit Chastity as the funniest thing that had ever happened to her. Here she was in her own parlor, and this rather intimidating man was claiming that he could prove a better lover than the man who had brought her to such pleasurable peaks of joy that she knew it impossible to climb any higher. Her laughter bubbled over; she held her hand up to her lips, trying to contain herself as she saw the man turned to face her once more. "I am sorry," she giggled, "it only strikes me that you are a fool to even suggest that you are a better man than Deke Saxon."

This was the most insulting thing that had ever happened to Randolph Beauclair; no woman had ever laughed at his manhood before. This bitch would pay, he swore to himself, his face turning purple with anger.

Chastity laughed even more as she viewed his features. He was truly angry, he truly thought himself a great lover. He was beyond being insufferable. Her loud, gay laughter followed him out of the parlor, into the foyer, and the yard.

He took his anger out on his horse as he grabbed the reins and beat the beast harshly with his riding crop. The bitch would get hers; she would pay; he would see to that, he stormed, leaving the plantation.

Chastity was still laughing, dabbing at her eyes with her lace handkerchief, when Ellie came into the parlor with Jake only a few steps behind. The large black man's features were a storm as he rushed into the room, but he was brought up short as he viewed his mistress.

Ellie also was dumbfounded. She had heard the angry shouting in the parlor, so she had rushed out to the barn to find Jake to help if the mistress was in need of his assistance. But now instead of the gentleman and her mistress shouting angry words she found instead her mistress all alone and laughing as though she could not stop. "You all right, Miss Chastity?" she questioned, thinking that perhaps the man had so angered her mistress that she had completely lost all reason.

"I am fine, Ellie." She tried to contain herself, finding the job more than she could do at the moment. Every time she saw Randolph Beauclair's face in her mind, she again burst out into peals of laughter.

Jake also was grinning now that he saw that no harm had come to his mistress. He rather liked this small white woman, even though he thought white people a bit peculiar.

After a time Chastity sat back down upon the settee and controlled her laughter. She did not even care what the man had thought about her laughing at him. She still could not believe the whole affair had taken place, as she sat and went over what had occurred only a few minutes before.

Randolph Beauclair posed no threat to Chastity; she still felt as safe as ever on her own property. Her days were as always, her routine not changing, the only difference now was that she no longer thought about what would happen when Deke came back. She knew now that she would never willingly be able to give him up. If Randolph Beauclair had accomplished anything with his rude visit, it was to reinforce the love that Chastity held in her heart for the man she loved.

"I shall be back later this afternoon, Ellie," Chastity shouted, as she grabbed a sweet roll off a plate on the stove on her way through the kitchen.

"Yes, mam," Ellie answered, not bothering to look up from her work. "Do you be wanting to take along a small lunch?"

"No, I do not think so. Perhaps I shall go to the beach and swim for a while. It is a beautiful day and I hate not spending some of it near the water." With this she left through the back door, on her way to the barn and to her horse.

Ellie grinned widely. She sure did enjoy this pert young mistress. The days now were never boring as they had been in the past. Miss Chastity kept them all hopping. She remembered last week when that gentleman had come calling and the grit her young mistress had shown. This was a woman that a body could be proud to work for.

Chastity had donned one of the lightest riding gowns that Madame Nadine had made for her. It was light blue and sprigged with tiny darker blue flowers. The neckline was cut low, revealing much of her bosom, and letting the cool air caress her satin-smooth skin. This outfit was of a thinner material than her usual velvet habits, and Chastity found herself loving the feel of the soft cloth next to her body. She had worn nothing beneath, thinking it a waste of time to have to put her heavy underclothing on when she would be taking it off as soon as she reached the beach.

This day seemed different from the others. She had felt it the minute she had awakened. She felt alive and vibrant, sure that something good would be happening to her.

It did not take her long to reach the white sand of the beach; her mare was fleet and surefooted, loving nothing better than to be given her head, and to let her long, slender legs race with the wind.

No sooner had she gotten to the beach than Chastity was out of her riding habit and swimming in the deep blue water as though she were a dolphin. Her strokes were strong and sure, and when she tired she turned on her back and let her body soak up the sun. How she loved this island. Never would she have had this freedom if she were still living in New Orleans.

Her thoughts were completely wrapped up in herself and the warm, silky water she was floating upon, so she did not hear the bushes near the edge of the beach part, nor did she see the figure peering upon her luscious form. But her eyes flew open as she heard a splash near where she was floating. She twirled about, peering around to see what could have caused such a great stir in the water.

She did not see a thing but her terror mounted as she felt something near her leg. She swiftly started toward shore, hoping that her imagination was playing tricks on her, but this hope was short-lived. She felt something grab for her leg and she kicked out, her lungs filling with warm salt water as her head went under.

As she felt her leg being grabbed she also felt hands encircling her body; sheer panic took over. She fought like a tigress, scratching at the head that rose above her. But her fighting ceased as quickly as it had begun when she looked into a pair of light blue eyes and a smiling, wicked face.

"Deke," she whispered, not believing her own sight. "But how did you find me?" She completely forgot about the fright he had caused her as she felt his familiar, strong hands holding her close.

"I went to the house only minutes after you had left; at least that is what Ellie said. She told me where to find you. God, I have missed you." His voice was like a silken caress, filling her whole being with its warmth.

Chastity's arms wrapped about his neck and she buried her face beneath his neck. "And I have missed you also," she whispered, still not believing that he was standing there in knee-deep water, holding her tightly against him.

He carried her to the bank, at the water's edge, his hands and lips a-tremble, feeling the soft skin that had been denied him those long, starving weeks. All the thoughts of how he had been deprived of this woman came to his mind, and all the dreams that had plagued his mind aboard the *Sea Wind* stormed him at the feel of her in his arms. It was as though this were the very first time he had lain beside her. He kissed her soft pink lips in wonder, knowing that no other woman could taste so sweet and cool. No other had ever captured his heart and held it for all the world to see.

She was as no other. Chastity Blackthorn was a woman of rare beauty and one he would forever be grateful for finding.

His hands, admiring and loving at the same time, roamed over her tender flesh. His whole being wanted nothing more than to worship her, to adore her for being there and for being the one whom he loved.

Chastity sensed something of Deke's mood, and small crystal tears came easily to her eyes. She loved this man and the time away from him had been torture for both of them. She reached out and boldly stroked his muscled chest and arms, desiring nothing more than for him to come down upon her there in the sand and to make her one with him.

Deke prolonged his desire, wanting to savor and enjoy the moment, wanting to imprint on his mind that his weeks without her had come to an end. So he plied her body from head to toes with nibbling kisses, lingering on her breasts and the tempting valley between her thighs.

At this sweet assault upon her body, small moans of pleasure escaped Chastity's lips. She called softly to this large, passionate man to take her now and put an end to her tormented wantonness, but again and again he denied her, wanting to bring her to a peak of desire that was nearly more than she could bear before he would finally fulfill her body's wishes.

Finally Deke, not able to contain his own passions any longer, rose above Chastity, and spreading her silky thighs to allow his entry, he plunged his sword into her warm, loving sheath; losing his senses and all reason he rocked back and forth upon her beautiful body.

Neither spoke; their feelings were beyond tender and loving words. They let their bodies do their talking in the age-old act of love, only theirs was not the usual love-making; it was a desperate love. Each sought out and claimed a part of the other, to hold and keep and never have to render up again.

They soared higher than the birds in flight overhead; they touched upon the clouds and dared the very heavens with their loving. So flaming and so intensifying were their feelings for one another, that they brought each other to peaks of rapture neither had known before.

Then they lay exhausted and trembling for a time after their all-consuming love play. "Did you truly miss me, love?" Deke asked, as his hands still roamed over her body, lingering on the soft peaks of her breasts, teasing and tempting. With the nodding of her head, he thought he would lose his very mind. She had missed him as he had her those many long nights. Once more his mind returned to the nights aboard the *Sea Wind* when he had lain awake dreaming and wishing for this woman to be at his side.

He truly had to be the luckiest man on the face of the earth, he told himself, pulling her tightly against his chest. "I cannot leave you again, no matter what the reason," he whispered as his lips took hers with a tender assault. "I promise you that this will be the very last time. If I must go to sea you shall be beside me on the *Sea Wind.*" He had finally made up his tormented mind. He had wished time and again on that lonely voyage that he had asked her to come with him, but now he knew that he would not leave her again.

Chastity thought herself in complete heaven. This man truly loved her, and all the pain and suffering that she had felt since meeting him was worth the price.

"I have decided to leave Nicole for good and you and I shall never again be separated."

With a look of shock, Chastity shook her head. "There shall be no talking me out of this, Chastity. I love you and will no longer be away from your side."

"But surely your wife will object." Chastity sat up now on the sand; she had not truly thought this far ahead.

"You do not know Nicole, my love. She cares naught about me. Her only care is for herself."

Chastity shook her head. "I do not believe that, Deke. She does care about you."

There was something in her voice that drew Deke's attention. He sat up and looked at her closely. "How do you know this, Chastity? Have you perchance met Nicole?"

Chastity's face flamed at the reminder of her near mishap with Nicole Saxon. "No, I have not met her " she answered lightly, her head hanging. She did not wish him to see the blush that she knew must be on her features.

Deke knew now that something had, indeed, happened during his absence. Someone else, if not Nicole, had spoken to Chastity about him and his wife. "Who did you see while I was gone?" His eyes probed her own, not letting her get by without the absolute truth.

"Randolph Beauclair," she murmured, almost making Deke think that he had misunderstood her.

"You did say Randolph Beauclair?" He made sure of her answer. What could his wife's friend want of Chastity? His type preferred older, more experienced women.

"Yes," came her reply. "He came out to the plantation under the pretext that he was interested in purchasing the property. Chastity did not truly know how to lie; she had never before had to, and to lie to the man she loved seemed impossible to her now.

Deke was flabergasted. "You say he rode all the way out to your house? And he said that he wished to purchase the plantation?" He could not believe what he had heard. Why on earth would the Frenchman ride all the way from Fort-de-France to ask about buying a piece of property that he would not wish to own and for which he certainly did not have the finances to pay. Deke knew all too well the Frenchman's assets; he had glanced at enough of Nicole's bills to know that she was all but supporting the man. As though a bolt of lightning had hit, he knew why Beauclair had visited Chastity. Nicole had sent him to see what was going on with the girl and her husband. "What did he say?" Deke watched her features closely.

"Not too much." The blush returned once more to her creamy cheeks. Deke's large hands grasped her chin and looked into her face. "What did Beauclair say?" His tone now was like steel; he would not be put off; she would have to tell all.

Chastity felt tears come to her eyes at his tone. "Do not be angry with me." She would rather die than have this man angry with her for any reason.

Deke saw what he had done with his harsh tone of voice. His arms encircled her and brought her tightly against his naked chest. "How could I be angry with you, my little love? I love you; but wish to know what Beauclair said to you."

Chastity swallowed hard and tried to recall all that had taken place that morning in her parlor.

Deke remained quiet all through her story, his arms holding her and his face stony.

At the finish, his breath seemed to leave him in a single gasp. "You laughed at him, did you? I can see how that must have deflated him, my precious." His voice now seemed to hold some merriment.

228

"I am afraid I did lose my temper somewhat and he may, in fact, report back to your wife the things I said about you."

This woman he now held was all innocence to him. She had defended him against an wicked attack. He only wished that he could have been there to see her in all her fine anger, and to have smashed that French dandy in the face. He smiled slowly and kissed Chastity on the lips. "Thank you for your defense, madam. But do not worry yourself about Nicole. I shall take care of her, and you and I shall live in peace."

His silken promises filled her with a pleasant joy. She had done right that morning in her parlor, she told herself, and she would in a minute do it again if only to see the pride in her lover's eyes for her once again.

Deke reached down and scooped her up into his arms, running out into the water and falling with her into its depths. His mood all playful and loving now, he would put the affair of Randolph and Chastity to the back of his mind. There would come a time and a place where he would be able to meet the Frenchman face to face, and then they would see who was the better man.

The rest of their day was spent at the beach, playing in the water and drying out on the sand with lovemaking and whispered words of love.

Deke saw Chastity home, explaining that he had to see to his ship and crew in Fort-de-France. He would be back no later than tomorrow afternoon he promised her as he lifted her from her horse and set her on her feet, keeping her locked prisoner in his arms. His lips took hers in one last farewell kiss as he turned and mounted his large black stallion. "Come, Lacey, let us be off." He patted the horse's neck fondly and turned him from the plantation.

Chastity stood on the front veranda, her hand shading her eyes as she watched until he was out of sight. She found herself exhausted as she entered the house. She felt happier than she had ever been in her whole life, but all she wanted now was a tray sent to her room and to lie down upon her soft pillow.

Deke rode into Fort-de-France. He had promised his men that he would return that evening, and return he did, with his head in the clouds and his heart staying behind with the woman he loved.

Jamie Scott met him on the deck of the *Sea Wind* with a smart salute and a large grin. "Everything's been made ready, sir. The men have taken all the cargo to shore and I gave them their pay and shore leave."

"Thank you, Mr. Scott," Deke returned, thanking his good fortune that he had a man as able as Jamie Scott to take care of things in his absence. If not for the young man he would be hard pressed to find a minute for himself. "Come to my cabin and let us share a bottle, Mr. Scott. It has been a long time since the two of us have sat together." Deke led the way to his cabin.

Jamie Scott made himself at home, easily stepping into the personality of friend and not just first mate to Deke Saxon. He truly liked this man he shipped with; no other had he ever seen who could compare with his captain. He was a fair and able sailor and even better as a friend with whom to laugh and drink.

"Fill the glasses, Mr. Scott, while I change my shirt. Perhaps later you would care to join me in town? Mayhap we shall find us some sport, ha?" His true hope was that he would find Randolph Beauclair. He had thought about the Frenchman and nothing else all the long ride back to Fort-de-France this afternoon. He would not be able to wipe the bastard from his mind until he had found him and felt his fist smash into Beauclair's slim body.

"Sure, Captain, that'll be fine with me," Jamie answered, going to the table and pouring liberal goblets of brandy.

"Where is the boy Christopher? I didn't see him about when I came on board," Deke questioned, taking the proffered drink in his hand, and sitting back upon a chair.

"I sent the lad to find us something for our supper. I wasn't sure if you would be back in time, but I went ahead and told him to get some extra."

"Good, good. I find myself starving. Christopher's a fine boy, do you not think?" Deke wanted the other man's opinion of the boy whom he had grown to love. He had never asked this question before, but for some reason he now wished to know his first mate's opinion.

"Aye, Captain, I find the lad more than able. He's always ready to learn and does more than his share. I think one day he will become a fine captain himself," Jamie Scott answered truthfully.

Deke nodded his head as though deep in thought. "One day he will own the *Sea Wind*. He will have to be more than good; he will have to be the best. My attorney has already drawn up the papers, leaving all I own to the boy. I do not intend to leave this good earth soon, but, Mr. Scott, I would wish you to know that I shall be counting on you to see after the lad if for some reason something should happen."

"Aye, Captain, you know you can always count on me." Jamie Scott did not like the turn of this conversation. Talk of death had always made him uncomfortable, and for this man whom he had known for years to be hale and hearty, to be talking in this manner brought cold goose bumps along his arms. He had served under Deke Saxon for the last eight years and had seen him in all manner of tight places; but always he had survived. Once he had even been shot in the shoulder by a pirate; that time Jamie had thought that they would lose their captain, but as always, he had pulled through. Now, though, his speaking as he had seemed so out of character that Jamie wished for nothing more than to bring him to a happier mood.

At that moment the boy himself entered the cabin, so their conversation ceased.

"Captain, I was not sure you would be here."

The boy's face lit up with delight as he saw the big man sitting at the table. He put the food down and hurried to fix his captain a plate.

Deke had noticed that in the last few months the boy had not seemed his usual gay self. He seemed moody and sullen most of the time, but Deke had put this down to growing pains. He had to admit that since meeting Chastity he had not had too much time to spend with the youth; perhaps this was the problem. Well, he would cure that. As soon as he and Chastity were settled in, the boy would come and live with them. Chastity would more than likely take the boy under her wing and treat him as her own. She was nothing like Nicole; her heart was kind and tender.

The three of them ate their dinner, laughing and joking about their life aboard ship. Afterward Deke told Christopher to bunk down in his cabin. He did not wish the boy to return to his and Nicole's house; he would explain tomorrow to the boy about leaving his wife. But now he wished for nothing more than to be about town and perhaps to find a certain Frenchman.

Their first stop was at a small tavern, where Deke saw a good portion of his own men, drinking, gambling, and chasing after the women serving drinks.

The place smelled of sweat and alcohol, but both the captain of the *Sea Wind* and his first mate seemed to enjoy the hearty shouts of the men and the buxom barmaids. They would start their drinking here, where they could feel comfortable and perhaps enjoy a good fight or two; then Deke's plans were to go about the taverns more frequently used by the rich or those who wished a night on the town and did not wish to rub elbows with the more common people of Fort-de-France. Deke thought to find Beauclair in such a place, swilling down the shillings that he had swindled out of his wife.

As he sat beside Jamie Scott and drank glass after glass of potent alcohol, his thoughts were consumed with hate for Randolph Beauclair and his own ice-cold wife. "Let's go, Mr. Scott," he mumbled, getting up from his seat, and half-knocking the chair off the floor.

As the two men reached the door one of Deke's crew members caught a glimpse of him. "Ah, come on, Cap, have one drink with some of your boys before ye leave us."

"Not tonight, boys." He grinned. "I have more important things to be about, but here, let me buy you all a round." He threw a fistful of coins upon the bar, and left his men shouting and pushing to get their drinks. "Are you ready, Mr. Scott?" He smiled at his men.

"Aye, Captain. You lead and I'll follow." Jamie Scott was also feeling in his cups, but he knew that his captain was about something pretty important to refuse to have at least one drink with his men. Perhaps it would lead to a pretty good fight, he thought, rubbing his fist with anticipation.

They entered three more taverns and sampled their brandy before Deke finally found the man for whom he was looking. He had almost thought that the evening might be wasted, for it had not appeared that the Frenchman was out and about this fine evening.

But, as the two men entered the last tavern that boasted of good food and excellent wine, Deke caught a glimpse out of the corner of his eye of the man he sought.

Randolph sat off in a corner to himself and upon his lap sat a tempting wench, bending her head to hear his low voice; and his black eyes, making no pretense, looked straight down her bodice.

"You spend my wife's money well," Deke casually remarked, walking up to the table.

"What?" Randolph was taken by surprise.

"Must I repeat myself?"

"Oh, it is you, Monsieur Saxon." Randolph let go of the girl who immediately jumped to her feet and fled, going and standing next to the bar and quickly cozying up to another gentleman. She wanted no part of whatever it was that was going on between the two at that table. She was not deaf and had heard what the big fellow with the angry-looking eyes had said as he had approached.

"Would you perhaps care for a glass of wine?" Randolph questioned, holding up the bottle.

"I would not drink with the likes of you. Though I should, seeing as how my own money is more than likely paying for the bottle." Each word Deke uttered seemed to be laced with deliberate contempt.

Jamie Scott saw now what had been eating at his captain. This man must be the one about whom the rumors of Deke's wife and a Frenchman had spread. He did not blame his captain for being angry. He would more than likely kill the Frenchman, he knew, if it were him who were being made the cuckold. He knew he would not sit idly by and take it.

"How dare you say such a thing to me?" Randolph sputtered, his complexion turning even paler than it usually was.

"I dare the same way you dared to go to the Blackthorn plantation under the pretext of being interested in buying it, when I know as well as you that you do not even have the funds about you for your next month's rent." Deke was truly getting angry now and his whole body seemed to be straining to burst free of his control.

Jamie Scott was dumbfounded. This affair was not about his captain's wife, but about his mistress. Did the man truly love the woman so much? And what about Nicole Saxon? Did his captain not care at all that she was supporting this man? If she was giving him coins surely she was giving him more.

"It is none of your business about my affairs, Monsieur Saxon, and I would appreciate it if you would kindly take yourself and your man here away from my table." The Frenchman tried to hide behind a wall of arrogance.

As Deke's cold, chilling laughter trembled off the tavern walls, all heads turned toward these three men.

"I suppose that you think it none of my business that you tried to compromise Miss Blackthorn also?" His dark brows rose, awaiting an answer.

"The woman is not married and I dare say a married man such as yourself certainly can lay no claim to her."

Randolph felt fear grip him as thought it were a physical being. He had never been confronted before by a man like this one and especially not over a bitch of a girl who had laughed at him. He could well understand it if the man had been angry about his wife; after all the two of them had been lovers now for the past five years.

"I lay claim to her," Deke Saxon growled, lifting the Frenchman up by the front of his shirt. "She is mine and what is mine I protect."

His huge fist smashed into the fear-filled face before him, sending the Frenchman slamming into the wall.

Randolph Beauclair staggered to his feet, leaning on the wall for support. He knew in that moment that all of his past mistakes had been nothing compared to the one had had just made. This large, animallike man was going to kill him if he did not protect himself.

But before he could even cover his head another fist came at him, this time hitting its mark with a sickening crunch; his nose was broken and blood poured down and into his mouth.

He slumped to the floor, but was pulled up once again by the hair of his head. "Never—do you hear? Never let your vile mouth even talk to my lady again. For the next time, I shall kill you." There was a promise of death in the voice of the man who stood before him. Randolph knew that he would live this time, though he might feel like dying tomorrow. Still, he would live and Deke Saxon would live to regret that, he swore as he once more sank to the floor and felt a heavy boot kick out at his ribs, causing his breathing instantly to become pained.

Deke turned about, putting the Frenchman out of his mind. He had done what he had set out to do and the man had better not make the same mistake again. "Are you ready, Mr. Scott?"

Jamie nodded his head. He had seen his captain angry before, but never with this deliberate cold anger. "Aye, Captain. You lead, as I said before, and I shall follow," came his answer.

"Good man, Mr. Scott," his captain answered. "I wish all men were as loyal."

Deke did not go on to the *Sea Wind*. He went instead to the stables and saddled his large, black stallion. Mr. Scott was sent back to the ship for the night and was told to expect him sometime tomorrow. He had a lot of business matters to attend to, but tomorrow would be soon enough.

Deke, once more, like a moth to a flame, was drawn out to the Blackthorn plantation. His loud voice filled the night air as he sang a lively ditty to his horse, Lacey. His mood was carefree and the night air felt good and refreshing to his clouded mind. "Ah, Lacey, take me to my love," he whispered to the horse as he finished his song.

He remembered back to another night when his horse had brought him to the front of the large, two-story house, a night of love and the awakening of his soul. The first night of his life, he thought, as he once more started his climb up the tall tree in back of the house. There was no sense in awakening the whole house, he reasoned, slipping into Chastity's bedchamber window.

He now knew every inch of the room by heart; not a stick of furniture was unknown to him. The form on the bed moved in her sleep and a small sigh escaped his love's lips. Quietly, he undressed and climbed into the fourposter, drawing the covers up about Chastity and wrapping her in a cocoon of his love. He would not wake her until morning; it was enough just to hold her close and to let his senses fill with her soft, sweet scent.

In Fort-de-France another scene was being enacted as the couple at the Blackthorn plantation slept peacefully. Randolph Beauclair made his way slowly up the back stairs of an old boardinghouse. Each step he took

237

sent sharp, piercing pains through his ribs. With one hand he held the rail and with the other he clutched a cloth to his face, pressed to his nose to catch the still-dripping blood.

As soon as Deke Saxon had left the tavern he had staggered outside, holding onto a post in order to keep himself upright. He watched the streets in front of him, first this way and then that, his mind wanting only to get even with Deke Saxon. He would make him suffer and suffer long and hard, he swore to himself as he let loose of the post and staggered down an alley.

He had quite a way to go in his condition, but finally he found the old building he sought. Mike Bragget lived in this boardinghouse and Mike would do anything asked of him—if the money was right. He and his henchmen were the worst of the lot on the docks of Fort-de-France and nothing was ever too hard for them to do. Randolph had had other dealings with Mike Bragget and always the man had worked quickly and quietly.

He tapped on the door before him and heard loud scampering coming from inside the walls.

The door was thrown wide and a huge, gorillalike man, with one ear missing and a scar that ran over one eyelid and completely covered one side of his face, stood in its portal. This man was the type mothers used to threaten their bad children, telling them that if they did not behave they would turn out to look like this beast of a man.

Randolph's only greeting was a grunt. If not for the fact that he had used him on other occasions, Beauclair would have been more frightened of him than perhaps of Deke Saxon, he thought, as he stepped into the room.

"I have some work for you and your men if you're interested?"

"Sit," came his answer. This man, he had learned, did not waste his words.

Seated at a small round table were Mike's henchmen, Theobald and Snake. They also were dangerous-looking men. Both were much smaller than their leader, but their smallness only added to their crafty appearances. Snake was the smaller of the two and also the quietest; Randolph could not recall ever having heard the man talk. What stood out about Theobald the most was his hand; never had Randolph seen a hand such as this and whenever he was in the same room with this man his eyes, as now, automatically went to his fingers. He was missing three of them—the middle ones—but what stood out so boldly was that he had had made up for himself a steel point which stood about three inches tall. This was strapped to the hand and was placed where the missing fingers should have been. He could almost feel the point of the steel hit into his own flesh each time he was near this dangerous-looking man. He would feel only pity for anyone who got in his way.

"Ye say ye have me some business?" Mike filled a glass of cheap liquor and slammed it down in front of Randolph.

Randolph shook his head, unable to drink with his nose in such a fix. "Aye, business that I cannot do myself, gentlemen, but for which I shall pay quite handsomely if the deed is done exactly right." Randolph leaned over the table, getting the trio's full attention. His choice had been a wise one, he told himself. These gentlemen would kill their own mother if the price was right.

Deke spent the rest of the next day at Chastity's side, and then when he could put it off no longer, he once again rode Lacey into Fort-de-France. He told

Chastity that he would try to finish up all of his business in the next couple of days so they could be together without any interruptions.

Jamie Scott and Christopher were still on the *Sea Wind* when Deke arrived late that afternoon. Christoper had cleaned and polished his cabin to a high sheen and Jamie had watched over the crew as they had scrubbed the decks and made sure all was put in order after their voyage at sea.

Deke smiled to himself; his ship would be the sharpest on the sea if left to his men. He had to admit that he would be lost without the pair of them.

Without any delay Deke went to his desk and started on his books. If he was quick about his work, perhaps he would be finished before morning, he thought to himself as he thumbed through all of the papers. He had let the paperwork go for too long and now he was going to pay. He sighed.

Christopher looked in his captain's direction with a smile of pity on his face. If possible, the youth would have done the captain's papers also, that is how much he loved the older man. Anything he could do for Deke Saxon he would always do, but this one thing he had not yet been taught to do, so he could only smile his sympathy to this fatherlike man.

"Go ahead, Chris, and see if Mr. Scott has something else for you to do. I'll probably be here quite some time," Deke told the boy, then quickly involved himself in his work.

"Yes, sir." Christopher left the room in search of the first mate.

It was indeed quite late when Deke finally leaned back in his chair and surveyed all that he had accomplished this afternoon and evening. Christopher and Jamie had already retired for the night and, as he finished, he felt the quiet of the ship surround him. He rose to his feet and stretched, raising his arms high in the air. He felt his stomach growl from hunger; he had not even touched the dinner tray that Christopher had brought earlier, so engrossed was he in his work.

Perhaps he would go and find himself something to fill his belly, then perhaps have a drink or two in a tavern nearby, he thought, going to his wardrobe and pulling out a clean shirt.

Before he left the room he blew out the light, leaving the cabin in complete blackness. He pulled his watch from his waistcoat and struck a match as he reached the dock. It was too quiet this evening, he thought as he looked about him. Indeed, it was late, already past the midnight hour; no wonder that it was so quiet.

Most taverns stayed open until the early hours of the morning, so he would not have too much of a problem finding something to eat.

As he walked in front of a huge warehouse near the docks something made him uneasy. He felt the tiny hairs on the back of his neck prickle and his sharp, blue eyes looked about him. The only things that he could make out in the dark were two large crates sitting against the front of the building.

Almost immediately though, he heard a noise, as if someone were singing. And then from around the corner appeared a large man, stumbling in the shadows and singing in a drunken voice under his breath.

Deke figured him to be a sailor, left on his own for the night, who, after filling his gullet with rotgut, wished only to find his ship and sleep off the evening.

The drunken man approached Deke swerving and stumbling, and now his deep voice was louder. They were almost abreast of each other and also even with the two large crates. Deke moved a bit toward the crates in order to avoid the man falling upon him. This was the last Deke Saxon moved, for at that instant he felt a blow on his head so devastating and powerful that he was brought to his knees. For one moment his thoughts were only of Chastity; then nothing, as he hit the ground.

Chastity Blackthorn was awakened from her sleep the next evening by the harsh sound of someone beating upon the front door of her house. She quickly wrapped a robe about herself and rushed down the stairs, thinking that perhaps Deke had returned and wanted to get in.

Ellie and Jake, who now lived in the two-story house, were already at the door to let the night caller in.

Chastity was surprised to see that her visitor was a rather stony-faced Jamie Scott. "Come in, Mr. Scott," she said, thinking that Deke must have sent him with some sort of message.

"Yes, ma'am, I will."

His answer did not set right with Chastity and she started to feel that something was wrong.

"Come into the parlor. Ellie, perhaps you would fix something for Mr. Scott to drink. After his long ride I am sure he will be needing something."

She led the way into the parlor and sat down upon a chair, folding her hands upon her lap. She tried to put off what she knew deep down was to come.

"Mr. Scott, it has been some time since I have seen you. I hope you have been doing well? I have been enjoying myself immensely here on Martinique. The people here are so friendly and the beauty all about one is all but unbelievable." She rambled on, not able to help herself, but not wishing to know what terrible news this man had brought with him.

"Miss Blackthorn." His voice interrupted her, bringing her own to a halt. "I'm afraid I came her with some unpleasant news."

Chastity rose from her chair and walked to the hearth. She was completely unprepared for what was to come.

"Captain Saxon, ma'am, has been killed."

His voice cut through her heart as if it were a wickedly sharp knife and her knees crumpled beneath her.

Mr. Scott was quick on his feet and caught her in his arms before she could hit the floor.

This is how Ellie found her mistress, in a dead faint, lying in a stranger's arms. With lightning speed she was at their sides, calling for Jake to come at a run. "What be happening here?" she demanded of this strange man.

"I am Captain's Saxon's first mate and I have brought your mistress the news of his death," Jamie answered in a voice that sounded as though at any moment he would burst into tears.

Ellie was dumbfounded; Captain Saxon was dead. What on earth was this poor little thing to do? She knew better than any how much her mistress had loved the man. There would be no getting over this terrible affair, she thought to herself. "Bring her to the couch please, sir."

Jake had entered the room and helped Jamie to lay his mistress upon the soft settee. He also had heard the bad news and his heart went out to this small white woman.

It was some time before the group around Chastity could get her to her senses. She sat as though she were a frightened child, not seeming to hear what was being said to her or what was happening around her.

Jamie Scott tried to explain to her how they had

243

found their captain's body in the water near the dock that very morning. He left out telling her how badly the man he had truly loved had been beaten, so that he was completely unrecognizable. Only his clothing and the color of his hair had they been able to identify him as the captain of the *Sea Wind*.

When he had finished his story, he sat and watched this woman's face; she seemed truly devoid of all emotion. His captain had loved this woman with all his heart and now he knew just how deep that love had been. She would never get over this blow to her heart. He could not leave her here by herself, he told himself. Only a few days earlier his captain had told him of the trust he held for him where the boy Christopher was concerned. Would he not trust him even more with this woman's care? This woman had meant so much to him that he had fought a man, and had he not proclaimed his feelings for her to the whole town of Fort-de-France? Had he not said those words that even now burned in Jamie's own heart? "I lay claim to her," he had shouted out to the Frenchman. Jamie's eyes burned with unshed tears as he remembered even more. "She is mine and what is mine I protect." No man would have said these words without some great and lasting love burning deep inside him.

"I will take her back to New Orleans and to her mother," he told Ellie, not leaving any room for argument. He had worked for and gained, over two years ago, his captain's papers; but he had not wanted his own ship; he loved sailing with Deke Saxon. But now with Deke's death things would be different. If what Deke had said the other day about leaving the boy his ship was true then the *Sea Wind* would set sail for New Orleans as soon as she was provisioned and a cargo could be put into her hull.

Ellie wept, but did not say anything. She knew that

the girl needed her mother now more than she needed her.

Chastity did not say a word. She was too consumed by pain to think. She tried to banish from her mind Jamie Scott's previous words. She could not let those words be repeated in her brain or surely she would run from the room, pulling her hair out and finding a means to her own end.

Jamie Scott told Ellie to have all of Chastity's belongings packed and ready to be loaded aboard the *Sea Wind* within the next three days. He himself would come back for her. He was rather uneasy about the way the girl just sat and stared, as though she were not truly understanding what was going on about her. If something were to happen to her also, he would not be able to forgive himself.

Jake carried his mistress up to her bed and tenderly pulled the coverlet up about her chin, and for the next three days that is where she stayed. She neither talked, nor in any way acted as though she knew when someone entered her room.

Dabs tried daily to get her mistress to say something; she went to her room and pleaded with her to recognize her. The girl thought that her mistress surely must have been put under some deep, black spell and she did not try to hide this opinion. She told Ellie this one morning and was swiftly slapped for her evil thoughts.

"The mistress is but ill with grief," Ellie admonished. "When she be getting back home to her kin she be her old self once again. Now I don't be a-wanting to hear any more of that there talking of spells and black magic. It all a bunch of nonsense; you hear me, girl?" Her black, stern face glared into Dabs's.

"Yes, ma'am," the black girl sullenly said. She wouldn't say any more, but she sure could think what

245

she wanted. The mistress scared her to death each time she went into her room and looked into her blank, staring eyes.

On the third day after the evening when Chastity had been apprised of Deke's death, Jamie Scott returned to the Blackthorn plantation. He had gotten the cargo he had wanted and had loaded the food and water kegs necessary for the trip to America. Now the only thing left to do was to fetch Miss Blackthorn. His captain had been true to his word; he had indeed left all he owned to Christopher, even leaving the boy his last name, Jamie thought. How his wife had looked at the reading of the will would stay with Jamie Scott the rest of his life. She had risen from her chair and shouted vile accusations at Captain Saxon's attorney, swearing that she would get even with the man for his part in Deke's underhandedness. She had been left only one house in Fort-de-France; not the plantation house, but a small house sitting on one of the main streets of the town. The captain had not even left her enough money to pay the servants for another year, she had screamed. But all her shouting and fuss had been for naught, the attorney said the will was good and valid and that she was not living with Mr. Saxon at the time he had signed the papers. Nicole Saxon had stormed from the room, her skirts flying with her anger.

Now, thought Jamie, he had another unpleasant affair to tend to. He brought his team of horses up to the front veranda of the house. He would have to see this girl brought safely to her family, as he knew his captain would wish. Each time he looked at her he would be reminded of the love the man had held for her and again and again he would see the face that had been fished out of the water. If only he could put that completely out of his mind, he thought as he jumped from the carriage and reached the front door.

Ellie answered the door and led the young man into the parlor. "Would you be caring for something cool to drink?" she asked, knowing that he more than likely would, after his long ride.

"Yes, thank you, I find my throat dry as dust." Jamie felt uncomfortable in the parlor and pulled at his collar. He only felt at home upon the sea, with a ship rolling and careening under his feet.

Ellie was gone only a few short minutes and returned carrying a tray of lemonade and iced cookies.

As she placed this down upon a low table, Jamie asked after her mistress.

Ellie had known from the moment she had opened the front door that this man was going to ask this question and though she hated the answer she would have to give, she also knew there was no way out. She would have to tell him how her mistress just lay abed and did not seem to recognize anyone.

Jamie was truly upset; never could he imagine a love so great that it would affect a person so to be left without it. "She shall have to be tended to then," he told Ellie. "She certainly cannot stay here when she has a family in New Orleans. I shall carry her out to the carriage and then aboard the *Sea Wind*. Perhaps she has a maid who would be willing to go along with her? I know when we rescued her from Captain Altman's ship she had a girl with her."

"Yes." Ellie nodded her head. "Her maid be Dabs and the girl shall be leaving with the mistress, though I don't be knowing what good that there girl be doing Miss Chastity." Ellie did not approve of Dabs and she did not mince her words where the girl was concerned.

Jamie took her meaning well and assured her he would see that she tended to her mistress.

"I think Captain Saxon would approve of what I am doing." He said this more to himself than to the black woman standing before him.

Ellie agreed with this young man. Perhaps if Miss Chastity would get off this island and try to forget some of her memories of the captain, she could once again be her old self.

Jamie carried Chastity, wrapped in her coverlet, out to the waiting carriage. Dabs followed, her arms burdened with her mistress's baggage, and mumbling under her breath about a body having to work from sun up until sundown.

Jamie at once saw what Ellie had meant about this girl and he reminded himself to keep a watchful eye on her. He was not about to let anything happen to the woman in his charge.

Chastity did not seem to mind in the least that she was being carried down the stairs and out into the open vehicle. In fact she did not even seem to notice what was being done with her or who the man was who held her in his arms. She reminded Jamie Scott of a small child lost from everything she had ever known or loved.

The carriage puled away from the Blackthorn plantation, with Dabs the only one looking back at the beauty they were leaving behind them. She would miss this island, she thought to herself, and most of all she would miss Jake's big, strong back. It might take some time for her to find another as good as he; but then, she reminded herself, she had plenty of time.

It was late in the evening, and hardly a sliver of the moon showed as Jamie Scott carried a bundled form up onto the deck of the *Sea Wind*.

Christopher Brice Saxon, now the owner of the *Sea Wind*, met them as they boarded. His somber, tawny eyes beheld the couple as they came aboard, but his expression was not one of sympathy as he saw the woman in Jamie's arms. If anything, his eyes became even harder in her presence. He had told himself over and over since they had found Deke's body that it was the woman, Chastity Blackthorn's fault. He had heard of the fight in the tavern between Deke and Randolph Beauclair and he had also heard what that fight had been about. He held no doubt that Deke's death in some way resulted from that fight. And if that was true, his young mind figured that the woman had all but helped to kill his captain, the only man he had ever loved.

Jamie took his burden into the cabin in which Chastity had at one time stayed—but then the circumstances had been different; her young world had held only beauty and the budding of a first love. Now she did not even act as though she cared where she had been placed, as he lowered her into the bunk that she had shared one night with Deke Saxon.

Not knowing what else he could do for the woman, Jamie tucked the blankets tight beneath her chin and left as he saw her shut her green eyes tightly. He would go right on deck and send her maid to her; he'd tell the girl that she was not to leave the cabin for any reason. If his memory served him right this was the same black girl who had on that other trip been spending most of her time with the ship's doctor. Well, she would find out shortly that the ship's doctor of that voyage was no longer on the *Sea Wind*. Deke had fired him off the ship after that trip; the man had stayed drunk most of his time.

The *Sea Wind* lifted anchor and set sail for America in the dark of the night. The crew were rested from their days of shore leave, but none felt too lively. This would be the first voyage the *Sea Wind* would be taking without Captain Saxon.

During the days that followed, Chastity stayed in the cabin she had been taken to by Jamie Scott. Some days Dabs would think that her mistress must surely be getting better, for she would seem more alert and even look about herself; but then she would once more become withdrawn. One day as Dabs had sat talking to her mistress about inconsequential things, Chastity had sat straight up, in the bed and looked directly into the black girl's face. "Did Captain Saxon arrive yet, Dabs?" she asked, looking about her, her green eyes scanning the cabin. "Be sure to call me when he gets here." These few words had seemed to completely drain the young woman and she had fallen back upon the pillows and slept.

Dabs had stared, wide-eyed at her mistress. Was she really mad? Did she not understand what everyone had already told her, that the captain had been found dead? The black girl did not know what to do, so she just sat there watching for any movement from the form upon the bed.

But that night as Jamie Scott brought in their tray, he asked after Chastity, so Dabs stepped outside the door, calling the first mate after her. She told him about what had taken place that afternoon; even now as she remembered, she felt cold shivers course over her body. "She be thinking that the captain still alive," she said hardly above a whisper.

Jamie Scott's heart when out to Chastity Blackthorn and he wished that there were more he could do. But he could think of nothing which he would dare do or say to the woman; he was not about to go in there and tell her once more that the man she had loved was dead and gone.

"Just leave her be, Dabs, and let her talk all she will, even if it doesn't make any sense to you."

This would be all they could do for her.

After the first day that Chastity talked about Deke, she seemed to notice more about her. Dabs even, on occasion, caught her smiling when the black girl told her something funny. But more often she talked about Deke Saxon, scaring Dabs half out of her wits, for she always talked as though he would at any moment step into the room.

Chastity talked mostly about the things the two of them had done on the island and after a few days of being on the *Sea Wind* she began to spend most of her days in a dreamlike state, once in a while mumbling as though she were talking to someone.

Chastity truly lived in another world; in her mind, only she and her lover existed. She dreamed mostly of their days together and often she would talk to Deke Saxon aloud as though he stood facing her.

One morning on awakening Chastity had relaxed back upon the bed and dreamed about the day that Deke had returned from sea and had found her on the beach.

It had been a glorious day for the young couple and one that had stayed fast in Chastity's mind's vision. They had made love on the pure, white sand and had swum together as though they did not possess another care. That love play upon the sand became vivid in Chastity's mind, standing out starkly and plainly. She saw her love tanned and strong when he had brought her to such tender peaks of love. Tears stung her eyes at these thoughts, and they would not leave. It was as though she was once again on that beach and could feel Deke's strong hands and sweet, cool lips upon her body. She moaned with desire as he rose up over her and filled her with his manhood.

"You promised me that day that you would never leave me again, Deke." Chastity sobbed with a racking sound that filled the cabin of the *Sea Wind* and also

251

made cold, shivering goose bumps along Dabs's arms.

"Do not leave me long. I shall wait for your return." Tears coursed down her soft, creamy cheeks, but now Chastity was in the large bed within the bedchamber of the inn at Fort-de-France and Deke was once more telling his love that he would have to be leaving her for a short time.

Once again, she saw Deke in her arms and her mind filled with his love-making as though he were next to her. His hands and lips played over her body leaving her gasping and weeping from her craving for him.

In her mind's eye she could see him boldly lying naked and full of life upon the large bed within that room and her heart raced. "I shall be waiting, my love," she whispered aloud, and then as though she were totally exhausted she fell back upon the bed and slept.

Dabs never doubted to whom she was talking and she wished with all of her might that she could leave this cabin. She even told Jamie Scott that she was expecting a baby and that she was afraid that her mistress would scare her into marking it with her wild talk.

Jamie had laughed, telling the girl that this belief was only an old superstition. Nothing could truly mark a baby.

Dabs did not believe him for she had been brought up on such superstitions. But she had also been brought up knowing that she was never to argue with white people; so she held her peace.

The *Sea Wind* pulled into the port in New Orleans on a bright and sunny day. Jamie hired a carriage to take Chastity and her maid to the Blackthorn house.

This carriage ride was different from the last one Chastity had taken. She did not need to be carried or wrapped in a blanket. She sat straight, looking out the window at all about her. Yet even the most common observer could notice at first glance that the girl was not truly taking in what was before her eyes.

Jamie jumped down from the carriage as it pulled in front of the large imposing house. He would make sure that someone was there to receive Miss Blackthorn before he helped her down and up the steps.

The butler answered the door and soon Cora stood in the portal. Tears streamed down her face as Jamie told her who he was and who was sitting out in the carriage in the street. She rushed by him and to the vehicle, pulling the door open and calling Chastity's name.

Chastity did not in the least seem surprised to see the woman at the door of the carriage. "Deke shall be here soon, Aunt Cora." These were the only words which came from her mouth.

Cora stepped back a step, and felt the reassuring arm of Jamie Scott.

"You did not give me time to explain all to you, miss."

"Let us get her into the house and then perhaps you and I could have a cup of tea and a small talk. I am afraid I also have some bad news to relay. You see, Mrs. Blackthorn died over a month ago from congestion of the lungs."

"My God, the poor girl." Jamie sighed, helping her down from the carriage.

Cora smiled at Dabs and patted the girl's hand. "You have had it hard I am sure, dear girl, but you are home now." She had not known the black girl too well, but she supposed her to be terribly concerned about her mistress.

Dabs smiled her thanks, accepting all the sympathy she could get, no matter from what quarter.

Chastity was quickly taken in hand and helped up-stairs to her bedchamber. Cora led Jamie Scott to the parlor and told her girl to bring a tray of tea for her guest.

"I wish to know all that happened to the girl." She came directly to the matter at hand.

Jamie let out a large breath of air and then began to tell all he knew, beginning with the rescue of the *Carry Queen,* at sea, and ending with the death of his captain, leaving out nothing and hoping that this woman who seemed made of iron would be able to help the poor girl.

Cora listened patiently and quietly, her features turning paler as this young man's story progressed. The poor, poor child, she thought. She remembered the shy, quiet girl she and Christine had waved good-by to that day on the wharf of New Orleans. She would never have thought that Chastity would have led such a life as this Mr. Scott was outlining before her. The girl had fallen in love so hard and fast that she was completely shattered, not knowing who she was or what was happening about her.

She had always loved Chastity, almost considering herself the child's mother instead of Christine; but now she realized that she was completely baffled as to what steps she should take next.

Jamie Scott had finished his story and now rose to his feet, his hands wringing his hat this way and that. "I am sorry to hear about Mrs. Blackthorn's death, ma'am. If there is anything at all I can do just let me know."

"No, no," Cora said absently, not rising to see the young man out. "There is nothing for you to do here, young man. I shall see to Chastity. I am sure her mother would wish her to get the best possible care. Even to the last hour her mother worried over the child." Cora thought back a month ago to that week Christine had lain sick. For the last year Christine had seemed to weaken and then when she had caught a slight cold she had become ill with a fever. The doctor had been sent for, but said there was not much that he could do for the ailing woman.

Christine Blackthorn had not lasted long after the doctor had been called in. About a week, Cora thought, and most of that week she had been delirious from fever. A great deal of the time she did not even recognize her best friend, Cora. She would fight the covers and any hands that would lay hold of her, calling loudly for Edward Blackthorn and at other times calling for Chastity. For a few days after her best friend's death Cora had been hurt to the quick. It had hurt deeply that Christine had not once called out her name; but this feeling passed as Cora realized how ill Christine had been. She had known all these years how much the woman had loved her husband. Even though he had been dead for so long she had stayed true to his memory, never going out with other men. In fact, she did not even appear to notice other men around her.

Jamie Scott cleared his throat to draw the attention of the woman sitting on the settee.

"Oh, excuse me, young man." Cora rose to her feet and started to Jamie Scott.

"I must be on my way, ma'am."

"Yes, yes, of course. I cannot thank you enough for bringing Chastity to me. Are you sure there is no way in which I can repay you?"

"No, ma'am. What I have done I did for my captain. He loved the girl with a love I never before have seen the likes of."

"Thank you, Mr. Scott, thank you," Cora said, taking the young man to the door.

Cora leaned against the door after closing it tightly. She let out a large sigh. She would have to see to the girl. Perhaps she would be better off out at Iva Rose. Cora remembered how much Chastity had loved the plantation and had not wanted to leave that safe haven to begin with; and for a moment, Cora could not help thinking that if the girl had been left alone, she would not be in this sorry condition.

It was several weeks before Cora made the final decision on what to do with the young woman who had been thrown into her charge. She had hoped for the first few weeks that with time Chastity would come to her senses, but it was evident that there had been no mental change in the girl. What really forced Cora to decide was the fact that there was without a doubt a physical change in the girl she had loved since she had been born. Chastity Blackthorn was, for a fact, pregnant. At first, Cora was worried over the reports brought to her every morning of the girl upstairs being ill in the mornings; and then as the girl's abdomen began to swell there seemed no doubt. Cora at once brought in a doctor to verify these suspicions, and he confirmed them with a smile and a nod of his old gray head.

For a time Cora thought to keep Chastity in New Orleans at the town house that Christine had left to her in her will, but on reflection she decided that the best care the child could get would be out at the plantation with Miss Tam and the other servants. Also, Cora thought that perhaps with the fresh country air and in the surroundings in which she had grown up, the girl would regain some of her senses before the birth of the child.

Chastity was far along with the child in her womb when Cora, along with Mr. Courtly, took her out to Iva Rose. The girl did not react in the least to her surroundings as her aunt had wished, but instead had to be led about as thougha child; and every once in a while she would make some mention of Deke Saxon or the island, Martinique. Cora wondered that day for the first time if the girl even knew that she was expecting a babe. She seemed not to know anything that was happening.

At first, Miss Tam was delighted to see Chastity returning to her old home; but after her first look at the girl, large tears formed in her black eyes and she looked to Cora.

After Dabs had led Chastity up to her old bedchamber Cora explained to Miss Tam all that had happened, and she was assured by the old black woman that the girl would receive the best of care as long as she was around to see after her.

Cora and Mr. Courtly left Chastity that same afternoon in the hands of the servants. Mr. Courtly had made plans to come out to Iva Rose at least once a week to check on the girl and to make sure all was running smoothly. The Blackthorns were his most prosperous clients; and though Chastity Blackthorn was not too sound in her mind, she was the only living Blackthorn left—until the child she carried was born. And then, he thought, it was more than likely that the child would be the heir to the Blackthorn fortune.

On a chilly, damp morning at the onset of winter, Chastity Blackthorn was taken to her bed for the delivery of her child. Cora and Mr. Courtly were sent for and arrived in plenty of time before the birth.

Cora was amazed when she went up the stairs to visit the girl she had loved as a daughter all of these years. Chastity did not seem to be in pain. In fact, she did not seem even to notice all of the servants running about or the midwife who coaxingly talked to the girl upon the large bed.

At that moment, Cora realized that there was no hope for the girl. She knew then that Chastity Blackthorn would never regain her abilities or be her old self. Cora seemed to sag with this realization and to age with her knowledge.

She sat down in a comfortable chair in a corner of the room and watched as the people about the room prepared for the new heir to Iva Rose.

The labor seemed to drag on for hours; and though Chastity still remained quiet, Cora now could see some of the young girl's pain reflected on her features. She prayed silently to herself that the birth would not be much longer; and as the Lord answers all prayers, before long, a wailing cry resounded off the cold stone walls of Iva Rose.

Cora let out a long sigh—her first thought of Christine not getting to see her first grandchild. If only her friend had been able to live a bit longer, perhaps she would have been able to enjoy this child as she had not her own.

"It be a girl, Miss Cora. It be a girl baby," Dabs shouted across the room from the side of the bed.

Cora rose and made her way silently to the midwife's side. Indeed it was a girl, and she looked to be as tiny and perfect as any infant that Cora had ever seen. As Cora looked at Chastity, she saw that the girl had already fallen into a troubled sleep. "Let her rest," she told the servants. "Clean her up and change her clothing and then leave her. Dabs, you stay here and sit quietly beside Miss Chastity in case she awakes and needs anything."

"How about the babe?" Miss Tam questioned, taking the infant out of the midwife's arms.

"Take her to the nursery, Miss Tam, and send for the wet nurse."

"Yes, ma'am." Miss Tam went from the bedchamber and down the hall.

Cora stood for a moment and watched the pale woman upon the bed. She felt tears starting to form in her eyes. What would happen to this child? she wondered to herself.

As she left the room she walked down to the nursery. Miss Tam was fussing around a bundle in a cradle and Cora walked silently over to view the contents.

In the center of the small bed lay a tiny, blond-haired being. Cora smiled fondly as she looked at her. She was beautiful, so pink and perfect. She would have to be the one to name the poor child, she thought. She would think of a name that would help to shape this young thing's destiny. For a moment as she looked on at the infant, Cora felt as though she could almost see into the future. Though the babe was but a short time born, she knew with a sudden clarity that the child would grow into a beautiful young woman and that her destiny was already plotted out before her.

Cora leaned down and touched her lips to the soft, pink cheeks. She would pray to the Lord above that this Blackthorn female, no matter what her course or fate, would find more happiness than the Blackthorn women before her.

Danielle

(1748)

Chapter Nine

"You be standing still now, Miss Danielle," Sara, the black woman who was now the housekeeper and the ruler of the old house on Iva Rose, scolded the young girl standing before her. "Hold up this here arm, child."

Danielle brought up the arm and let out a long, drawn-out sigh from soft, pink lips. "How much longer, Sara?" Her tone was of annoyance and boredom, not masking her feelings one bit.

The tall, thin black woman smiled to herself as she took a straight pin from between her lips and stuck it through the material. This girl would never change. Though she was no longer a girl but a young woman, she still acted as she had at ten years old—so impatient and always in a hurry. "You just be standing still for a few more minutes. You be wanting something pretty when that Mr. Davinport comes this here week."

"Oh pooh, what does it matter what I wear? I have known Mr. Davinport since a child. And he certainly could not care less what I wear. He only comes out to Iva Rose to check to make sure all is running right. It is his job, Sara, and you know this."

"Why sure, I be a-knowing that, child. But still you can look your best when he comes out here. And don't you be forgetting yourself while he's here. I don't be wanting the gentleman to think that you ain't been brought up proper."

Laughter filled the black woman's ears. "Oh, Sara,

you are a card. Mr. Davinport, I am sure, knows as much about me as you do."

"Just the same I be wanting you to promise that you behave yourself?"

"I promise, I promise," Danielle laughed, bringing down her arm and stepping off the small table that Sara had made her stand upon as she fitted her gown.

Sara looked fondly at the girl before her. Indeed the girl had grown up in the past few years. Her body had become that of a woman, not that of the young, skinny girl she had once been. A full, tantalizingly high bosom pressed against the thin material, and her hips softly molded and outlined her perfect shape. Even her heart-shaped face had seemed to mature; her always-smiling pink lips seemed to have become fuller and more inviting looking and her slanted violet eyes held now an allusive, alluring look within their depths. Sara once again reminded herself as she lifted the gown over her young charge's head, her dark brown fingers contrasting drastically as they glided over the girl's golden, wheat-colored curls that it was time something was done with the girl; she was too full of life and too ripe for the future to be wasted out here at Iva Rose.

Danielle herself held thoughts along this same avenue. Mr. Davinport would be coming out to Iva Rose and perhaps once again he and his wife, Linda Sue, would invite her to spend another two weeks in New Orleans with them. She had gone two times in the past and truly had a marvelous time on both occasions. They had given a ball in her honor on her eighteenth birthday and they had taken her to the theater. The large city had been another world to Danielle after being raised on Iva Rose. And though she loved this large, cold fortress and all the people who lived here on Iva Rose, she found herself wishing more and more to be able to go into the big town. She enjoyed the attention that was lavished upon her by the gentlemen. And she also found that she more than enjoyed the light flirtations in which she indulged with these young men.

Danielle, as her mother before her, had had tutors hired to come to Iva Rose, but unlike her mother she had excelled in her subjects and had rather enjoyed the company of these teachers, especially if they happened to be young men. Though she never let herself go too far with her flirting, she had already in her short span of life turned many gentlemen's heads.

"That be fine, honey." Sara patted her on the arm, bringing her out of her daydreaming. "Why don't you go out to the kitchen and see if your mamma's tray is ready. You can take it on up to her if you like." Sara saw the look of wounded pain enter Danielle's eyes the minute she had mentioned her mother, but she knew there was nothing she could do for the girl; things could not be changed.

"All right, Sara." Danielle left the room and headed to the kitchen. She hated this time of day more than any other, the time when she was expected to go upstairs to Chastity Blackthorn's room.

In a few minutes Danielle stood outside the door holding a tray laden with food. There was no need to knock for there would be no answer, as there had never been in the past, so the golden-haired girl pushed the door open and stepped into the room.

Her mother, Chastity Blackthorn, sat across the room, sewing on a small sampler, her eyes downcast, her mind not truly on what was in her lap, but somewhere far away.

"Mother, I have brought you your dinner." Danielle as each day in the past, tried to reach into some hidden recess in her mother's mind. But as always, she was rewarded by cold silence. "I shall put it here on this table, Mother." The girl set the tray within arm's reach of the woman sitting in the chair.

Chastity looked up to her daughter with only blankness in her green eyes. "Thank you, Dabs."

Danielle felt the tears once again fill her eyes, and unbidden came the memory of a small girl coming into this same room and calling this woman mamma. But the small girl had been led out of the room by servants and told that her mamma was sick and that she mustn't bother her. It had been years later that she had found out the truth about her mother. Chastity Blackthorn was not right in her mind and the doctors said she never would be. Danielle had grown up with an aching pity for this woman.

Only a year ago Danielle had gone in search of this Dabs after whom her mother called all of the servants and even her daughter. She had been sent from the main house by Miss Tam, who had died years ago, and the woman had been put to work in the cotton fields. At first Dabs had been reluctant to speak to Danielle, she still felt a sharp resentment for being displaced from her mistress's side. But after some light persuasion the old black woman had told Danielle all she knew about Chastity Blackthorn.

Danielle had kept what the woman had told her to herself, not even confiding in Sara as she always had in the past about anything major in her life. But what Dabs told her about her mother and all that had happened to her on the island of Martinique was not something that she could share with anyone.

The young girl looked to the woman sitting in the chair and tried to imagine her in the arms of a man. It was true that Chastity Blackthorn was still a beautiful woman—in fact one could never guess that she was the mother of a grown daughter—but still, for Danielle to picture her mother alive and in love, as Dabs had told her she once had been, seemed impossible for the young girl to envision. She wondered for the thousandth time what exactly had happened on the island of Martinique. How could the place have changed this woman so?

"Well, Danielle, how have things been running out here at Iva Rose?" Jonathan Davinport questioned, peering over his thick-rimmed spectacles at the trim young woman across from him.

"As you can see, Mr. Davinport, things here never change," came the answer, the girl's blue eyes staring into his dull, listless ones.

"At times, child, things that never change and stay at a regular pace can be a blessing." He abstractly waved her words away, as he thought about the thriving business that his uncle, James Courtly, had left to him. He was truly hard put these days to keep all his affairs in order. He had even had to hire two office clerks and he found himself more often than not trying to watch over their shoulders to make sure that they were not cheating him.

"True, Mr. Davinport, I am sure that you would think along these lines." Danielle could not keep her resentment out of her voice.

Jonathan Davinport was not a stupid man, though he did view life in a different context from that of most men, and now he could easily tell that something was bothering this young lady. "Is something the matter, Danielle?" he questioned apprehensively, not sure that he wished to involve himself in whatever was bothering the girl.

Danielle sat a minute looking at this man, her insides seeming to want to burst forth and tell him exactly how she was feeling, left out here in the wilderness all to herself with no one but an ill mother and a house full of servants about her. She had felt this morning when she had awakened that something was going to change for her and now all she had to do was to state how she felt and leave it to this man to take care of things. Was he not paid well for his assistance to her family? She had known for the past few years what Mr. Davinport and his uncle before him had done for the Blackthorn family. So now, as she took a deep breath, she tried to find the words in her mind to say to him, "I do have a problem, yes."

He looked on expectantly, not saying a word.

"I wish to leave Iva Rose for a while," she blurted out.

The room remained quiet for a time while Jonathan Davinport absorbed her words. She wished to leave the plantation? But where was she to go? What was he to do with a young girl? He certainly could not be held responsible for her. He and his wife, Linda Sue, were older now and they enjoyed their privacy. He thought for a minute about when he had taken her to New Orleans and put her up for two weeks. Why, she had nearly worn both him and his wife out with parties and going here and there. With his business he just could not have a house guest as young and as needful of attention as this one. "Do you know what you are saying?" he finally got out. "Do you not see what has happened to your mother in the world out there?" He attempted to change her mind.

Danielle thought for a moment of her mother and then, as though a bolt of lightning had hit her, she rose to her feet. "Precisely, Mr. Davinport. I wish also to go to Martinique."

Jonathan Davinport's eyes enlarged visibly with her words. "You must be jesting." He could not believe that this young girl who had never before been a bit of trouble was saying this thing to him. He had heard over the years about her fire-headed grandmother and how she had ruled the Blackthorn dynasty, but he had always thought of this girl as taking more after her mother. The thought struck him that perhaps with age she had changed.

"I assure you, sir, that I am not jesting in the least. I think that I am at an age where I should be taking an interest in the Blackthorn affairs and I cannot think of a better place than the plantation on Martinique. No one from my family has been to the island since my mother, and I think it is about time that someone did go there." Danielle truly had no idea why she was saying all of this. She had never even thought about going to Martinique; it was as though someone other than herself had control of her tongue.

"Well, I see," Jonathan Davinport answered, rubbing his hands together in great vexation. "I cannot argue with you about being of age, but I certainly never expected you to declare your wish to leave Iva Rose."

Danielle wanted to laugh out loud. Did this man think that she would stay out here on the plantation for the rest of her life, remaining a spinster and caring for her mother? Instead of giving in to her hilarity though, she stared at him eye for eye. "I shall be moving into my aunt Cora's town house within the next two weeks. You may send word to me when you have made the arrangements for my trip." She would not be dissuaded now that she had voiced her wishes. She would carry out all that she had said even though the thought of the venture on which she would be starting out truly did give her a fright. She had never before done anything besides tend to the people on Iva Rose.

"Very well then, miss, I can see that your mind is already made up and that I can not change it so I

269

shall be in touch with you at the town house. And by the way, Danielle, the town house is yours. Your aunt Cora left it to you in her will." Mr. Davinport rose to his feet.

Danielle felt a bit contrite now that she had said all this to the man who had always been so kind to her, but she stopped herself just in time before she told him she was sorry for her words. She now was the head of the Blackthorns and she should be taking part in her inheritance. "Thank you, Mr. Davinport," she said instead and saw him to the front door.

As she saw him out of the house she felt her body racing with her excitement. Had she, Danielle Blackthorn, truly said all of those things in the parlor? Was she really going to go through with the trip to Martinique? Why of course, she scolded herself. From this day on, she would have to take her future in her grasp and make of herself what she would.

Three days later Danielle found herself in New Orleans and residing at the town house that once her Grandmother Christine had shared with her Aunt Cora. She remembered her Aunt Cora only vaguely, for she had been but a child when the old woman had passed on, but she had heard great stories of her grandmother and her aunt.

On that first day there as she trailed from room to room, she tried to envision the life the women must have had behind these beautiful walls. Gay and flamboyant affairs came to her mind. The house must have been alive with lights and laughter, she thought as she sat down upon the white sofa in the parlor. She could only think that the two women living all to themselves had enjoyed life to its fullest.

She had heard much about her flaming-haired grandmother from Mr. Courtly, and even Mr. Davinport at times made mention of her as a fine lady.

Danielle looked about herself and sighed, wishing that she also could have shared in some of the adventures the two women must have had.

Her grandmother had been wealthy and had remained single. Never did it enter the young girl's head that her grandmother may have been lonely, with only Cora as a companion and not trusting to any men other than Mr. Courtly. No thought such as these entered the mind of this young girl, first setting out on an adventure and, perhaps, to find a romantic love that she could remember in the back of her mind when she herself became old.

Two of the servants from Iva Rose had been ordered by Sara to accompany the young girl to the house in New Orleans. And Sara, knowing the mind of a young inexperienced girl such as Danielle, had sent two of the older servants who would be able to give her young mistress some advice if the need should arise.

So, after indulging her dreams a bit longer, Danielle rose from the sofa and found the black woman called Marcie upstairs airing out a room for Danielle's use.

Without hesitation Danielle began to help the girl, by putting away some of her belongings that she would be needing while she stayed in New Orleans.

Danielle had been taught while growing up on Iva Rose to help whenever she could, so the woman, Marcie, did not rebuke her mistress, but she gave the young blond-haired girl a tender smile. All who lived on the plantation loved this girl and Marcie was not of a different mind. "You be needing to find this house a woman that can cook, Miss Danielle. I be able to get us through this here day and tonight, but I ain't no cook."

271

"Tomorrow, the first thing in the morning, I shall go and talk to Mr. Davinport; perhaps he can help us." Danielle smiled, stepping back from the dressing table and viewing the assortment of perfumes and other toilet articles that she had arranged neatly.

"Yes, ma'am, that be fine then," Marcie agreed nodding her head. "I not be a-wanting you and old Sam out there to be a-blaming me if'n you be going hungry."

"Don't you worry about a thing, Marcie. "Danielle laughed at the woman, finding nothing to dampen the joy she was feeling at finally being on her own and answerable to no one but herself.

That evening after sharing a meal of fruit, cold meat, and bread with Sam and Marcie, Danielle retired to her chambers. She had at first thought that she would go to bed early, but after a time she found that this was not to be the way of things.

The only other time she had been away from Iva Rose and the safety of the bedchamber she had grown up in was when she had visited with Mr. Davinport and his wife. She had felt secure and safe under the man's roof and had had no trouble sleeping, but this night as the dark closed in about her she became aware of her vulnerability with only two servants in the house.

She would see to hiring another man to do light jobs and help Sam, she thought. But then she scolded herself for being a fool. Was she going to fill this old house with servants when she did not even know how long she would be here in the town house?

She was nervous and excited, she reasoned with herself as she lay back against the satin pillow covering. Things would settle into a normal pace after a few days and she would feel completely at home.

As she shut her blue eyes, thoughts of the voyage

which awaited her went through her mind. What would she be finding when she reached the island of Martinique? The very name of the island sparked off romance and adventure in her soul. What had happened to her mother and her father on that island? she wondered for a few minutes. What a strange attraction and pull the name of the island held for her! It was as though nothing else mattered in her life but for her to go to this place that had ruined her mother's mind and life.

Though her mind was willing to stay awake and go over all of the thoughts plaguing her for some time, her body was not. As thoughts of the island swam before her mind, her eyes grew heavy and she slept.

The first thing that Danielle did upon awakening was to send a note to Mr. Davinport that she would dearly like to meet with him today if it were convenient with him. She sent this with Sam, who assured her that he knew his way about New Orleans.

She had eaten her breakfast of last night's leftover fruit, meat, and bread and had changed into a mulberry-colored gown with low-cut bodice and flounced sleeves when Marcie entered her chambers with a note from Mr. Davinport, inviting her to have lunch with him at a small French restaurant.

She smiled her pleasure after reading the short message. She would be delighted to join him for lunch. She certainly hoped he would be able to help her find a cook; fruit, meat, and bread only went so far for a steady diet.

For the rest of the morning she went over the rest of the large town house. She still found herself amazed that she was at last residing in the same house in which her grandmother Christine had lived out her life. She had always been intrigued by the other woman. She had heard vague stories of her grandmother's past and had grown up thinking her to be some romantic heroine of long ago.

At the appointed time Sam drove Danielle to the restaurant where she was to meet Mr. Davinport. With little difficulty, she spied the attorney sitting in a small alcove within the restaurant.

Going directly to his table, she stood for a minute waiting for him to look up from the paper he was reading and notice her. She began to tire of her wait, so clearing her throat she greeted him. "Ah, Mr. Davinport, I see that you are on time."

The elderly man looked over his thick-rimmed glasses, his face turning red with his embarrassment as he stuttered and rose to his feet. "Miss Blackthorn, it is a pleasure." He pulled her chair out. "You look quite lovely this afternoon." He thought that a compliment was in order after his rude behavior.

"Why thank you, Mr. Davinport," Danielle responded, delighting in his discomfort. The man had always been kind to her, but she found that his abstractedness bothered her at times.

"Tell me how you found the town house?" he questioned. He had hired servents to go over the house every two weeks to be sure that the house stayed in good order and now he thought that he could find out if the people he had hired had done all that they were supposed to.

"The house is lovely. I find, though, that I am in need of a cook. I only brought two servants with me and I am afraid that neither can cook."

Their conversation stopped as a waiter came and took their orders.

After the young man left the table, Mr. Davinport responded to Danielle's predicament. "I shall have a woman sent to the house this very afternoon, Danielle.

Is there anything else?"

Danielle smiled sweetly, berating herself for wishing to prick this man with her rudeness. "No, indeed not, Mr. Davinport; everything else seems to be fine. Have you found out anything about a ship leaving for the island?" She was anxious now to be on her adventure. Thoughts of Martinique crowded her mind, teasing and tempting her.

Mr. Davinport had not yet searched out a ship on which to book passage to the island for this young woman. Up until this morning when her servant had brought him her message, she had been the farthest thought from his busy mind. He had, after leaving Iva Rose a few days past, reasoned that the girl was just bored, and given a bit of time she would find something with which to occupy herself and would forget about going to the island. "Why, no." He cleared his throat. "I'm afraid I have not found a suitable ship yet. Miss Blackthorn, I was wondering, do you intend on making this voyage by yourself?"

"Why of course, Mr. Davinport." Danielle had thought that all of this had been cleared up and that he would find her passage and she could be going in a short amount of time.

"I am afraid—" The waiter brought trays of tempting food at this time and this stopped his speech until his plate was before him and the man had left the table. "As I was saying, I would not be the one responsible for sending a young girl, with um"—he looked across the table at her, his dull, nonregistering eyes lowering to her bodice, and his face turning a dark red—"with your beauty, to an island that you know nothing about; and where you do not know any of the inhabitants."

Danielle looked across at the man who had been her family's attorney for years. "Whatever are you saying,

Mr. Davinport? If you think that I am going to change my mind, you are misguiding yourself. I intend to go to Martinique — with your help or without it."

Jonathan Davinport saw the determined look in this young girl's eyes and knew that he could not dissuade her in any way. "Perhaps then, a companion." This was the first thing that came to his mind. He certainly could not send her on her own. He was, after all, caretaker to the Blackthorn estates.

Danielle digested this news slowly and then began to eat some of the delicious food on her plate. "Fine then, Mr. Davinport, a companion it will be. Only I do hope that I shall not be waiting long."

Jonathan Davinport smiled slowly at this young girl and he also began to eat from his plate. Perhaps things would not be too bad if he could find a responsible person to take charge of her.

After the meal was over Jonathan Davinport, before helping Danielle up from her seat, told her that a friend of his was having a party at the end of the week and that if she would like to go, he and his wife would be more than pleased to take her.

Danielle was delighted; she would be more than glad to accompany them to the party. This was what she needed; she would be able to meet people and renew old acquaintances whom she had met while staying with the Davinports.

After promising to call upon her at eight o'clock Saturday evening, Mr. Davinport escorted Danielle out of the restaurant and to her waiting carriage.

She smiled her satisfaction as she sat back within the vehicle. She would be going to a party at the end of the week, her house would be gaining its cook; and though she would be having a traveling companion, she at least would still be going to Martinique. What more could a young girl want? she wondered to herself with sheer joy.

The next few days Danielle spent replenishing her wardrobe. She had not had much experience in the past with shopping, most of her clothes had been made from material sent out to Iva Rose; and Sara, who had a talent for sewing, would fashion Danielle gowns from the latest magazines that Mr. Davinport sent out to the plantation once a month. So Danielle, as she roamed the market streets of New Orleans finding the best and most expensive dress shops that the town had to offer, was in sheer heaven.

She delighted in the feel of the soft, satiny materials that the shops held, and she spent mornings sitting and looking in the books of sketches of gowns that had been designed in Paris. Never had she felt as carefree and wonderful.

Danielle liked one dress shop better than the others she had visited. And though the woman who ran the establishment was rather a large-boned and not too friendly woman, she did sew beautiful creations. This was where Danielle would have the gown that she would wear to the party this week made up, she decided as she viewed some of the woman's work hanging on a rack at the back of the shop. They were delicate, flowing gowns, looking to be fit for queens, Danielle thought as she ran her hand lovingly over the materials.

The shop was busy as Danielle looked about, but within a short time the large woman was at her side. "Can I be of help to you, miss?" Her voice was cold and anything but friendly.

"Why yes." Danielle decided that the best way to approach this woman was to hold a cool and lofty manner herself. "I am in need of a gown and after having viewed some of your work I think I would like to have the gown made up here."

"Well, I don't have all day. As you can see, I have only one girl to help me." She pointed a long, beefy finger at a small girl who was tending to a customer at the front of the store. "So tell me what it is you had in mind and be quick about it."

Something in the woman's voice struck a cord with Danielle that made her back stiffen. "I had in mind a gown for a party, something such as these you have hanging. A sheer, wispy material, perhaps of a rich cloth."

The woman eyed Danielle with her head slanted. "You would do better in a soft, pale color. When do you need this gown?"

"Why, at the end of the week." Danielle could not believe the nerve of this woman. She knew the colors that she wished. She supposed that next the woman also would be telling her the style of the gown she should be wearing.

"That is too soon. I have not the time to have a gown ready in that short amount of time."

Danielle had not thought of the time it would take to create a gown. She had thought that she only had to tell the shopkeeper what she wished and she and her assistants would sew up a gown in a short time. "I must have a gown." For a moment she thought of all the gowns in her wardrobe, but to her none of them would do. She wanted a gown made by this woman.

"I am afraid not, lady." The woman started to turn her back on the girl.

Danielle could not believe this woman and she also turned. Perhaps she could find another shopkeeper who sewed as well as this woman.

As she reached the door she heard a call from behind her. "Young lady. Miss."

Turning, Danielle saw the large woman hurrying

down the aisle toward her. For a moment a feeling of fright came over her, but then she reasoned, the woman could not possibly do her harm when her shop was filled with customers.

"Young lady, come to the back room of my shop. Perhaps there is something there that will suit you." She did not wait for Danielle to answer, but turned about and hurried back down the aisle, at the end of which she disappeared through an open door at the back of the shop.

Danielle, having followed, found the room dark and cluttered. Gowns hung about and material lay on different-sized tables.

"Sit down, sit down." The woman waved Danielle to a chair against the wall and away from the congestion of the room.

She went to a rack of gowns and then, once again standing in front of Danielle, she held out a beautiful gown of a silvery, shimmering blue.

"Oh," Danielle breathed, one hand reaching out to lightly touch the gown.

The woman for the first time smiled. "I know what you mean. The material is one of a kind. A girl came here months ago and ordered the gown made, but then, due to unfortunate circumstances, she was not able to obtain the coins to buy it." She also stroked the gown. "Perhaps, though, it will not fit or you may not like the style." She looked Danielle over noticing the high-necked, dark-blue gown she now wore.

"May I try it on?" Danielle's heart raced; she would give anything for this gown to be hers.

"Why, of course. There is a dressing screen." She looked about the room as though not ever knowing where things would be. "There, it is over there." She pointed to the back of the room. "I shall be out front; if you need anything you only have to call." She left the room, leaving the gown draped across Danielle's arm.

As Danielle went behind the screen and began to unbutton her gown, she could not take her eyes off the one she had laid across a chair. Never had she seen anything like its color, and the feel of it made her think of something so delicate and fine that she could not wait to have it next to her body.

And she was not disappointed. The gown circled her like a soft, sheer cloud. Its silvery-blue color brought her eyes to a dark, violet blue and was a perfect complement to her golden hair.

She sighed as she stepped from behind the screen and stood in front of a full-length mirror. It was beautiful; she had never seen herself looking so well, she told herself. Though the bodice was cut lower than any gown Danielle had ever worn before and the sleeves were only small straps of material holding the gown on her body, still she stood breathless, viewing herself.

The large woman who owned the shop came back into the small room at this time to check on the girl she had left trying on a gown. She also stood as though thunderstruck. The girl in front of the mirror was a vision of unreality. Never had she seen such beauty.

She must have made some small noise for Danielle turned about and saw her standing watching her. "The gown is lovely, madam." She turned once more to look at her reflection, not being able to keep her eyes from the gown.

"Quite lovely indeed," the woman breathed, stepping closer. "It is as though it were made for you."

"I shall pay whatever the price, madam." Danielle turned once more to the larger woman.

"Aye, I imagine you would," came her reply. "But do not fret." She seemed to pull herself from the trance of beauty she had been pulled into. "Usually I do not charge full price for a gown that has not been claimed."

"I can afford the price, madam." Danielle began to take the gown tenderly from her body.

The woman looked more sharply toward Danielle. She had not thought the girl wealthy; in fact she had supposed her to be either a working girl or perhaps one being supported by a gentleman with limited means. Her clothing was not rich, it was of a rather heavy, enduring material worn by plenty of women who had not the coins to throw away. "What is your name, my dear?" she questioned, hoping to throw some light on this woman.

"Danielle Blackthorn," Danielle answered, pulling the gown over her head and paying little attention to the larger woman.

At this answer, the woman looked more sharply at the young girl. "Blackthorn? Would you be a Blackthorn from Iva Rose?" She could not believe that this girl was one of those Blackthorns. Why, they were rich. She certainly could afford better clothing than what she had if she were related to them.

"Yes, ma'am, my mother is Chastity Blackthorn and my grandmother's name was Christine." Danielle now looked to the woman.

"Well, will you beat that?" she exclaimed. Then, taking the gown out of Danielle's hands so she could dress herself, she quickly regained her composure. "Will you be having any more gowns made up, Miss Blackthorn? I shall have a chemise of the sheerest material made for this gown and if you leave it to me I shall also have slippers made."

Danielle at once noticed the difference in the woman's tone and she cocked her head at an angle toward her. Had her name made the difference? she wondered as she dressed herself. A name such as Blackthorn and the wealth that came with it, she soon discovered, could change anyone.

She left the shop shortly after that, telling the woman that she would have several gowns made up and that she would return again in two days to pick up the gown, slippers, and chemise.

The large woman was all smiles now as she led Danielle to the door, promsing that she would have the objects ready on her return.

The next day Danielle spent relaxing and reading at her leisure in her town house. She had been so busy the past few days that she thought herself deserving of a day's rest. Her pace at Iva Rose had not been hurried, but since arriving in New Orleans she had been going constantly.

Mr. Davenport had been true to his word and that same day he had obtained a cook; a large, jolly black woman who began to reside in the room adjoining the kitchen.

Danielle truly liked this large woman called Mae, and she more than liked the woman's cooking. She could even cook better, to Danielle's thinking, than the cook at Iva Rose. So this day, besides resting, she also enjoyed some of the good food that the woman prepared.

The party was a lavish affair, almost a ball, Danielle thought as she entered the foyer of the Thambridges' home with Mr. Davinport and his wife, Linda Sue.

The house glowed with lighted chandeliers, music greeted their ears from the ballroom, and the guests were plentiful and lively.

Mr. Davinport's chest swelled as he saw the envious

looks on the faces of the men as he entered the front door. All were amazed at the beauty of the woman who held his arm.

Danielle smiled at one young man and then the other as they approached Mr. Davinport and talked to him in order to make the acquaintance of the vision beside him.

Erin Thambridge, an elderly gentleman of some means, along with his wife, Maureen, were among the first to greet Mr. Davinport and his wife and the woman who accompanied them. Mr. Thambridge had seen beautiful women in his time, but he found that his old, gray eyes were drawn to Danielle as is a moth to a flame. "It is nice to make your acquaintance, madam." He bent over her hand and lightly kissed it after Jonathan Davinport had made the introductions.

Danielle graced him with her sweetest smile, her head flying in these surroundings. Never had she been to an affair such as this. She let the elderly man kiss her hand and nodded her head toward him, but she was not truly paying any attention to what the gentleman was saying.

"I see your companion is anxious to be on the dance floor, Jonathan," Mr. Thambridge said, noticing where her eyes were glancing. "May I beg this dance with you, my dear?" he questioned, not caring that his wife was standing next to him.

Danielle gladly nodded her head, wishing nothing more than to be dancing. "I would love to dance with you."

Erin Thambridge gave Danielle his arm and with some aplomb he swung her out upon the floor.

Danielle, as her mother before her, had been taught to dance by her tutors, and during her earlier visits to the Davinports she had had her only other occasions to dance. She loved the feel of gently being swept across a dance floor on the arm of a gentleman in the midst of swirling couples.

As soon as the dance finished Danielle was once more swept up into the music on the arm of another gentleman. And this, for the next couple of hours, was her routine. Before she could catch her breath another young man would request the privilege of dancing with her. Danielle was flattered by all of the attention that was lavished upon her and accepted all invitations that were offered to her until finally, with feet that felt as if they would at any moment fall from under her, she begged her partner for a moment's reprieve.

"But of course, madam." The young man gallantly swept her a courtly bow and took her arm. "Would you like to sit over there?" He pointed to a group of chairs that lined one wall, upon which sat some elderly dames. "Or perhaps you would care for a seat in the gardens?"

The choice between the two was an easy one for Danielle. The thought of sitting in the gardens on a night such as tonight with a young man as handsome as the one at her side was too tempting an offer. "The gardens sound inviting, sir," she said, letting him lead her out the French doors.

The night was lighted with a full moon and the gardens abounded with fragrant-smelling flowers. Danielle could make out the scent of roses as she left the room and breathed in great gulps of air.

Other couples were standing about, so as the young man led Danielle toward a bench not far away, she willingly went along.

The young man's name, Danielle had found out, was David Whiteman. He was handsome and well-dressed in a pearl-gray suit with light-blue pin stripes;

he was also quite attentive.

He helped her to sit down and then handed her a cool drink of champagne. "You are new to New Orleans, Miss Blackthorn?" the young man ventured, watching this lovely girl through his dark lashes. "I have heard of a family called Blackthorn who own a large plantation some way out of town."

"Why yes, I am one of the same Blackthorns. You must be talking about Iva Rose. That is my family's plantation." She looked at the young man with more interest now.

"Your family also owns a large shipping line and other interests here in New Orleans?"

This young man seemed to know more than he wished her to know, Danielle thought fleetingly for a moment. She did not answer, but nodded her head and waited for what more he would have to say.

With hardly any notice, David Whiteman slipped his arm about the back of the bench and began, "I am pleased that you decided to come from your plantation and to stay in New Orleans for a time, Miss Blackthorn. Our small town is in need of beauty such as you possess."

Danielle was beginning to feel a small bit uncomfortable as she sat here in the gardens with this man. "Perhaps, sir, it is time that we join the others in the ballroom?" She noticed now that the other couples had gone in and they now seemed to be the only one out here in the gardens.

"We do not need to hurry, Miss Blackthorn." Danielle felt his hand lightly touch on her shoulder. At his slightest contact, Danielle jumped in her seat.

"I think I would prefer to be dancing, sir." She stood to her feet and started back to the French doors, not waiting or watching to see if her companion was following. She wanted romance and adventure, but she did not want it at the expense of what her family's money could buy.

Once back in the ballroom, Danielle was again swept about the dance floor, though now she avoided David Whiteman every time he started toward her. She had not liked the way he had mentioned her family's wealth; it was as though he were calculating her advantages.

The rest of the evening was filled with gay laughter and light flirtations but Danielle now looked at each young man with different eyes. She would have to protect herself, for there was no one else to do the job for her, she told herself. She could not lightly succumb to any gentleman's charms here in New Orleans. Most knew of her family's fortune and she would not be used.

For the next few weeks, Danielle found herself to be the center of attention of most of the young men of New Orleans. Wherever she went it seemed that swarms of young men vied for her favors.

Since the night that she had gone to the party with the Davinports she had been invited to numerous parties and to other affairs. These invitations she had gladly accepted, wishing to enjoy herself to the fullest.

But even though she had been raised on Iva Rose and had mostly remained cloistered with no more than servants for company, she seemed to be able to tell what kind of man held her in his arms as he swung her across the dance floor to a waltz; or what exactly a daring young man had in his mind as he told her flowery words of love and devotion and begged for her to think kindly of him. She was no one's fool, as at first the young men of New Orleans had expected of a young innocent who had led a sheltered and secluded life. They soon found that she was not easily led astray. Her grandmother's wild blood surely must flow through her veins, she told herself more than once after she had set a young man back upon his heels with the palm of her hand, because he had tried to take more of an advantage than Danielle would allow.

She found that she enjoyed these affairs, but she also found that she was growing weary of the never-ending frivolity and gay times.

So it was with a happy heart that Danielle opened the short note Mr. Davinport had sent to her one morning.

He sent word that the ship that would take her to the island of Martinique was now in the harbor. He also said in his message that he had acquired a chaperone for her—a woman who lived on the island of Martinique—and that this woman would be more than glad to act as a companion for Danielle.

Danielle had been quite ecstatic with the news, and she spent the next few days packing, going to the dress shop to pick up some gowns and other apparel which she had not yet gotten, and seeing that all would be in order in her town house upon her departure.

Chapter Ten

"And this is the young lady, of whom I have been telling you, Vanessa. I hope the two of you will get on well."

The small, portly lady looked in the direction where Jonathan Davinport was looking and there, striding up the gangway, was one of the loveliest girls she had ever set eyes on. A large smile came over her features. No wonder Jonathan had wished this young lady chaperoned. With her fair looks she would be bestirring the gentlemen right and left.

As the young woman came to a halt in front of the couple standing on the deck, Jonathan Davinport made a large bow in her direction. "Good afternoon, Miss Blackthorn. I hope you find yourself in a fit mood for sailing this day."

"Indeed I do, Mr. Davinport. Have no fear; I would not miss this day for all the world." As Danielle's vivacious voice filled the couple's ears, her eyes took in all aboard the sleek-looking clipper that was to be her new home for a time.

Mrs. Delmar's smile did not leave her face. She certainly would not be finding this cruise boring. This young Miss Blackthorn was so full of life and fun she found herself wishing that she herself were so young with the world lying in wait for her. But she tolerantly smiled and reminded herself that she had already lived a full, exciting life, the memories of which she kept tucked away in her mind. But this young thing before her was only now starting out and by the looks of her she more than likely would set Fort-de-France back on its heels.

"Vanessa Delmar, this is Danielle Blackthorn." Jonathan spoke interrupting her thoughts.

"It is a pleasure, my dear." Vanessa held out one plump, gloved hand to the young lady before her.

Danielle Blackthorn's twinkling, violet-blue eyes shone brightly at this friendly woman. "The pleasure is all mine, Mrs. Delmar. I wish to thank you for agreeing to be my traveling companion. I do not know what I would have done without you."

"Nonsense, child. I am more than glad to have you with me. I have found that there is nothing worse than traveling by one's self," Vanessa truthfully told this charming young girl.

A member of the crew stood aside and waited, holding several of Danielle's bags. He had been assigned the job of showing this beauty to her cabin and as he stood and waited he decided that this was one job he could do all day.

Jonathan Davinport was quick to notice the man standing and watching their small group. "Well, ladies, I believe it is time for me to be leaving the ship. I wish you both a good voyage and, Vanessa, be sure and tell Henry for me that I missed him this trip."

Vanessa Delmar smiled fondly at the man before her. "Of course, Jonathan, and I know Henry will be disappointed that he missed you, but he felt he could not leave Martinique at this time; perhaps next year." She then turned in Danielle's direction. "I believe this young man is waiting to show you to your cabin."

Danielle looked with a glowing face in the young man's direction. "I believe you are right, Mrs. Delmar. I cannot thank you enough, Mr. Davinport, for all your help. You will not forget to get word to me as quickly as possible if there is any kind of change in my mother?"

Vanessa Delmar was quick to notice the change which came over the young girl at the mere mention of her mother. She had heard that some tragic event had caused the elder Miss Blackthorn to seclude herself for the past several years on her plantation. Something about a young man's death that all had supposed to have taken place on Martinique. Well, she for one did not care for idle gossip. She had learned early not to believe half of what she heard unless the information was coming from the doer of the deed.

After Jonathan assured her that her mother would be well cared for, and left the ship, Danielle was shown to her room.

Vanessa told her that she would call back at her cabin in an hour and they would go to dinner together.

Danielle was afforded one of the best cabins on the ship. She sighed with relief as the young man put down her bags and left her room. This would be her first time truly on her own. She could feel her blood pumping faster and faster at the thought of finally being free.

She twirled about the room, her skirts flying about her and her golden hair falling out from under her hat. She felt so jittery and excited inside, she could barely suppress herself.

She fell back upon the bed and lay flat on her back for a few minutes. She was completely overcome with the power of her freedom. She would be able to do what she wanted for the first time in her life.

She rose and without hurrying changed her gown for one a bit fancier for the evening ahead.

She wished to be ready by the time Mrs. Delmar knocked on her door. She had no wish to keep the good lady waiting. She felt herself imposing on her as it was, to burden this kindly woman with the thought that she was in any way reponsible for her care, but Mr. Davinport had insisted that she could not under any circumstances make this trip without the company of an older woman.

At first Danielle had resented the idea of having anyone looking after her, but now she realized, after meeting Mrs. Delmar, that perhaps the trip would be more enjoyable with someone to whom she could talk and with whom she could share her experiences.

A knock sounded outside her cabin just as Danielle was putting the final touches to her hair. "I shall be right out, Mrs. Delmar," she called, glancing one last time at her reflection in the mirror.

"I thought that we could take a small stroll about the ship before dinner, if you would care to. We have plenty of time before the dinner hour."

"That sounds delightful to me, Mrs. Delmar." Though Danielle's family owned a fleet of ships, this was her first time at sea and she had never before looked over a ship such as this.

The two women walked about, talking to one another, trying gradually to get to know one another.

As they arrived in the dining area and took a seat, Vanessa Delmar was telling Danielle about the island to which they were heading.

Danielle sat spellbound, barely touching her food, so enraptured was she with the other woman's words.

She described Martinique as a tropical paradise, with lush jungles, vibrant colors, and warm friendly people.

Danielle could almost shut her eyes and imagine herself lying upon a sandy beach, with soft, sensual music playing in the background and her senses filling with the lushness about her.

Vanessa could tell by the girl's dreamy, blue eyes all of her deepest thoughts. Ah, to be that age once again, she thought. To have all those romantic thoughts of love and life.

"You make your island sound so wonderful, Mrs. Delmar. I can hardly wait to arrive."

Vanessa Delmar patted Danielle's hand. "You will love it, I am sure. I can barely wait to see you mixing with the Fort-de-France society. You will have every eligible young man on the island crawling at your feet. And the women—oh my dear." She laughed aloud. "They will simply be green with envy."

A bright red flush covered Danielle's clear creamy complexion.

"I do not mean to embarrass you, child, but you

291

will be by far the loveliest thing to touch foot on our island in quite some time." Vanessa laughed lightly, trying to pull the girl into her gay mood. "You will have to stay for a time with me and Henry."

Danielle started to reply but she rushed on. "But of course you will stay with us. We shall have a party in your honor and introduce you to everyone. And oh, my dear, wait until my nephew, René, gets a glimpse of you; he will be the first one begging for your favors."

Danielle laughed gayly with her friendly companion. She had never thought this woman would be so kind, but she was soon learning that Vanessa Delmar was not only kind but truly wonderful.

Vanessa walked Danielle back to her cabin, reminding her, as she would every evening aboard ship, not to forget to lock her door. Danielle was to learn in the next few weeks that though her chaperone was always gay and light-hearted, she also took her job of watching over Danielle quite seriously.

The two women were always together when outside of their cabin. They shared their meals in each other's company and would usually spend their afternoons sitting in lounge chairs on the deck of the ship, talking and laughing their time away.

Danielle thought it funny that whenever a young man would approach her, Mrs. Delmar would always seem to be near, watching like a mother hen over her only chick.

There were several other passengers aboard the ship so the women never lacked for company. In fact, they found some of the passengers quite tiresome, mostly the younger gentlemen who tried to make themselves known to Danielle.

Danielle enjoyed all of this attention better than when she had been in New Orleans. There, most of the young men were after the Blackthorn fortune and when she saw the greedy looks in their eyes, she would feel her blood run cold. But here on board this ship, she told herself, no one knew her and all the flattery that was lavished upon her was truly for herself and not for what she could bring to a man.

"Are you listening, dear?" Mrs. Delmar tapped Danielle lightly upon the arm with her ivory fan, pulling the girl from her train of thought.

"What? Oh, I am sorry, Mrs. Delmar." Danielle started.

"That's all right, dear." She knew the way of the young; they were forever daydreaming. "I was saying that we should be back at Fort-de-France in time for carnival night. Granted, I am sure it is nothing compared to what you have in New Orleans, but, my dear, what fun! The streets will be full of merrymakers and revelry. We shall have to get you a costume if there is time; and oh, we can have my nephew, René, escort you about. Henry and I always stay home and oversee the servants this night. We have so many friends stopping by for drinks and food; so you see you will have to have an escort." Mrs. Delmar rambled on.

"A carnival? Why, how wonderful," Danielle exclaimed, clapping her hands together gayly. "I have never been to one."

"Why, you poor child," Vanessa Delmar cried. "Every young person must participate in a street party. Why, that occasion holds some of the fondest memories of my youth. You grow old so quickly, my dear; you must learn to grab all the fun things coming your way."

Danielle more than agreed with this kindly woman. She herself had been having these same thoughts for the past several months. She was ready to live, to laugh, and to put all cares behind her. "Oh, Mrs.

Delmar, I can barely wait." She sighed.

"It will not be too much longer, child. We should be arriving on Martinique in only a few days."

The remainder of the time aboard ship for Danielle was spent in dreamy expectation of what would be awaiting her on the island of Martinique.

With her first glance at the green spot rising out of the blue ocean water, she knew she would not be disappointed.

Mrs. Delmar stood close to Danielle's side. She had viewed this same sight on numerous other occasions, but still, each time she stood at the rail of a ship and looked toward Martinique, she felt her breath come in tiny gasps and her heart begin to race.

"It is breathtaking," were the only words which came from Danielle's mouth, as she clasped the hand of the other woman to her own.

"Those are precisely my own sentiments, my dear. Quite breathtaking indeed."

Danielle watched the once-green dot on the water, turn gradually into a large mound of earth, boasting of lush, green jungles and huge mountains jutting from its interior.

Their boat docked swiftly and efficiently and from then on, Danielle found herself pulled into a whirlwind of excitement.

"Yoooohoooo, Henry," Mrs. Delmar shouted, waving frantically to a distinguished, elderly-looking gentleman on the wharf. He was waving at the two women with just as much enthusiasum.

"There is Mr. Delmar, now, Danielle," she said taking hold of her charge's arm and pulling her behind her. "Come along, child, let us not keep him waiting all afternoon out here in the sun."

Danielle smiled in agreement, thinking it sweet that the elderly married couple were so anxious to see each other once again. She was to find, though, in the next few days, that Vanessa and Henry Delmar shared a very rare love. They truly cared a great deal for each other and though they had been married for over twenty years, their eyes still lingered on each other and their words were always loving and soft.

"Henry, Henry." Mrs. Delmar rushed into the open, waiting arms that were held out for her. "Wait until I tell you all the news and wait until you meet this beautiful young lady I have brought home with me," the spritely, elderly lady rushed on after she had hugged and kissed her tall, gray-haired husband soundly in plain view of all on the streets of Fort-de-France.

Henry Delmar smiled fondly down at his wife, used to her hurried manner and lack of decorum. His look slowly went over the girl who stood at his wife's side. He was not shocked by her presence either. His wife was well-known for her kind heart and if there was someone in need of her protection she would always be willing to give it. "And who, my dear, is this lovely young girl?" he questioned his wife fondly.

"Come here, child, and meet my Henry." Her plump, ringed hand pulled Danielle before her husband. "Why, Henry, this is Danielle Blackthorn. She will be staying with us for a spell, before she goes out to her plantation."

"Blackthorn you say, my dear? Would you perchance be one of the Blackthorns who own the Blackthorn shipping line?" He looked at Danielle, but his question was promptly answered by his wife.

"Why, but of course she is, Henry dear. And she has come to Martinique to add some color and charm."

Henry Delmar's smile never vanished, though he thought it strange that this young girl would wish to visit such a small island as Martinique. With all of the

Blackthorn money one would think that she would wish to visit London or Paris. "You will be going to your own plantation then?" he questioned Danielle. But before she could answer he had bidden the two ladies to step into the waiting carriage, for he swore that they would all fry if they remained much longer standing in the open sun.

As the carriage took the occupants to the Delmars' house, Danielle explained that she planned to stay for a time at the same plantation house where her mother before her had resided.

Danielle was shown to one of the large guest rooms and promptly water was brought up for a long leisurely bath.

That evening, Danielle found that the Delmars had invited a guest. Vanessa Delmar's nephew, René Beauchamp was present for the evening.

Wearing a light, organdy, low-cut gown, with her golden curls piled atop her head, Danielle found herself smiling and flirting gayly with this dark, handsome gentleman. His features, sharp and true, were set off by coal black eyes and hair of the same hue. Even his long, tapered hands bespoke his being a gentleman, and Danielle found herself completely pulled into his charming ways.

Vanessa Delmar also smiled fondly toward her nephew; he had always been her favorite. Since she and Henry had never had a child of their own, she automatically had lavished all of her motherly love and attention on her charming nephew. And she had to admit that the young man had been quite properly spoiled. Between her and Henry and his own mother and father, the boy had never wanted for a thing in his life. Now though, his aunt decided that she was beginning to have special plans for him. She had grown in the last few weeks to love this young girl,

Danielle Blackthorn, as though she were her own daughter. Would it not be perfect—her thoughts went astray—if this young couple sitting at her dinner table were to find themselves in love and to marry?

And indeed by the end of the evening René Beauchamp was completely enamored of the young beauty sitting across from him. She was completely enchanting, he thought, and what was more, she would be the possessor of a great fortune. He did not usually associate a woman with her wealth, but this vision before him had it all—great beauty and charm *and* wealth. He could look long and far throughout his life, but he truly doubted he could find another woman so fully to his liking.

Danielle fell asleep that evening with exciting dreams of the following day. It would be the carnival night and René Beauchamp had gallantly asked permission to escort her about the streets of Fort-de-France.

Danielle's gown was a shimmering, aquamarine silk; its bodice was cut low and fitted snugly, causing Danielle's tiny waist to appear even smaller and her high, firm bosom to be pushed upward and to seem fuller. The sleeves were puffed, rising above the elbows and reaching to meet silk gloves made of the same shimmering material as the gown.

Her shining golden curls were piled atop each other and in each of her perfect ringlets sparkled a small glimmering, emerald hairpin. At first glance, this sparkling effect in the golden coiffure was breathtaking.

She had not had the time for a costume to be made up, but Vanessa, with sure-mindedness, had gone out that very morning and purchased a half-mask, nearly the same material and color as Danielle's gown. This covered the top portion of her small, heart-shaped face, leaving only her pink, petal lips and small rounded chin to be seen.

Standing back and looking critically into the full-length mirror, a small smile appeared upon Danielle's features. She really felt like spinning about the room and laughing aloud from her happiness. Never had she felt so carefree before and if not for the black girl standing near her with a lace shawl ready to be placed across her shoulders, she indeed would be expressing some of this pent-up happiness.

Slowly her smile faded as the young girl standing before the mirror thought for a moment of another girl who, twenty years before, had been on this same island. Had her mother also dressed as she, expecting to find excitement and perhaps a romantic and dashing man to storm into her life? Danielle wished briefly that she could have known her mother better, but all she truly knew about her was what she had learned from Dabs and some of the other servants at Iva Rose.

At this moment she felt that she would have given anything to know if her mother, beautiful and full of anticipation, had gone to a carnival or ball. Perhaps one day she would know more of the woman whom she called mother. She sighed, allowing the black girl to wrap the shawl about her shoulders.

A knock sounded and the door to Danielle's chambers was thrown open; in a brilliance of red taffeta, Vanessa Delmar swept into the room. "Lord, child, you are simply ravishing." The kindly woman looked Danielle up and down, not believing her eyes.

"Thank you," Danielle murmured.

"Why so glum, dear?" She had instantly noticed the girl's quiet pallor. "I thought to help you on with your mask."

Danielle was holding the small half-mask in her hands and gladly gave it over to the older woman. She would put her tragic mother from her mind for this night and just live for the moment and herself, she decided promptly, not wanting to hurt this woman who had done so much for her. "I am fine, Mrs. Delmar. I suppose I am just a bit nervous, this being my first affair of this kind."

"Stuff and nonsense to nervousness, my dear. Think of all the fun you will be having and what a handsome escort you will have at your side. Speaking of whom, that is why I hurried up. René is downstairs sampling Henry's best wine and prancing about; I suppose anxious to see you, my dear." Mrs. Delmar was pinning the half-mask to each of Danielle's temples, with more of the emerald hairpins. "That should do. We do not wish for your mask to fall off your face at an unlikely moment." She placed one more pin for good measure on the side of the mask.

Danielle could only smile, knowing that Mrs. Delmar hardly left room for answers to her questions; her light and frivolous talk went on and on.

"You look divine, child." The older woman stepped back from her handiwork. "I doubt that even René will know you."

"Thank you, Mrs. Delmar, for all you have done." Danielle hugged the small woman tightly to her.

"Posh, child, no thanks are needed. You have brought back some of my own youth. All I ask is that you enjoy yourself."

"I promise I shall." Danielle twirled gayly about, not being able to suppress the gaiety glowing within her.

"Let us go down and join the men for a glass of that wine before you are swept out into the streets by René." Mrs. Delmar put her arm about her young charge and left the room with her, anxious to view the effect this woman would have upon her nephew.

The older woman was not to be disappointed, for when the two ladies stepped into the parlor, René Beauchamp's mouth fell agape and, rushing to his feet, he quickly was at Danielle's side, offering her his arm.

"And what do you think of my young friend's costume, René?" Mrs. Delmar wanted to hear for herself what her favorite nephew thought of this girl for whom she had grown to care.

"I can hardly say, Aunt Vanessa. Miss Blackthorn, you are truly a vision and I, with my lacking tongue, could not so much as begin to express the beauty that you have brought before me."

Danielle's blush rose under her mask. "Thank you, Mr. Beauchamp, but I am sure you are exaggerating with your compliments."

Vanessa Delmar preened and smiled at her nephew's words. She knew him to be not exaggerating, for she knew he always said what he thought. And surely they were the perfect couple, she thought as she viewed the pair standing before her. René had dressed all in black; he also was carrying a half-mask. And with Danielle's golden and his dark good looks, they seemed to be made for each other.

"Let me get you a glass of wine, Miss Blackthorn." Henry Delmar brought both ladies small crystal glasses of the deep-red liquid that he and his nephew had been sampling already.

Danielle smiled her pleasure at its sweet, fragrant taste.

"I can see that you like it." Henry grinned, knowing no greater pleasure than watching someone enjoying something that was his own. "I dare say everyone will be bringing out his best vintage this fine evening." He placed one arm loosely about his wife's waist.

"You young people must not stay here with us old folks now." Vanessa took the crystal glasses from their hands; her intent, to rush them on their way.

"You are quite right, Aunt Vanessa. If I wish to show Miss Blackthorn all of Fort-de-France, we must be on our way." He gallantly placed a small kiss on his aunt's cheek and then turned and took Danielle's arm. "Are you ready?" he questioned softly, once more struck by her unusual beauty.

"Oh yes," came her answer, for Danielle was quite ready for the evening ahead. She felt something deep within her, telling her that to miss this night would be to miss living. Something seemed to be driving her onward and she knew this minute that if she had not had this young man for her escort, she would have ventured forth on her own. There was something out there in the night awaiting her, something she could not miss.

"You young people enjoy yourselves now," Vanessa Delmar called to the couple as they went through the front door. "Are they not just gorgeous together Henry?" she sighed when they were gone from the house.

The revelry along the streets of Fort-de-France was deafening to Danielle's ears. All about, there were loud voices and throaty laughter.

René kept hold of her elbow, leading her up the streets, following one group of party seekers and then another. At every house where they stopped they were served wine and food; René seemed to know everyone.

Danielle's head was a-swim as he introduced one group of costumed people and then another. Danielle fleetingly wished her escort would not reveal her name or those of the others so easily. This whole affair to her would have a much more romantic flavor if no names were mentioned and all had to wonder who was standing next to them.

But as one set of eyes and then another looked toward the beauty on René Beauchamp's arm, Danielle told herself that no secret would be kept and all of the town would know her identity before the evening was at its finish.

Danielle felt René's hand loosen and fall away from her arm, as they rounded another corner. "Forgive me, Miss Blackthorn, but if I could leave you for just one moment. I see an old acquaintance whom I know would love to meet you. I do not think he will turn back this way, but if I hurry I am sure I can catch him."

"Of course, Mr. Beauchamp. I shall stand here and watch the participants in the parade." She smiled and turned from his direction to watch the people along the streets.

What fun everyone seemed to be having! Gay, brilliant colors flashed before her eyes and laughter filled her ears. She stood watching as a large man dressed as a matador, threw his cape about and shouted aloud, "Olé, Olé." Then, to the sheer delight of the onlookers, he wrapped the black cape about a passing dairy maid, whose squeals of pleasure resounded loudly as he threw cape and girl up into his arms and started on his way.

Danielle's bell-like laughter came softly to the ears of passers-by. Ah, to be free to do what one wished to do, she sighed.

Suddenly something next to her drew her attention. Her blue eyes looked up into the smiling face of a black-haired, copper-eyed sultan. His costume, including turban and half-mask, were of the whitest satin. His torso was a dark, rich, leathered tan with which his golden, tawny eyes contrasted dramatically, making him appear by far the most attractive man she had ever before seen.

Danielle felt her breath start to come in short erratic gasps as his scorching eyes traveled over her, making his own appraisal.

The sultan indeed was feasting his lions' eyes on the lovely woman before him. Who could this beautiful creature be? he wondered, taking in her beauty from the top of her golden curls, set with the twinkling stones, down over her silk gown. His hot, bold eyes lingered on her full, rich breasts which were amply displayed and continued down to her narrow waist and rounded, trim hips. Even though her mask covered a large portion of her face, he knew he had never seen her before. With her bearing and rich manner of dress he could tell she was of the gentry, but he had met at one time or another, all of the unattached young ladies in Fort-de-France, but he knew without asking that he did not know this one. "A pleasure, mademoiselle." He boldly bowed, never taking his tawny eyes from her own.

Even his voice made Danielle's heart race. She nodded her head slowly in his direction, forgetting all about the crowded street and the noise about her until she was shoved from behind, causing her almost to stumble into the stranger's arms. "Oh, I am sorry," she gasped as she felt his arms reach out to steady her.

"I'm not." His deep-throated voice filled her every pore and the heat from his fingers lying against her arm, seemed to penetrate her gloves and to char her very flesh.

The two were pulled into the large mass of people who crowded the street, and the sultan's rich laughter blended in with that of the people about him.

Danielle's own small smile came to her face as she

was gayly pulled along, the stranger never leaving her side.

Soon the two were talking; laughing and shouting with the revelers about them; tasting more wine and nibbling at the various foods brought out for them.

In the presence of the sultan and the excitement of the fun which was all about them, Danielle had completely forgotten about the young man, René Beauchamp.

The potent wine which had been passed about so freely this night must have completely gone to Danielle's head, for she soon found herself enjoying this stranger's company, and when his arm slipped about her waist she felt only warmth and security.

The farther the crowd pushed, the less familiar Danielle's surroundings became; then, without any warning, a large gust of wind swept through the streets followed by a pelting rain shower.

The streets cleared instantly, everyone running for the nearest shelter to be found. Danielle, laughing along with the rest and getting soaked to the skin, was pulled by her sultan into the doorway of an inn.

Her laughter died in her throat as she felt his warming lion's eyes appraising her body through the sodden gown.

His strong fingers, which were long and neatly manicured but fully used to a day's hard work, reached up and slowly unpinned the tiny, emerald hairpins which secured the mask at Danielle's temples.

Danielle felt only pride as he brought the mask away. She was glad at that moment, that she was beautiful and totally a woman. No one had to tell her these things, for the sultan's eyes blazed across her face, and mirrored his every thought.

The sultan was completely taken off guard. He knew the woman whom he had followed the night through was beautiful, and had even expected as much when he would take her mask from her, but this vision, with her clear honeyed complexion and her blue eyes looking up to him as though she were alive only for this moment, was beyond belief. If he had traveled the world over and searched for true beauty—and indeed he had been all about the world—he would have always come back to this woman standing before him now. Never had he seen anything as beautiful. Slowly, clutching her eyes in the depths of his own, he brought his dark head down and took the trembling lips before him.

Time and reason seemed to stand still for Danielle as she felt his lips descend upon hers; warm, sweet lips, filled with the promise of tenderness, her mind thought as she gave her mouth over completely to this stranger.

The sultan felt her awakening response and pulled her tighter into his embrace. "I wish I could take you up and sail away with you, my lady." His husky whispered words evoked a strange feeling of almost sensual desire from Danielle's body and the man holding her felt her quiver.

"We had best find a warm fire," he said softly, before once more plundering those tempting, pliant lips.

Without a will of her own, Danielle felt her head nod in agreement to his words. She felt no shame or remorse; she only felt the need to be close to this man.

The sultan once more pinned her mask upon her face. He felt a moment's regret as the small, slightly upturned nose was hidden from his view.

Danielle followed willingly at his side, into the inn and up the stairs. Nobody paid any attention to the young couple, for the inn had now become as noisy as the streets were earlier.

As the sultan unlocked a door halfway down the hall, he let Danielle pass before him.

"We had better start a fire to get rid of the dampness." He leaned over the hearth and started to pile it with logs.

The room was in complete blackness except for the glowing fire. And as the sultan rose to his feet his eyes fell on the woman in his room.

The very air seemed to be alive with a sensual current as with slow, pantherlike strides he came to her. Reaching up, he began to painstakingly remove each of the emerald pins from her hair, feeling its silky threads slip through his fingers.

Each pin he lovingly set upon the bureau, until Danielle's golden curls lay down about her waist. Then he pulled her tightly to him, rubbing his face in her fragrantly sweet golden strands.

Danielle was lost; beyond the point of being called back or of actually wanting to be. This man before her was offering something new and alive, and without any reason, she knew she must accept all. Perhaps this was why she had been pulled with a desperate need of the unknown to come to this island paradise; perhaps all that had ever happened in her past had been leading to this one night of love in a stranger's arms.

She felt his sure fingers undoing the buttons that ran down the back of her gown and she shut her blue eyes, letting him have his way.

Standing in the flickering light of the hearth in only petticoats and chemise, Danielle heard a faint gasp come from the sultan's throat.

Once more his lips took hers, but this time they did not stop with her mouth. He covered her face and throat, lingering at the swell of her bosom.

Danielle knew with certainty that if not for his

strong arms holding her upright, she would have been reduced to putty and slipped to the floor.

As though he were practiced in the art of undressing women, her petticoats and chemise soon followed her gown across a chair, and she stood naked and beautiful to this stranger's eyes.

"You are beautiful." These simple words, coming from this man's mouth, were the sweetest that Danielle had ever heard.

His tanned, strong hands gently, as though taming a wild mare, roamed over Danielle's body. He filled the cups of his palms with her swelling breasts, went down lower over her flat, tight belly and then farther to the triangle of love.

A groan of sheer passion came from the sultan's throat and Danielle, feeling fire and ice coursing through her veins from his merest touch, felt her breathing become ragged, uneven.

The sultan's strong, capable arms lifted Danielle and carried her to the bed, his mouth greedily tasting the soft, sweet taste that was hers alone.

He laid her upon the sheets, standing back and letting his lions' eyes roam freely. She was absolutely beyond any kind of beauty he had ever seen before and he could barely believe his luck in her freely wanting to share this beauty with him, a stranger.

As he had undressed her, he now started to remove his own costume and Danielle, with her senses fully aroused leaned upon one elbow and watched with hazy, dreaming eyes.

His turban was first unwound, revealing a head of rich black hair, reaching down below his collar. Then he removed his shirt; this had been open to the waist already but as it was taken from his body she inhaled deeply, noticing for the first time the thick short dark hairs upon his chest and his tanned, bronzed muscle-rippled back and chest. As he lowered his white pants and let them drop to the floor, Danielle felt her heart all but stop. She had never before seen a man's body, but now she knew what real beauty was. Dark crisp hair grew down his flat belly and around his powerful, throbbing manhood; his body was supported by muscular, well-proportioned legs. His whole presence was raw, powerful man, but his eyes, as he watched Danielle's reaction to his body, allayed all fear.

This man would be gentle, giving, and loving. She would find only pleasure in his arms. For a moment Danielle thought of how she had been brought up. Nothing had prepared her for this. Women who did what she was about to do were called wantons.

The sultan saw the look of uncertainty cross her face, and quickly he was lying at her side, his fiery lips making a scorching path from toe to head.

Let her be called a wanton, she thought as she felt her body respond to his. This would probably be her only chance to have a man such as he. Tomorrow she would once more be the proper Blackthorn heiress, but for tonight she was going to be a woman, finally made complete by this man.

Strong, probing, and plundering fingers roamed freely over Danielle's body, bringing her passions to a flaming peak.

The sultan's mouth seemed to be in all places at one time; opening to take a full, ripe breast; its demanding tongue making delicious patterns across her engorged, rose-tipped nipples; his lips going lower and his tongue now going over her stomach, bringing soft moans from her as he tasted of the sweet ambrosia of her body.

As his head went even lower to the triangle of her passion, Danielle felt herself slipping from the sane world. Her body was a throbbing, volcanic storm, aching for something beyond her reach.

His mouth and tongue seemed to plunder her very core of existence, to drained her of substance and then to raise her once again to the pinnacle of pleasure. She was taken up hills and valleys of feeling that she had never known before, then swept into a world where only she and he existed.

As he rose once more above her and lay at her side, prolonging the sweet fulfillment which was to come, Danielle reached out her hands and boldly ran them over his body. She felt the corded muscles of his chest and belly, and when her small white hand roamed farther down and gently held on to his throbbing member, she heard and felt his catch of breath.

"Oh, no more, love," he moaned, taking her hand and bringing it to his lips. He had no desire to waste himself; he wished now only to lose himself in the sweet folds of her body.

Danielle's eyes were passion-filled as he rose above her, spreading her thighs gently, his manhood probing the recesses of her innermost secrets. Then she felt a sharp, piercing pain the minute his love tool pushed into her body.

The sultan felt the tight membrane protecting this woman's maidenhead break at his entrance. What kind of game was she playing? he wondered as he looked as closely as he could in the dimming light, into her eyes. By her actions he would have sworn that she was not a virgin. And by all that was right, what in the world was a young virgin apparently of good background doing on the streets at night alone and why was she so easily misled?

For a moment he considered questioning her, but all such thoughts flew as he felt her arms wind about his back and her body arch seductively against his own.

Danielle had been mildly surprised by the sharp pain she had experienced, but Sara had told her some facts about what happened between a man a woman, so she had not been completely in the dark. Sara had also told her that sometimes the pain of losing your virginity would last, but Danielle found that in her case this was not so. Oh, she was a bit frightened now, but as she wound her arms about this man's back she felt her wish to know more far outweigh her fright.

The sultan's body slowly developed a sensuous, luring rhythm. He did not wish to hurt this lovely creature who had decided for no reason that he could see to give to him the jewel of her virginity. So his movements were tender and gentle; his lips kissed her throat and face, and from his throat came sweet love words, praising her beauty.

Soft, languorous words of love came gently through the open windows; somewhere out in the dark night another lover was singing to his beloved.

The music seemed to heighten the passion of this couple on the bed enflaming them ever on.

The sultan wrapped Danielle's satin legs about his waist, striving deeper and deeper into her nether regions; making her body one large unquenchable force striving for fulfillment; pulsating, sweating, and straining for the earth-shattering pleasure that was near.

And when it came, she gloried in the feeling, wrapping her senses in sheer, pulsating pleasure.

The sultan out of a sense of knowing women, knew the instant the woman beneath him reached the peak to which he had striven to bring her, and his whole being swelled with an unreasoning pride. His body, for a few short moments longer, drank of her body, and then he also felt that feeling of sheer brilliant delight start at the center of his being and expand in a mighty, plunging storm of rapture.

His body stilled and his breathing was ragged, but his lips roamed over Danielle's face and throat, not seeming to be able to get enough of her passion-drenched body. "You inflame me beyond reason, my little mysterious angel." He smoothed back stray curls from her face and watched her features, waiting to see if she felt he was due an explanation.

But if he truly expected one, he would be surprised. Danielle felt no remorse for what they had done now that the deed was finished. She reasoned with herself that her maidenhood had mattered little to her, and if not this man now atop her, another would have done the same. But something in his look told her that she was deceiving herself. No other could take this man's place. She brought his face close to hers and gently placed a honey-soft kiss upon his mouth. "I know the questions that you wish to ask, but I pray you to still them before they are uttered. Let us hold on to this short time we have together."

The sultan was lost in her soft voice and delicious mouth. And the thoughts that had been plaguing his mind, of who this creature was and where she came from, were not asked. It indeed would destroy this magical evening, he thought, if he did know more about her. Perhaps she was right.

Twice more the couple on the bed delved into the act of making love. The sultan was thrilled at being the teacher of such an apt and willing pupil. And Danielle bloomed like a ripe flower under his expert hands, shedding all restraints and inhibitions as he showed her the glory of his body.

They finally slept for a time, their bodies entwined.

Danielle awoke with a jolt, startling the man at her side. "What is it, pet?" he asked in a satisfied, sleepy voice.

"I must not stay any longer." She rose and started to dress; she had been dreaming about Vanessa Delmar and in the depths of her sleep René Beauchamp's face came to her.

The sultan also rose from the bed and pulled from his wardrobe a clean white shirt and a pair of dove-gray trousers. He was just as appealing in these clothes as he had been in his sultan's costume, thought Danielle. He was by far the most dashing man she had ever met.

"I'll go and get us a carriage, love." He came to her, his manner still that of the gentle lover. "Stay put until I get back." He lightly placed a small kiss on the tip of her nose.

As soon as he left the room, Danielle's hands flew to pull up her stockings and pull her hair back into a knot at the back of her head. There was no way that she would be here on his return. If he accompanied her back to the Delmars' residence, he would surely find out her identity. And what if someone were to catch them together? What if René were to chance upon them? She would be placing herself in a most unwise situation if she waited about.

Going to the door she looked both ways. Making sure that no one was in the hallway, she hurried down the stairs. Going through the now-deserted kitchen, she found and went through the back door. Circling the inn, she cautiously approached the street; and clutching up the hem of her aquamarine gown she quickly ran, hoping that she was going in the right direction.

Only moments later she ducked into an alley as she heard the wheels of an approaching carriage, coming from the direction of the inn. The man she had spent the last few hours with was frantically searching the streets of Fort-de-France for the beauty who had disappeared.

Back out in the open once again Danielle hurried down one street and then another. She froze in her tracks as she went around a corner and there, directly in front of her, was a carriage, just turning the corner.

"Danielle." René Beauchamp's voice filled her ears. She fell into his arms, her relief and exhaustion apparent.

"Where on earth have you been?" He held her tightly against his chest. "I have been frantic. Uncle Henry and I have both been searching every street in Fort-de-France." He held her at arm's length, appraising her diligently from head to foot.

Danielle saw all too quickly what his eyes were seeing. Her hair, the last time he had seen her, was piled high and in perfect order. Her gown now was rumpled from the rain and having been casually thrown over a chair, and she had left behind her shawl, her half-mask and the emerald hairpins. "Oh please, René, do not make me relive these past few hours," Her eyes were pleading as they looked into his. She would need time to formulate a believable story, she told herself.

René Beauchamp was lost as his eyes met those before him. This was the first time she had called him René. He would not push for an answer now; he would let her catch her breath in the carriage and slowly he would learn what had happened.

He gallantly helped her into the carriage, covering her lap with a cashmere rug. This gave Danielle plenty of time to think up a passable story.

She sat across from René Beauchamp, and with glittering tears in the depths of her eyes recounted how she had been pushed along with the crowd of party-goers and had not realized her whereabouts, then the downpour had come, making everyone run

313

for shelter. She said she had gone into a close-by inn and sat down by a warm hearth. She then told of how she must have fallen asleep, rumpling her gown and mussing her hair. When she had awakened she had fled the inn in search of the Delmars' house. Most of what she said, she told herself, was the truth. She was only omitting the sultan who had wondrously shown her the joys of becoming a woman.

She hurried up to her room, after quickly repeating to Vanessa Delmar the same story that she had told the woman's nephew.

Once behind the secure doors of her chambers, Danielle once more relived the hours long past. Had it been true? Or had she been dreaming? But no, she told herself, her body still ached sweetly from her love-making.

Slowly, she took one piece of clothing and then another off her body, doing the same thing that a strange man had done only hours ago. When nude, she stood in front of the mirror, looking at herself from different angles. She had not changed; the only difference that she could see was that her body glowed with a delightful tingling glow. Something new, she told herself; something that the sultan must have left behind for her to remember him by.

Not dressing her body, letting it keep the wicked, languorous feeling unhampered by bindings, she climbed between the sheets, her eyes shut, and her mind filled with the handsome vision of the stranger she had met.

Golden eyes set in a dark, devilishly handsome face bore down upon her. Even in her dreaming mind she felt her body reaching out to that of the stranger. Her last thought was that she did not even know her sultan's name. A wispy, faint smile came to her passion-swollen lips.

Chapter Eleven

The town of Fort-de-France was as interesting as Danielle had imagined. The day after the carnival night, René once again paid a call on Danielle. He gallantly asked if he could escort her about town. And bubbling over with the thought of seeing some of the sights of the island, she eagerly accepted.

First they walked down the main streets which boasted fine, little shops and romantic, out-of-the-way cafés. René, as he had done the evening of the carnival, introduced the woman on his arm to everyone whom they met that he knew.

After stopping at one of the small cafés for a light lunch, René proceeded to show Danielle some of the busy activity along the waterfront.

Tall-masted ships crowded the dock and everywhere one looked people were hurrying about.

Danielle's eyes were pulled to a large vessel with the name *Sea Wind* boldly painted on her sides. And for a moment as she stood, shading her eyes with her hand, she thought she saw a familiar face upon the deck of the ship. But as quickly as she caught a glimpse of the man, she also lost sight of him. René pulled her arm, wishing her to come along and not to stand, looking at the ships, out in the sun. A woman with her own shipping line need not stand and watch boats all day, he thought, pulling out a handkerchief and wiping his brow. "Blast it, but it is hot," he swore aloud.

Danielle did not really think she had seen her sultan of the other evening. Her every thought seemed now to be of the strange man, and more than once this day she had thought she had seen him, but on closer inspection she had been proven wrong.

Perhaps she would see him again at the Delmars' party. Everyone was supposed to be there according to Vanessa Delmar. And if Danielle had but known the man's name, she would have without reservation spoken out and asked Vanessa about him.

Now that time had passed, Danielle wished fervently that she had found out more about him. She was the one who did not want to let him know who she was, but now she found herself wishing that he would somehow appear before her and tell her all she wished to know.

René brought her back to the Delmar's house, promising to return that evening. Danielle enjoyed the young man's company, but she could not help but wish that he had golden eyes. In everything he did or said she seemed to compare him to the man she had held tightly to her bosom the night she had become a woman. And though she hated herself for it, at the same time she could not stop doing it.

The chandeliers were all ablaze and music filled the lower portion of the Delmars' house.

Danielle stood off from the foyer, smiling and making charming small talk to everyone who passed by.

Vanessa Delmar had insisted that she and René stand with her and Henry to form a receiving line to meet their guests.

Danielle stood first on one foot and then the other, impatient to be able to go into the ball room and circulate among the many guests who had already arrived.

Vanessa knew how anxious her young friend was

and when she noticed the girl shift her feet for the tenth time, she thought to let her go. "Go ahead, child. You and René go out there and enjoy yourselves. Henry and I shall greet the rest of the guests, but by the hour and the number of people already here, I would say that we should be joining you very soon."

René grabbed hold of Danielle's hand and the two young people fled the foyer and hurried into the ball room.

Danielle, her lovely face smiling, wore a watered-silk blue gown, with a daringly low-cut bodice, seeming to just barely cover the tips of her full breasts. The gown was a light blue, bringing the color of her eyes to a dark sapphire. A small diamond necklace hung seductively between her breasts. Matching tiny diamonds were at her ear lobes; her hair was swept up into an elegant coiffure, drawing much attention to its shining, yellow mass.

René who held this vision of loveliness tightly in his arms was also quite elegant this evening. His jacket and trousers were of a light-gray material, his waistcoat a creamy ivory satin with different colored birds embroidered on it. His head was held high as he, all concern and tenderness, led the young woman through the steps of the dance.

As the music came to an end and René brought Danielle over to stand near the French doors, a score of young men rushed to her side, all of them asking for the next dance.

René smiled at them as he would at smallchildren. This girl at his side was all that he could ever wish for and he felt his chest swell with pride when he noted the reactions of the other gentlemen as their eyes came to rest upon her.

Danielle was flattered by all the attention given to

her. She flirted wickedly, enjoying herself whole-heartedly; and then finally, acting as though it was the hardest decision that she had ever had to make, she held out her hand to a young auburn-haired gentleman whose face was lightly speckled with freckles.

The young man wore a grin from ear to ear as he took the hand offered him and led the girl out onto the dance floor.

The evening continued in much the same vein as it had started. Danielle was swept from one pair of arms to another until finally once more René made his way back to her side.

"Perhaps you would care for a glass of something cool? If you wish we could sit this one dance out."

His words were a lifesaver and her features showed as much. "Oh, thank you, René." She gladly took the proffered glass of liquid. "I thought I'd never have a chance to rest." But as she said this sentence her eyes were gayly looking about her, anxious already for her next partner.

As Danielle, at René's side, stood looking at the dance floor, she felt a presence behind her, and as she turned she found herself lost in a pair of lion's eyes.

His hand, the same hand that had known her so intimately the other night, reached out and took her own, leading her out onto the dance floor. He did not ask her consent or care what anyone thought of his brash actions. His only desire was to feel her soft, yielding body once more pressed against his.

Danielle found herself speechless as she stared up into the face she had been dreaming about nightly. She felt her knees begin to tremble and her heart begin to race as his breath whispered sweetly against her hair. She had wanted this very thing to happen, she told herself. She wished this man to find, to claim her as his own. There was something too powerful for her to deny where this man was concerned.

"You have led me a merry chase, my golden rebel." His husky voice filled her very soul. "When I found you had fled my room I took this town apart looking for you and here you were under my very nose all the time." He sighed with relief at having finally found the woman who had been plaguing his every thought day and night since carnival night.

Danielle looked at the man who now held her tight and she was not surprised to find that this man was by far the best looking she had ever seen. He was dressed in a royal-blue jacket and trousers, snow-white ruffled shirt and a lighter blue waistcoat with silver threads running through it. His jet-black knee boots were so brilliant that one could see oneself in their depths. Pure virile masculinity seemed to vibrate from this man, a throbbing animalism which no woman could long resist. "You were looking for me, sir?" Her voice held innocence.

"Do not play the coy maiden with me, my lovely." His words sent delicious little shivers of pleasure running down her spine.

"And pray tell, sir, now that you have found me what do you intend to do?" She felt more at ease now as he glided her around the room.

"Ah, my lovely, what do I have in mind for you?" His words were a silky caress. "I thought to offer you a king's ransom for the gift you have given me."

"Gift, I can think of no—" Her sentence was left in midair as she suddenly knew exactly what he had meant. Her face flushed brightly; she had not believed that he would dare to bring up that night. But she was learning fast that this roguish man before her would dare anything he pleased.

Ah, the lass truly remembered and knew exactly

what he was talking about, but now the real question was, what was he going to do now that he had found her? He had not let himself think this far ahead, having been absorbed by his frantic thoughts of seeing her once again. He only knew that once again he held her in his arms, her head resting lightly against his chest. She was a perfect fit, held tight against him, and he was not about to lose her a second time.

As the dance came to an end the man still clasped her hand, afraid to let loose and find her gone from him again.

René Beauchamp approached the couple, feeling a knot of nervous anticipation in his stomach. Throughout his life, he had not felt any true jealousy that he could remember until the minute he had seen this man pull this woman out onto the dance floor. As he had stood leaning against the wall he had felt something in the pit of his stomach, something warning him that to leave this man with Danielle could be very dangerous. "Ah, Danielle, I see that you have met the good captain?"

Danielle looked from one man to the other. René had said captain. Could this mean that her sultan was the captain of a ship or some other kind of captain? Her eyes questioned his.

Golden, copper eyes held hers softly, his mind saying over and over again, the name Danielle. What a beautiful sound the word had. But he had known all along that she would not have a plain name. A woman such as she would have to have a name befitting her. "Good evening, Mr. Beauchamp." His lions' eyes moved to the man who had intruded upon them. "I'm afraid I have not been properly introduced to the lovely lady."

René Beauchamp was puzzled for a minute. He had never known or even heard of this man's having been

320

interested in any woman. In fact, everything he had ever heard, had indicated just the opposite; that he did not care in the least for the fair sex. But then, Danielle was a very different type of woman. He could not imagine any man not being pulled into her charms. He would have to be on his guard, he cautioned himself. "Then let me be the one to have the honor of introducing you to her." René came to Danielle's side as though he belonged there. "Miss Danielle Blackthorn, may I present to you Captain Christopher Brice Saxon, captain of the ship called the *Sea Wind* and also owner of a very large plantation here on Martinique."

His words seemed to have a strange effect upon the couple. Danielle's eyes widened and her body trembled. René had said her sultan's last name was Saxon. Had that not been the same name, she had been told, that her father had claimed? Was he somehow related to her? The thought became magnified in her brain. "Christopher Saxon?" Her voice seemed tiny and far away even to her own ears.

"At your service." The clicking of his heels was like a thin wall of ice encircling him. Blackthorn, how could this woman be a Blackthorn? Had he heard correctly? But, of course, he had heard right. Was this woman releated to the Blackthorn woman who had caused the death of Deke Saxon? His golden eyes were no longer warm, but instead seemed to be measuring her with a frigid, calculating gaze.

The small group was quiet. It seemed as though an eternity had passed before Danielle heard the deep, thrilling voice for which she had come to care so much. But now that voice was not tender and full of love words; it was cold and hollow.

"Are you then one of the Blackthorns who also own a plantation here on the island?" Christopher asked, hoping that her answer would be no, but knowing beyond any hope that he would be proven wrong.

Danielle did not understand what was happening. Her world seemed to be crumbling down about her feet in these few minutes. She nodded her head yes. "My mother is Chastity Blackthorn; she stayed here on Martinique some years ago. But I do not understand how that can concern you." She felt suddenly desperate for an answer, as she stood facing this angry man. Something was happening, she did not know the reason for it. Why was he looking at her in this way? How could the fact that she was a Blackthorn affect him in the least?

René Beauchamp had noticed the strange interplay going on between the two. Both of them had seemed to react quite strangely when he had spoken their names. He had always thought of this Christopher Saxon as being a bit odd. He had heard many stories circulate about the island concerning his cruelties and ruthlessness out at sea. But why on earth this cold, hard anger had passed over him because of this girl, was beyond him. "Come, Danielle, let us dance." His voice broke the quiet; his hand reached out and took Danielle's. He thought it better to take her away from this man's fiery anger before something happened that could not be corrected.

Danielle followed René without question, feeling those lions' eyes following her across the floor. Why would he be so angry with her? Had she done something wrong? Had it been because she had not told him who she was sooner?

She felt it the minute Christopher Saxon left the room. She could no longer feel his eyes upon her and she felt in their place a cold unreasonable finality; one that told her he no longer wished her to partake of his life.

Perhaps René could tell her more about him. "René, could we not get a breath of fresh air?" she asked, wishing to question him in a more secluded spot than this crowded ballroom.

"But of course, Danielle. It would be my pleasure." He had not realized the full extent of Danielle's reaction to Christopher Saxon; but when he put his arms about her he felt her body's slight trembling. His sure feet danced them out of the French doors and into the flower gardens. Perhaps the fresh air would revive her flagging spirits.

Going to the middle of the gardens, Danielle sat down upon a small stone bench, fanning herself delicately.

"René, that gentleman, Christopher Saxon, do you know much about him or his family?"

By his worried look, Danielle could tell that René did not like her questioning him about another man, but as René was a true gentleman, he saw no way out of answering.

"I am afraid I am not that intimate with the gentleman. Uncle Henry, on occasion, had dealings with him, using his ship to transport cane from his plantation yearly. His life is quite different from my own, I am afraid. All I really know is that he is the captain of the *Sea Wind* and I feel I must also say that I do hear he is a bit of a hard man to deal with."

"And his family?" Danielle asked once again, listening avidly to each word that came from René's mouth.

"I know nothing of a family. And what I do know is only what I have heard over the years." Due to her questioning eyes, he continued. "They say that years ago a man was murdered along the docks, and that this Christopher was left his ship and his plantation on which he hardly ever lives, by this same man."

Murdered on the docks; that must have been her father. Hadn't Dabs said that Deke Saxon had been found right before they had left Martinique, that he had been killed and left floating near the docks. "You do not know who the man was who was killed, do you René?" She held her breath awaiting his answer.

Her pallor was growing by the minute, it seemed to René. He had thought the fresh air would quickly bring her to her normal self, but by the look of her, this was not to be the case. "No, Danielle, I do not know the name of the man. The whole affair took place years ago. I really do not understand your great interest in this Christopher Saxon, Danielle." He sat beside her and one of his hands went over her own. He wished for her thoughts to be of him and not this ship's captain.

Danielle thought kindly of René Beauchamp, but she, unlike him, held no romantic notions for the pair of them. Her thoughts were completely taken with Christopher Saxon. "Thank you, René," she absently said, thinking that perhaps Vanessa would be able to tell her more about the captain of the *Sea Wind* tomorrow. She could not let this lie; she would have to find out who her sultan really was.

Shortly after the end of their conversation, René led Danielle back into the crowded ball room. But for her, the evening was ruined; the feel of those cold lions' eyes seemed to be all about the room.

Christopher Saxon left the Delmars' home with a visage that was blacker than the night. His anger was such as he had not felt in years. How could he have been so blinded, he raged at himself.

His long pantherlike steps resounded off the brick sidewalk with each stride he took, and at each sound his fury increased. Shortly he found himself at the waterfront and, without hesitation, he pushed open the doors of the Pheasant Inn, shoving aside a large, dangerous-looking man who was just on his way out.

He was usually not a drinking man; he had seen too often the effects that strong liquor could have on a person. But this evening, he reasoned with himself, was far different, and that the only way to clear his mind of his black thoughts was with a bottle.

How could he have been so blinded by a pair of high, full breasts and rounded, soft hips? How could he, after all these years, have fallen into a trap set by a pair of blue bottomless eyes? How could he, of all the men on the face of God's green earth, have been the one to become enamored of Danielle Blackthorn?

His mood was such that a fight would have suited him well. He could work off some of his pent-up fury if he had someone to use his fists on, but this evening he was not to be obliged. All those who had resided in Fort-de-France and especially those who hung about the docks, knew of Christopher Saxon and not too many wished to tangle with the captain of the *Sea Wind*.

All within the inn readily saw for themselves the type of mood the large man was in, and as quickly their eyes lowered to their own affairs, not wishing to provoke this man with even a glance.

Christopher lowered his frame into a chair near the back of the room and called out roughly to the barmaid who was approaching his table, "Whiskey, bring me a bottle."

"Aye, govna, be back in a mite." The buxom, friendly woman grinned, making Christopher grimace at the sight. Most of her teeth were blackened; their appearance outshone her good features.

She was back in only seconds, placing the quart of whiskey down in front of the man and stepping behind him, her hands idly rubbing the back of his neck. "Me name be Milly, govna. And to tell ye the truth, I be a-liking what I be a-seeing." She made her meaning quiet clear.

"Leave me." Christopher's voice, a low rumble, the girl step back a pace.

"Aye, govna, whatever ye say; only don't be forgetting me name now." She smiled once more, knowing that soon he would be into his cups and most gentlemen were not as choosy after a few drinks when a woman was within easy reach.

Leaving the glass on the table Christopher brought the bottle to his lips, tossed his head back, and let the fiery liquor pour down his throat, leaving a warm path and setting fire to his insides. It served him right, he told himself. He should have found a better place to drink the night through than an inn where only the cheapest liquor was served and which only the roughest men in Fort-de-France frequented. But truthfully this atmosphere fitted his mood to perfection. His eyes went across the bar, glancing over the girl Milly and then over the men standing about. Lord, the chit had a hungry look about her, he thought; even from afar she looked capable of eating him alive.

He leaned his chair back against the wall and once more brought the bottle to his lips, taking a long draught from the heady brew. Once more golden hair and blue eyes danced before his mind, making him curse aloud and bring the bottle to his lips to empty its contents.

With the bottle empty, the girl Milly returned with another. Christopher grinned up at her, knowing that she must have been watching his every move to be so quick about her job. "That's the girl." He tossed her a coin upon her tray and spoke loudly. "Keep them coming." As she smiled and turned to leave, he gave her rump a light pat and she in return gave him a broad wink.

After this bottle he would be more than ripe, she thought as she left him once more to his drinking. She could wait, she told herself. It was not every night a gentleman as well set up and as fair to look upon entered the Pheasant Inn.

Christopher's eyes were glazed and his mind was a bit foggy as he tried to sort out what had brought him to the state that he was now in.

"Ah, the wench," he breathed aloud. The golden-haired beauty whom he had thought to find and offer all he owned, that she should think him worthy of her love. A sour taste came to his mouth, and trying to kill it, he swigged down more of the vile-tasting liquid.

What a laugh, he present her with all he owned. Laughter rippled from his lips. She with her Blackthorn wealth needed nothing he could offer. What a besotted fool he had been, he scolded himself harshly. Letting himself fall for a damned woman was bad enough; that the woman was a Blackthorn was even worse.

His mind went back to years ago and another Blackthorn woman he had known. A fine black film seemed to cover his thoughts of the woman who had caused Deke Saxon's death. Chastity Blackthorn. The mere thought of the woman brought a cold hatred to his mind, and he, like some great fool, had now been duped by another Blackthorn.

His thoughts went back to a few hours earlier. She was truly the most beautiful woman he had ever seen; even with his hatred he had to admit this. She floated across his brain in a light-blue cloud, her sweet, innocent face looking trustingly up into his own, blue eyes full of budding passion meeting and holding yellow, tawny eyes.

"No!" He slammed his fist against the table, drawing every pair of eyes in the room in his direction. he would not let himself be taken in so easily as that, he swore to himself. No Blackthorn would ever claim him in any way. He was not to be taken in as easily as Deke Saxon had been.

"Ye be wanting another bottle, luv?" Milly rushed over, wondering what kind of devil was riding this man.

"Aye and be quick about it," Christopher brought the half-empty bottle up and finished the contents in one large gulp. He would have to put the golden-haired witch from his mind. She was a Blackthorn; that very name made his anger visible to any who happened to view the manner in which his large fists clenched and unclenched and the pulsating muscle in his cheek throbbed with his violence.

His thougts went to the man who had found him as a mere lad, taken him aboard his ship, and loved him as though he had truly been his father. But he had been much more to Christopher as a lad; he had been a friend and a teacher, and he had also shown him the only love he had ever received. Everything which he owned today Deke Saxon was responsible for and by God, he told himself, he owed the man more than taking to bed a woman who was a member of the family, and more than that, the daughter of the woman, who had caused his death.

He thought all Blackthorn's shallow and wealthy, not caring who they hurt as long as they gained that which they wanted in the end. He had had twenty years to think over what had happened to Deke Saxon and what had transpired from the moment Chastity Blackthorn had been brought to the island of Martinique. She had deliberately set out to entrap

Deke Saxon, making the man become enamored of her beauty and her soft-spoken words so that he had forsaken all to be at her side, giving up his home and his wife, thinking of nothing but to have her as his own, but where did that lead him? Christopher's drunken mind questioned. It led him to his death, his body beaten and dumped in the ocean.

And then the fine Chastity Blackthorn had gone on her merry way leaving Martinique and all thoughts of the man who lay cold in his grave. She had not cared what trouble she had caused during her stay on the island, only having desired to get back to her fancy plantation in New Orleans. This is how Christopher's grieving mind had pictured things twenty years ago, he being a young boy and not fully understanding what had taken place—except that the man he loved had been killed. And though Jamie Scott had tried to tell him the facts and that it had been none of the young woman's fault, he had needed someone to blame and the easiest place to put this blame had been on the woman who had disrupted all their lives.

For a moment his mind filled also with the vision of Randolph Beauclair. But quickly thoughts of the man were gone. He had no proof that the man had had any part in Deke's death; it was merely his own opinion and if for some reason he were to find out that it was true, the French bastard would get all that he deserved.

Now another Blackthorn was on Martinique, but this time her prey would be wary. He would not be taken in by a soft, yielding body.

For a moment he thought back to the night of the carnival. Never had he been so taken with a woman before. She had woven a silver curtain of desire and passion over his very soul, making it impossible for him to think clearly, or to function normally. His every moment from that splendid night until this, had been filled with thoughts of her loveliness. Even in his sleep he had been plagued with thoughts of her. The day after the street party, he had sent out several of his men, including Jamie Scott, to see if they could find out something of a golden-haired beauty who was new to Fort-de-France.

What a fool he had been, he stormed at himself. All this would be put to an end now that he knew her identity, he told himself, drinking once more of the bottle.

Milly, as sly as a cat licking her lips over a large bowl of cream, stood next to the bar, eying the large, handsome man who sat alone at the table drinking himself senseless. At about the same time he took his last swig of the bottle of whiskey, she thought it was time for her to make her move. "Ye be wanting more, luv? Or perhaps ye would like to go up those stairs." She shrugged her shoulder to the stairs leading up to a hallway boasting of private rooms. "Milly will bring ye more pleasure than ye be finding in that there bottle, I guarantee ye." She rubbed her body against his side, her voice almost a purr.

"Aye," Christopher mumbled, picking up the new bottle by neck of the glass and throwing his free arm about the girl standing next to him. "Lead on to paradise, my lovely." His voice was a drunken slur as he started up the stairs. But his aim was to erase the golden image in his mind by losing himself in the soft folds of another's body.

The room was empty except for a small cot under a window and a dresser sitting agiainst one wall. There were no rugs or other comforts. Milly's profession did not allow her to buy extras with her few coins.

As soon as the door shut behind them, Milly's strong hands roamed over Christopher's body. What a man, she breathed feeling the strong muscles beneath his shirt. "Ye be something, govna. Let me help ye." Even before she finished, her fingers were unbuttoning his shirt and unbuckling his belt. Her breath caught as she pulled his breeches down from his hips. What a magnificent body. Her eyes glowed as she watched his throbbing manhood pushing up into the air.

Christopher, drunk and swaying slightly about the room, was mildly pleased with the girl's reaction. He had had plenty of women like this one before him. She was typical of all the other whores about Fort-de-France and every other town he had ever been in. Throughout his life Christopher had sampled many women, his looks seeming to draw them as a bee is drawn to a fragrant flower. Never had he refused any who acted in the least interested. All were treated the same; they got the use of his magnificent body, their pleasure being as much as his own—with an added extra. They also received a few shillings for their favors.

Milly now began to undress herself, pulling her gown and then her woolen shift over her head.

Christopher, for a brief minute, thought of another body that had been naked before him. Danielle had been a golden goddess. This girl's body was on the heavy side and with her clothes off her overpowering scent hit his nostrils; cheap perfume liberally splashed upon a sweaty body did not appeal to Christopher in his present condition. Nauseated, he sat back upon the cot. "That's a luv; ye just lie yerself down. Milly will do everthing that's needing to be done." She walked to the dresser and poured a bit of water out of a pitcher into a bowl. Therein she proceeded to wash her body.

Christopher watched as her washrag went over her ample breasts and to her armpits. The whole time her dark eyes held in a steady gaze on his body; for a moment he felt somewhat the feelings a defenseless chicken must under the steady perusal of a large hawk. She seemed ready to devour him with only her glance.

Christopher's manhood, which minutes ago had been large and throbbing, wanting nothing more than a woman to slack itself upon, had grown limp as he watched the woman in her toilet. An image of Danielle Blackthorn sitting back in the folds of a luxurious tub, up to her chin in delicate bath bubbles, her golden body glowing softly in the candlelight, came to his mind. For a second he even imagined that he could smell the sweet rose perfume that had seemed to cling invitingly about her. He shook his head, trying to clear his senses. What was the matter with him, could he not even while drunk enjoy himself and not be plagued with visions of the golden-haired witch?

"Move yerself over, milord." Milly's soft, white body came to the cot and she started to lie down next to his stretched-out form.

At least she did not smell quite as bad, Christopher thought, as he moved over and felt her skin making contact with his own. At this touching of their bodies, Christopher's mind seemed to be completely clear and free of all traces of the cheap whiskey he had been consuming all evening.

Milly's mouth and hands roamed freely and expertly over Christopher's body, bringing him once again to a hardened state.

A wicked smile appeared on Milly's face in the dark room, as her hand encircled Christopher's love tool. What a pleasure this was going to be! It had been a long time, indeed, since last she had had a man such as this. Without warning she threw a beefy leg over her lover and rose above him. "I am in the mood to ride this evening, my great powerful steed," she murmured, giving Christopher no choice but to lie back and take that which she was offering.

For a fleeting minute Christopher thought of pushing her from him and off the bed, grabbing his clothes and leaving; but truthfully he did not seem to have the strength to do the deed. His legs seemed leaden and the rest of his body too heavy to raise. The only thing about himself which seemed to have any life at all was his manhood and its vitality and life amazed him.

Milly, too, was amazed at her luck this evening as she rode her gentleman visitor as though there would be no tomorrow. It was not every day that a girl was lucky enough to come across such a fine specimen of a man, she told herself over and over again as she pumped her heavy body up and down and ground herself on top of the man lying on her cot.

When it was over, and Milly, exhausted, rolled off Christopher and lay at his side, he none too steadily sat up and rose to his feet.

"What ye be about, luv? There ain't no rush. I'll not be charging ye any extra for another go at it."

Christopher grimaced at her words. Another round like the one he had just undergone and he would more than likely go running from this room as though a madman. She had truly been more than he had expected, he admitted to himself. She seemed to pull everything out of him and now that she had over-exerted herself, her body odor once more hit his nostrils and seemed to wrap about his very senses. "I must be off and see to my affairs." His voice was rather harsh, telling her he would not stand for any pleading or begging. As he dressed himself with her eyes upon him, he reached into his wallet, pulled out

333

some coins, and threw them upon her dresser. Hurriedly he opened the door and left the room, not waiting to be cornered into a conversation with the woman with whom he had just shared a bed.

The morning after the ball Danielle awoke earlier; even with the dreges of sleep still pulling at her she knew she must rise and try to talk with Vanessa. All night through she had been plagued with thoughts of Christopher Saxon and she knew she would get no rest until she set matters straight between them.

She knew now that she would never meet another man quite like her sultan and the merest thoughts of the one night she had spent lying in his arms set her heart to soaring and her pulse quickening. She could not let things stay as they were, with his hate reflected deep within his eyes. She would have to know his reasons. And if she could find out no other way she would confront him herself and demand to know what she had done wrong.

Danielle was not so fortunate as she had hoped when she finally caught up with Vanessa Delmar that afternoon. The dear lady had stayed abed, ordering the servants not to allow anyone to disturb her. The ball had been a success and she was exhausted.

When Danielle did get to talk with the kindly woman there was not much she could tell her about the Saxons. She did confirm that the man who had been murdered and left floating in the sea had been Deke Saxon, and this man, Danielle had been told by Dabs, had been her father.

Vanessa did know a bit more, but she claimed that the affair had taken place so many years ago that her mind was foggy. As she remembered, this Deke Saxon had been married to a French woman, but the story about the island was that he had left her and was in love with someone else.

"They say, my dear, that this Deke Saxon was a very handsome man and that his wife refused him her bed and openly flaunted her lover under her husband's very nose." Vanessa repeated what she had heard in a shocked tone. "I will not divulge this man's name who was supposed to be her lover, because he still lives on Martinique and, in fact, is married to a dear lady with whom I have made aquaintance."

"But to get back to this Deke Saxon, from what I heard at the time, the boy Christopher—he was but a lad then—was the sole inheritor in the man's will. There was plenty of gossip in those days I shall tell you, and that is why I am truly reluctant to tell you all of this. I am not sure how much of this is truth and how much fiction."

"Oh please, Vanessa, do tell me all you know," Danielle asked, her hand fondling her teacup absently as her rapt attention was focused on the other woman.

"Well, my dear, if you are sure . . . Though I see no reason why you should wish to know anything about Christopher Saxon, my dear. Why the stories that circle the island about that young man are enough to make a decent woman's ears turn red. It is beyond me how the young man stays alive with all the fighting and carousing that he does."

"Yes, Vanessa, I have heard," Danielle said impatiently, wishing her to get back to her earlier story. "You were saying that this Deke Saxon left all he owned to Christopher?"

"Why yes. That is what I heard, and I suppose it to be the truth for the woman who was his wife left the island shortly afterward. They say she had family in France and returned to them. I heard she made such a ruckus about the will that when she left Martinique she was still in a fit of anger. That is why they say she left her lover her instead of taking him along with her. Though, as I said, I do not know how much of this is the truth, my dear."

"Then this boy, Christopher Saxon, he was related to Deke Saxon?" Danielle felt a tightening fear grip the bottom of her stomach.

"I am not quite sure. I remember at the time that this is why his wife tried to contest the will. She claimed that the boy only borrowed the name Saxon and that he was not truly a blood relation to her husband," Vanessa continued, watching Danielle's face for any kind of emotion that would explain her wanting to know about the Saxons. But she could only put it down to a young girl's foolish curiosity, for Danielle gave away none of her feelings.

At the end of Vanessa's story, Danielle felt somewhat relieved. If the story was true, then she was not related to Christopher as she had feared. She had thought that this might be reason for his anger. But still, if this was not his reason, then what could it be? she asked herself. Suddenly Danielle felt so tired and weary that she only wished to go to her bed, and lie down, shut her eyes, and sleep a dreamless sleep; one that would last for days, not just a short night.

"Thank you, Vanessa," she wearily said. This whole affair was proving too demanding. Too much had happened to her since arriving on this island.

"Why that is quite all right. I only wish I could have told you more, only I am afraid that is all I know."

"That is quite enough. You see, I met this Christopher Saxon last evening and I must admit that he has intrigued me." She felt it better to tell this good woman some reason for her curiosity rather than to leave her to wonder at its cause.

"Oh, my dear, I understand, but you must not let yourself be fooled by a man of his sort. He is quite ruthless and I hear dangerous, too." Vanessa's face was all concern. She had hopes of Danielle and René becoming more than just friends, but if the young woman were to lean toward a man of Christopher Saxon's notoriety she would not be the right woman for her nephew at all.

"You are right I am sure, Vanessa. It was only my curiosity, piqued for the moment, that made me question you. I do think, though, that it is time that I went to my own home here on the island and did not abuse your hospitality any longer." The idea had just come to Danielle that perhaps if she left this town and was alone on the Blackthorn plantation, she would be able to better sort things out in her own mind.

"Nonsense, my dear, you are not in any way abusing my hospitality. I had thought that perhaps you would wish to remain here with Henry and me. We have so enjoyed your stay and I know that René will be very disappointed to see you leave."

"Thank you, Vanessa, but I truly think that it is time for me to see what the plantation is like. I promise you, though that if I do not find things there to my liking, I shall return to you. And I shall come into town as often as possible."

"I guess if you must, you must. But I shall hold you to your promise and shall be expecting to see you quite often. I shall have René take you out to your property whenever you are ready, dear." The kindly older woman patted Danielle's hand.

At the end of that week Danielle was ready and packed to go out to her plantation. René had volunteered to drive her in his carriage, though upon hearing of her decision to move, he expressed his dismay that she wished to leave his aunt and uncle's house so soon. He had hopes of having more time with her in which he could court and woo her and then present his suit for marriage. He was sure that he wished her to be his, and with her all the way out at her plantation it would be much more difficult than he had imagined.

It was another hot day; though by the looks of the clouds it might rain by the late afternoon. Danielle relaxed against the cushioned seat of the open carriage with her lace parasol opened, protecting her somewhat from the cruel sun. She sighed softly as she looked at René, resting upon the opposite seat. What a truly wonderful friend he had proven in these past few days. What she would have done without him she had no idea. He had helped her to keep her mind off Christopher Saxon. René had come to the Delmars' home daily; he would take her for short outings and for lunch and then he would arrive each evening for dinner, not giving her much time to think of anything more than what outfit she would change into before he would once more be coming to see her.

Danielle was not quite sure if he was doing all of this out of his sense of duty for his family or if he were attracted to her for herself. He had been the perfect gentleman so far, not daring anything more than holding her hand.

"You look exceptionally lovely this morning, Danielle." His voice seemed functional, always saying the right things.

"Thank you, René." Danielle also automatically responded, her eyes going in all directions as they headed out of town.

As they left the town behind them and were riding down the rutted, dirt road, which wound about small mountains and through lush jungles and eventually led to the Blackthorn plantation, two horseback riders came toward them. One was a huge black beast and the other on a big brown.

Danielle shaded her eyes with her hand, trying to make out who was approaching. René also looked off in the riders' direction.

As the two pulled abreast of the carriage they slowed their pace.

René called to his driver to halt as he recognized the pair. Danielle, seeing who one of the riders was, felt her face flush, but not from the heat of the day.

Christopher Saxon sat straight and arrogant upon the back of a magnificent black stallion. He did not speak a full minute, but instead sat looking down at the two within the carriage. Finally though, out of necessity Christopher spoke. "Good day, Miss Black-thorn, Mr. Beauchamp."

"Good morning, Mr. Saxon, and you also, Mr. Scott," René responded rather coolly. He still had not forgotten the affair at the ball with Danielle and this ruthless-looking man, but Mr. Scott, on the other hand, he rather admired. He had met the first mate of the *Sea Wind* on more than one occasion and liked the man immensely.

"Aye, Mr. Beauchamp, it is good to see you again." Jamie Scott doffed his hat to the couple.

"I do not think you have met Miss Blackthorn, Mr. Scott." René introduced Danielle to the man.

"Why no, I have not, but what a pleasure it is, ma'am. I believe I knew your mother; that is if she was called Chastity Blackthorn?" Jamie had heard that the girl had come to the island and he held his suspicions about his captain and the young woman. It seemed much too much of a coincidence that the girl had arrived on Martinique on nearly the same day that Christopher had ordered several men, including himself, to search the town of Fort-de-France for a blond-haired beauty with dark blue eyes.

"You knew my mother?" Danielle's soft voice filled Christopher's ears, making his body tighten visibly. "How wonderful to find someone who remembers her. And right when I am to leave for my plantation. I would so have liked to have gotten the chance to talk to you about what you remember of her."

"Why, ma'am, it would be my pleasure to visit with you anytime you wish. I have no aversion to the ride out to your place."

"Perhaps you could visit me one day soon then?" Hope shone on Danielle's face.

"Why, ma'am, it will be my pleasure. Perhaps in a few days after you have settled in." Jamie had thought, when he had first heard that the Blackthorn girl was on the island, that perhaps there could be a chance that the girl could have been sired by Deke Saxon. This had only been a fleeting thought and one which he had quickly squelched. But now his thoughts, after meeting the girl, were reinforced. She had a look about her which his old captain had and her eyes were almost the exact same blue as Deke's had been. There was no mistaken that she indeed was Deke Saxon's daughter and if his young captain were not so stubborn and bullheaded he also would notice the resemblance she held to the man they had both loved.

"Oh, that will be delightful." Danielle smiled. "I shall be awaiting your visit."

Christopher was held totally frozen for a moment as he watched the joyful animation on the young woman's face. He had to harden his heart against her beauty, for still his dreams plagued him. From the moment he shut his eyes at night until he would open them in the morning, he was tortured with her beauty.

"Mayhap I can talk my captain here into accompanying me out to your plantation, ma'am," Jamie Scott added, pulling Christopher out of his thoughts and back to the group around him.

"Fine," Danielle said, all to quickly, before Christopher could object. "I shall be expecting the two of you then." Perhaps, she thought, she would get her chance to talk with Christopher and find the reason for his coldness.

Christopher scowled darkly at his first mate. "If you are ready Mr. Scott, let us be on our way." He tipped his hat to the couple in the carriage, jerked the reins on his horse and started toward town, his first mate following, after saying once again that he would be seeing Danielle soon.

René once again, as he had been the night of the Delmars' party, was struck by the thought that something was not quite right between Danielle and Captain Saxon. There seemed to be a tension-filled current running through the very air between the two. He hated to question Danielle, but if things kept on the way they now were he would be forced to ask her what the captain meant to her. He had plans to ask her to be his wife. He was going to give her more time to adjust to the island and to get to know him a bit better before making his proposal, but under these conditions he thought himself right in believing that he should know all that went on with her. There would be no secrets between himself and his future wife. And if this Christopher Saxon in some way had offended this woman for whom he had grown to care, he would have to think seriously on matters to defend her honor and his own.

He would not speak to her now about Christopher Saxon; he would bide his time and wait for the appropriate moment, he decided after thinking the matter over fully.

The rest of the ride out to the Blackthorn plantation was mostly silent, both occupants of the carriage having thoughts of their own and not wishing to be disturbed by idle talk.

Danielle had been overwhelmed with the desire to shout out to Christopher and ask why; why he seemed to look through her with icy, golden eyes; why he would not even say a civil word to her and what it was that she had done to deserve this treatment. With these thoughts chasing about in her mind she barely noticed René sitting next to her. When her thoughts were of Christopher Saxon she had no room in them for anyone else.

The view that met Danielle's eyes as the carriage pulled away from the tree-lined road and pulled in front of the large frame house, was the same one that had greeted her mother twenty years before and her grandfather before that when they had had their first looks at the Blackthorn plantation.

Nothing had changed. The flowers were in full bloom, sending a heady scent in all directions, and the house seemed to sparkle in the sun. It's cleanliness and relaxed atmosphere were obvious. but Danielle did not fully appreciate what was before her; she could not shake off her thoughts of Christopher. And as René led her up the stone walk she merely glanced about her, barely taking any notice of the lush surroundings and the colorful birds flying about the house.

Ellie met the couple on the front veranda, her face alight as she gazed at the young woman before her.

"You must be Ellie," Danielle said, already knowing her answer. As soon as she had arrived on Martinique, she had sent word with a messagenger boy, about her arrival and her plans to stay on the plantation. She had told the boy to tell the woman called Ellie to have the house ready.

"And you, child, must be Miss Blackthorn. You look so much like your mama, I be knowing you anywhere." Ellie smiled brightly and took the bag her new mistress was holding tightly in her hand. "You-all step on in the house out of this heat. I'll sent Jake out to unload your baggage." She included René in her invitation.

"Thank you, Ellie." Danielle smiled, already liking her. She tried for a minute to figure out the old woman's age, but she thought it impossible. She looked to be as old as the island itself, but what threw Danielle off was her apparent agility and posture-straight frame.

The house was cool and Danielle sighed with relief as she sat back upon the settee in the parlor.

René smiled fondly down at her, thinking her beautiful in her rumpled state. "I think you will be fine here, Danielle. The old black woman seems friendly enough, but before I leave I think I shall check out back at the cabins and see the mood of your people. There has been some rebellious talk among the blacks lately and I would not want to leave you if something not right is in the air."

Danielle looked up with worried eyes, pondering what had just been told to her.

In an instant René saw her look. "There is nothing to worry about; talk such as this has been traveling the island for years." He had not meant to worry her but as he glanced at her he entertained the thought that perhaps this situation would aid him in his courtship. It would give him a perfect excuse to ride out to check on her as often as he wanted and perhaps she would realize the foolishness of a woman such as herself staying out so far all to herself.

He sat with her for a short time longer, enjoying a

cool glass of fruit juice and trying to put her back in her light mood before he took his leave.

As soon as René left the house, Ellie showed Danielle up the stairs and to her room. "You be comfortable here, ma'am." She smiled. "You mama slept right her in this same bed."

Danielle looked at the bed; her blue eyes were full of wonder. Her mother had slept right here in this same room. She wondered for a minute if she had also shared this bed with the man she had loved, and for a second she was tempted to ask Ellie if she knew, but she thought better of it. What would this old black woman think if she were to ask such a question? It was not the type that most young women asked.

As though reading some of what was running through the young girl's mind Ellie softly said, "Miss Chastity was happy for a time here in this house."

"Was she really? I never knew my mother when she was happy." Her tone was wistful, as she sat down upon the soft down bed and tried to imagine her mother at a time when her life was a happy and care-free one. The woman she had grown up knowing was only a shell of a person, living in her own small world.

"Why, honey, your mama was different, that was all; being quiet and keeping to herself. But before that awful day she was as happy as a young schoolgirl."

"What day are you talking about, Ellie? What awful day?" Danielle's heart fairly raced in her breast. She had not expected to find out any information about her mother for a time. She had thought that she would have to ask cautiously all the questions she wanted answered, but here this kind, black woman was practically telling her the minute she met her, all she knew of her mother.

Ellie, who had started to unpack Danielle's gowns

from her trunks, turned and looked sharply at the girl. "Your mama didn't tell you what happened here, child?"

"No, Ellie. My mother, I am afraid, has not been herself since her return from Martinique. She does not realize what is happening about her. She seems to live in another world." Danielle felt she must tell this woman the truth about what she knew of mother and she only hoped that she would not decide to withhold all she knew. "Dabs told me as much as she could remember, Ellie," she added, hoping this would put the black woman more at her ease.

"Bah, that black girl, she weren't worth the food it took to feed her. I never could figure why your mama kept that girl for her maid; she was one sorry girl."

"She works in the fields now. Miss Tam thought the same as you and sent her from the big house years ago, I am told."

"Well, that sure was a smart move. This Miss Tam must be a smart woman, that's fer sure." Ellie went to another trunk and started putting away its contents. "Well, let me see. You were wanting to know what happened to your mama. And I can't see no reason why you shouldn't be hearing the truth of the matter."

Danielle sat upon the bed as though on pins and needles; she could barely stay still. She wanted to jump up and walk about the room and to ask Ellie a thousand and one questions.

"Well, honey, what happened to your mama happened that morning when she was brought the news that the captain had been found dead in Fort-de-France. You be knowing about Captain Saxon?" She looked to Danielle and let out a sigh with the nod of the young girl's beautiful blond curls. She surely wouldn't want to be the one to tell Danielle that her mother had had a lover. Someone else must have already told her this, she decided, as she looked over to the bed and saw the truth written upon her features.

"Why, honey, your mama was so happy before that day. Captain Saxon and her were together as much as the captain could get away from his duties in Fort-de-France. I ain't saying what them two did was right, but I tell you, never did I see a couple more right for each other than the two of them." She looked up from her work once more, directly toward Danielle. "It surely broke her heart and even more, I believe, it broke her mind that day they come and told her that her man done been killed."

Danielle felt the tears slowly make a path down her cheeks. "What was he like Ellie, this Captain Saxon?"

Of course, the girl would want to know about Deke Saxon, Ellie told herself, as she tried to find the words to say. She had known the minute she had laid eyes on the girl that afternoon, that Deke Saxon was the child's father; there could be no mistake. "He was a handsome man, honey, and good, too. You could tell in everything he did that he loved your mama. Why, his eyes, I can still remember, when they would look to Miss Chastity, they would light up with a special warmth and anyone standing in the same room with them would feel like an intruder."

Danielle's breath gasped from the woman's words. "He truly loved her that much?" She asked the question, but already knew her answer.

"Why, he sure did, honey. You're daddy loved your mama with all his heart," Ellie replied, finishing with the last of the unpacking.

Danielle looked hard at Ellie, trying to see if the woman was judging her parents. But all she saw on the old black face was years of knowledge and love.

Chapter Twelve

For the first few days, Danielle stayed close to the plantation house, getting to know Ellie and the other servants and becoming better acquainted with the climate and the surrounding area of Martinique.

All the servants went out of their way to satisfy her every want and the large black man called Jake was always about explaining the running of the plantation or answering any questions she might have. She was soon to find the man a wealth of information and invaluable with his services.

When she asked about the other blacks on the plantation and how they fared with the heat and their work, she was told that they did indeed work hard; sunup until sundown they bent their backs in the cane fields. Many died from snakebites and many more from illness. Her heart went out to these people who labored for her family. She had often visited and even tended the people on Iva Rose and she asked Jake if he thought that her presence would be a welcomed one here with his people.

At first Jake did not know how to answer his new mistress. The other white lady, whom he had found out was Miss Danielle's mother, had never even once asked about the poor black humans who gave their life blood in order to keep her plantation going but now her daughter wanted to surround herself with his people and to tend to their children and old folks. He had no idea how the blacks would take to her presence, and he confessed as much to her. They, for the most part, had never been around any white people before. They might take her offer of wishing to see them as an affront. But she was the mistress of this estate and he had no right to keep her from visiting the small structures that sheltered his people.

Danielle gave no thought to his warnings. She knew that the people here were her responsibility now and she fully intended to see that they were cared for.

The next morning after her talk with Jake about the slaves, Danielle, after breakfast, asked Ellie to see that Jake had a horse saddled for her and also himself, while she went upstairs to change into more suitable clothing for riding.

While Ellie hurried to do her mistress's bidding, Danielle reached her room and quickly pulled off her taffeta gown and all other embellishments down to her chemise.

Danielle had always shunned riding habits, thinking them almost as clumsy as a gown, so at an early age she had taken to wearing men's breeches and a shirt. She wore high knee boots to protect her legs and tied a white scarf about her neck. Her hair she wore pulled back; and a ribbon, tied and knotted, kept the golden curls from her face.

Ellie had looked askew at her young mistress as she had descended the stairs in tight-fitting trousers and white silk shirt. At first glance Ellie had been reminded of a woman she had seen years ago, before she had been brought to Martinique. She had been sold off the island of Grand Terre and there on that island pirates abounded; and that is exactly who her mistress reminded her of now—a woman pirate. There had been several on that infamous island and one woman, who had stuck all these years in Ellie's mind, was dressed just like Miss Danielle, standing now before her. Slowly a smile came to her old black face. Why should she not do as she wished? Ellie questioned herself. Had her mother been more like the daughter perhaps she would now be in a different state.

Danielle sighed with relief. She had thought that Ellie would perhaps try lecturing her on the proper attire for a young lady, as she had been daily lectured by the servants at Iva Rose. But the old black woman's smile told her that this would not be the case. "Did you talk to Jake, Ellie?"

"Yes, ma'am, and he be guessing where you be wanting to ride. He done told me of your talk yesterday about those blacks out yonder in the shacks."

Danielle's look was sharp. "Do you object, Ellie?"

"No, ma'am, I just not wishing any harm to be coming to you." Ellie softened her face and her voice.

"Do not worry yourself, Ellie. Jake and I shall be back by noon. So have a large dinner; I am sure I will be starving."

"Yes, ma'am, I sure do that." Ellie's smile shone back on her face. She had been wrong to worry about this mite of a woman; she could see that she was more than able to take care of herself. And besides, Jake would be with her and she trusted him as fully as she had ever trusted anyone here on Martinique.

Danielle left the kitchen and walked out back to the barn, from which Jake was leading a sorrel mare toward her; and following behind was a darker colored stallion.

Danielle at once reached for the horse's reins. She started to pet its velvety nose and whisper soothing words into the mare's ears. She wished the animal to be at ease with her and offered it the lump of sugar she had brought with her from the kitchen. The mare greedily munched the sugar from her hand.

Jake smiled affectionately at the young girl. She

seemed to think about everyone, he told himself, even horses. He would soon see how her kindness would pay off, he reminded himself as he helped her to mount and then jumped upon his own steed's back.

The cabins of the slaves were set quite far from the big house. Jake led Danielle through a well-worn path surrounded by thick foliage that was almost jungle-like. It was some time before they came to a clearing full of fairly neat, well-kept small cabins.

Danielle noticed at first glance that most of the cabins had small vegetable gardens in the back. And from the largest cabin in the circle of buildings she could hear the loud laughter of the children.

"Are your people happy?" she asked Jake as they brought their mounts into the village.

Jake knew where her thoughts were; with the laughing children. "Children do not find the pain of adults until they grow older."

Danielle sensed his strong resentment and tried to put it from her mind. She had felt this same strong feeling numerous times before in New Orleans, when she had asked questions of certain slaves. She had found that she had reasoned with herself long ago that slavery was not right; but she also found that she alone could do nothing about it except to see that all people owned by the Blackthorns were treated fairly.

She kicked the swelling sides of her mount, going ahead of Jake a bit.

"Missy, would you like to meet my mamma and family?" Jake called to her, sorry somewhat for his harsh words. He could not blame her for the faults of others and a cruel society.

Danielle jumped at the chance to meet Jake's family. If she could become friends with one family, the others would follow in time. "Oh yes, Jake, that would be wonderful. Besides your mother, do you have a wife or any children?"

"Yes, missy, I gots a real good woman; her name be Wren. And we got us five sturdy younguns. My mamma's pretty old now and can't be seeing or hearing too well, but she helps Wren with the younguns and helps with tending our garden. My woman, she tends to most of the younguns in the big cabin, while's theys mamma's working in the fields." He led his horse in the direction from which she had heard the laughter.

The two horses pulled to a halt in front of the largest cabin and several children of various sizes ran out of the door, shouting the words "papa" and "Jake."

Jake laughed loudly and swung first one and then another into the air, and amid these peals of laughter Jake's wife, Wren, stepped to the door.

"What you be doing here, Jake? You be in some kind of trouble up at the big house?" Then her eyes came to rest on the golden-haired woman, with men's breeches on, smiling down at the children. "You children you run on in to Grandma Em," she scolded, scooting all the small black figures to the door, like a mother hen.

"This be my woman, Miss Danielle." Jake grinned at the woman now standing, hands on hips, waiting for an explanation from her husband, as to what was going on here.

"I am glad to meet you, Wren." Danielle smiled, trying to put the fiery-looking black woman at ease. "Jake has told me all about you and the rest of your family."

Wren knew at first glance that this woman had to be the Blackthorn girl about whom her husband had told her. But she could not figure out why Jake would bring a white lady all the way out here to the cabins.

She always imagined the white's as being too good to lower themselves to looking in on their slaves. She had been born and raised here on this plantation and had only had small glimpses of any white people, one being the overseer who lived on the plantation and mostly stayed drunk and to himself, and the other had been years ago when she had been a young girl and she had first met Jake. He had just started up at the big house and another white lady lived there then. She had heard a rumor that there was a black girl who lived up at the big house and tended to the mistress, and she also was supposed to have been attracted to Jake. Wren, on impulse one day, had gone up to the barn and hidden herself away hoping to catch a glimpse of this girl and to spy out her competition. But instead of seeing the girl she had wished for, she had herself been surprised and had hidden herself farther back behind the bales of hay, holding her breath as the mistress came into the barn and stood for a time petting a horse's silky neck and cooing softly to it. Wren had been surprised and frightened that she would be caught so she had never told a soul about that day; not even to her husband whom she loved with all her heart would she confess this secret.

"Wren, the missy here, she come to see if she can be getting anything for our people." Jake's voice seemed to harden; he knew his wife well and he did not wish her to offend this woman who seemed only to want to help.

"Why you wishing to help our people? None of the others wanted to worry themselves."

Jake's black face seemed to resemble a thunder cloud. "Woman, you hold your tongue. Excuse her, missy, she not been feeling well lately and she not knowing what she be saying."

Danielle knew at once the kind of illness Wren was

suffering from, mistrust and a willingness not to believe that anyone cared about their plight. "That's all-
right, Jake, I understand. Wren," she turned her
attention to the woman, "I care about all human
beings and especially those who are suffering."

Something in this woman's voice rang with the truth
in Wren's ears and quickly her face became brighter
and a small smile replaced the frown. "What you be
keeping the missy out here in the heat for, you big
dumb man?" she jokingly chided Jake. "You welcome
to come into the cabin, missy. The children stay here
while theys mamma's out working and a few live here
all the time. Grandma Em, she lives here with them
that need her." Wren stepped away from the doorway
and waited for Danielle to step into the room.

Jake stood dumfounded. He would never understand this woman he had married. One minute she
was as hard as nails, the next she was as soft as clay.
Well, no matter, he told himself, at least she was
being kind to the missy now.

Wren swept her calico skirts aside, allowing
Danielle into the large single room. The walls con-
tained crude beds, built one upon the other in bunk
form. There was a large table in the middle of the
floor, reaching from one end of the cabin to the other,
and against one wall was a huge hearth and bubbling
upon this was a delicious-smelling stew.

"Sit yourself down." Wren indicated the stool
pushed under the table. "You children behave yourselves in front of the missy," she scolded two small
boys who were pummeling one another.

Danielle smiled at the boys and called them to her.
Slowly, with the shyness of small children, the boys,
with large saucer, brown eyes approached the beautiful woman with the kind smile, sitting at their table.

Within minutes Danielle had the children, one on

one knee and the other bouncing gayly on the other, as she visited with Wren and Grandma Em. She asked them of the other blacks' needs and made a mental note to have Jake go into Fort-de-France tomorrow to purchase these items. Medical supplies were most needed, for some of the children had open sores and others had colds. Some of the elders were ill from the rain and the heat of the island. She also noticed that the children and the women could use new material for clothing and shoes. She could well imagine the condition of the people in the fields.

The noon hour came all too soon and Danielle realized that she would have to be getting back to the big house; Ellie would be worried if she lingered much longer. She had made good friends of the women whom she had met today, she told herself, and she would not go back on their trust in her. She promised to return again in a few days, when both Wren and Grandma Em expressed their disappointment at her leavetaking.

The rest of the afternoon, after Danielle reached the house, flew by in a hurried rush. She wrote a list of all the things that she could think of for her people in the back cabins; she gave this list to Jake and instructed him to leave at first light the following morning for Fort-de-France and to return before nightfall with the supplies she requested.

The next evening right before sundown, Jake drove up the long drive to the plantation house with the wagon bulging with much-needed supplies.

Danielle happily searched through the contents as Jake held high a lantern. Everything seemed to be there, she sighed as she plundered through the last box.

Barely able to wait until the next morning, Danielle retired to her bedchambers that evening.

True to his word and with his captain in tow, Jamie Scott arrived at the Blackthorn plantation the next morning. Christopher had at first refused any part in his first mate's harebrained idea of visiting a Blackthorn, and especially Danielle Blackthorn. But after prompting him a few days and finally accusing his captain of being pigheaded and afraid of a mite of a girl, he had finally consented. Though grumbling and ranting at Jamie Scott for being an interfering old fool, he had shaken his dark head in agreement.

The pair had set out from Fort-de-France early that morning in order to avoid most of the sun's penetrating glare. So it was that Danielle had just finished her breakfast and was standing outside the barn next to the wagonfull of supplies when she saw two riders coming down the lane to the big house.

She knew instantly who the large man on the huge black stallion was and she felt her knees starting to tremble at the mere sight of him. She had tried for the past few days to exhaust herself with work and exercise so that she would not be awakened with dreams of this man. But no matter how hard she tried to quell them and no matter how tired she was, she would sleep restlessly, with Christopher Saxon always in her mind.

Jamie Scott and Christopher also saw Danielle at the same instant. But their view of her was quite different from that which they had expected. Before them stood a willowy, strong-figured woman dressed in men's clothing. Christopher's eyes were automatically drawn to the tight-fitting breeches and the white silk, form-fitting shirt.

Jamie Scott smiled broadly, not letting any of his shock over the young woman's attire show on his

355

features. "Good morning, Miss Blackthorn. I hope you are well and find everything here on the plantation to your liking."

"Indeed, Mr. Scott. I find the plantation most satisfactory. Though I admit I do miss New Orleans." Her voice sounded rather stiff and unyielding; she tried to keep her eyes on Mr. Scott to prevent them from wandering to his handsome captain. "I am afraid I was not sure when you would be arriving and I was just about to ride down to my people's quarters."

At that moment Jake brought out her mare and jumped up to the seat of the wagon.

"If you would like, you are welcome to join me or you can go up to the house until my return. I should not be gone long. I have only to take these supplies to some of the women and to make sure that they know how to administer the medicines."

Christopher had stayed quiet, his eyes going over the lushness of her body. And as she spoke his dark brow rose archly. Did this woman with the last name of Blackthorn truly care about someone other than herself? He would have to see this to believe it. "We shall ride along," were his only words.

The two men followed close behind as Jake started the team of horses, pulling the wagon onto the path that wound its way to the group of cabins.

As the small party rode up to the group of cabins, low-voiced shouts were heard, saying that the mistress was coming. And before long all the children from within the large cabin were surrounding the group on horseback and grinning up at the mistress and Jake.

Christopher as well as Jamie Scott was surprised at the children and also at the adults who came out to greet their mistress. Their faces registered trust and in some they saw the beginnings of love.

Danielle touched each child fondly and to each she

spoke a kind word. "I see all is well, Wren," she called as she dismounted her horse.

"Yes, ma'am," was her answer, as Wren tried to keep the children under control. "You younguns run along and play. Let the missy catch her breath."

"They are all right, Wren. Let them stay; I brought each a small present."

The children shouted with glee at these words from their mistress, then stood quietly, though expectantly.

Danielle laughed as loudly as any of the children as she climbed onto the back of the wagon and started handing down the boxes.

Without much preamble Christopher and Jamie were drafted into helping Jake carry the packages into the cabin which housed the children.

Danielle soon left the unpacking to the men and she and the women went inside and started to take each item out of the boxes. When she found the one she had been looking for, the boxes with the combs and ribbons for the girls and the small knives for the boys, leaving Grandma Em and Wren to finish the unpacking and putting away, she grabbed them up and headed out the door.

Danielle called the children all to her and led them out to a large tree a small distance from the cabins. She then sat down upon the grass and all the little ones followed suit.

The faces about her were free and gay as she handed each the treasures she had brought them; and for most of the children these were indeed treasures, and the only ones they had ever known.

The girls looked in wonder at the many different-colored ribbons that were before them and Danielle had each pick the color they most liked. All the combs were the same style and color so these were easily distributed.

The boys could not believe their eyes as each was handed a pocket knife. Their eyes were larger and Danielle noticed that their smiles were even larger as she handed each his present.

The children could not seem to thank their mistress enough and as they sat around her feet they repeated over and over their gratitude.

Christopher, finished at last with the unpacking, stood against the cabin and watched Danielle with the children. There was something special about the woman, he had to admit. For a moment a fleeting smile came over his features as he watched Danielle, a small girl on her lap, combing the girl's hair and tying a red ribbon in a bow in her braids. He would never have believed her capable of such a generous heart. She certainly did look quite fetching sitting their laughing and playing with the children.

Jamie Scott pulled him from his thoughts as he walked to where his captain was standing. "That's the last of the boxes." He also watched the young girl for a moment. But he was not as surprised as Christopher; he had known that the girl would be exactly as he was finding her. "It seemed as though there might be a storm brewing." He looked to the sky and at the dark clouds forming quickly overhead.

"Aye," his captain replied, not taking his lions' eyes from the girl near the tree. "Tell the black to get the wagon ready. His mistress should be ready soon."

Jamie sensed that Christopher wanted to be to himself as he watched the girl and turned quickly to do as he requested.

As though drawn by some power beyond her, Danielle's eyes rose from the child on her lap to the man standing against the cabin. His eyes were compelling, drawing her out and to him. She felt her breath start to quicken and could barely stop the trembling of her hands.

Christopher watched and then slowly, with halting steps he strode to the tree.

Danielle could not break contact with the golden eyes before her and as the man came to within feet of her she felt she would swoon from his closeness. How could a mere man have this power over her? the thought went through her mind.

"I think it is time to leave, if you are ready, Miss Blackthorn?" His words came out hard and without feeling, as he tried to hide the effect she had over him.

Danielle shook herself from her feelings of being lost in the lions' eyes. How could he be so unfeeling and cold to her after what they had shared together? she questioned herself.

"It looks as if it will rain soon," he added sensing some of her rejection.

"Yes, yes of course, you are right," she murmured, setting the girl from her lap and onto her own feet and telling the children to run along and show Wren and Grandma Em what they had received.

The children all scrambled to do as the mistress had told them, all squealing with laughter and trying to outrun the others to get to the cabin and to show the women first.

Christopher offered her his arm, but mustering all of her wits about her, Danielle turned her head and started to the wagon, leaving a grinning Christopher in her wake.

Jake and Jamie Scott were ready to leave by the time Danielle reached the front of the large cabin. Wren was standing at the door with several children about her, showing her the fine gifts they had received.

"Thank you, missy," she said to Danielle as tears filled her eyes. "You be making Jake bring you back here for a visit," she made Danielle promise.

The ride back through the thick forest was made in

silence. Danielle barely felt the large, cool droplets of water raining down upon her and her horse. Her thoughts were solely of Christopher Saxon and she was hard put to rebuke herself for her mind's betrayal. He obviously did not care at all about her and for some reason he seemed only to want to inflict some sort of hurt on her.

Christopher himself was also having troubles with his own thoughts as he rode his stallion directly behind the golden-haired beauty. The woman seemed to have some form of accursed hold on him that he did not understand. Merely watching her from afar brought back fond memories of her during carnival night. She seemed to have bewitched him, to have entrapped him with her golden looks. And as he watched her back and her white silk shirt being pelted with the rain, he caught his breath; her every contour seemed silhouetted by the clinging material.

The downbeat of the rain was almost overpowering as the group pulled out of the winding trail and back of the house. "You run on to the house, Miss Danielle, and I'll take the wagon and your horse on to the barn," Jake yelled over the noise of the rain.

"Aye, and I'll take your mount on, too, Captain." Jamie Scott gave Christopher no choice in the matter but to run along with Danielle.

Reaching the back door to the kitchen, Christopher held it wide for Danielle to make a plunge through.

"You two just be staying right there where you be at," scolded Ellie. "Me and the girls just this very morning done mopped this here floor and I ain't about to do it all over again." She hurried from the room.

Christopher and Danielle stood inches apart as they waited for Ellie to bring back towels. Christopher felt his breath inhaling sharply from this close contact and as he glanced down he noticed at first look Danielle's pointed nipples straining against the silk material of her blouse.

Danielle also looked to where his lions' eyes had roamed and saw to her horror what was plainly visible before him. But her pride was stronger than her sense of modesty so she stood with her head held high and all but dared the man to move.

With a sigh of relief, Ellie returned to the room and bustling like a mother hen, she handed first Danielle a large, enveloping towel and then Christopher. She also saw the condition of Danielle's clothing and with a sly glance she studied the face of the man who stood so near to her mistress.

"You had better hurry upstairs, Miss Danielle. It seems this here is the day for visitors." At Danielle's look of inquiry she finished, "There's another gentleman caller in the parlor. He been there quite some time now. Him knowing the rain about to come he decided to stay here instead of chasing after you to the cabins."

"Who is it, Ellie?" Danielle questioned, drying herself off the best she could.

"That Mr. Beauchamp that brought you out here that first day, honey," Ellie supplied, watching intently for any movement on Christopher's face. And when she saw the fleeting dark scowl which came over his features before he could control them, she smiled to herself. "You go on up and change your clothes. Don't you be a-worrying about this gentleman here. I'll show him up to one of the guest rooms and have his clothes pressed dry in no time at all."

"Thank you, Ellie." Danielle flew from the room, not bothering to turn another time in Christopher's direction.

"You come on up the stairs with me, Mr. —" Ellie

did not know his name and waited for him to supply her with her answer.

"Saxon," Christopher said absently, not noticing the sharp look given to him by the old black servant.

Danielle rushed about her room, pulling sodden clothing off and throwing it into a corner and pulling gown after gown out of her armoire until she found the one to suit her mood.

A dark, royal-blue velvet was the color that struck her for this occasion. And the low-cut bodice of the gown, she thought, would keep both of her gentlemen callers' attention from wandering.

The material itself was a bit heavy for the climate of the island, but with the coolness brought on by the rain she saw no reason for herself to be overly worried.

And with her toilet completed she stood back and smiled a slow, delighted smile. She looked her finest. Her hair she had brushed near the hearth—in which Ellie had build up a blazing fire—until the golden tresses were dry and curling perfectly at her will. She wove it atop her head and caught its mass in a dark-blue snood, leaving only tendrils dangling at her temples and a few loose curls at her nape.

The gown itself was a rich affair, her bodice cut far lower than most she owned and seeming with each breath she took to gape a small bit more. The sleeves were snugly fitted to her wrists and a small line of white lace encircled each. Also, at the neck was a small line of lace, but this only enhanced the gown.

As she reached the door to the parlor she heard voices coming from within. She had hoped to be alone with René for a few minutes before Christopher would arrive, but it seemed that her plans had been set astray. She must have taken longer than she thought with her toilet. She did not know what she truly wanted, perhaps to have Christopher walk in on a fawning René; perhaps she wished to make him jealous and then to treat him as harshly as he had her.

She had no more time to think on such matters as she heard the men within laughing at some private joke. She gathered her skirts together and swept into the room.

René was first on his feet. "My dear," he breathed as she came into the room. He rushed gallantly to her side and took one of her hands, bringing it to his lips.

Danielle glanced over his lowered head into the smiling, lions' eyes of Christopher Saxon, and as quickly brought her glance back to René. "Oh, but it is delightful to see you again, René. I had no idea that you would be back out to see me so soon."

"The time away from you has been quite harrowing I am afraid, so I decided without a second thought this morning to rush out as quickly as possible. I am afraid, though, that I did not expect to find you already with a guest." His voice now sounded strained, as his eyes left her face and went to Christopher's.

"Why, you know that Mr. Scott and Mr. Saxon promised to visit as soon as I was settled." Danielle smiled sweetly at René, as she walked over to the settee and sat daintily upon it.

"Why, yes, of course," René answered, though he was seething inside. He had hoped to find Danielle all alone and his to entertain for the afternoon.

Christopher had not as yet joined in the conversation, but after Danielle had seated herself, he also resumed his seat. Damn, he swore to himself, she was a lovely bit of womanhood. That gown seemed to make her blue eyes even bluer than they usually were and her swelling bosom was more than an eyeful for any man. For a moment there, when she had first entered the room, he had wanted nothing more than to knock René Beauchamp's eyes back into his head and to shout to her to leave the room and fetch something else to wear. A slow smile crossed his features at these thoughts. What was happening to him? Was the girl turning him into an old, grouchy man who could not enjoy the sight of a beautiful woman?

René also had resumed his seat, but his attention was fully wrapped up with Danielle.

"Tell me how Vanessa is faring, René?" Danielle questioned, now feeling somewhat uncomfortable because the two men were both watching her closely.

"She is fine and Uncle Henry also. They told me to mention how much they missed you and that they expect you to visit them soon."

"Of course, tell them that as soon as I am able I shall come and plan to spend a few days with them. I have been so busy with my people here I have hardly had the time to plan anything other than being sure that they have all that is needed for their health and comfort."

Rather shocked, René looked at Danielle. "You surely are not mingling with your blacks? Why, you have an overseer for matters which concern your slaves."

Danielle felt her anger flare, but kept a steady rein on her control, reminding herself that René had become a good friend to her in Fort-de-France. "Yes, I do have an overseer, René, but I have not as yet met the man. I was told by one of the blacks that the man stays drunk most of the time. So I do not know if I shall ever see him. And if he does not even care to show himself to the mistress of the plantation he works on surely you can reason that he does not care about the people who reside on that plantation."

René did not know that he had caused her to use that tone of voice but thought her overseer to be its cause. "You cannot believe these blacks on these islands, Danielle. They will tell you anything that comes into their heads. I am sure your overseer is just too busy with the work in the fields and has not had a moment to meet you."

"No matter. I intend to send Jake tomorrow with the man's wages for the rest of the year and to inform him that he is no longer needed. I find that there is too much that needed his care and he did not tend to it."

"You cannot be serious." René was completely shocked now. "Mr. Saxon, please tell Danielle the seriousness of such a move." He appealed to Christopher to side with him.

"I am afraid not, Mr. Beauchamp. I agree with the lady completely. If the man is a drunkard and the lives of her people are in his hands, then the man must be relieved of his duties." Christopher smiled toward Danielle, his eyes teasing but gentle.

René was outraged and it showed on his face as he started to stand to his feet.

"Now, gentlemen, let us not discuss such taxing subjects; no one will tell me how to run what is mine." She also rose to her feet, but went to the bell cord and pulled. "Let us have a cool drink before dinner." She hoped that Ellie would come swiftly before René did something to really anger Christopher or herself.

Ellie, as though knowing that something would be needed soon, entered the parlor, bearing a tray with tall glasses of fruit juice, and a decanter of brandy for those who would wish for stronger drink.

"Oh, thank you, Elle," Danielle exclaimed a bit too joyfully, making the black woman look toward her.

"Dinner will be ready shortly, Miss Danielle. I took the liberty of being sure that there would be plenty for your company. It don't look like this here rain is going to be letting up no time soon."

"Fine, Ellie. Call when you are ready. I am sure these gentlemen will do justice to anything you have prepared." Danielle played the regal hostess, though she was still a bit angry over René's words.

"This weather can certainly be a bit boorish at times," René said to no one in particular, but filled the quiet room with his words.

"Yes, it can be trying to those who are not used to it," Christopher added, looking at Danielle for a moment and then rising from his chair and going to a window. With his hand propped against the glass, he stood staring at the droplets of rain hitting against the leaded pane.

" 'Tis nothing like New Orleans," Danielle breathed, once again feeling homesick. She had more than once felt this feeling hit her, the desire to be back at Iva Rose. Perhaps she would cut her visit short, she told herself, as she sat there and sipped at her drink. What need was there of her staying here on an island she cared nothing about anyway?

"Have you ever been to New Orleans, Mr. Saxon?" René asked the solemn man standing next to the window.

"Years ago," came his soft-spoken reply. But Christopher was thinking of that time years ago when he had taken his ship to transport this very woman's mother back to where she belonged. His anger seemed to be fed by his thoughts. But before he could express himself more fully Ellie once again came into the room.

"Dinner is ready, Miss Danielle."

René stepped quickly to his feet and offered her his arm, leaving Christopher to follow after them.

René and Danielle made up most of the conversation during the meal, Danielle finding that she could not stay mad at René for long because of his kind and gallant ways. Christopher sat at the end of the table and mostly watched the couple while he ate his dinner. He did not contribute to their small talk and they could only guess at what his thoughts were.

With the meal completed, once again the group went to the parlor. The rain had not let up in the least. In fact, it seemed even harder than that afternoon.

"I took the liberty of asking Ellie to make up a guest room for each of you," Danielle told the men as they entered the parlor. "I am sure you would not care to venture out into this foul weather when you can be comfortable here."

"That is most kind of you." René bowed in her direction. Though he would have wished for this Captain Saxon to decline the offer of her hospitality, he certainly was more than fond of having the chance to stay the night. Perhaps tomorrow when the captain would leave he would be able to have a few minutes alone with her.

Christopher did not answer, but only nodded his head, his eyes watching all. As they lingered on at Danielle's face he saw her slight flush and a small quirk of a smile came to his features.

The meal had been served rather late in the evening so it was well past dark when Danielle begged to be excused for the night. She felt herself completely drained after her day of nerves with Christopher Saxon.

Both gentlemen also said that they would like to be shown to their rooms so Danielle, before going to her own, showed René to his first and wished him a good night. It was obvious that he would have wished to have been alone with her, but Christopher stood his ground and waited for her at the door of René's room.

Saying good night to Christopher Saxon was more than Danielle had thought it would be. "In God's name, how can you abide that popinjay?" were the first words out of his mouth as René shut his door and the pair stood in front of the next door down the hall.

"How dare you?" Danielle whispered harshly, not wishing for René to hear her arguing out in the hall.

"I dare what I please," came his answer.

Danielle started to walk away, but her arm was held in a tight grip. "You flaunt yourself prettily for the snob I see, but a real man you can only turn your back upon."

"And you, I suppose, are a real man?" This was beyond belief. The insufferable bore thought that he could be hateful and cruel to her and she was supposed to take it as a lady.

"I thought I had already proven to you the powers of my manhood."

Danielle's face turned to flame. "How dare you throw such a thing into my face. If you were any kind of gentleman you would not mention that night. It meant nothing."

"I have told you once, my fine beauty, that I dare what I will. And we shall see what that night meant in due time."

Danielle pulled with all her strength and finally was rewarded by his releasing her arm. "Do not ever touch me again. I shall not be so easily led astray as once I was. I know what kind of man you truly are."

"And I, my Blackthorn lady, know exactly what kind of woman you are." Her words came back to her, only striking with a vengeance.

Her hand rose to strike his arrogant face, but was swiftly caught in a viselike grip. "Do not tempt me to teach you here and now a well-deserved lesson. Your friend in the other room may not understand." His finely chiseled face was only inches from her own. His warm breath caressed her cheek and left her panting for breath.

As though her arm were contaminated, he threw it down from him. "Good night, Miss Blackthorn." He opened the door to his chamber and entered, leaving her gaping after him.

Danielle was beyond anger as she stomped down the hall and went through her bedchamber door, slamming it soundly behind her. Who did the arrogant, self-centered, conceited oaf think he was?" she ranted aloud to the empty room. How dare he talk to her in this manner and in her own home at that. She would not stand for this. She stomped about the room in a fine, raging anger.

A few hours later, after fitfully trying to sleep, but not being able to shut her eyes without the vision of Christopher Saxon coming to mind, Danielle got up and dressed in pants and shirt. She would go to the barn and try to find some peace, she told herself.

Quietly, lighting one small tallow candle to light her way, she went down the stairs and out the front door. The rain had slackened somewhat now.

Danielle had thrown a cape over her shoulders before leaving her room, so upon reaching the security of the barn she was dry and comfortable.

A lantern had been left dimly lit and it scattered dark shadows about the big room, but for the most part Danielle could make out where she was going. She went directly to her mare and the horse, sensing her presence, whinnied softly.

Danielle rubbed the soft nose that was pushed at her through the stall and then she climbed the wood enclosure. She would just pet the animal for a time, she told herself. This would take her mind off her own troubles.

The animal scents and the fresh-smelling hay set her mind at ease, and after a time of speaking and petting the mare, Danielle found herself hardly able to keep her eyes open. She decided to lie down in the hay. No one would know of her indiscretions; she would surely wake before dawn and go to her own chambers. But at that moment the thought of her chambers and the haunting memories of the past few hours were too vivid in her mind for her to wish to return to them so soon.

Finding a warm, secluded spot in the corner of the barn, she lay down, curled into a ball, and immediately fell asleep.

Sometime later, she awoke with a start. Something was touching her lightly on the face and in her sleep she had been pushing the unknown substance away.

Christopher, not finding any rest either in the large house, had decided to go in search of Jamie Scott. He had not seen the first mate since that morning and wished to talk to him, for lack of anything better to do.

The barn was quiet when he entered. His lion's eyes searched the corners for Jamie, but to his amazement he did not find the man for whom he searched, but the woman whom he had tried to scorch from his brain these past few hours.

He approached cautiously, not wanting to awaken the golden creature from her sleep, but only to view her and keep the pleasure to himself.

She seemed even more beautiful in slumber if possible, he thought as he stood to the side and watched her even breathing. He wondered for a moment what she was doing sleeping out here in the barn; she must have been restless as he was.

God, she was lovely. If only she was not who she was, perhaps things could have been different. He stood some time watching her and then on sudden impulse he squatted down on his haunches and picked up a piece of hay. This he gently swiped across the bridge of her small nose. He smiled patiently when she feebly swatted at the offending bit of disturbance to her sleep. She reminded him of a small child as she now lay.

When her eyes slowly opened and she saw who was plaguing her, she started up on her elbows. "You?" she breathed. "Can I find nowhere that is safe from you?"

"No," was his simple reply, spoken softly as his yellow, tawny eyes gently held her.

Neither said a word for a time, but looked on at each other. Slowly, as though in a dream, Christopher lowered his form down upon the hay next to hers.

His arms encircled her and his lips sought out those below his own. He felt complete lying there in the bed of hay. He had not felt so at ease since the night of the carnival, when he also had held this graceful creature in the circle of his strong arms.

Danielle also sighed aloud. This seemed right, to be in the this man's arms. To be near and protected by him from the outside world.

But all too quickly their dreams were dashed as Christopher, taking his lips from Danielle's, looked deep into her dark-blue eyes and whispered as though to himself, "If only you were not a Blackthorn."

Those simple words affected Danielle as strongly as ice water had thrown into her face. She froze and stared at him. "You hate me so much?"

"Aye, I hate you that much. Though I am powerless to control myself when I am around you." His voice was soft and Danielle could tell that he was speaking the truth.

"But I have done nothing to make you hate me so

371

much." She sat up.

"It started years ago, before your time." He knew he made no sense, but his feelings were his own and he could not change them.

Tears had started to flow in earnest down Danielle's flawless cheeks. "I had hoped—"

Christopher did not give her time to finish. "Do not mislead yourself, Danielle. I can not be taken in so easily as another was years ago by Chastity Blackthorn." Anger now filled his voice as he thought of Deke Saxon.

Danielle stood to her feet. She knew who the other man was that he was speaking of—her very own father. But in her fury, she was not going to give him the satisfaction of hearing her say those words. She started to the door, barely able to see now from the tears. "I shall try not to mislead you again then, sir." Of a sudden the thought struck that she wanted to hurt this man who had meant so much to her; to hurt him deeply, as much as he had hurt her. She dashed the tears with the backs of her hands, and turned about. "I shall tell you now then, that this will be the last opportunity of this sort that we shall have. I had only thought to try out my charms one last time." She was not getting caught up in her story as she saw the reaction coming to his dark face. "René has asked me to be his wife and I have accepted him."

Her words hung in the air for a full minute. It had worked, she told herself. He had not expected this, and his face showed it. She turned then, as though her blood flowed with royalty and started to the door. But as her hand touched the latch, Christopher was at her side and pulling her forcefully against his chest.

"Do not deceive yourself or Mr. Beauchamp. You will never belong to another." He was even surprised at the boldness of his words, but he knew them to be the truth. Though he did not wish her, he could not bear the thought of her in any other man's arms.

"How dare—"

"I shall say again I dare anything I wish." He brought his lips down and covered the pink morsels before him.

Danielle struggled in his grip, but it was to no avail; he was a powerful man and she was a mere woman.

After drinking his fill of the nectar that was this woman's alone, Christopher released her and set her from him. "You shall belong only to me." His voice was a command; then turning, he left first, through the barn door.

For the second time this evening Danielle was seething with outrage. She brought her hand up to her bruised lips and glared her hatred out the barn door, directing it at the arrogant blackguard who had just left. How could one man be so dishonorable? she ranted. How dare he say that she would never belong to another, when he admitted even to himself that he does not want her? He was the most presumtuous, perplexing man she had ever had the misfortune to meet.

Before going back to the house she sat down upon the floor of the barn and tried to sort out what had just happened. How could she have told him such a bold-faced lie, to say that she was to marry René? What if he were to confront René with this story? Her shame would know no bounds if this were to happen. And even if he did not confront René she would have to do something; he would be expecting her to announce her engagement and then to marry.

She would leave Martinique, she decided quickly and decisively. She would find the first boat leaving the island for New Orleans and she would book passage on it. It was foolish of her ever to have made this journey, she scolded herself. She had had nothing but trouble since coming here. And she missed Iva Rose; no matter how good the people on the plantation here, she would always love Iva Rose best.

Having made these plans, she felt a weight lift from her shoulders. As soon as René and Christopher both left in the morning she would send Jake into Fort-de-France with a letter to her shipping office. She would advise them of her needs and wait until they sent her word of the ship she sought.

With her mind made up she left the barn and went back to the house. Once in her room she found herself easily falling into sleep, no dreams hindering her now that her mind, for the first time since stepping foot on Martinique, was made up.

The next morning Danielle awoke later than usual, but felt refreshed and invigorated. When she made her way downstairs and out into the kitchen, Ellie informed her that Mr. Saxon had said to tell her of his thanks for her hospitality of the night before, but he could not wait around all morning and had business to tend to so he had left right after breakfast.

Danielle had snorted, "Business indeed," drawing Ellie's attention, but the wise old woman held her peace.

"The other gentleman, he said to tell you that he be waiting for you in the parlor after you finished your breakfast," Ellie added, and for some reason Danielle got the distinct impression that Ellie did not care for René Beauchamp.

After eating a light meal of jam, rolls, and a piece of fruit, Danielle left the kitchen to find René. As she entered the parlor he rose to his feet. He had been sitting comfortably, thumbing through a book, with his feet stretched out.

"Ah, Danielle, you look quite lovely this morning,"

he murmured, taking her hand and eying her body which was clothed in a light muslin morning dress.

"Thank you, René, but to tell the truth I hardly expected to find you still here. On arising so late I naturally presumed that you would have left for Fort-de-France."

René felt a hint of irritation at her words. Did she mean that she had hoped him to be gone when she awoke? "I had thought that perhaps we could have a private conversation this morning. If you remember correctly there was not much chance for me to speak with you with Mr. Saxon underfoot.

René's tone irritated Danielle this morning and she hoped that he would get on with whatever it was that he wished to say and have an end to it. If not, she would plead a headache, which she expected to be coming down with shortly as it were. "I am sorry, René, but as I told you yesterday I had no idea that you were coming for a visit."

"I know and of course, I do not blame you." He drew her by her hand to the settee. "I know how hard it must be for a woman with your beauty to be all alone. Why, any ruffian or intruder could find his way out here to your plantation." He was referring of course to Christopher.

"I assure you, René, I am not besieged by men trying to break down my door." Danielle laughed at the thought. "Why, I have Jake and Ellie here to protect me. So do not let that thought concern you." Perhaps he was truly frightened for her safety, she told herself.

"It is not only your safety that concerns me, Danielle, but also your business dealings. It seems to me that you are in need of a man to help you in these affairs." He did not give her a chance to reply before he went on. "I have given the matter some thought and I think that I should be the one to help you concerning your slaves and other taxing duties." He held up his slender hand for her not to interrupt. "I do not mean to just walk in and take over, but I hope that you will consider me as a husband and then you will be free to leave all in my capable hands."

Danielle felt herself holding back her laughter. Who did he think he was? Did he not know how obvious his ploy was? Did he think her so stupid that she would agree willingly to let him have all that was the Blackthorns'? No, the man who would gain all her wealth would have to be far more worthy than René Beauchamp. Another thought struck her as she sat thusly; she had only last evening told Christopher Saxon that she was going to marry this man who now sat proposing. How ridiculous this whole affair seemed to her now. "I am afraid not, René." Her laughter started to bubble out.

René sensed her joviality at this serious moment and looked sharply at her. "Perhaps you do not understand. You would not only be pleasing me, but also my aunt and uncle would be greatly thrilled with your consent. In fact, before I left Fort-de-France I made a special trip to their house to tell them of my intention of proposing to you."

"I am afraid you will have to tell them that my answer was no then, René, for I do not intend to marry you or anyone else for some time. I have only recently decided to leave Martinique and to go back to New Orleans."

René's sense of reason all but deserted him upon her confession. He had always been given what he wanted and now he wanted this woman to become his wife. She could not refuse him. His face turned red from anger and he sputtered uncontrollably. "You shall be my wife. You cannot mean what you are saying."

Danielle saw his imbalance immediately and stood

up from the settee. If he did not gain control of himself shortly she would have to call for help. "René, you are a dear friend, but I have never given the matter of marriage between us any thought." She tried to reason with him.

"Dear friend?" He laughed. "Dear friend indeed. Did you think I only wanted for us to be friends? Do you think I waste my time on any little bit of fluff who comes along? Did you not know from the minute that I set eyes on you that I had to have you?"

This was unbelievable; it could not be happening to her. "René, I do not know what to tell you," was all she could get out.

"Tell me that you will be mine," he implored, his eyes glazed as he took a step her.

Though he frightened her beyond endurance, Danielle could not let him go on with the thoughts he now harbored. "I cannot René. I wish I could consent to be your wife, but I do not love you. You are only a friend and I think that now considering both of our feelings, even that should be put to a standstill."

With a control that seemed to come from some hidden recess René pulled himself to his full height and sneered. "You think you are too good to be the wife of René Beauchamp. You will wish that you had given this matter some thought. But now that I have seen your true character perhaps things will be better off without a marriage between us."

Danielle felt a threat in his words and a cold, unreasoning shudder went up her backbone. "René, try to understand," she ventured as he started for the parlor door.

"I understand all too well and perhaps so will you one day."

There was an implication of something close to a threat. "I am sorry," she murmured as he stormed

377

from the house.

Sometime later that day, Danielle called Jake to her and told him of her plans to leave Martinique. She could read in his eyes that he would be sorry for her leavetaking, but she promised to do all she could for his people before she left. She handed him the letter she wished him to take to the shipping firm, but thought it best that he not leave now until the following morning. She did not wish him on the road after dark; there was no telling what could happen to a black man all by himself at night.

So the next morning after Jake left the plantation, Danielle started to ready herself for her departure. She hoped that since she had made up her mind to do the deed, she would not have long to wait before a boat was ready to take her to New Orleans.

After the scene with René, she would truly almost be glad to be gone from the island. She had thought of him as being one of her best friends here on Martinique, but now she knew that she was all but friendless in her strange surroundings.

That evening Jake returned with a note from the shipping firm stating that a ship now in the harbor would be leaving in only a matter of four days and by a lucky chance would indeed be stopping in New Orleans.

Danielle was relieved that she would soon be leaving, but at the same time she was saddened. She would miss the people on this plantation; she had made some very good friends among the black people here.

Before leaving she would see that the overseer was fired. After some thought on the matter she had decided that she would offer Jake the job. Who better would know how to treat the people than a black himself? She would once again leave the estate in the hands of the Blackthorn attorney in Fort-de-France and for a sizable fee she was sure that he would make monthly visits to see to it that everything was going smoothly.

Jake and Ellie were both ecstatic at the idea, though Ellie burst out weeping when she heard that Danielle would be leaving and that the house once more would be empty of mistress or master. She had hoped for a time that that good-looking Mr. Saxon would realize how he felt about Miss Danielle and that before long they would marry. But now, even these hopes seemed futile, she thought as she steadied herself to face caring only for herself again.

Danielle decided that it would be best to break away quickly, so that evening she packed her belongings and readied herself for the carriage ride into Fort-de-France. She would go the next day into the town and stay in a motel room until the time of the ship's departure. She would also visit with Vanessa and Henry; they at least deserved to hear from her why she could not marry their nephew.

The next day seemed identical to the one when René had first brought her out to the plantation, except today she sat in a closed carriage and Jake sat upon the driver's box.

The drive seemed endless as the day wore on, but finally, before the sun lowered in the sky, Jake pulled the carriage up to the hotel and handed her down from her seat.

Danielle was exhausted and after being shown to her room by the portly innkeeper and saying her farewells to Jake, Danielle fell upon the bed, not even bothering to take off her travel-stained clothes, and slept immediately.

The next day after a hearty breakfast Danielle penned two notes, one to her attorney on the island, expressing her wishes about the plantation, and the other to Vanessa Delmar, requesting a convenient time for paying a visit. Both notes she gave to a young boy who stood about the inn, hoping to run errands for the patrons. For a coin he promised to hurry right along and to await a reply from the Delmars' home.

The boy returned within the hour, out of breath and eager that she would find no fault. Danielle smiled fondly at the youth and gladly gave him two coins.

The note he gave into her hand was in Vanessa's own handwriting. Danielle hastily tore the envelope open and read the contents. With a sigh she lowered it. At least her fears had been groundless; she had thought that perhaps the Delmar's would be angry with her for not accepting René's proposal, but either he had not told them of her refusal or they were not too upset by her turndown of their nephew, for Vanessa had invited her to their house at one o'clock tomorrow afternoon for tea. She also chattered on about other things that did not matter, so Danielle took this as a sign that they were still good friends.

For the rest of the day Danielle went about some of the streets and shopped, wishing to purchase presents for those of the servants who lived in the house at Iva Rose; and also she looked for something special for her mother.

The next morning Danielle anxiously awaited the time to go to the Delmar's home. She would be leaving the day after tomorrow and she wished to spend some of her time with Vanessa. She was sure that when the woman heard that she would be leaving the island, she would plan her schedule so that they would have at least one more afternoon together.

When the time came for the appointed tea, Danielle left the inn wearing a light-blue gown with silver pin stripes. She wanted to look her best for the occasion so she had left her hair down and flowing freely to her waist.

It was only a short walk to the Delmars' house and after being greeted by a maid at the front door, Danielle was shown out to the back gardens where tea had been set on a round, glass table top.

Vanessa was nowhere to be seen, so Danielle took a seat and waited, thinking the woman too busy about the house somewhere.

However, it was not Vanessa who greeted her a few short minutes later, but René Beauchamp.

"René," Danielle said slowly. "Where is Vanessa? We had an engagement for today." There was something odd here, she cautioned herself.

René took the opposite chair across the table. "Aunt Vanessa sends her regrets, but she and Uncle Henry were called out to their plantation late last night. Something about sickness with the slaves." He started to pour the tea into the china cups.

"Perhaps I should leave then." Danielle started to stand, but was rooted where she was by René's cold voice.

"Stay where you are, Danielle. There is no reason why the two of us cannot have tea." His tone was an order and something in his eyes told Danielle that she had best, for the time being, do as he told her.

"Very well then, but just one cup. I really have a million things to do." She tried to sound calm and not to let him see her fear. For some reason she sensed that he would take delight in seeing her cringe before him.

"So I hear that you are indeed leaving the island?" he asked, stirring cream into her tea.

"Why yes, I told you that day at my plantation that I was not going to stay on Martinique." But how did he know about her leavetaking? she wondered.

Some of her perplexity must have shown on her face for his next words were too close to her own thinking. "This is a small island and news travels fast when one knows where to seek out information."

This seemed like a sly René, one that Danielle had never met before; and she felt her nervousness mount by the minute. She picked up her tea in shaky hands and tried to finish quickly, wanting any excuse to be gone and away from him.

René's slow, steady grin told her he knew all too well her thoughts.

Danielle started to rise once more after she had set the china cup down. "Please tell Vanessa that I was sorry to miss her, but I really can not stay any longer."

René also rose and started to walk her to the front door. "Have you thought over and perhaps reconsidered what we talked about the other day?"

Danielle looked at him in wonder as she stood before the door. "No, René, I have not reconsidered. I thought I had made myself quite clear the other day, and shortly I will not even be on the island any longer."

"That is too bad but if you insist on being unreasonable. . ." He took hold of her arm as she was about to step through the portal.

Danielle turned about and pulled, but her arm was firmly held. "Let go of me, René," she hissed, not wanting any passing stranger to see her struggling with a man on the Delmars' front stoop.

But as she turned she saw something gleaming in his hand; she looked down to find herself staring at a small derringer held firmly in the palm of his hand.

"Do not cause a scene," he warned, pulling her closer to his body.

"What do you intend to do with that?" Her voice was trembling with her fright.

René laughed aloud harshly, the sound grating upon Danielle's ears. "Just do as you're told, my high-and-mighty lady. Go down the steps and up that road." He half-shoved her and pulled her in the direction he had nodded toward.

"Where are we going?" She now felt fear that she had never known before settle over her. Was he so mad that he thought to kidnap her and force her to marry him? He would find himself very much mistaken if these were his intentions, she told herself. But she was no longer as sure of her feelings as she had been in the past.

"You will see when we get there," he ground between clenched teeth, as he shoved her before him.

They wound down one street and then up another. Danielle had never been in this section of town before. The buildings were older and looked more run-down than those to which she was accustomed. Even the smell in the air here held a tinge of uncleanliness.

The smell of the sea air was stronger here though, she noticed and she looked about her, trying to find something familiar.

As they came in front of a two-story, deserted-looking building, René hissed, 'Up those stairs and be quick." He glanced anxiously over his shoulder to make sure that no one was watching.

"René, what do you plan to do?" Danielle tried one last time.

"Just shut up and do as you're told." He pulled her along, the gun pushing cruelly into her ribs.

How was she to get out of this deranged maniac's

hands? she frantically thought as he opened the door to the building and shoved her inside, slamming her hard against the far wall.

This man who stood over her holding a gun was far from normal, she realized. He was dangerous and she had to find a way to escape from him.

"Get up," he shouted, grabbing hold of her arm once more and starting to pull her up the stairs.

"René, if you think to force me into marrying you after this you had best think again."

His laughter filled the room he was now dragging her into. "Marry you? After what you have put me through? No, Miss Blackthorn, I would not stoop to marrying you now. I will use you as I please and no one will be the wiser. The only friend you have in this town is my aunt and I have only to tell her that you left me to go back to New Orleans."

"No." Danielle clutched at her throat, and shook her head. She could not believe what was happening to her.

René was leering openly now at Danielle and the message in his eyes was not lost upon his victim. "You will be mine without the bother of a marriage ceremony."

Danielle pushed with all of her strength, knocking René off balance and sending the derringer across the room. But quickly he was steadied and in control again. He went to the door and locked the latch, not concerned that the gun had flown under the cot which rested against the wall.

Danielle stood across the room from him and held a chair in front of herself as though this would afford her some protection. "Please, René." She gasped as he started toward her."

He seemed to delight in her fright, as though he were being fed by her fear. His eyes shone brightly as he advanced. Each step seemed to bring Danielle closer to her doom.

But just as Danielle was face to face with the madman a disturbance could be heard downstairs and then the door to the room that kept Danielle hostage flew open, shattering into a thousand pieces.

She could not believe her eyes and sagged to the floor, almost in a dead faint. There, as though he were a knight of old, stood Christopher, glaring his fury in René's direction.

He advanced slowly toward the thin, dark-haired man, wanting to crush him, to squeeze the very life out of his body as he saw what was taking place in the room. He had sent a youth from the hotel that morning to follow wherever Danielle went, promising the young lad a gold coin if he did as told. The boy had been more than willing and had followed Danielle to the Delmar's house. Then he had come running to Christopher's ship with the news of René's taking the beautiful woman to this old deserted building. Christopher had had Danielle watched, wishing to know if she were truly going to marry René Beauchamp, for he had promised himself that he would not let her go through with such an affair. She belonged to no other than himself. And when the boy had brought the news of her whereabouts, Christopher had been perplexed. Why would René bring her to such a place as this. No one except those of bad reputation ever ventured into this side of town, let alone brought a woman whom they intended to wed to such a sleazy place.

The moment he had stood outside the building and looked up at its massive ruin he had known something was not right. When entering and not at first finding Danielle, he had considered leaving; perhaps the boy had been mistaken. But then his attention had been pulled up the stairs by some slight noise. His steps were quick as he ran up. He turned the knob, but found the door locked tight. Some unforeseen fear gripped him and without another thought he brought up his foot and kicked the door open. What met his eyes brought red-hot anger coursing over every portion of his body. Danielle stood clutching a chair to herself and quaking before René Beauchamp, but the minute her eyes beheld him, she sank to the floor.

He grabbed hold of René by the collar and jerked him off his feet. "You dare to do harm to the lady?" he seethed, in a deathlike tone.

"It is none of your affair." René gulped and tried to squirm out of the large man's grip.

"How say you that it is none of my affair, you scum? She is mine."

René realized his mistake and pulled hard, falling to the floor. "She is not yours," he said, trying to regain his footing. "I know she had naught to do with you."

"Then you do not know as much as you think for the woman there before you is mine now and forever." Christopher once more reached down to grab the culprit, but René was quick and wiry and squirmed out of his grasp, running as quick as his feet could carry him to the door and out of the house.

Christopher did not waste his time on René, but bent down and picked Danielle up in his arms. "Did he harm you in any way?" he gently asked, seeing the fright on her face.

Danielle could only shake her head as she clutched Christopher's shirt front as though she would never let go. She wept then, great wrenching sobs, that tore at Christopher's heart. She had not meant to lose control, but the past few hours had been too much for her after everything else that had happened to he since she had arrived on Martinique.

Christopher carried her from the building and to his ship, her tears still coming down, his shirt now soaked to the skin, and his throat one large lump.

He entered his cabin and laid her gently on the bed. He seemed to sense that she had finally had more than she could bear. He left her to herself and after a few minutes checked back to find her fast asleep. He smiled softly to himself; this is how he most liked watching her, while she slept and he could view her at his leisure. But now was not the time, he reminded himself. He had affairs to attend to before she awoke.

Chapter Thirteen

The gentle, swaying motion of the *Sea Wind* brought Danielle out of her deep sleep. She awoke with a start and jumped into a sitting position. Christopher sat in a chair that he had pulled to the side of the bed and was relaxing and sipping a snifter of brandy.

"Ah, it is nice to see that you have come back to the living." He grinned at her.

"Where am I?" She did not recognize this room she was in or whose bed she lay upon.

"You are on my ship, the *Sea Wind*, Danielle," came his answer.

"What am I doing on your ship?" She was fully awake now, remembering all of that afternoon when René had kidnapped her and the vile threats he had made. If not for Christopher's bursting through the door when he had, there was no telling what might have happened to her. "I want to thank you for your help today." She rose as if to leave the safety of his cabin.

"There is no need for thanks. I told you before that you were mine and what is mine I protect."

Danielle was in no mood to argue with yet another madman and said softly, "If you would be kind enough to help me leave your ship and to reach the safety of my hotel, I would greatly appreciate it."

"I am afraid not." He still sat relaxed, with legs stretched out. "I have decided that you are not capable of caring for yourself."

"And you think you will do the job for me, do you?" She could not help the sarcasm that filled her voice. "What of your hate for who I am?"

"Aye, I do intend to do the job and as for the way I feel we shall get that settled from the start. I find that you have some strange hold over me. I tried for a time to fight it, I must admit, but now I see no reason to fight what is natural between a man and a woman. My feelings for you have not changed, nor will they ever, but I have come to reason with them. I want you, Danielle, like I have never wanted another, and I intend on having you." He had risen to his feet and stood nonchalantly as though what he was saying was an everyday occurrence.

"First René and now you. Is there no end to you men and your cruelties? I shall fight you as I did René. Never again will I be used by you." She stood determined, facing him.

"I will not take you by force; nor will you fight me. You will become my wife and submit to your husband."

Danielle thought she had misunderstood. "Marry you?"

"Exactly. I find the idea quite simple. I do not wish for any other woman and I assure you that while I am held by this power you have over me you *shall* not belong to any other man. So the simple solution that I came up with is to marry." He walked to her and now stood looking down into those fathomless blue eyes. "You do not truly have much say. I deem what happens aboard my ship."

"You would force me, then? You would take a wife by force, knowing that she does not wish you?"

"Aye, I have no care for how you feel about me."

Danielle could not believe her ears. He was more insane than René. "And if I refuse?"

"I told you, you have no choice. The priest is aboard ship now and if the need arises I shall have you bound and gagged throughout the ceremony. I have known the good father for some time and he likes my gold for what it can buy for his orphans."

"You would truly do that?" How could this be happening? How could a man who professed to hate her want to make her his bride? What could be the real reason behind all of this?

If Christopher were forced to give an honest answer he would reluctantly admit that he truly did not know why he wanted to take this woman to be his wife. The idea had come to him as he had carried her to the *Sea Wind* and her tears had been shed so soulfully upon his chest. At first he had wanted to protect her from something like this ever happening again, but then he had remembered that she was a Blackthorn and the idea of marrying her for a form of revenge hit his mind. "I would do that and more to get that which I want."

"But—"

"There are no buts. I went to your inn and brought your trunks." He indicated her piled-up trunks, set in a far corner. "I shall leave you for a time and when I return, be dressed befitting my bride. Do not forget, if necessary I shall use force." With this he turned on his heels and left the cabin.

What was the matter with the men on this island? Danielle wondered as he left the room. Were they all bent on dragging a woman against her will to where they wish and then trying to verbally force her into doing acts that were not of her own will?

For a second a small portion of Danielle's brain said, Would it not be fitting to marry the man who took your proof of virginity? Would not the joke be on him, marrying you and you not caring a farthing for him in return? But then another portion of her brain scolded, But do you care about him? Remember those lips, cool and strong against your own on carnival night? Can you forget that muscular, and all-powerful body next to your own?

"Stop," Danielle wanted to scream, but instead paced the room, holding her head in her hands. What was she to do? You have no choice, the daring part of her mind said. You have no choice in the matter but to submit; and though you pretend to all the world that you do not care, you will once again have those arms encircle you and hold you close.

"No." But even she could not lie to herself. She wanted Christopher Saxon and though he thought he was forcing her against her will, she knew the truth of the matter. Under different circumstances, had he come to her as René had and pleaded for her hand in marriage there would have been no hesitation on her part; she would have gladly told him yes. Why, now, did she hesitate? Was not the offer still the same? She would marry the man she loved and perhaps in time he would learn to love her also. Could it be so hard to warm a cold heart, like he possessed?

Father Durphy was the next person to enter the captain's cabin aboard the *Sea Wind*. And as the good father went through the portal, he was stopped in his tracks, his mouth gaping wide. What beauty and innocence the young woman sitting across the room seemed to possess. She sat primly, her complexion fair and gleaming, her hands folded demurely in her lap and her eyes lowered.

Father Durphy had known Christopher Saxon for years and he had to admit that he had not expected this type of woman to be awaiting him in Christopher's cabin. He was not sure what type of woman would meet his eyes when Christopher first told him of his desire to wed, but surely he had not expected the rough and at times ferocious captain to have found himself such an angelic beauty.

Danielle had expected to raise her eyes and to meet those of Christopher so she was surprised to find a father of the church standing and watching her closely. From first glance she knew that she would like the father. He was small and angular, but his face drew one's eyes directly to it; his eyes were warm and giving and the smile that encompassed his features welcomed all.

He held out his hand and his voice filled Danielle's ears with his compassion. "Come to me, child."

Danielle rose and did as bade her, accepting the father's hand willingly as though one of his lost sheep.

"I thought that you would care for a small chat before the ceremony was performed. Christopher told me that it would not be necessary, but I insisted."

"Yes, Father," Danielle answered, as he led her back to her chair.

"Is this marriage of your will, child?" For a moment the thought of Christopher forcing this young woman into becoming his bridge came to the father's mind, but quickly thoughts such as these were dispelled as Danielle nodded her head.

"Yes, Father, I am willing." Her words sounded strange and Father Durphy had to bend down low to hear them.

They talked for some time before the cabin door was once more opened and a magnificent-looking Christopher Saxon strode into the room. Danielle looked in amazement toward the man who was to become her husband. His attire was perfect in cut and fashion. His jacket and trousers were light, fawn-colored, and his vest was shot through with strips of gold; his high black knee boots fairly gleamed from their recent polishing and his hair also, Danielle noticed, had been trimmed for the occasion. "Does everything meet with your satisfaction, Father?" He smiled at the man sitting across from Danielle.

"Indeed, my son, you have gained yourself a lasting treasure here." His eyes tenderly rested on Danielle for a moment before going back to Christopher. "I must admit I was surprised."

Christopher also was surprised and his face showed some of his discomposure. He had expected to step into the room and be berated by the father for trying to force a woman against her will, but instead he found Danielle beautiful in a pale-yellow gown, her blonde curls twined about her head, and talking companionably with the father. He had to admit that she was a lovely woman, by far the most beautiful he had ever seen. Most other women would have needed at least a full day to make themselves ready for their marriage, but this one in just a short amount of time was able to transform herself into a vision of desire whom any man would be proud to claim. He stood with hands folded behind his back and grinned down at the father. "Surprised, Father Durphy? Come now, you have known me for a time and must have known that I would not settle for anything less then perfect."

His lions' eyes roamed over Danielle's form from head to toe, not caring that the father was in the room and witnessing what he was doing.

Danielle flushed a deep scarlet, more from his eyes than from his voice, but a warm fire was beginning to grow in her depths. He had said that she was perfect; could this not be a good beginning for a marriage?

The marriage ceremony was performed on the deck of the *Sea Wind* with all crew members standing at attention and watching as their captain married his lady.

Jamie Scott displayed a grin that seemed to go from ear to ear. He could not have wished for anything more pleasing than to see his captain marry the lass who was the daughter of Deke Saxon. He knew his captain still did not know that the girl's father was also the man whom he had claimed as stepfather, but he thought that in time when the young man's anger diminished, perhaps then he would realize the truth.

Danielle stood small and delicate next to the tall, virile captain, her body trembling with each word the father said and when Christopher took her hand and placed a large diamond upon her finger, he had to hold her trembling small white fingers with his other hand.

In a short space of time the ceremony was over and the crew were shouting and giving the captain and his lady their well wishes. None dared more than a slight nod of the head and a brief smile at Danielle for fear of arousing their captain's wrath.

Christopher was well satisfied with the day and his gay mood proclaimed to all his satisfaction. He watched as each one of his men paid their respects to his wife and when it was Jamie Scott's turn, Christopher was a bit more touched than he would let show.

"You have truly got yourself a fine man, missy. I know him ever since he been a lad and you won't be finding another like him." The first mate had been bolder than the rest and placed a tiny kiss upon Danielle's cheek. As his face came down close to hers, for her ears alone he whispered, "Your father would be proud of this day, lassie."

Tears came to Daniell'e eyes from the dear man's words. She had thought that perhaps Jamie Scott knew about her parentage, but she had not been sure until this moment. "Thank you," she breathed as he left her side.

Marriage to Christopher Saxon was not what Danielle had imagined. He did not come to his cabin that first night or the next or next; in fact he seemed to have forgotten about his new bride completely.

After the marriage ceremony, when all had given their well wishes, Christopher had escorted Danielle to the captain's cabin. Stepping inside the door he had told her not to expect him for he had matters to tend to aboard the ship, but Jamie Scott would be bringing a tray to her shortly.

Danielle had not answered him, but had turned to the porthole and stared out at the vast blue sea. Her mind kept going over and over the fact that now she was Mrs. Christopher Saxon, as her right hand automatically turned the large stone, so alien to the finger of her left hand.

Christopher had stood for a moment viewing her back, his thoughts unreadable, before he turned and left the room.

That was the last Danielle had seen of her husband for several days. Jamie Scott came daily with her meals and straightened out the cabin, staying each time for a while and talking to his captain's new bride. Never once though, did he venture to speak of Christopher, and Danielle as though by mutual consent could not broach the subject of her husband either. Every soul on the *Sea Wind* knew now that the captain was ignoring his beautiful, young wife and whenever she passed one of the crew in the companionway or one of them were sent to the captain's cabin on an errand, his eyes automatically dropped, not being able to stand the sight of the pain that would be in the young woman's face if he were to look. As much as the crew avoided the woman aboard the *Sea Wind* they tried with all their might to avoid its captain.

Christopher Saxon was in a vile mood. The day of the wedding, after leaving his bride to herself in his cabin, the full impact of what he had just done hit him full in the face. It was as though his mind scolded him; he had married the enemy. He surely must be possessed, he told himself all the day and night long as his very soul was in torment from knowing that the woman he most desired was within arms' reach aboard his ship and in fact he had every right to go to her and claim her as his own. But a part of him warned against going too quickly to her; he wanted her to think that she was of little value to him. He had to hold himself in check at night while his body screamed out in agony to go to her.

Several nights had gone by and Christopher, awakened by some inner need, stood on his feet. His tension had mounted to a final breaking point. Even his dreams as he lay sleeping on the deck of his ship were of the woman who now laid claim to his name; it was impossible to sate himself any longer with his thoughts of revenge.

His moves were sudden and without thought as he pushed open the cabin door that separated him from the woman he wanted. He looked to be a large angry beast standing there outlined against the moonlight which came in through the porthole.

Danielle stirred in her sleep, but did not fully take in what was happening. She thought she was dreaming as this man stood brazenly before her. But the minute she felt a hand touch her and lay hold of her, she knew her dream had come to life. "What?" she gasped, jumping into a sitting position, fright apparent on her features.

"It is me, Danielle. Do not shout so or the crew will think that you are coming to some harm." His voice was harsh as he glared down at the vision upon his bed.

Danielle shook her head trying to clear it of sleep and to make sense of what he was saying. "But what do you want?" Her words were innocent and went straight away to Christopher's heart.

"If you remember, you are my wife." Still his words came out harshly, but his yellow eyes had grown to a deep warm color as he viewed Danielle with the covers pulled down to her waist and her bosom heaving with her breathing. Slowly he reached for his belt and pulled it from his trousers, and then he dropped his boots and pants.

Danielle now held no doubt concerning the business that had brought her husband finally to his cabin, and her anger mounted by the minute. "What do you mean by coming in here in the middle of the night for your own selfish reasons?" Her words came like a hiss in the dark night, and they brought a grin to Christopher's lips.

She still had retained the fire that he had seen her display before. For some reason he had thought that perhaps marriage would change this woman and mayhap with the change she would lose the power she seemed to hold over him. He sighed with relief; the thought of her changing from what he had known before was not one that he relished.

"You sound like a fish wife; one thing I cannot stand in a woman is nagging," he mumbled as he sat upon the bed and peered closely down at her.

Danielle pulled the heavy cover up to her chin and turned her back upon her husband. "Humph," she snorted. A nag indeed, she would show him. She would be cold and unresponsive and see how he liked her under those terms.

Christopher, naked, climbed under the covers, and the feel of his flesh against hers brought a scorching fire race through his loins. His large hands roamed freely over her back and buttocks. Even through the material of her nightgown Christopher could feel the bountifulness of her body.

He pulled her to him and felt her reluctance, but this only further inflamed his passions. "Ah, does the rose have thorns?" He chuckled and with one heave had her facing him and his arms tightly encircling her body.

"No!" Danielle sneered between clenched teeth, as his lips forced themselves upon hers.

"Yes," was his mumbled reply. Christopher's lips descended upon hers with a towering urgency.

Danielle fought those lips for she knew that she would be powerless in a mere few moments under his powerful assault, but all too quickly the power that they held and the magical way in which his hands roamed at will over her entire body turned her from ice to fire.

Her body seemed to melt against his own; her skin tingled where his hands trailed and molten liquid erupted in her very depths.

Christopher felt her resistance weakening and at once doubled his assault. He might like a woman who

397

could show a little fight, but more than that he liked a woman with passion and one such as he knew this one to be was a rare find. His lips and hands searched out her body, finding all her secret places of love and delight. Within seconds he had her naked to his bold yellow eyes and as soft, sensual moans came from deep within her throat, he reinforced his attack, knowing now that his anger was gone and all that remained was a desire for pleasure and the passion that his body could evoke within her own.

Danielle, like her husband, succumbed to the wanton desire of the flesh. Her hands roamed over his muscular form, her tiny fingers tantalizing and playing as they had never done in the past. All struggle and fight were gone from her mind now; the only thoughts which prevailed were those of another night when she had lain with this man. That night he had not known her identity, but he had brought her to peaks of abandoned passion which she had not known existed. And though he might for his own reasons not wish to care for her, she knew that there was this between them, this thing of their bodies which could not be denied. To her there was no shame as she felt this man's hands upon her naked form. This was her husband and the man she had already admitted to herself that she loved.

As Christopher's large, tan body rose up and over Danielle's pale and creamy form, his lips and tongue played with and taunted her rose-taut breasts and his leg gently nudged hers apart.

Danielle was swept into stormy desire, wishing only for completion, to have done with this soul-shattering teasing of her body. She wanted what was to come more than she had ever wanted anything in her life.

Christopher's lips rose to Danielle's ear, lightly nibbled it and softly spoke delicious, sensual words of love. As their bodies fused it was as though no feelings of animosity had ever been between the two. All hatred and hurt disappeared, their bodies saying what their mouths could not.

The first sparks of flame began to ignite within Danielle's body and without control she moved against her husband with a frenzy of desire, wanting what he alone could give her body, wanting to feel that same overpowering, all-consuming feeling of rapture that she had felt that other night in his arms.

Knowing much about women Christopher strove to bring this small slip of a woman to the highest pinnacle of pleasure that he could. She was like no other, he thought as he looked down into her passion-clouded violet eyes. Her body trembled and pulsated with his every movement, her arms wrapped about his neck; and he with a care brought her into a world of unreserved and uninterrupted passion.

As their love play peaked, both were brought to a towering climax at the same time. Then neither spoke, but both drank in what had just occurred. The eyes of each devoured the other.

After a time Christopher relaxed back upon the bed and, pulling his wife tightly into his arms, he rested his head upon the pillow. He lay silently for a few minutes and as he turned his head to say a few soothing words to her, he smiled tenderly. Her eyes were shut tightly and her breathing was light and even. She seemed to be caught in a deep sleep, but Christopher noticed as he looked down upon her that a tender smile touched lightly upon her pink, soft lips.

There was something about this woman, Christopher thought, but for now he would rest. He shut his own eyes thinking how soft the bed was and how warm the body next to his own.

The next morning Danielle awoke to her husband's warm breath hitting lightly upon her cheek. Her eyes fluttered open briefly, seeing who it was that lay next to her and that the sun was not yet up. For a moment she gazed at her husband's handsome features. In sleep, he seemed somewhat softer, as though he were only a young boy with no troubles to bother him. For a moment she remembered how hard and cruel he could be at times. But how vulnerable he seemed at the moment. Her eyelids once more grew heavy and sleep came to her.

The next time she awoke she was alone in the bed, her husband's side where he had slept the night away had now grown cold and was empty. She could almost think herself imagining the happenings of the night before. Not a trace of the man who had slept beside her remained in the cabin. But she held no doubt of the previous night; her mind went over what had taken place only hours ago.

Sometime late in the afternoon Christopher entered his cabin once again. Finding Danielle cleaning and straightening up the room he went over and sat down at his desk, his tawny eyes never leaving her form as she went about her duties.

Danielle felt those eyes as though they were physically burning her skin. Why had he come back? she questioned herself. Did he intend to torment her with his presence? She began to feel nervous and unsure as the time grew longer and still he did not move. Had she somehow done something to displease him or was he being plagued by some evil spirit and did he wish to take his bad mood out on her?

As Danielle finished her cleaning, sat down upon the bunk, and folded her hands in her lap, Christopher loudly cleared his throat.

"I thought that you might perhaps be interested in knowing where we are going?" He raised one dark brow in her direction.

As Danielle looked at her husband a frown creased her own brow. She felt somewhat guilty as she gazed over at him; she had not even thought for a moment of where this man was taking her. She had been too wrapped up in the happenings of the past few days.

Taking her responsive look as an affirmative answer Christopher rose from his chair and walked about the desk. "I thought that it would be best for me to tell you now that we would be leaving the *Sea Wind* in a few hours." He sat his large frame down upon the edge of the desk.

Still Danielle could not seem to find her voice, but she stared at this man who now had the right to tell her where she would be going and where she would not. She could not imagine where they would be docking for they had not been out to sea long enough to be going too far from Martinique; but as she sat there she realized that she did not truly care where her new home would be. She was tired of the island and did not truly wish to live there anymore anyway.

Christopher's golden eyes slowly raked over his wife's body, while his mind went over what he had found under all those clothes with which adorned her form. "Father Durphy is anxious to be back at his rectory." Christopher pulled himself from his pleasant thoughts and continued with what had brought him to his cabin in the first place. "As I said, we shall be leaving the ship within a few hours, but what I wished to tell you was that you need pack but a small bag. We shall be staying but a week or two on the island."

"What island is it that we shall be going to?" Danielle softly questioned, her eyes still lowered to her hands.

"Why Martinique, of course," came his answer, his voice holding surprise at her question.

"I had hoped, I-I mean I had thought that we were far from Martinique."

Christopher caught something more in his wife's voice than she had wished for him to hear. "You do not wish to return to Martinique?" Then it hit him, perhaps she was afraid that René would accomplish his evil intent toward her if she were on the island. "Danielle, if you are frightened of returning to the island, do not be so. I am your husband now and will protect you with my life. No harm will be done you ever again." His tone was hard and promising.

"Frightened, sir?" She had forgotten almost completely the affair with René. "I assure you I fear nothing on Martinique. I had only had hopes of leaving the island. I fear I did not find it as I had hoped."

An unreasonable anger started to spread over Christopher as he watched his wife defend herself. He knew all too well of her wish to leave Martinique and he also knew where she wished to go, but she would learn that she would do as he wished. No other wishes, she would find, mattered in the least to him. "Ah indeed, madam, I had forgotten for a moment your desire to return to your kingdom. Yes, I recollect now that you had told me once before that you were going to leave the island and go back to New Orleans." His tone held a nasty sneer.

Danielle picked up his tone at once.

"I assure you, sir, I have no kingdom." Her own anger began to flare. "I just find your island not quite to my taste."

"Perhaps you also find your husband not to your taste?" His dark brow rose threateningly. "If I recall correctly you also, on that same evening of telling me that you were going to leave the island, told me of your intention to marry René Beauchamp. You never did quite explain what you were doing in that building with the man you intended to marry that day I came to your rescue." Christopher now stood back on his feet and strode to within inches of where Danielle sat on the bed.

"Why you uncouth, unfeeling barbarian," she shouted, jumping to her feet. Who did this man think he was and what right did he have to insinuate that she had wished for René to treat her as he had? "You are correct, I do find you lacking and not up to my taste."

Christopher's hands reached out and grabbed her by the shoulders. For a moment Danielle thought he was going to throttle her, but as quickly as his anger had come, a small smile played about his sensuous lips. "Do not fool youself, madam. Your René could never have taken you where I did upon that bed last evening. You need a man to flame those fiery passions burning deep within your soul." His lips descended, warmly slanting over her own.

His strong arms, without any effort pulled Danielle close against his chest and his lips and tongue strove penetratingly over her mouth, bringing his wife's senses to a shaking discomposure. "No other could ever make you feel this hungry desire." He stood back from her, leaving her wobbly and unsteady. "Do not play me for the fool, Danielle. I know your needs, perhaps even better than you yourself; so wipe René and every other man from your mind. For even if you do not admit that I am your master, you shall learn that you belong to only me and I do not share in the least what is mine; even your thoughts I will not share." He turned then and started to the door, leaving Danielle staring wide-eyed after him. "Be ready to leave the ship when I return," he called over his shoulder and then went through the door.

Danielle sat back down upon the bed as the door shut. What had she gotten herself into? she questioned herself. She thought she loved this man, but how does one love a man such as he? She had hoped to change his thoughts of her, but how could she ever hope to change a man such as he? He overpowered her at every turn and his looks simply melted her. She seemd to be falling deeper and deeper into the web that he had spun instead of inducing him to fall for her charms; so far her ploy seemed to have backfired. He was just as arrogant and ruthless as ever. And what pained her most was that he was right about all he had said before leaving the cabin; no other *could* ever take his place and she knew this.

As the sun began to lower in the heavens and light dimmed in the cabin aboard the *Sea Wind*, Danielle Saxon sat silently upon the bed, not even noticing the darkness filling the room, so deep was she in her thoughts.

With a dark scowl written across his features Christopher entered the cabin and bumped about, trying to find a candle to light. As he lit the tallow lantern and looked about the room he saw his wife sitting quietly upon the bed. She seemed so tiny and withdrawn that for a moment his heart gave a lurch, but quickly he reminded himself of the events of this afternoon and also that this woman was Chastity Blackthorn's daughter. He would have to be on guard for her acting abilities; he could not let himself be pulled into feeling sorry for her. "Are you ready, Danielle?" His voice was gruff.

Danielle stood up and nodded her head. "Yes, I have packed a bag."

"Good, then come along, the small boat is waiting."

Danielle, having felt chilled all day, had dressed in a dark-brown, long-sleeved gown, and still, with the start of evening, she felt the cold seep into her body. Her dress was made more for the cooler climates of New Orleans than for a tropical island, but Danielle was to find as she was handed down the rope ladder on the side of the *Sea Wind* and climbed into the smaller boat that she had made the right decision. As the boat was rowed ashore the cool air and the icy sprays of salt water hitting upon her face had her shivering against her husband's side.

Feeling his wife's quaking body, Christopher pulled his dark-blue seaman's jacket from his body and wrapped it about Danielle's shoulders. He barely gave his wife a second thought as he absently performed this deed; his tawny eyes were watching the *Sea Wind* grow farther and farther away from the smaller boat.

The only other occupants of the boat were Father Durphy and two men of Christopher's crew, and as the men's large, muscular arms stretched back and forth upon the oars, Martinique came closer and closer.

Danielle noticed at once that they were not docking in Fort-de-France. Her mind frantically experienced a thousand different thoughts as the beach of the island came into view, but she dared not ask her husband about them for fear that he would answer her once again in anger.

As the boat touched shore Christopher jumped out and handed Danielle's bags to one of the men. Then he took hold of Danielle and before she knew what she was about he had pulled her up into his arms and started carrying her to the sandy beach. "You would not want to get your slippers wet," was his only explanation as he set her on her feet.

"Thank you," she whispered and reached out to the large man for her bag.

Christopher strode back to the boat and helped the priest out, then having gathered up his own bags and tucked a few rolled-up maps under his arm, he started back to his wife's side.

"Father," Christopher called to that kindly man. "These two men will see you safely back to Fort-de-France. It is only a few yards to my home and there we can have a carriage readied."

"Thank you, my boy. I shall not refuse, seeing how far we are from Fort-de-France, and I am rather rushed for time."

Christopher smiled down at the other man. Then, placing his arm about his wife, he started up a well-worn path from the beach through a group of trees.

They must be going to Christopher's house, Danielle thought, idly wondering why they had not put into Fort-de-France if they had to return to Martinique. What did Christopher have in mind? It was as though they were sneaking to his home in the dead of the night.

She did not have long to ponder these thoughts before the path came to its ending and the group stood on the grounds of a large plantation house, lit up brightly.

Christopher walked the group to the barn a distance from the large, two-story house and called loudly to the groom, who came running from the back of the building.

All this time Christopher held to Danielle's waist, and after giving instructions to his man to help his two crewmen rig up the carriage, he and Danielle said their farewells to Father Durphy.

Danielle fondly told the older man that she would miss him and asked him to return to pay her a visit whenever he could arrange to do so.

The father seemed disappointed as he sadly told

Danielle that he did not think a visit would be possible in the near future. He had much too much work to take care of at his rectory.

Their conversation was cut short as the two crewmen announced that the carriage was ready and waiting.

After saying good-bye once more Father Durphy climbed into the back of the vehicle and the men whipped the horses out of the barn and out into the dark night.

As soon as the carriage disappeared from sight Danielle once again became very aware of the presence of her husband at her side and of his hand gently resting at the small of her back.

She was surprised when she started to the front of the house and Christopher steered her around the large fragrant gardens to the back of the building.

It was dark and almost eerie here and for a second Danielle wanted to question her husband about his intentions, but as he led her through a small group of trees two smaller houses came into view.

These must be guest houses, Danielle reasoned, but she could not understand why Christopher would be leading her out here away from the main house if this was indeed his plantation.

"Stay put for a minute while I light a lantern." Christopher, leaving Danielle standing in front of the second house, opened the door and made his way within.

To Danielle this man grew more curious with each hour. But she had no choice but to do as he bade her.

Danielle was indeed surprised when her husband returned and escorted her into the building. The house consisted of only two rooms, a front room, containing comfortable-looking furniture at one end; at the other, across the glistening wood floor, was a desk and a whole wall containing books. The large room was comfortable looking at first glance, although it had a definite masculine feel to it.

The wood floors shone with a gleaming well-polished look and brightly patterned rugs were scattered about. The room had a number of large open windows; they gave it a cool, airy feeling. Danielle stepped farther into the room and sighed her pleasure. It seemed to suit her mood. The house was airy, fresh smelling, and neat — all important aspects to Danielle.

Christopher had left her in the front room and had taken the bags through an open door. Danielle wandered about touching a ceramic figurine here, or picking up a book from the desk and rubbing her fingers over its expensive binding there. She did not understand her husband's moods or why he would prefer to reside here in this smaller house rather than stay at the large house. But she herself would be completely satisfied, she was sure.

Hearing Christopher making quite a bit of noise and singing a light tune in the next room, Danielle slowly walked to the open portal. She stopped, surprised, as she saw Christopher stand before the hearth and pour water into a large cauldron upon the fire.

The room was beautiful; deep, plush carpet of a light multicolored pattern adorned the floor. Drapes of the same light colors hung over the large windows on the opposite wall from the hearth. In the center of the room was a large fourposter brass bed, with light-blue, sheer netting draped from its canopy, forming a soft, sensual-looking enclosure.

Christopher looked up from his labor and saw his wife standing in the doorway. A slow, lazy smile crossed his features as he saw where her blue eyes were resting. "I shall have water readied for your bath in a short time, Danielle." As her eyes went back to his and he noticed their inquiring look, he continued. "I thought that you would appreciate a long, hot bath. I know that aboard the *Sea Wind* the only baths you were able to have were sponge baths, and those only with sea water."

Danielle was surprised at his tone; she had heard it before in the past but not too often. Usually he used a hard, almost gruff manner of voice whenever he was addressing her, but on a certain number of occasions he had shown a different manner, such as now. He seemed softened and almost tender.

"Thank you," she murmured. Not truly trusting his pleasant mood, she stepped into the room.

"Your bags are over there near the bed. Perhaps you would like to hang up your gowns before they wrinkle too badly. Tomorrow I'll have one of the girls from the big house come out here and do the things that you wish done." He went behind an Oriental dressing screen and dragged out a large, round, brass tub.

Danielle quietly went about pulling her clothes and personal things from the bag she had packed aboard the *Sea Wind*. Her gowns she lightly shook out and hung up in the closet and her brushes and perfumes she set upon the small dressing table, placed near the window.

Christopher had stopped what he was doing and stood watching his wife setting about her work. She was a beauty, he had to admit. She seemd to be able to bring his blood to a roaring boil by merely walking by him, swishing her skirts.

As he saw her finish he took the water, now hot and steaming, from the fire. "Your bath is about ready," he called across the room to Danielle as he emptied the last of the water into the brass tub.

Danielle did not quite know what was expected of

her as she looked from her husband to the steaming, inviting tub of water. Did he expect her to simply undress in front of him and to leisurely take her bath?

Christopher must have sensed her discomfort for he, as though with reluctant steps, went over to where the dressing screen was and brought it over to place about the brass tub. "Perhaps this will put you more at ease, Danielle," he murmured loud enough for her to hear.

She had hopes of his leaving the room, but she was to be disappointed on this score, for Christopher walked about the bed and stood within a few feet of her. "If you would turn your back, madam, I would be delighted to play your maid this evening."

Danielle slowly turned her back to him and waited with increasing discomfort for him to perform his services. His fingers softly touched the nape of her neck as he tried to unbutton the first clasp of her gown, and Danielle felt small delicious shivers of delight pass through her body. How could this man affect her as he did, she wondered as he finished the long line of buttons. Though she had admitted that she loved this man, still she berated herself for letting herself swoon and be his willing pawn whenever he snapped his fingers.

As he slowly lowered his hands, for a second longer than was needed he let them linger at her tiny waist. Danielle stepped quickly away from his strong masculine body and, with some amount of dignity, tried to reach the safety of the Oriental dressing screen.

After undressing Danielle chanced one small glance around the thin screen, wishing to see what her handsome husband was about. With a sigh she slid into the warm, soothing water. Christopher was unpacking his own bag and putting his clothing away. She would have plenty of time to relax and enjoy her bath.

Her reprieve was short-lived though, for when

Christopher heard the splash of water, indicating that she had indeed stepped into the tub, he came around the screen.

His breath caught in his throat as he viewed his wife in the folds of the silky soft water. Her creamy skin gleamed in the candlelight; her full, rosy breasts tempted him with their game of hide-and-seek as the water covered them one minute and left them to his full view the next. Her long, golden hair was pinned atop her head, leaving small curls dangling about her heart-shaped face and the nape of her neck.

Danielle looked up with fright written on her features. She had not expected him to intrude on her privacy, but she was quickly learning that this man did precisely as he wished.

The silence that came between them was thick and noticeable, Christopher's yellow, lions' eyes tenderly caressing her body and Danielle trying her best to sink her form into the warmth of the water.

"I brought you some soap." And as he said this he also poured a dark, rose-scented liquid into the bath water.

"Thank you," Danielle murmured softly, reaching up for the creamy pink-colored soap he held in his hand toward her.

Christopher could not bear to part from the sight that was filling his eyes, so rather than leaving after handing her the soap, he stood and watched as, after smelling the rose-scented soap, Danielle smiled her appreciation and started to lather the pink soap onto her sponge and wipe the creamy substance along each arm and down her graceful neck. This was sheer heaven to her after the days on board ship where she had had only the soap aboard the *Sea Wind* and salt water to keep herself clean.

Danielle lost herself in her small pleasure and for a

few minutes forgot all about her husband, but she was once again made aware of those lions' eyes because Christopher, having left the side of the tub, returned within a few minutes, carrying a small chair and a large fluffy towel.

To Danielle's amazement her husband settled his large frame on the chair and without any kind of hesitation let his eyes once again indulge in their pastime of a few minutes earlier, that of watching his wife in her bath.

Realizing that he indeed had the right to sit there and watch as she bathed, Danielle tried to ignore those lions' eyes that seemed to be burning a fiery path upon her body.

Christopher seemed to lose control of himself as he sat and let his vision fill with the loveliness before him. His hand reached out and caressed a small tendril of hair that was now soapy and damp. "Ah, you destroy me at every turn, Danielle." He sighed, barely loud enough for Danielle to hear.

Feeling her face flush, Danielle took the sponge and tried to cover her redness up by scrubbing at her cheeks. "I am about finished, sir, if you would be good enough to hand me the towel." She wanted to get out of the tub now before her husband saw how his closeness was affecting her.

"Step out, Danielle." Christopher rose from the chair and held out the oversized towel.

At first Danielle thought to refuse, but then once again she realized that she did not have the right. This man standing before her was her husband and held all rights over her, body and soul.

She stood up and stepped out of the tub.

Christopher stared, spellbound. Water droplets ran down her body making it shine with a glistening radiance.

Danielle started to take the towel from his grasp, pulling him from his dazed reaction.

"Your beauty is breathtaking, my love." His voice was a husky caress that sent a blush over Danielle's entire body. He held onto the towel since he intended to dry his wife's body. "Come before the fire, love, so you do not take a chill."

And there before the firelight Christopher slowly began to dry Danielle's body, delighting in the feel of her womanliness and smooth curves.

Drowning in his tender words and gentle caressing through the fleecy towel, Danielle let herself be led as though a lamb to the slaughter, where her husband pulled her.

The firelight from the hearth cast a sensual atmosphere about the room which was not lost on the couple.

Danielle felt all but faint as Christopher's hands roamed over her body and when his lips lightly nibbled at the nape of her neck she felt her body lean toward his, and wanted desperately to feel his hands enfold her and to again show her the delights that his body could bring to her.

Christopher was no less lacking in desire than his wife and as though he could bear the torture no longer, with a loud groan he bent down and gathered Danielle up into his arms, his mouth bearing down upon hers with a force which told of his complete hunger and desire.

Losing herself in his soft, sweet lips and probing tongue, Danielle wrapped her arms about Christopher's neck and arched her body toward his, her own mouth seeking out and trying to capture a portion of the sweet ambrosia that was hidden from her sight. Her breasts strained against his chest as though twin burning flames, scorching where they touched and

413

bringing Christopher quickly to the side of the bed.

Laying Danielle upon the soft coverlet, Christopher, without any delay, began to undress himself. As he finished with the last of his clothes, he looked down into his wife's face. She lay as he had placed her, but now her eyes were shut tightly, her features still holding the look of desire she had earlier possessed.

With no more hesitation Christopher lay down next to the woman upon the bed—and woman she was. As his body molded against hers, Danielle let her hands roam as they would, her mouth finding her husband's, and if he was somewhat surprised he did not show it as he relaxed back upon the bed and let her have her way this night upon this large magnificent bed.

The rose scent of the bath oil and soap wrapped about Christopher's senses and as Danielle rose above him his large hands pulled one by one the pins that held the golden mass of her hair upon her head, leaving a golden curtin draped about the pair.

Danielle's woman's body moved seductively over Christopher's towering form, her silken thighs wrapped about her husband's torso as though he were a mighty steed; and with an instinct born from the beginning of time, she began to love her man.

Christopher's breathing was ragged and shallow as Danielle began to move up and down upon his body. His hands reached up and began to mold and fondle her breasts, and as she began to moan with ecstatic sob of pleasure, he increased his efforts, making his body move with a rhythmic, never-ending motion; his lips and hands seemed to ravish Danielle's body, not leaving one tiny spot untouched, rendering her senseless and gasping upon him.

From deep within Christopher's chest Danielle could hear light laughter erupting as her head rested, limp and damp from her exertions, upon the dark mat of thick, rich black hair. "Ah, my little flame, you are not finished yet. This is only the beginning." And at the finish of these words Christopher gently eased Danielle upon her back.

Danielle felt drained, completely lacking the will to move.

But Christopher would not long let his wife stay in this state of complete relaxation. Soon once again she lay moaning and writhing under his expert handling. He stormed her body as though a knight of old storming a resistant castle. His hands roamed at will, seeking and caressing; his mouth and tongue were like a fiery brand where they touched. Danielle seemed to completely melt. And then as his fierce and throbbing love tool bore down and filled her almost to bursting, Danielle's world seemed to explode with a multicolored brilliant explosion, stemming from deep within her belly and erupting from the very depths of her being. And still this was not to be the end. The fire upon the hearth burned down to light embers and the moon slowly moved above in the heavens, and still the couple upon the bed lay clasped together, their cries and moans of passion filling the dark bedchamber..

The afternoon's bright light streamed into the window between the drapes, and with a small moan Danielle opened her eyelids. As she looked about her she saw that her husband was not beside her in the bed or in the room. She at once saw that the hour was late and stretched her arms over her head and arched her body. She felt completely content this day with her life and all about her. After last night's love-making and this morning's sleep she felt that there was not a care in the world that she could not handle. Her husband had to care for her, she told herself. Though Christopher had not told her in so many words last night, she knew there was something between them that was not usual, something unique that only the two of them possessed.

As she sat up on the bed and pulled the pillows behind her head, she heard light footsteps coming toward the bedchamber door. Within minutes Christopher was standing in the portal, holding a tray of delicious-smelling food and grinning broadly.

"I thought you might appreciate something for breakfast, even though it is already past the noon hour." His mood seemed to be jovial this day.

Danielle looked toward him with some concern. "You should have awakened me. I do not usually sleep this late." Danielle did not want this man to think that she was a lazy laggard.

"Do not concern yourself, love. I even slept a bit late this morning." His eyes were full of devilment and his voice was hinting at something that he was sure Danielle would understand.

And, indeed, she did. Her face flushed to a bright scarlet as she thought of the night before and her display of wanton behavior.

Christopher chuckled loudly as he set the tray down upon the bed. "Do not be embarrassed, pet. What we did is done by most married couples."

Danielle felt her face grow even darker at his words.

"Here, sweet, let us see to this food; I fear I am starving. I have not eaten a thing since yesterday." Christopher sat down upon the coverlet and took the covers from the tray.

Within minutes Danielle had forgotten all about her embarrassment as she put her full attention on the food set before her. She was reminded harshly by the first bite of that wonderful repast that neither of them had eaten since the day before on the *Sea Wind*.

As Christopher finished, he sat back against the

post of the bed and sipped silently at his coffee. His lions' eyes watched Danielle but she still did not notice anything about her except the food on her plate.

Shortly though, Danielle looked up from her plate and with a small smile began to apologize. "I am sorry, but I, too, have not eaten a thing since yesterday."

"No need to apologize; I enjoy watching you," he answered truthfully, not caring about her reaction. "I thought that perhaps when you finished we could take a walk about; that is, if you care to see my plantation?"

"Oh, yes. I would be delighted." Danielle pushed the plate of food from her and started from the bed.

"Take your time; I am in no rush, Danielle." Christopher lingered at his coffee, and his eyes once again, as on the night before, filled with the lovely vision of his wife. Last night had more than surprised him. He had known from the other times with this beauty that she was more than enough in bed, but last night had shown him just how much she was. She had more than pleased him. He had never before met a woman with as much passion as he himself possessed, but he found that there was more than enough passion in her and with luck being on his side she now belonged to him.

Danielle was not to be calmed; she wanted to be out and about and perhaps to find out more about this strange man who was her husband. There were so many things she wished to know, but dared not ask him. Quickly and under the watchful eye of her husband, she went to her closet and pulled forth a light-pink day dress with white lace at the sleeves and neckline. She chose slippers to match and then brushed her hair out long and glowing and tied it securely with a pink velvet ribbon. Noticing the admiring shine in her husband's topaz eyes, she knew she

417

had chosen correctly.

The plantation, which at one time had belonged to Deke Saxon and now belonged to Christopher Saxon, was large and thriving and, Danielle found, absolutely beautiful.

The rest of their afternoon was spent going through the large, sprawling house and the beautiful, exotic surrounding grounds.

The house was a huge three-story structure, but for some reason as Danielle stood outside the veranda, she thought that it looked somewhat cold and forbidding. Large white columns rose up and dominated the front portion; they added to the chilling feeling that Danielle experienced.

Inside, she was no less uncomfortable. The whole house held a cold feeling. As Christopher took Danielle through the rooms on the first floor, his earlier mood seemed to change; he became stiff and withdrawn. He spoke only when necessary to explain the history of each room.

Even the servants, to Danielle, were cold and uncaring. Seeming to be almost frightened as she and her husband entered the front door, they quickly left the couple to themselves and headed to the back kitchen.

As the pair went up the stairs and Christopher showed Danielle the bedchambers and adjoining sitting rooms, Danielle could feel cold chills coursing over her entire body.

Christopher noticed, after he had entered the room that at one time had belonged to Nicole Saxon, his wife's pallor and also the way in which she held her arms about her as though she were freezing. "Is something the matter, Danielle? Come sit here for a moment." He led her toward the large canopied bed and helped her to sit on the fluffy, white spread. He could only imagine that he had tired her out in some way from his hurried pace. He had always been uncomfortable in this house, but he did not think that she would be having these same feelings.

"I am all right," Danielle murmured. She did as her husband bade her, then looked about the overelegant room. "Whose room was this?" she questioned him softly, as chill bumps rushed over her arms.

"This was Nicole Saxon's room. She was the wife of my foster father, Deke Saxon. Her taste was rather frivolous." Christopher looked about the gold-and-scarlet room.

"Why do you not live here in this larger house?" Danielle ventured.

"I am afraid that this house is not too much to my taste. And I have never had the time, or truly the desire to refurbish the place. I prefer something smaller and less extreme," he answered truthfully.

"I also find this house distasteful," Danielle added. "I think you would like Iva Rose, the Blackthorn plantation in New Orleans. The house is comfortable and loving, though it is quite large."

Christopher looked at his wife as though he had not truly seen her before, and something in his lions' eyes caught deep within Danielle's heart. His anger was apparent; she had truly made a mistake in mentioning her home. "If you have regained yourself, madam, I am ready to be on my way." He rose to his feet, not waiting for her reply, and started to the door.

Danielle watched his ramrod-straight back. He seemed so unyielding and unattainable at this moment that Danielle wanted to burst into tears. Was she to be forever on guard and watching what she said around this man? She slowly rose from the bed and followed her husband. She did not regret leaving the house behind as she stepped out into the sunshine, but she did regret her earlier words. She and Christopher had been on agreeable terms for a while and she had rather liked the easy way in which they had communicated one with the other. But now she could see, as he walked around to the back of the house, that things once more would revert to how they had been in the past.

Christopher had brought in two servants from the big house to tend to their needs while they stayed here on the plantation. The elderly black man with a head full of kinky gray hair was called Enoch and the young, pert, light-colored black girl was called Obadell.

Danielle at once took to the pair, finding the girl a lively companion and willing to anything that she was asked to do. The elderly man was polite and by the large smile he bestowed upon Danielle as the pair entered the small guest house, she knew that he was of a friendly nature.

It was late when Danielle and Christopher came back to their house and as they entered the front door they could smell the aroma of tempting food coming from the direction of the kitchen out back, a distance from the guesthouse.

Enoch met them at the door and, grinning broadly, he took Christopher's hat and told the couple that dinner would be served directly.

Christopher only grunted at the man and after introducing him to Danielle he left the front room and entered the bedchamber.

Danielle, not wishing to disturb her husband, and frightened that he would in some form show his temper toward her, walked about the front room, acquainting herself with the surroundings. She let her eyes roam over the books and, after much debating, she reached up and found one that caught her eye. It was a book of sonnets that she had not read before. This would be just the thing to help her quiet her shattered nerves, she told herself as she made her way over to the sofa at the other end of the room.

Christopher had gone into the other room and had for a few minutes thought that Danielle might follow behind. He was glad that she had not, for his mood was ugly and he knew that at the slightest provocation he was sure to burst into a storm of abuse.

He sat back upon a chair and lit a tapered cigar. It was amazing, he thought to himself; he had almost forgotten who his wife was. He took a long drawn-out puff on the cigar and his yellow eyes went over to the large fourposter bed. After last evening's play upon that bed and most of today spent in a companionable manner with the woman who was now his wife, he had all but forgotten that she was a Blackthorn. Well, he would not forget again, and if, in fact he dared, he was sure that she would remind him as she had done today. He slammed his fist down upon the arm of the chair and then rose to his feet. What was he to do with the wench? He paced the floor, trying to clear his mind of her bewitching golden looks.

He had thought that he would in a short time grow tired of her, but from that first night when he had seen her with her half-mask pulled over her face, standing all alone on the streets of Fort-de-France, he had been bound up in her unusual beauty and now instead of growing bored with her as he had with other women in the past, he found that he could not force her from his mind.

As his pacing increased, his thoughts took flame. He would have to do something with her; he could not play the doting husband to a woman with the last name of Blackthorn. And what of his crew and ship? Right this minute instead of being on the *Sea Wind* captaining her about the small islands and picking up cargo, here he was in a bedchamber worrying about his wife. Thank God he had a good man like Jamie Scott, whom he could trust with his ship and men. Jamie would get a good deal with the cargo and be back within two weeks to pick him up; and in this short time he would have to decide what to do with Danielle.

As Christopher entered the front room, his mind still in a turmoil with his scrambled thoughts, he stopped short in his tracks as he went through the portal. His wife sat, curled up on the sofa, with a book in her hands, her head laid back against the back of the couch and her eyes shut. She was sleeping and to Christopher's eyes she was the most beautiful creature he had ever seen.

For a few more minutes he stood, not making a move, just staring at Danielle. But all too soon Enoch came through the back door and started to call out to his master. Christopher stopped him short by lifting his arm. He did not want Enoch to wake his wife; this thought seemed to ease the black thoughts from his mind.

As Enoch turned and left the room, Christopher with silent steps made his way to Danielle's side. Bending down he took her soft, plaint lips with his own.

Danielle awoke with a jump, but found herself pinned to the sofa by her husband's strong arms.

As she struggled to awaken Christopher bore down upon her with a vengeance, as though wanting to punish her. His lips pressed harshly upon hers and his arms took hold of her shoulders, not letting her move from her position.

His grasp broke, though, when he heard Obadell and Enoch enter the back door to bring in trays of food.

Christopher stood straight and tall, his lions' eyes angry and taunting as they bore down upon Danielle. "It seems our dinner is ready, madam." He gave her his hand and helped her to her feet. He could feel her trembling under his hand and a tiny smile of satisfaction came over his lips.

Dinner was delicious, but Danielle could not fully appreciate the good repast. Every time she glanced up from her plate, Christopher's dark scowl would be signaled out in her direction. "You are awfully quiet this evening, love." Christopher could not seem to control his urge to hurt this woman who shared his name.

Danielle did not answer, knowing that no answer was expected of her. Her husband was doing nothing more than trying to provoke her, but she was determined not to let him get the best of her.

Finding that his wife was not going to step into his trap, Christopher once more attacked his plate.

After dinner was finished and Obadell had cleared away the plates, Danielle once more went to the sofa and opened her book. Christopher, seeing that his wife was thus entertained, went to his desk and pulled out a stack of papers that were in need of his tending.

The room remained quiet until the dark of evening. The only sound that disturbed the couple was that of Obadell entering the front room and lighting several tallow candles. She also went to Christopher's side and asked if there would be anything else needed this evening, and if not, she and Enoch would be going back to the big house.

Danielle waited a space after Obadell had left the room. Then making sure that her husband was fully occupied with his papers, she slipped from the sofa and softly made her way to the bedchamber.

She was exhausted and only wished to fall upon the

large comfortable bed and to shut her eyes and sleep. This game of wits that she was forced to play with Christopher was more tiring than one would think.

Going to her wardrobe, she pulled out a light-yellow nightgown and went behind the Oriental dressing screen. With some difficulty she proceeded to unbutton the row of buttons at the back of her gown. As she finished and stood naked, having pulled chemise, stockings, and shoes off, she heard a slight noise in the room.

Stepping behind the screen Christopher found his wife standing naked, her gown clutched to her bosom and her eyes large blue circles.

Christopher took a step closer and reached out to take the gown from her hands, but he found resistance. "Do you intend on denying me, madam?" His dark brow rose over a sardonic glare.

"I-I. . ." Danielle could only stutter and hold tightly to the material between her fingers.

"Madam, if that is your intention I shall at this minute set you straight. I have the right to do as I wish and I wish for you to stand in front of me and hand me this offending gown." Christopher's voice rose and his hand gave the material a tremendous jerk, tearing it from her hands.

Danielle felt all her calm reserve come to a boiling rage at his pulling her gown from her person. "Do you think you own me as you do your horses or your blacks?" Danielle shouted, throwing her hand out and toward the direction of the barn area. "By what right do you dare to order me about in this fashion?" Her breathing was ragged, causing her naked bosom to rise and fall rapidly.

Christopher welcomed this display of temper and admitted to himself that this was what he had wanted to see all the afternoon and evening. He relished the thought of a fight with this woman, and more than the fight he could see in his mind his conquering of her body. "Aye, madam, you *are* mine as my horses and my servants are. Even more so, you *belong* to me. Your name now is Saxon, not Blackthorn and I shall not let you forget this fact. And when I say to stand before me, you shall." Christopher dropped the gown upon the floor and with his empty hands he grabbed hold of Danielle, stroking her arms.

Danielle struggled in his grasp, his stroking inciting her to a roaring fury. "Take your hands from me, you simpleton. I will not have you pawing me."

Deep, roaring laughter filled the room and Danielle's ears. "You say to me you *shall* not have? Nay, madam, you are wrong. Your years as a Blackthorn taught you to play the haughty lady well, did they not, love? Well your future will be spent doing as I," — Christopher tapped upon his chest — "Christopher Saxon, say and nothing else will matter to you."

"You pigheaded fool, you unspeakable oaf." Danielle brought up her fist and attacked the large chest that was directly before her.

Christopher was caught off guard for a second and felt the wind leave him when her fist hit his chest. "You shall do as I say!" His mood was becoming angry and he caught her hands in his own, pulling her tightly against him. "You are mine." His lips came down hard upon Danielle's soft mouth.

Pulling and struggling, Danielle could not daunt this giant of a man who held her captive.

Christopher picked her naked body up from the floor and as easily as though she were a newborn babe he bore her to the bed. As he threw her down upon the mattress he began to pull his clothes off.

Danielle could see that what he held in his eyes was not the tenderness that he had shown her in the past.

On the contrary, he was angry and was in the mood to show this woman that he was her master. Thinking she had an opportunity to get away, Danielle tried to scoot to the other side of the bed and jump to her feet. But she soon found that she was not fast enough, for Christopher fell full-length across the bed and grabbed her about the waist. "You shall not fly from me, my pet." His words sounded like doom to Danielle's ears.

He pulled her fast against his hard, masculine body and all her struggling now was in vain. This night Christopher did not, as he had done in the past, try to arouse Danielle. He roughly rose up over her, spread her thighs, and with an urgent thrust he entered her dry and unwilling body.

Danielle cried out with the pain of being taken in such a brutal manner and once more her fists began to pound out at her husband.

Christopher laughed aloud in a cruel manner. "You shall not forget that you are no longer a Blackthorn, but now are my wife and a Saxon." He attacked her lips as harshly as he had the other portions of her body.

Danielle felt tears rain down from her eyes from the hurt she was feeling, but Christopher pumped up and down with a relentless force, his hips moving up and down until finally he relaxed upon her, spent and exhausted.

Danielle rolled over to the far side of the bed and wept silently into her pillow. She now had no hope of their marriage ever being more than what she had just seen. She would be forever a pawn in this man's life; he would never care for her feelings or whether she cared for him. There was something unnatural about Christopher Saxon, and she thought, before falling into an exhausted sleep, that she had made a terrible mistake. She should have fought him to the very end before agreeing to become his wife. Now, as he had just shown her, he could do as he wished with her.

Lying flat on his back, Christopher looked up in the dark at the ceiling. He could hear Danielle's light sobbing into her pillow and now that he had shown her his manly strength he felt himself not as proud as he had thought he would be. He had never before forced himself on any woman, let alone the woman who carried his name. He considered reaching out to comfort her, but something held him back. This woman was playing havoc with his soul and mind. He wanted to hurt her and to show her that he was her master; but at the same time he wished to take her and to show her the tenderness he held stored in his heart. He truly did not know which way to turn.

The next morning Danielle awoke to the sound of Obadell straightening up the bedchamber. Upon looking about she noticed that her husband was nowhere to be seen, so with a smile for the black girl she sat up upon the bed.

Obadell smiled back at her mistress. "Morning, ma'am. I be bringing you some breakfast shortly." She held the gown that Christopher had thrown on the floor the night before.

"Thank you, Obadell." Danielle fluffed the pillows and placed them behind her head.

"Mr. Saxon, he say to tell you that he be back this afternoon. He got some business to tend to in Fort-de-France," the girl threw over her shoulder as she hung up the gown and started out the door to fetch her mistress' breakfast.

Danielle felt some small relief at the news that Christopher was not in the small guesthouse. She would not have to face him after what had happened last night. She doubted that she would be able to look him in the face without feeling hurt and even a small bit of fury.

Obadell was gone only a few minutes and entered the bedchamber carrying a large tray of food.

"Thank you, Obadell. Perhaps you would care to sit and talk for a bit?" Danielle felt the need to talk to someone this morning.

"Yes, ma'am, if you be wanting to talk, I sure be the one to talk to you. My mamma always did say that I could talk more than any other young girl she ever did see."

Danielle started on her breakfast, as Obadell sat down upon the edge of a chair, and between bites of food Danielle questioned the young girl about all she knew of the plantation and its master.

Obadell could not tell Danielle all that she wished to know for the girl had, only five years ago, been brought to the plantation, along with her mother and three sisters.

She did tell her mistress though how she and all the blacks on the plantation felt about their master.

To Danielle's surprise the girl was full of praise and had only good things to say about her husband. All of the people here loved their master and Danielle found that they would do anything to please him. At first she had been shocked at the girl's words. How could these people love a man such as her husband? But then, after some reflection, she realized that she was truly not being fair. Christopher had only shown *her* that he could be a tyrant and a bully; he more than likely had never had to show this side of his nature to his people—unless she herself was the only one to bring these qualities out in him, she reasoned to herself thoughtfully.

Obadell also told Daniell that her mother was the

housekeeper at the big house and that she and her sisters helped to keep the house in order. Most of the people on the plantation worked in the fields and lived in the cabins on the other side of the big house.

Danielle did not bother to ask the girl if she knew anything about Deke Saxon or his wife, knowing that she and her family had not lived on the plantation long enough to know anything of them.

She was still curious about her father, and though she knew now about his death, she still wished to know more.

After breakfast she changed into a light, flower-printed dress, took her book of sonnets under her arm, and headed for the gardens. The sun was warm upon her as she sat down on the ground with her skirts spread about herself and began to read.

She sat reading thusly until noontime and then, once again entering the small house, she took a piece of fruit from a bowl in the front room and went into the bedchamber and sat upon the bed.

The heat had caused her to become a bit weary and so with nothing else to do after eating the fruit she lay back to take a small nap.

When a slight noise pulled Danielle from her sleep, she realized that it was already beginning to become dark. She jumped into a sitting position and looked about.

"I see you have enjoyed your day of leisure." Christopher's voice filled her ears, making her sigh with some relief. She had heard a noise in the room and had for a moment been frightened, not knowing what had caused this sound.

"Obadell tells me that she let you sleep and that you have not eaten supper. Nor have I, so I told her to just bring some cold meat, cheese, and bread."

Danielle did not answer, still feeling angry about the treatment he had handed her the night before.

Christopher did not seem to notice, but went to the brass tub and began to fill it with buckets of water that Enoch had brought into the room. "Would you care to bathe first, love?" he questioned, pulling his shirt off and throwing it across a chair.

Danielle of course wanted to bathe, and with some difficulty she swallowed some of her pride and stood down from the bed. "Thank you," she said and went to the dressing table and started to pin up her long, golden curls.

After filling the tub, Christopher sat down upon a comfortable chair and lit a cigar. "Are you not interested in my day, love?" He seemed to have forgotten or put from him what had occurred the night before in this very room.

Danielle glanced at him with a look of wonder on her features. Could this man be so unfeeling that he had forgotten that he had raped her last night? Was she now to play the loving wife as though none of what had happened upon that bed had truly occurred?

She was not too far off from what Christopher had had on his mind. Of course he had not forgotten what kind of savage he had been the night before. Could any man forget treating his wife in such a manner? All day in Fort-de-France he had had one thing on his mind, and that was the harsh treatment he had inflicted upon this lovely creature. Her vision filled his head at every corner, making his day a disaster. He could barely conduct his business, and when he had gone to lunch with a gentleman and tried to discuss the manner in which he would be handling his cargo aboard the *Sea Wind,* he could hardly keep his thoughts on the gentleman's talk.

This wife of his was proving more than a handful.

She was presenting a problem at every turn. But each time he had thought of her during the day, he once again saw her as he had the night before, weeping into her pillow. Her soft sobs had lingered on in his ears after his own eyes had shut. And though the purpose of his treatment of her had been to show her that she would do as he bid and to teach her that she was no longer a Blackthorn, Christopher somehow had the disturbing feeling that he was the one who was being taught the lesson.

Danielle, still not answering him, went behind the dressing screen and began to undress.

Christopher stepped to his feet and walked behind the screen. He pushed her hands away from the neck of her gown. "Let me do this for you, Danielle."

"I am quite capable of undressing myself." Her words sounded hollow and a bit chilled.

Christopher did not say anything further, but finished undoing the row of buttons. When he had finished he once again went around the screen and sat back down upon the chair, picking up his cigar and enjoying its flavorful taste.

Danielle was stunned as she sat down in the tub of warm water. Her husband was leaving her to her privacy. Was this the same Christopher who thought nothing of bullying and threatening her? After a few minutes Danielle realized that he was indeed allowing her to bathe in peace so she began to lather the fragrant soap over her body and enjoy herself.

Christopher felt tortured as he sat there and heard the splashing from his wife's bath and her sweet voice lightly humming a lively tune. He was a man who was used to having things his own way, reaching out and taking what he wished. But for some reason he felt he owed himself this small punishment of keeping himself from what he wanted most, for he would not again be such a brute as he had been last evening.

Danielle lingered, it seemed to Christopher, overly long in her bath and when she finally did step from behind the screen she was wrapped in a long, velvet dressing robe.

Christopher sat for a few more minutes in his chair and watched as Danielle sat in front of the dressing table and then proceeded to pull the pins from her hair. She brushed the golden mass out until it glistened. Christopher gave a soft, satisfied sigh as he watched his young bride. She is ravishing, he thought. He rose from his seat and went behind the dressing screen where he pulled off his boots and breeches and places his large frame in the brass tub.

The water was already beginning to lose its warm feeling so Christopher hurriedly washed himself and toweled dry. As he stepped from behind the screen he glanced about to see were Danielle was. But the room was empty; except for a glowing candle there was no movement. As his yellow eyes went to the bed he spied through the netting a form. There she was, he sighed with relief. She had not flown from him as he had feared.

Striding to the bed with nothing but the towel wrapped about his middle, Christopher sat down upon the edge and from a side table once more reached for a cigar. Lighting this from the candle flame he then snuffed the taper out, lay back down, and puffed thoughtfully on his cigar.

At the instant that her husband had gone behind the dressing screen, Danielle had made her way to the large bed and buried herself deep within the coverlet. Presenting her back to her husband's side of the bed, she tried to find some sleep.

Her ears, though, heard the slightest movement made by the man who shared her life. There seemed no getting away from Christopher; even sleep would not come to her to give her a reprieve.

Sometime later Danielle thought she heard Christopher's voice tender and soft saying the words, "Sleep peacefully, my little love." She fell back to sleep and before the morning's light she once more awoke to find herself snuggled up tightly to her husband's body. Even in her sleep she was somehow strangely drawn to this man, she fleetingly thought before shutting her eyes again.

The next day was somewhat like the first one the pair had spent at the guesthouse. Christopher brought a tray for their breakfast and he and Danielle shared this upon the large bed.

All the tension and bad feelings of the day before seemed to have disappeared from Danielle's mind and she and her husband enjoyed sharing the meal together.

Christopher, as he was sipping on his coffee, began to tell Danielle some of his plans. He had so far not confided in her, so when he did Danielle was a bit surprised.

"Jamie Scott should be arriving back with the *Sea Wind* at the first of the week and we shall then be going to England to get rid of our cargo. Jamie has been going to a couple of smaller islands in the Caribbean to take on cargo that will be of the highest value."

"To England?" Danielle sat up straighter on the bed, her eyes aglow at this news.

"Aye, to England," Christopher replied, noticing the excitement these words had brought to his young wife. He had originally decided to leave her here on his plantation, but now he was not so sure. His plan had been to make one more trip to Fort-de-France and to visit René Beauchamp to set the matter straight about his wife. The thought of meeting the other man for a minute set Christopher's blood boiling. It would be more than a pleasure to meet the villain who had dared to abduct Danielle. He would teach that French dandy a well-deserved lesson and one he hoped the other woud carry with him for some time.

But now, though the desire to face René was still hot in his mind, he was not so sure about leaving Danielle here on the island by herself. More things than René Beauchamp could happen to this young beauty.

"I have never been to England." Danielle's voice was wistful.

"It is not too much; in fact it is rather crowded and noisy." Christopher tried to soften the blow that she would be receiving by not being able to go along.

Danielle's smile filled his head. "Aye, my lord, I am sure you would think in this manner. You have been on this island for a time and a man does not feel the confinement as a woman does. I have always dreamed of visiting England."

Christopher was lost in the blueness of the eyes before him and found that he was unable to tell this beauty that he did not intend to take her along. Perhaps, he thought, it would be for the best if she did go with him. He still had not grown tired of her and she did warm his bed as no other had ever done. Mayhap by the time they returned to Martinique he would have grown weary of her and could more easily set her from him. He found himself smiling back at her. "Aye, I think you may find England to your liking."

Their next few days were devoted to leisure and pleasure. The young married couple spent most of the day together, Christopher hardly leaving his wife's side for a moment other than to check on how his plantation was running. And Danielle found that Christopher's actions as the gracious husband were much to her liking. His temper had not flared again as it had that dreadful night when he had shown her the strength he possessed. Indeed, now all that he did was with tender concern for her. At times she still found that when she was not expecting it she would turn and find his yellow lions' eyes watching her as though expecting to find something that was hidden from his view. And when this happened, Danielle could feel a chill course over her body. But mostly, he tried to be kind and thoughtful.

Danielle realized that she could almost be lulled into a sense of security, a feeling of true affection coming from her spouse, but as these feelings came to her she would again remind herself of the times he had riled and berated her for no apparent reason. She felt as though she were walking on eggshells, ever ready for his mood to change from one of lovingkindness to that of a storming beast.

Now Danielle sat in the gardens and watched as a pair of birds went about the job of gathering twigs for their nest. How peaceful it was here on the island this morning and how peaceful was her inner self. She had risen early, even earlier than her husband, and had escaped the house by coming to the gardens. As she sat upon the grass with her head resting lightly against a huge, gnarled old tree, she relived the evening that had just passed.

It had proceeded much as the previous evenings, except that when she had been in her bath, Christopher had joined her. Their love-making had been wild and carefree. Never had she known anything like Christopher Saxon; he had come into her life and had completely turned her mind and soul upside down. His hands and mouth last evening had played a sensual tune upon her flesh that still left her breathless. The silken water had added a certain exotic atmosphere to their love play, for Danielle had never experienced such feelings of pure pleasure before in her life.

She saw herself as she was last night, naked, her body glowing in the candlelight, and she saw Christopher's magnificent bronzed body stepping into the brass tub with her and pressing close against her. As he sat down in the warm water, his arms circled under her breasts and pulled her down upon his lap.

Danielle could feel his manhood large and throbbing against her thigh and the sexual tensions of her surroundings and of the man who held her tightly drove her to a heady, anticipatory delight.

Their love-making was a frolicking, wild, surge of passion. As Christopher stormed her body and opened wide the floodgates of her desire, she felt herself slipping into another world where only she and her large, handsome husband existed.

Then, her climax completed, Christopher carried her to the bed, and there, their bodies naked and still wet from the tub, he made tender, consuming love to her.

Danielle felt her breathing grow ragged and shallow as she sat with her eyes shut tightly and her head against the tree. Oh what sweet, sweet love Christopher knew how to arouse.

"What are you about here at this time of the morning, pet?" Christopher stooped down beside her and lightly kissed the tip of her pert, little nose.

Danielle smiled tenderly up at this man who, though he might not know it yet, held her heart wrapped in the palm of his large, strong hand. "I was only dreaming, my lord."

"Aye, dreaming you say?" Christopher sat down and boldly pulled Danielle's form against his chest. "You

436

have certainly found the best place to dream, my love."
He looked about at the profusion of beautiful flowers
and leaned back against the tree. "I wonder at times
what thoughts go through a lovely woman's head." His
tone was reflective, not that of wanting answers, but
thoughtful.

"Perhaps you would not care to know the thoughts
of another, Christopher." Danielle's tone also was
softly spoken.

"Aye, you may be right. I fear that for a woman
your wisdom is far above most."

"Nay, my lord. I wish 'twas truth you be speaking,
but most women are far brighter than most men give
them credit for being."

"Ah, my fair beauty, I cannot agree with you
there." Christopher gently brushed a blond curl away
from Danielle's cheek. "Most of the women I have
known have been far from bright; indeed the opposite
is more often the case if the truth were out."

"Perhaps some, my lord, but surely not all. In my
own family there have been women who have been far
superior to men and have done quite well on their
own." Danielle had not meant anything by her words.
She was thinking of her Grandmother Christine and
how she had handled the responsibility of the huge
Blackthorn fortune all by herself. But with the tightening of Christopher's muscles she knew at once she
had erred again.

"Aye, I know full well of the Blackthorn women and
their cruel ways. And if your intentions is to follow in
the footsteps of those before you, I warn you now to
have a care." Christopher's anger was apparent and
devastating as he pushed his wife from him and stood
up.

"How dare you talk of my family in that manner!"
Danielle also was angry. She brought her hand up to

slap the offending face that was glaring down upon her.

Her small, dainty hand was easily caught by Christopher's larger one. "I had thought by now that you would have realized that I dare what I please. It seems that I have told you this before. Must I prove again to you this simple fact?" His lions' eyes were shooting angry sparks from their depths as he brought his face to within inches of hers.

Danielle could control her emotions no longer. Ever since she had known this man her world had been turned upside down and she never knew when or where he would turn on her. So now as he glared his hatred down upon her, she burst into tears. "You are a brute and I hate you," she cried, trying to pull free from his grasp.

Christopher held her for a moment longer and then of a sudden released her. "I shall teach you at another time how to control that waspish tongue of yours, my wife. But for now I have not the time." He turned about and started from the gardens. "Do not hold dinner for me. I shall be late."

Danielle, on hearing his words, ran back to the house and to the safety of her room. What a mess she had made of things once again. But how was she to be constantly on guard for what she said? She knew now that what had sparked off his towering anger was her mentioning anything about the Blackthorns. At that simple slip of her tongue he had become a thundering wild beast. She wept harshly into her pillow.

What hurt her most was the contented bliss that they had shared these past few days; but once again she reminded herself that though she had felt the same happiness before, she also had felt this same pain despite her caring.

For the remainder of the day Danielle stayed locked

up in her bedchamber, claiming to Obadell that she did not feel well and only wished to rest. She even skipped her meals, not feeling up to eating the food upon the trays that were brought to her chambers.

Christopher himself was in a furious mood as he rode his big, black stallion into the town of Fort-de-France. What did the wench mean to do? he questioned himself, keep throwing her mother up in his face? Was all her warmth and loving some kind of farce? Was she truly cold and unfeeling, only waiting for the right minute to thrust the barb of her biting sword deep into his flesh?

For a minute he was reminded of Nicole Saxon. This was the type of woman she had been—cold and calculating. Even her home had held that same cold feeling and for that reason he had never been able to live in the big house. Was his wife truly this type of woman? Her mother also had appeared sweet and innocent on the surface, but she had been the cause of Deke Saxon's death, had she not? And was not his wife's last name Blackthorn? Though he could try, he knew that he would never be able to change this fact.

He rode his horse along the waterfront and tied him up in front of a tavern he frequented when in town. He felt his stomach growling for its meal and, entering the building, found himself a table.

Before he was finished with his breakfast, he spied a gentleman with whom he had done business in the past and asked him to join him. It was too early to start drinking!—and that is precisely what he felt like doing—so instead he conversed with the gentleman and inquired of him if he would be needing anything transported to Europe in the near future.

And indeed the gentleman did have some valuable pieces of china and silver which he would have Christopher carry with him if the price was agreeable.

Christopher left the tavern with the man and the rest of the afternoon was spent going over what the man wanted shipped and then having a few glasses of brandy with the gentleman in his home.

Upon taking his leave of this man Christopher returned to the same tavern in which he had breakfasted, but now as he had not before, he ordered a bottle of whiskey.

He had tried to put his wife from his mind all day and now he wished to wash her beautiful face from his thoughts witha bottle of liquor.

Sitting in a far corner all to himself he drank slowly and reflectively of the liquid. But he found that the more he drank the more his mind became plagued with demons. Danielle's face rose in and out of his brain; she was laughing, smiling or lying in his arms on the large brass bed. These were tormenting thoughts for him to bear and the more they persisted the more he drank.

The hour was growing late but still Christopher sat in his lone corner, and whoever chanced near him could hear the large, dangerous man mumbling in his cups.

For the past few hours, the barmaid had refused to bring him any more to drink, so the proprietor was the one who braved the lions' den. Christopher had roughly ordered the girl from him when she had offered him her services upstairs. His temper had seemed to snap at her invitation. "Damned women, all they think of is to ensnare a man," he cursed loudly, shoving her halfway across the large room.

He did not have to take a hag, such as the one who had been bringing him whiskey, to bed, he thought drunkenly. He had a far more tempting morsel awaiting him at home. Again Danielle's golden locks and small perfect-shaped face came to his mind.

As he was sitting like this with his head bent down and his thoughts on his wife, a small group of men entered the tavern. Their loud, boisterous voices caused Christopher to throw a glance in the direction of the door.

His lions' eyes, hooded behind his dark lashes, watched as the group made their way to a round table and the four men sat down and shouted for a bottle. Christopher could not believe his good luck, for René Beauchamp was among them. And with his black mood there was not another man in all of Fort-de-France he would rather have seen this night.

Without a second thought, he pushed his chair from him and approached the group of men. René's back was to him so he did not notice the large, angry man come up behind him, but his companions were immediately aware of the angry set face and storming yellow eyes on the man who strode in a few short paces to their table.

Two of the men stood up, their faces revealing their concern about what this fellow wanted with their group.

Christopher, emitting a bellow of rage, grabbed hold of René's jacket and shirt at the nape of the neck and brought him to his feet, his chair falling in the process.

"What the—" He never finished as he glanced around and saw who had hold of him.

"Did you think I would let your dirty work go unpunished?" Christopher's angry voice cut through him like a knife.

René tried to twist out of Christopher's grip, but all he could do was half-choke himself by his efforts. "Wait a minute, Christopher, let me explain," he tried to reason.

"You scum, save your explanations for some other fool. I know your kind, René Beauchamp, even though some innocent females may not."

By the tone of Christopher's voice, René knew that all was lost and when he felt the pain on his chin and himself being flung across the table he had earlier been sitting at, his thoughts were to pray to the Lord.

As Christopher jumped over the table and grabbed René's shirtfront, once again the three other men and the proprietor tried to intervene. But like an angry lion Christopher shook them off. "Begone. This is between me and this offal that calls himself a man," he shouted at the group of men.

"Mr. Saxon, be reasonable," the owner of the establishment shouted, grabbing Christopher's arm as he was about to smash it down on René's face once again. He did not wish this kind of affair in his tavern. Too many bad repercussions could be aroused from a man such as this Mr. Saxon doing damage to René Beauchamp. "Take your fighting from my building if you insist on having this affair out." The proprietor was a large man himself and his face was now a beet red from the exertion of trying to keep Christopher's arm in the air.

One of the gentlemen who was in the group with whom René had entered also pleaded with Christopher to come to his senses. "If you must test the better man's mettle, have some care and do it as gentlemen," he shouted.

For some reason this thin man's voice reached into Christopher's drunken mind and he eased up some on his hold on René. "As gentlemen you say?" He eyed his opponent. Then he threw back his head and deep loud laughter filled the inn. "This man is no gentleman by any means, sirs." He stood to his feet, leaving René where he had dropped him with his first punch.

"But as you say, this thing should be settled in the proper way. I shall meet you in the morning before dawn, Mr. Beauchamp, on the outskirts of town. You may choose the weapons. It matters little to me, for you shall not see another sunrise."

René stared on in horror. "You are jesting?" he got out.

"Jesting? Nay, I am serious. Unless you would rather take your punishment now?" He cocked his head toward the man, wishing that René would say that he would. Christopher rather enjoyed the feel of that soft flesh upon his fist. "You dallied with the wrong woman and now you will have to pay."

"How so? She was not attached and surely you saw that I did her no harm." René tried to get himself out of the predicament in which he found himself. There was no way he could fight Christopher with sword or pistol, even fists. The man was a killer and if he even for a moment thought that he could win with any of these weapons he knew full well that he would be only fooling himself and would not live long to enjoy his life after tomorrow morning.

"You ask how so? Let me tell you, René." Christopher bent down and spoke with a deadly, savage tone. "The woman you abducted is my wife."

All in the tavern who were within hearing range became quiet, and watched René's face turn a beet red. "Danielle Blackthorn, your wife?" René sputtered, not believing his ears. The little baggage had spurned him and become this blackguard's wife?

Christopher saw his look of disbelief and was quick to reassure him. "Aye, my wife. And no scum such as you shall touch her and live long. Tomorrow morning I shall be awaiting you." He then looked to the man who had told them to settle this affair as gentlemen. "Do not let him forget this appointment."

The gentleman nodded his head. "I shall be his second and make sure that he is on time, sir."

"Good." Christopher nodded, turned from the group, and retrieved the bottle still sitting on the table he had earlier occupied. "Innkeeper," he shouted toward the group. "I shall be in need of a room for the night."

The large man hurriedly made his way to Christopher and led him up the stairs to a small room. Before leaving, the man turned and spoke. "I did not know what the fight down there was about. Had I known that it was concerning your wife I would not have come between the two of you."

"Do not concern yourself. All will be out in the morning." Christopher entered the room, sat down upon a chair, and started to pull his boots off his feet.

"I shall come up myself and wake you in the morning. Perhaps you would let me have the honor of being your second." The man truly was concerned and wished for Christopher to know that he in no way condoned René Beauchamp.

"Fine then, man," Christopher replied, taking another long drink from the bottle. "I'll see you in the morning."

"My name is Robbie, Mr. Saxon."

"Ah, Robbie be it? Well, Robbie, I had better get myself some rest now so I shall be fresh in the morning. Be sure to wake me." Christopher fell back upon the bed.

"That I will, sir, that I will," the innkeeper replied leaving the room and shutting the door tightly behind him.

Christopher beat his fist into the lumpy pillow trying to find a comfortable position to fit his head. His last thoughts were of his wife; in his mind he could see her lying soft and innocent in their large fourposter brass bed.

It seemed as though Christopher had no sooner laid his head upon the hard pillow than he heard Robbie knocking and calling to him from the outer door. "It's time, Mr. Saxon. You had best hurry; you don't want to be late."

Christopher grumbled a reply and sat up, rubbing his sleepy eyes. "Come on in, Robbie," he shouted as he stood up and pulled his pants on.

Robbie stuck his head through the door and stated, "I'll be downstairs, sir, in the main room fixing you a drink to clear your head; and I'll have my girl, Mat, fix you something to fill your belly. I woke you early so you would be having plenty of time."

"Thanks," Christopher mumbled as he poured a pitcher of water over his head; droplets scattered around the small room.

Only a few minutes had passed before Christopher was sitting at a large table, sipping a mug of hot liquid and eating cold meat and bread.

Robbie came around from the back of the tavern carrying a bag and humming a spirited tune under his breath. "I have something here for you, sir." He threw the leather bag upon the table.

Christopher watched with mild interest.

From within the bag Robbie pulled out a beautiful inlaid box and then proceeded to pull out a velvet cloth wherein was wrapped a fine hand-tooled sword.

Christopher's look was one of amazement now as he watched the man open the box and display two perfect dueling pistols.

"Aye, sir, I have all the tools you'll be needing for this morning's work." Robbie busily laid out the assortment of weapons.

"These are quite fine weapons, Robbie," Christopher murmured as he stroked the sword handle with admiration.

"They surely are, sir. I acquired them from a gentleman in Londontown, I did. I'm afraid that the gentleman offered his weapons and his life to me one fine afternoon."

Christopher looked with new respect at this towering man. "I'll thank you for their use, Robbie."

Robbie once again with loving hands wrapped the sword and placed the weapons back in the leather bag. "If you're of a mind to be on your way, sir, I have already had your stallion and me own steed saddled and they should be waiting out in the front."

Christopher now was anxious to be done with this affair and to be getting back home. In the back of his mind he worried about Danielle. He had not been separated from her since he had become her husband and the woman was so unpredictable and hard-headed he was unsure of how she would react to his not coming home all evening. "Then let us set to and be on our way." Christopher rose and, slapping Robbie on the back, he and the innkeeper left the tavern.

The streets of Fort-de-France were deserted at this time of the morning; the only sound coming to the two riders' ears was that of the steady clopping of their horses' hoofs.

Christopher and Robbie were the first to arrive at the appointed meeting place, and as they watched the sun just starting to rise they also spied three horses coming toward them.

Christopher felt himself become keyed up when herecognized the man in the middle as René Beauchamp. His blood was raging through his veins with a steady, pounding surge.

"Good morning, gentlemen." The gentleman who

last night had proposed this resolution, pushed his steed ahead of the others until he was in front of Christopher and Robbie. He dismounted and gave his salutations. "I wonder, Mr. Saxon, if I might have a private word with you?"

Christopher nodded his head and walked a few paces from where he had been standing with Robbie. "What is it you have to say?" He was in no mood to talk. He wanted this affair over and René lying dead.

"Sir, I am afraid that we have behaved rather hastily in this affair of honor. Things are no longer done in this form. Besides being illegal, quite a bit of talk could come out of this whole process. I beg you to consider what it is that I have to say."

Christopher stood relaxed and in control, watching this young man. "Go on, sir," he said as the man paused for a minute and ran a forefinger around his collar.

Arnold Bitely was not used to having to plead another's case, but he did feel some responsibility for what was taking place here this morning. When he had arrived at René's apartment, his servant had blocked the door and told him that his master was not at home. Arnold, finding this statement hard to believe, had pushed the man aside and made his way up the stairs and to René's room. There, René Beauchamp lay, snoring upon the coverlet.

He had harshly shaken the other man and pulled him from his sleep. "You must hurry, René, the time grows short and Mr. Saxon will be waiting for you at the edge of town."

René had sat up on the bed and with blurry eyes had lightly said, "I have no intention of meeting Christopher Saxon this morning or any other."

Arnold Bitely had looked at his friend with shock. "Man, your honor is at stake here. You cannot lie abed and act as though nothing is taking place."

"Quite right, Arnold, I do not intend to sit here or lie abed. I am glad you have awakened me. I found out last night that the ship the *Dawn Bell* will be leaving Fort-de-France this morning and will be heading to France and I, my good man, intend on being on her deck."

"You are not serious, René? I cannot believe that you would run away from this man like a common coward. Think of the rumors and your family. We shall all be affected by your infamous actions if you persist in this line of thinking." Arnold was more than outraged, he was becoming angry with this man who was lying abed and acting the coward. He had only known René a short time, but he would never have thought him capable of such conduct. Any man who was challenged to defend his honor or himself by another was obligated to do so or be labeled the lowest kind of coward.

René sat up now and glared at his friend. "You are not the one who has to face this Christopher Saxon. It is I who shall be the one who stands before him." René's face was a beet red, as he tried to defend himself.

Arnold tried to go about this in a different direction. "Perhaps I can talk this Mr. Saxon into accepting an apology, René. Perhaps he would call the affair to a halt if asked."

René seemed to become a bit more confident at this suggestion. "Do you think it possible?"

"The man was drunk last evening when he attacked you. Perhaps this morning he also realizes that to fight in this fashion would bring only bad results." Arnold doubted what he was saying, but he would tell this coward anything so as not to be labeled the friend of a man who fled to France to avoid a duel of honor.

René rose from his bed and began to dress. "Do you think it will work, Arnold? I have thought all the night of how to get out of this affair, but the best I could come up with was to board the *Dawn Bell*. I hated the thought of leaving the island and my mother and father, but for a time I did not think it possible any other way."

"Yes—yes, I am sure he will listen to reason," Arnold replied. "Only hurry we do not want to be late. James is to meet us at the end of this street."

But now, as Arnold stood before this huge man who looked as cool and composed as though this sort of affair happened every day to him, he was not too sure that his friend would live out this day. "Mr. Saxon, I know that your honor has been abused sorely by Mr. Beauchamp, but, sir, my friend wishes that you accept his humble apologies and call this whole affair to an ending." There, he had said it. Now it was up to this man whose yellow eyes were shining with almost an animal brightness.

A slanted, cruel smile came across Christopher's lips. "Your friend has much need to apologize, sir, but I am afraid that I am not the one for him to make them to. You see, sir, I have already been pulled from my warm bed at this early hour and I would not wish for my comfort to be disturbed in vain."

"Your answer, sir?" Arnold knew what this man meant by all his fine talk, but he wanted to be sure.

"My answer is nay."

"There is no changing your mind?" He felt he had to try.

"You are a true friend, sir, but I say nay once again. The culprit shall pay for his actions." With this, Christopher turned and made his way back to his second.

Arnold also turned and went back to the two men

with whom he had arrived. They had dismounted already and were standing at a distance awaiting him. As he told René the outcome of his discussion he thought for a minute that the man might faint dead in his tracks. His pallor turned to snow white and his lips began to tremble, but within a short time he seemed to regain himself.

"Fine then. I have given him a chance; if he refuses, then the folly is his own. Let us have an end to this wait," René told his companions, surprising them with his courageous talk.

The two groups converged in the center of the empty field and it was Robbie who questioned what weapons would be needed and pulled open his leather bag.

As he opened the gold inlaid box containing the pistols, René at once took hold of one. "This will do nicely." He checked the ball and prime. There was no way he would fight Christopher Saxon with a sword. He had heard too many stories of the many battles with pirates and other cutthroats that the captain of the *Sea Wind* had won. He would not be cut to pieces by this man's strong arm. At least with this gun he might have a small chance of hitting him before he himself could be shot.

Christopher grinned evilly into René's face. "Fine choice. I would have made the same." He also reached into the box and took out the other pistol.

René swallowed hard as he absorbed the meaning behind those few words. Christopher Saxon intended to kill him and there was no way out.

"Gentlemen, if you are ready?" Robbie questioned, shutting the box and putting it back into the bag. "We shall proceed."

Both men nodded their heads, René a bit more slowly than Christopher.

"Then if you will both stand back to back. Begin to walk at the sound of my voice counting out the pace of twenty, whereupon you will both turn and fire at will. Each gun has one ball within its chamber that is to be used." Robbie's words sounded loud and ominous in the clear, quiet field.

Both Christopher and René did as told and stood back to back, their legs moving a step further with each sounding of Robbie's large, booming voice.

On the sound of twenty Christopher swung about, aiming his pistol, but René did not even think to aim. His only thought was to fire before Christopher Saxon could and to try to harm him before he could shoot his gun.

This proved to be René Beauchamp's mistake. The bullet which came from his pistol cleared a good two feet from Christopher's head and as he saw what he had just done his legs began to tremble as he faced his deadly opponent.

Christopher's lions' eyes glared his hatred for this man he was facing, but he waited before pulling the trigger completely back. He wanted René to suffer for what he had dared to do to Danielle. He wanted him to squirm as he had made his wife do in that run-down building. He also wished to see the fear that was written on his face before he pulled the trigger. And all of this was plainly before him. René Beauchamp was a lowlife coward who could only stand up to woman and children. He squeezed the trigger, enjoying his view of René's fall to the earth.

With easy strides Christopher made his way to his opponent and glared down at his squirming form.

René's screams of pain could be heard throughout the clearing in which the group was gathered and in the surrounding woods. And as he writhed in pain, holding on to his arm he wept over and over. "You shattered the bone; the bone is shattered. Help me, help me."

Christopher was not quite done with this man. Though he had wished him dead he did not quite have the cold deliberate deadliness that was needed to aim his pistol at the other man's heart. As René writhed in pain, Christopher brought his boot down, pinned the bleeding arm, and bent low to René's pain-contorted face. "I could have killed you just as easily. Never again come near me or mine. If you do I shall not let you off so easily." He turned then and with his second, Robbie, he mounted his black stallion and left the two men to care for the screaming René.

After giving Robbie his profound thanks, Christopher left the other man who was headed into Fort-de-France and he reined his horse's head in the direction of his plantation.

He felt somewhat better now after showing René Beauchamp that neither he nor anything that belonged to him was to be trifled with. And indeed that little golden-haired beauty who was his wife did belong to him. Though at times he wished to strangle or throttle her, she was still his and nothing would ever change this fact. With his thoughts on Danielle, he kicked his horse on to a faster pace. Perhaps she would still be abed and he could with some maneuvering slip in beside her. He thought back to the last night they had lain together and his blood began to pound through his body.

As Christopher reined his horse within the barn and dismounted, he felt some apprehension wash over him for some hidden reason. He looked sharply about, but did not notice anything out of the ordinary.

It was still not very late in the morning so when he entered the small guesthouse he was somewhat surprised that both Enoch and Obadell met him at the front door. "Good morning, Enoch, and you also, Obadell. Is it not a bit early to be about?" he questioned. Still the feeling that something was not quite right persisted.

"Why, yes sir, it sure be right early," Enoch responded while quietly hanging his head. "I'm afraid, sir, that the missy ain't here if you be a-looking for her," he added after a few seconds.

Christopher's lions' eyes bored into the old gray-haired Negro's. "What do you mean by 'my wife is not here'? Where is she then?"

"Why, sir, I not be a-knowing. She woke up the first thing this morning, had Obadell help her to dress, ordered a horse saddled, and went on her way. I asked her if'n she wouldn't be a-wanting to wait until you returned and she didn't answer me, sir."

As he looked at the two black slaves, Christopher's face began to cloud with his anger. "Did she mention to you, Obadell, where she was going?"

"No, sir." The girl shook her head back and forth. "She sure didn't. But, Master Saxon, sir, she be dressed in the strangest outfit." With his questioning look, she added, "She have on a pair of tight men's breeches and a silky shirt." Obadell, as both men could see, was plainly upset by her mistress' behavior and so was her husband.

Swinging around, he stomped from the house, shouting toward the stable for the boys to saddle his horse back up. As he entered the building the second time he noticed something he had missed earlier. One of the mares which stayed in the barn at night was not in her stall. Danielle must have taken her for her escape.

And escape, he knew in his mind, she was trying. He would have to hurry if he wished to catch her. He knew without a doubt where she was headed. She would not venture toward town, for she might have run into Christopher on his way home, and the only other place where she could find safety would be the Blackthorn plantation.

He swung his leg over the horse's back and was galloping out of the barn. He would teach her this time who her master was and teach her good. She would not so easily again take up and run when she thought his back was turned. He whipped his horse to a faster pace as his eyes took in the tracks on the trail that were made by the smaller horse that Danielle was riding.

The sun was climbing steadily up in the sky and still Christopher had not caught a glimpse of his wife. Now that he had had more time to simmer down, thoughts of her hurt and alone, thrown from her horse, or having come to some other harm came to his mind. He now felt more anxiety for her safety than anger at her leaving. There were so many things on the island that could harm a young small woman like his wife. There were animals, and then there were men. Also, she did not know this section of the island and could become lost or thrown from her horse.

He pushed his mount to a harder pace and after a time with a sigh he reined up in front of the Blackthorn plantation house.

Hurriedly he ran up the front veranda and beat upon the door. His need to see his wife now tempered his anger; just the need to fill his eyes with her vision, to make sure that she was all right.

Ellie answered the door before Christopher had the chance to knock it from its hinges. "What you be a-wanting Mr. Saxon?" Ellie's face showed her surprise at finding Christopher Saxon beating at the front door.

"Where is she?" At Ellie's look of wonder he went

on, "Your mistress? Where is she?"

"Why, sir, she ain't here no more. She done left days ago to go back to her mamma." Ellie could not understand this; she would have thought that Danielle would have told this young man her plans to return to New Orleans.

"She hasn't been here then?" Christopher's face registered his concern.

"Why no, sir. If'n you be wanting to see Miss Danielle you going to have to do some traveling. She done gone like I told you."

Christopher did not stay to talk, but turned about and hurried to his horse. If Danielle was not here by now something must have happened to her. How he could have missed her was a mystery to him. After the sun had come up in the sky and dried the dew he could no longer follow her tracks, but her tracks as far as he had been able to follow them were headed in this direction. He kicked his horse's sides and once more started to backtrack the way he had come.

After a sleepless night Danielle had risen before dawn, not with the intention of running away from her husband, but with the thought of showing him that she was not a woman to be taken lightly. She had decided while lying abed that she would take a horse and ride over to her own plantation.

She would not be treated as lightly as he had so far treated her and because he had not come home the past night she was seething with anger. He more than likely had spent the night in the arms of some street wench. She stormed about the room, throwing clothes here and there. She was sure that with his sexual appetites Christopher Saxon had not spent the night alone. So she intended to teach him a lesson. She would not be here when he returned and he could worry about her for a change.

When she had finally found the clothes she was seeking she called Obadell into her bedchambers, wishing the other girl's help so she could hurry with her toilet.

Once in her breeches and shirt she left the house and entered the barn. Having picked out a chestnut mare and had one of the stable boys saddle it for her, she left her husband's property.

She followed the trail that led to the other side of the island, enjoying her ride through the cool, lush foliage. Her mind for the past few days had been so jumbled and full of worry that now she let herself go and relaxed upon her mount.

She was anxious to see Ellie and Jake once again, but as she was nearing the Blackthorn property she noticed a trail forking off from the one she had been on. It was one that she had never noticed before. She decided after only a second's thought to follow it and to see where it led. It was early and Ellie would more than likely still be abed so she had plenty of time.

Christopher also had found the same trail and after a moment's hesitation he, too, led his horse into the thick, lush jungle which encroached on the winding path. The tail led around a small mountain, which abounded with trees of all description and flowers of every color. It was as though he were in another world. He prayed that his wife had seen this path and had decided to take it, but he knew that he would follow it to the end to see what would be awaiting him.

It was quite some time before Christopher saw full sunlight from the end of the trail and when he reached it, he reined in his horse and caught his breath.

The view before him was beautiful, a large, glistening pond spread out and circled by deep, lush, green grass. As he cast his eyes about the area he saw tied to a tree, the mare that had been taken from his stables. A slow, lazy grin spread across his features as he also caught a glimpse of a golden sea nymph, floating near the pond's bank.

It was Danielle and she lay upon her back with her eyes shut, drinking in the sun's rays.

Christopher gently walked his mount back toward the trail. Near a tree he dismounted and shed his clothes. He himself would take a swim, he decided, his thoughts of his wife already turning to desire.

With silent footsteps Christopher neared the water's edge. He stood, bold and bronzed, his desire apparent as he watched his wife.

Danielle, who had been swimming for some time, had rolled over and lay floating on her back, letting the cool water soothe her and the sun's rays soak into her naked flesh. She felt no fear here in this secluded spot, but as she lay with eyes shut, for some reason she felt a presence near her. Cautiously she opened her blue eyes a crack and tried to see about her, and there, directly in front of her to her horror, was her husband. She jumped as though to run, but instead went under the water and came up spitting. "You!" she exclaimed, not believing it possible for him to be standing there.

"Aye, my beauty, it is your husband." Christopher's teeth flashed pearl-white as he grinned tauntingly at her.

"But how did you find me?" She now stood in waist-deep water, her bosom heaving with her exasperation as she glared her anger at her husband.

"Did you think that I would not find you, little pet? Do you after all of this time know so little of me?"

Christopher taunted her, wishing to teach her this time that nowhere could she hide from him, that she was his woman, and would do all at his whim.

"You do not own me, my lord. I am not your slave that you can lightly order about." Danielle tried to appear brave in front of this huge beastly-looking man.

"Come here to me, Danielle." His words were spoken softly, but his tone allowed no getting away from what he wished.

Danielle shook her golden, wet curls back and forth as she stared into his lions' eyes which were shooting dangerous sparks of anger daringly into her own deep-blue orbs.

"I said come to me." He took a step toward the water and his wife also took a step, but one backward.

Danielle felt true fear as she watched Christopher's every movement. She had already been a victim of his cruel anger and she had no wish for another scene such as that one, burned across her memory, of the night when he had raped her.

"Danielle, do not be lacking in wits. Do as I tell you." Christopher's anger now filled his every word and manner.

Without an answer, Danielle dove into the water and with sure strokes tried to gain the other side of the pond.

Christopher smiled with pleasure. Something about this secluded area and his wife's naked form kept his spirits high instead of clouding his mind with his anger. He would still have to punish her, but now his intent was to punish her with more pleasure than pain. He also dove into the crystal-clear water and with very little exertion he slowly gained on his wife.

Danielle glanced behind her one time and saw that Christopher was no longer on the pond's bank, but found him only a few feet away from her. She intensified her strokes, trying to put all her strength into each hand that went over the water and kicking hard behind herself.

But all that was to no avail, her husband was an expert swimmer and with little trouble and in no time he was upon her. The water was deep where they now were and, as Christopher reached out and grabbed hold of Danielle, she felt herself grow faint from her fear of reprisal for her actions, and almost with a desire for her own death she went under the water.

Christopher at first thought this a game of hers to obtain her freedom until he saw that his wife was not coming back above the water. But he still held her by the waist so he forced her up out of the water and with all of his strength he swam to the shore.

Danielle was half-unconscious when Christopher carried her and laid her upon the soft, cushioned grass. Tenderly he cradled her head and wiped the tendrils of hair from her pale face, his thoughts in a panic as he viewed her still form.

All too soon, though, Danielle sat up choking and spitting up the pond's water. As she breathed in large gasps of air, Christopher noticed that tears were coming from her eyes.

Gently he brought his hand out and wiped them from her smooth cheeks. He realized that her tears were due more to her fear of him than her near drowning and it cut him to the quick that he had caused such panic in her. "Rest easy for a minute," he whispered, holding her still against his chest.

Now that the floodgates of her tears had opened, Danielle seemed powerless to shut them. She wept openly with great wrenching sounds. The past days of living as Christopher's wife with the attendant conflicts and emotions all came to the surface at this minute, and without being able to stop, Danielle covered her face with her hands.

"There, there, pet." Christopher felt his heart melting because of her tears and he tried to comfort her as well as he could. He had never had to comfort another soul before and now he found himself not quite knowing how to give the tender consideration that a woman needed at a time like this.

Something in his voice that had not been there before caught in Danielle's mind. An understanding of which she had not thought him capable. For a minute her tears stopped and her eyes looked deep into his, trying to seek that which she had not known before.

Christopher also felt something different about this moment and as Danielle looked up into his face his lions' eyes probed deep into her blue, liquid pools. Slowly, as though all motion about them had ceased, Christopher brought his mouth down and covered the pink tempting petals which were waiting for his possession.

Danielle's body leaned toward her husband's, not wanting him to release her. Wishing for more and more food for her craving body, she wrapped her arms about his neck and pressed her bare breasts against the black, curly mat of hair on his chest.

The feel of Danielle's hard-tipped breasts and her velvety smooth skin drove Christopher into a frenzy of desire. His lips made small kisses over her face and along her neck, his tongue tasting and teasing, probing and plundering.

Danielle could taste the cool sweetness of his lips and moaned with her desire. She seemed inflamed by a world of bittersweet passions. How could she so easily be pulled into this maelstrom of lust and wantonness? her mind for the barest minute berated her. But as Christopher's hands roamed over her lower body all such thoughts fled.

The green grass smelled sweet and of the earth as Christopher lay Danielle down softly upon her back. His heart pulsated upon her heart, his mouth plundered her mouth, his thighs covered her silky smooth thighs and as one they were joined by the act of love.

Christopher's lips went to Danielle's ears into which he whispered husky, incoherent words of love and endearment. Anticipating their desired effect, his body worshiped hers with a tenderness and gentleness she had never known before.

Danielle was driven to a unique feeling, one that she had never quite known before. Her husband was making love to her as though she were all that mattered, all that he would ever care for, and this feeling reached deep within Danielle's soul, touched off explosive sparks in the foundations of her being, and brought them up as though an erupting volcano were melting all obstacles and barriers.

"Christopher—Christopher," she called out, holding on to his large, tanned back and crying over and over that one name as he brought her to the pinnacle of her womanhood.

At the same time she found this all-consuming climax, Christopher's lions' eyes gazed down into his wife's passion-filled face, and something in her look touched off a quickening feeling deep within his chest. He did not want to love this woman who was a Blackthorn; he had no desire to be bound to her by any strings on his heart, but there was something between them that he would not deny. And though he hated the thought of what this might be, he knew that one day he would be forced to face these feelings which came over him as he looked upon this golden creature.

His large hands tenderly stroked the creamy

smoothness of her cheeks. His lips once more sought out the honey taste of hers and his body slowly moved, so that he was brought to the peak of pleasure that only this woman could bring him.

Afterwards, both lay upon the lush grass in each other's arms. Neither spoke for a time, but each enjoyed the feel of the other and the solitude and beauty abounding about them.

Christopher did break the silence sometime later. "Do not think you can escape me, Danielle. I shall never let you go away from me." His words were spoken softly as he lay flat upon his back and watched the movements of the cloud overhead, but there was a tone in his voice that told Danielle these were not mere words said for the saying.

"I was not leaving you, my lord. I but wished to visit Ellie and Jake." Danielle's words were also softly spoken.

For a few minutes no reaction came from Christopher, but after a time he rolled back toward his wife and took her passion-swollen lips with his own. "Do not be hasty in your judgment again. I am not one to let my wife roam about at will and unprotected."

As a small spark of anger ignited deep within Danielle's blue eyes, Christopher was quick to add, "There are too many dangers on the island for a woman alone and with your beauty."

This seemed to calm Danielle a bit and once again her eyes became a deep, tranquil blue. "I truly did not think that my leaving would be that upsetting."

"Let us not make mention of the affair again." Christopher stroked her neck, her bosom, delighting in the way that her nipples swelled and in the flush that covered her face and neck. "I am sorry that I could not get back to the plantation last night, but I had business to settle the first thing this morning."

Danielle tried to put what his hands were doing from her mind and to concentrate on his words. "I was worried when you did not come home, Christopher," she mumbled not wishing for him to know that she truly had been furious and eaten green with jealousy.

"It will not be happening again. Jamie Scott should be coming with the *Sea Wind* tomorrow evening."

"So soon?" Danielle sat up, excitement in her voice.

"Aye, tomorrow evening," Christopher knew well her cause of joy. She was anxious to have her first visit to England. He, too, sat up and then rose to his feet, and giving Danielle a hand, he swept her up into his arms and carried her to the water. "There is no sense in wasting this beautiful day, my pet. We can worry about Jamie Scott, the *Sea Wind,* and England another time."

Danielle's laughter filled his ears as he jumped into the warm, tempting water with her in his arms. "Aye, my lord, 'tis a fine, beautiful day," she wholeheartedly agreed.

This night as she had in the past Danielle dressed in a warm, long-sleeved dress, knowing that the cool night air and the ocean spray from the oars on the boat would more than likely bring her a chill if she did not dress with caution. She had debated wearing a cloak, but decided that if she were to become too cold she would, as on that other night, wear her husband's sea jacket.

For a few minutes as Danielle stood at the dressing-table mirror combing out her long, golden hair, she thought of her husband. She felt her breathing catch as she went over the past days. Yesterday and this day had been the best days of Danielle's life. Christopher had never been so considerate or caring. She knew

463

with a certainty that this kind and gentle Christopher was the man whom she loved and wished to spend the rest of her life with, but at times like this as her thoughts roamed in this vein she was plagued with doubts. He had all too often in the past shown that his temperament was not always kind and gentle. He could change within a moment and become an angry beast who didn't care for her feelings or desires.

"Are you about ready, love?" Christopher walked into the bedchamber and strode to where his wife was finishing her toilet. "You look ravishing," he breathed kissing the nape of her neck.

Danielle leaned back against this powerful man and smiled into his face from the mirror. "Thank you, my lord, and all of my things are ready. Enoch can carry them back down to the beach whenever he wishes."

"It is already beginning to darken outside so we had best go down and await the *Sea Wind*. Jamie sent word that he would have the small boat sent ashore as soon as he arrived." Christopher himself picked up the bags that were sitting in the middle of the floor.

Danielle, as she started to the door, turned and glanced about the room. She had an ominous feeling that she would never again be seeing this bedchamber, so she let her eyes roam over all its contents. She had experienced some memorable moments behind these walls and she did not wish to forget them.

After Danielle said her good-byes to Obadell at the small guesthouse, Christopher, Danielle, and Enoch started out on the path that led to the beach.

As they stepped onto the white, sandy beach they could see the *Sea Wind*. She was already anchored and had sent her small boat, with two men rowing, in their direction.

As the men rowed their captain and his wife to the larger ship, Danielle watched Enoch grow smaller and smaller in the distance. She had no strong love for Martinique, so she knew that she would not be longing for this tropical island. She turned her head about and watched as the *Sea Wind* came closer. She would look to the future and try to have a happy life with her husband, she thought silently.

As Christopher and Danielle climbed aboard the *Sea Wind* by the rope ladder, Jamie Scott shouted out his welcome and gave them his hand. " 'Tis good to see you, lad, and you too, lass," he greeted them. "Our trip was prosperous and our hull is full, Captain." As he said this to Christopher his eyes took in Danielle. Her cheeks were flushed and she looked lovelier than he had ever seen her.

"Fine, Jamie, fine. I am glad I have a man I can depend on such as you," Christopher said, taking Danielle's arm and steering her toward their cabin.

Jamie followed along behind, telling his captain about their trip and the cargo they had loaded.

"I'll be getting you something warm to drink now," the kindly first mate said as they entered the cabin.

"That will be wonderful," Danielle rejoined. She had become chilled during the boat ride to the *Sea Wind* and still she did not seem to be able to get herself warm.

As Jamie started back out the door he turned and smiled at Danielle. "It is nice to be having you back aboard, ma'am. And I think that your visit surely did you some good. You look quite beautiful; you be reminding me so much of your mother at this minute."

Danielle smiled her appreciation at this dear man. "Thank you, Mr. Scott."

Christopher scowled darkly at his first mate as he

465

made his exit, and then with a penetrating glare, he turned his yellow eyes upon his wife. The words seemed to pound across his brain. "You remind me so much of your mother at this minute." It was true, and again for a time he had almost forgotten who Danielle's mother was. He harshly scolded himself for playing the fool over a Blackthorn woman. Without saying a word, he turned about and stomped from the room.

Danielle looked at her husband in wonder as he turned his hateful glare upon her and stormed from the room. What had she done now? She tried to search her mind for any slight misconduct on her part.

Oh, she was tired of this whole affair, she raged as she pulled her clothing from its bag and began to put it where it belonged. She just could not please this man to whom she was married and there was nothing that she could do to change this fact.

Jamie returned with a cup of hot, steaming tea and also a look of pity on his features. He, too, just minutes ago had tasted his captain's temper. What could have gotten into the younger man was beyond him, but if Danielle had changed on the island and had grown more lovely, her mate had indeed grown angrier.

For lack of anything better to do, Danielle paced about the cabin for a time after Jamie had left. Christopher had as yet not returned to their cabin and as the time of his absence increased, Danielle's anger also rose with it. How dare he do this to her? she stormed. To dump her in this room and then leave her without a word.

She angrily pulled a nightgown from her drawer and changed out of her dress. She chose a clinging, satin creation with daring splits up the sides that rose to her waist and were held together in the front by only tiny ribbons. She would tempt this angry beast who was her husband she thought, and then she would play the cool maid when he fell under her spell.

As this idea played boldly across her mind, she pulled the pins from her hair. She would wear it loose and flowing since Christopher had so many times in the past said that he liked it best that way. She brushed her golden curls until they glistened with a silken texture. She then splashed herself with a lilac-scented perfume and stepped back to look in the small mirror hanging on the cabin wall.

She would tempt him and whet his appetite, and then she would scorn him with her cold manner. In this way she would see how well he enjoyed being treated as though his feelings mattered not a whit.

As the room grew darker, Danielle lit a candle and placed it near a chair in order to be able to read. She would be sitting and reading her book of sonnets when her husband would enter the room and she would at her leisure give him her attention.

All of Danielle's plans had been played out finely in her mind, but as she sat and waited and the time grew later and later, she found herself yawning from her sleepiness. Her plans would be to no avail if Christopher were to enter the cabin and find her fast asleep, she warned herself sternly, sitting up straighter in the chair and trying to focus her eyes upon the print in the book.

It was dawn when Danielle jerked herself awake and out of the chair she had been sitting in throughout the night. Her blue eyes went about the room; she quickly noticed that her husband had never come back to their cabin.

With some anger mingled in with self-pity Danielle stomped over to the bed and flung herself down upon its frame. She felt an overwhelming desire to tear the gown from her body and rend it into a thousand pieces. How dare Christopher not even come back to their room so as to give her the desired vengeance she wished? her mind ranted furiously.

After a few minutes her weary mind and body fell back into a troubled sleep, that was filled with dreams of her handsome husband's arrogant face.

The next time she awoke she rose from the bed and dressed in a thin cotton gown. The weather on the *Sea Wind*, because they were still near the Caribbean, was warm and humid. For this reason Danielle donned a gown of light, pale peach with low-cut bodice and short sleeves. She brushed her hair down her back and pulled the thick mass back with a matching ribbon. She was indeed breathtaking this morning, though there was no one about to appreciate her sparkling beauty.

Shortly after she had finished with her toilet, a knock sounded outside the door. In response to her call to enter, Jamie Scott came bearing a tray of food.

He smiled a faint, apologetic smile toward her as he set the tray upon a table. "Is there anything else you be a-needing, ma'am?" he questioned, his sympathy plainly with his captain's wife. He truly felt that the lad was a cad for his treatment of this young woman.

Danielle shook her head from side to side, swallowing hard before she could answer. "No, thank you, Mr. Scott, this will be fine."

"All right, lass, I'll return later for the tray." The first mate left the cabin, his heart heavy because of the girl's treatment. He wished there was something that he could say that would ease her plight.

Danielle could tell by this kind man's tone and his mood that he and probably every one of the crew knew the whereabouts of their captain last evening. As he left the room she felt tears come to her eyes. She tried to harden herself and her heart to Christopher's harsh treatment, but she found that she could neither eat the food before her nor think of anything else but her husband.

Her days before going to Martinique and after her marriage to Christopher had been spent reading and sewing, but as this day drew on, her thoughts could not stay on either subject. They constantly strayed to her husband. More than likely, she thought, she would not see him again until he once more needed to slake his body of its built-up desire. But each time during the day when she would hear footsteps outside the doorway, she would expectantly be waiting for the door to the cabin to open and for Christopher to stride boldly into the room.

Once more, as on the previous evenings aboard the *Sea Wind*, Jamie Scott brought Danielle her dinner. But still Christopher did not come to see her. She looked sharply at the first mate as she noticed that his mood was not the same as it had been this morning. Instead he seemed rather gay and almost pleased with the life about him. How could he or anyone else be so happy when she was miserable? She did not voice these thoughts, but kept them to herself. Fortunately Jamie did not wish to converse with her for she thought that if he said one word about her husband she might just break down and tell him all her thoughts. She breathed a sigh of relief when he deposited the tray on the table and then left the cabin.

After eating a few forced bites of the food upon her plate, Danielle, as she had the night before, went to her drawer and pulled forth a nightgown. However, she did not choose this dark-blue gown as a means of tempting her husband, but rather for its cool and comfortable lines. She roamed about the cabin for a time, going for a minute to look over some papers that held Christopher's bold handwriting. Then, finding only boredom in this direction, she sat down and tried to read. This, too, she had no desire to do, and within a short time the book lay upon the chair and she was walking about once again. It was only a short time after dark, but Danielle decided that the only thing for her to do was to go to bed. Perhaps sleep would free her from her tormenting thoughts. Blowing out the candle on the table she lay back upon the bed. Her heart felt as heavy as a piece of rock. She did not know what she had supposed last night would have brought about between herself and her husband. She imagined to herself that she would have scorned his loving lips and skillful hands and that he would have fallen upon his knees and begged her for her favors. Tears, great crystal drops of water, streamed down Danielle's cheeks. This had all been a terrible dream; her husband would never fall to his knees and beg her for anything. And she also knew that at his first kiss, her own lips would turn traitor and melt under his desirable mouth. And those hands, just the thought of the pleasure that she had received from them in the past made her tears flow even heavier. She knew now that she would be forever this man's slave; he had only to snap his fingers and she would do his bidding — and she also knew that she hated herself for this weakness.

As she lay there weeping softly, an exhausted sleep came over her; in that sleep she was able to share the perfect happiness she wished to have with the man she loved. Her dreams were of soft words and gentle looks and strong tender arms circling her and protecting her. She willingly would have stayed within these dreams and never awakened, but as though her dreams were becoming reality, Danielle was pulled from her slumber and into Christopher's arms.

"No," she mumbled once more, though even in her

sleep-laden senses she knew that her resistance was of no concern to him. What this man wanted, he gained, and no amount of saying no could stop him.

"Go back to sleep," he scolded her, pulling her tightly up against his chest. "I find my bed softer than the floor of the deck of the ship." He held her tightly against him and breathed in the lilac scent of her hair, letting his own mind fall into a light slumber.

Danielle did not speak, but instead let herself be lulled into a sense of security, of being strongly protected and cared for. As though her dreams were coming true, she snuggled tightly against him.

Sometime later during the dark of the night, Danielle awoke to Christopher's lips and hands exploring her body and bringing her to ecstatic peaks of pleasure.

"Ah, love, you fairly drive me wild with desire," Christopher whispered, making Danielle think for a moment that she had not heard him correctly. How could he treat her as he did? she reflected as he stormed her body and soul. He seemed like fire and ice: one minute passionate and loving; and then the next, for no reason apparent to Danielle, he could be as cold and unmoving as a north wind. She told herself that she would never understand this impossible man, but for now she sighed from the pleasure he was bringing to her; she would not try to reason him out. She would take what tenderness he offered and gladly be his puppet. No other man was his equal; no other could fill his place.

The next day followed like the last, only on this day Danielle questioned Jamie about her husband's whereabouts. Christopher had not been in bed next to Danielle when she had awakened. After last night's love-making she had expected a kind word from him before his departure. At least a kiss before he left her side, or a good-bye.

The answer that the first mate gave Danielle was simple enough. "He must tend to the running of his ship, lass. The captain is a busy man."

When Danielle nodded her head to indicate that she now understood what detained her husband, Jamie Scott offered a bit more. "I'm afraid the captain can be a hard man at times, lass, but he's a good man at heart. As a boy he had a hard life and I'm afraid he finds it a bit difficult to trust people at times."

Danielle smiled her thanks to this man who showed that he truly cared for her peace of mind. "Thank you, Mr. Scott; I appreciate your taking the time from your busy day to talk to me."

"That's all right, lass, I enjoy talking to you," Jamie truthfully replied.

After the first mate left the cabin, Danielle found her day as she had found others aboard ship—boring and endless. She read and she paced and she wondered if tonight her husband would decide to sleep in his cabin or on the deck of the *Sea Wind*.

That night as she lay sleeping she felt the heavy weight of her husband lie down upon the bed and she felt herself being pulled into his arms.

This was to be the routine for Danielle for the next few weeks. Christopher always came to their cabin after Danielle had gone to bed; and always when she awoke in the morning she would find his pillow empty and cold.

The only person she ever had a chance to talk with was Jamie Scott and she valued these talks and his friendship.

The only event which broke the monotony of this trip for Danielle was the storm that awakened her one night to find her husband already gone from the bed.

She felt the ship pitching and rolling; then she heard the raindrops which bombarded the *Sea Wind*. Great roaring thunder and flashing streaks of lightning filled the cabin and Danielle burrowed deeper within her covers.

She had never before been on a ship during a storm and she did not much relish the idea now. She found that she mostly stayed abed for the next two days. The *Sea Wind* was a worthy ship, but the storm that had surrounded them was powerful and mighty, throwing the ship about at will, and Danielle found that when she tried to walk about the cabin she more than likely fell or stumbled and lost her footing.

She did not see her husband during these days of bad weather, but Jamie Scott came as often as he could to bring food and to assure Danielle of the *Sea Wind's* capabilities.

He knew that the young girl was frightened but that her husband could not spare the time to tend to his wife's fears; all of his strength and attention were needed on the deck of the *Sea Wind*. Many a ship had been brought to the bottom of the sea by a captain who did not put his full attention to her care.

The storm was a small one. It lasted only two days and another evening, but the captain neither rested nor stopped for a single moment until the last of the treacherous winds had died down.

In the morning that Christopher did enter his cabin, Danielle had already eaten and made her toilet, but she quickly ran to her husband's side when she saw the weakened condition of his body.

He looked fatigued and weary; his black, damp hair was strewn about his face, and his face itself looked years older. At once Danielle saw the piece of bloody cloth wrapped about his left forearm and she gasped aloud with her worry.

"Let me help you, Christopher." She wrapped her arm about his waist and helped him to sit upon a chair.

"I am fine, Danielle; do not worry on my account. I only need rest. The storm is over." He seemed too tired for even these few words.

"Hush and let me help you." She started tugging off his high knee boots and brought water and towels for him to wash himself with.

As she started to pull the cloth from his arm he pushed her away. "Get me a clean shirt," he ordered and himself undid the blood-soaked cloth. It was only a small gash, but the blood had flowed because of its depth. Christopher washed the offending cut with water and left it as though it were of no concern.

Going over to the bed, he lay down and as soon as his head hit the pillow his eyes shut.

His arm lay off the side of the bed and Danielle, seeing this, went to his side and pulled up a chair, after getting medicine and bandages from Christopher's sea trunk.

With quiet skill she wiped the cut clean of any blood and filth that Christopher himself had overlooked. Then she packed the wound with salve and gently bandaged his arm. For a moment her hand lightly caressed the strong bulging muscle on his upper arm. Even in his sleep he held a power over her body. It was an all-consuming power that gently swept all thoughts from her mind except those of her husband. Shaking her head she tried to clear her head. Christopher needed his rest; she could not chance waking him by her silly desire to feel him.

It was late that evening before Christopher once more opened his eyes. He stretched and yawned as he came awake and looked about with his tawny eyes.

Danielle was sitting across the cabin doing some light sewing and as his eyes filled with the gentle vision of her performing this easy task, his gaze softened. This is how he would have imagined a husband and wife behaved. She doing her woman's work and caring for her husband, and he trusting completely and fully in her generous heart and tender love. Quickly, though, he pushed these thoughts to the very back of his mind. This woman had the blood of her mother and he always would have to be on his guard while she was his wife.

Danielle's blue eyes rose, caught, and locked with those of her husband. She had been drawn from her sewing to look in his direction but as she gazed at his face she saw the anger and distrust with which he glared her way. She did not rise and go to him as she had earlier envisioned herself doing upon his awakening; instead she sat, frozen, watching his hate-filled features. She was the first to break eye contact as she lowered her eyes once more to her sewing.

Christopher sat up and as he did so he noticed that his arm was bandaged. His glance once more went over to his wife. It would seem that she must have been busy while he slept. With one quick glance he noticed the care she must have taken with the bandaging of his arm, but instead of softening toward her his scowl seemed to darken. He rose from the bed, and, pulling on his breeches, he left the cabin without a word thrown in her direction.

He was gone only a few short minutes and returned with Jamie Scott following in his wake, carrying a tray of meat, bread, and cheese and a pot of steaming black coffee.

Danielle did not get up from her sewing, but watched the two men talking while Christopher ate his fill. It seemed that the storm had not in the slightest

475

harmed their course; if anything the winds had pushed them long faster.

Christopher smiled at this news and seemed to relax somewhat; propping his feet upon a leather hassock he lit a cigar and sat back to let out a swirl of smoke.

"You don't need to worry yourself, lad. I'll be tending to the ship this night. You just rest yourself. You did enough during that storm," Jamie advised his captain as he started to the door.

Christopher did not answer his first mate, but only smiled his thanks to the man. When his mate had left, the captain of the *Sea Wind*, at his leisure, enjoyed his cigar, and as he had earlier from the bed, he watched his wife.

Danielle felt those cold topaz eyes upon her and after a few minutes of this unbearable torture, having stuck the needle twice in her finger, she threw her sewing into its box and stood up from the chair.

She felt her body's weariness from the past few days' of worry and sleeplessness due to the storm, so, with no further thought, she decided to go to bed.

Since she had been aboard the *Sea Wind*, this was the first evening that Christopher was present in the cabin when Danielle had to change and bathe before going to bed. And though she was not modest, she felt some embarrassment at having to change in front of this man who was sitting and watching her with his glacierlike eyes.

Obtaining her nightgown she placed it upon the bed and turned her back to her husband. Her small hands roamed up the back of her dress and slowly unhooked the buttons. Pulling the gown from her body, she stood in only her satin chemise; and with some ingenuity she brought her nightgown over her head. As it slowly went over her body she pulled the chemise down her form.

Christopher's loud laughter filled her ears and brought quick embarrassment over her features. "Take the gown off, Danielle, and come over here."

His words were like a whiplash striking out at Danielle's body. She stood paralyzed, not daring to do as he commanded.

"Do as you are told, woman." Christopher's impatience sounded in his voice.

With slow, trembling fingers Danielle gathered the gown to begin to bring it over her head. She knew that not to do as this man told her would only bring her harsh punishment. Had he not already shown her that she was barely more than his slave? As she brought the pale gown over her head, she did not turn about, but stayed standing with her back to her husband. Why did he wish to humiliate her in this fashion? Silent tears made a path down her face.

Christopher's eyes filled with Danielle's lavish curves, the gentle sway of her hips, her trim back, and rounded buttocks brought a rise to his manhood so that it nearly burst from its confinement.

"Come here." His order was a throaty, sensual sound coming from deep within his chest.

Danielle could not move; nor could she say him nay. Her head shook from side to side, her golden curls shining about her body as its only covering.

Christopher realized that his command was more than she could obey without thoroughly damaging her pride. On silent feet he came up behind her, his tanned, large hands going over the back of her body. He sighed aloud, pulling her up against his form.

Danielle could feel the heat and bulge from his manhood as he pressed hard against her and his hands reached around and cupped her breasts. Her tears now were not from the harsh treatment this man inflicted upon her, but from the feelings of passion that he evoked in her traitorous body by only the slightest touch.

Christopher had wished to show this woman once more that he was the stronger and that she would do as he told her. He would not for a minute let her think that her Blackthorn blood was special in any way. But with the feel of her soft body under his hands his harsher side softened as it always did, and he could not fully teach her what he wished. She was a woman with fire and passion, one made only for love and only for him. He turned her about slowly and looked deep into her face, trying to find in those violet-blue eyes the answers to his questions. How was this woman different from all of the others he had known? How could she hold this power over him, so that he could neither think nor sleep without her invading his mind? There had to be an answer to all of his questions, he told himself, as he slowly brought his hand up and wiped away a lone tear on her cheek. His heart tore when he thought that he had once more made this small golden beauty weep. His lips lowered and softly tasted the salt from her tears. It was a long and penetrating kiss, one that searched and sought out; as though Christopher thought that this was where he would find the answers to all of his questions. Perhaps those soft, pink petals held more than just gentle words.

As Danielle's lips were released she leaned, trembling and shaky upon Christopher.

Once more with his forefinger, he brought her chin up so he could view her pure, heart-shaped face more fully. "You blind me with the beauty before me," he whispered softly. "Never have I met a woman quite like you; I cannot seem to fill my eyes and body with enough of you."

These words of love surrounded Danielle with a

pleasant, hazy intoxication. She knew, deep within her heart, that he did not mean the words that he had whispered to her, but she needed them and craved them as she needed food and water to sustain her body. She reached up on tiptoe and gently touched her lips to his, her pride gone where this man was concerned.

With a groan, Christopher began hastily to pull his shirt and trousers from his body and then pushed Danielle down upon the bed, lying atop her.

Danielle lay pliant and soft beneath him, her will bent as though their minds were but one as he made the motions of love and she responded to each thrust and movement, bringing both their bodies to a flaming climax at the exact same time.

No words were said or needed as the couple lay entwined together in the after-throes of their love-making.

The pair fell asleep this way, and once more during the night they roused themselves and delved into the delights that only they could bring to each other.

For the next few weeks Danielle's life followed the same routine. She busied herself cleaning the small cabin during the morning hours; then she would read or sew, trying to fill her hours with something to occupy her hands. Late each evening Christopher would climb into their bed and make sweet, passion-filled love to her, filling her body's every need and never leaving her lacking. But as the morning's light filled the room she knew a sadness that replaced her husband's tender touch; she would find his side of the bed empty and disturbingly cold.

Her only conversation during the day was with Jamie Scott, as it had been since boarding the *Sea Wind*. She longed to become closer to her husband.

There had to be a way to touch his ice-cold heart. But as time passed her wishes did not become reality.

Then one day Christopher came to the cabin at noon. Danielle, who had been sewing on a sampler that she had started on Martinique, had looked up with surprise written on her features.

He did not favor her with a look or gesture for a moment, but went directly to his desk and sat down. He went through his papers, pulling out some charts and spreading them before him, he finally leaned back in his chair and looked at Danielle, his lions' eyes taking in her unique beauty.

She was dressed in a rose-print gown with creamy satin lacing along the border of the neck and sleeve cuffs. And from the top of her golden head to the tips of her cream-colored slippers, she looked to be perfection itself. "We shall be arriving in port soon." His soft words reached Danielle's ears.

Her face came alight. "How soon, Christopher?" To his ears she sounded like a child and a small smile came over his face as he watched her drop the sampler she was working on and run to the porthole, as though she would see land stretched out before her.

"It will be but a few more hours. I doubt you can see anything from there, my pet."

The disappointment was visible on Danielle's face and a small tug of pain came over Christopher's heartstrings.

"I'll come back for you when land is in sight and you can watch from the deck." He had allowed her hardly any freedom aboard ship, for fear of the crew paying some disrespect to her, and now he could see that the weeks of confinement in the cabin had taken their toll and that she was in definite need of this small treat.

"Oh, thank you, Christopher." She whirled about

and then walked over to where he was sitting. "I shall try to stay out of everyone's way." She and Christopher had barely talked in some time, but she found his mood pleasant now, so she expressed herself fully.

Christopher quickly rolled up the charts on the desk and gathered them under his arm. "I shall send my first mate to call for you when land is seen." With these words he once more was gone from the room, leaving Danielle to the quiet of the cabin.

She walked impatiently about the room, swishing her skirts as she went to and fro. In only a few hours they would once more be back on dry land; her heart raced with glee. She could not keep herself from going back time and again to the porthole, though now she knew she would see nothing.

To make time go at a faster pace, she, for the second time that day, dusted and went over the cabin, making sure that everything was in order.

Danielle's first knowledge of being near land was the sound of someone shouting, "Land ho."

A few minutes later Jamie Scott was at the door of the cabin telling her that the captain had sent him to escort her to the deck to watch the ship dock.

Danielle hurried after the first mate as though afraid she would lose sight of him at any moment. He directed her to a spot, near the rail, that was clear of the congestion made by the crew who were getting everything ready for docking, and there she hurriedly made her way.

She looked about and finally saw her husband, shouting out orders to his men and doing heavy work himself where needed. Once, while he was near, his eyes rose and met Danielle's and for a brief minute both were held as though by some magical string that pulled them toward each other.

But quickly Christopher looked back to what he was

doing and tried to put his wife from his mind. It was hard enough to keep his thoughts off her when she was encased in the cabin, let alone on deck and tormenting him, he thought harshly.

When the green land rose up and Danielle could make out the shapes of buildings and other landmarks of the town called London, Christopher came and stood at her side.

"We shall not be in port long." He said this as though to no one in particular.

Danielle looked at her husband with visible disappointment. "I had hoped to do some shopping and perhaps look at some of the sights. I have never been to Europe before."

"I shall not have the time for such matters." His voice sounded harsh, but when he saw the look of complete dejection on his young wife's face he softened his tone somewhat. "I have business matters to attend to, Danielle. Perhaps I can see if Jamie would mind taking you about where you would wish to go. Though I am making no promises."

Once more Danielle let her mood soar. She would be able to talk the kindly first mate into being her companion, she was sure. He was her friend and friends did small favors for one another, she reasoned as she looked on at the town spread out before her.

"Where will we be staying, Christopher? At an inn?" she asked hopefully, already anticipating the excitement of leaving the ship and setting foot on dry land once more.

Christopher answered truthfully, "I had thought to stay aboard ship, seeing as how we would not be in port for very long." But this, too, he decided against, after watching her gay features drop a little at his words. "But I suppose that we could take a room at an inn or a tavern. I imagine that you would find it a relief to be in a room which did not roll and pitch?"

Danielle instantly saw that he had changed his mind because of her and she at once tried to let him know that she would not be disappointed if they stayed aboard the *Sea Wind*. "An inn would be nice, but I suppose that it would be more practical to stay aboard ship, since, as you say, we will shall not be here overly long. Also, all of our clothing is here on ship."

"No, I have made up my mind; we shall stay at an inn. Mr. Scott," he called over his shoulder as he saw the man walking by.

"Yes, sir." The first mate stood at attention.

"See that some of my wife's things and my own also are made ready to go ashore." At the first mate's look of inquiry he added, "We shall be staying at an inn. You also may wish to bring along a few things."

"Yes, sir," Jamie Scott said and turned about to do his captain's bidding.

Less than an hour later the *Sea Wind* docked in London harbor and Christopher was soon handing Danielle down the gangplank.

With Danielle in the middle and Christopher and Jamie on either side of her the trio left the waterfront and made their way to an inn in which Christopher had once before stayed.

The inn to which Christopher brought them was clean and the proprietor was friendly, but Danielle felt dozens of pairs of eyes following her as she crossed the large downstairs front room where dinner was served and went up the stairs to their rooms.

Christopher also saw where the men's eyes rested and before going into the room with his wife, he told Jamie Scott to order dinner for them and to bring it to their room for this evening.

Danielle was surprised by the furnishings of the room; she had been in only one other inn and that had been on Martinique. And the rooms on the island, though well-appointed and neat, had been small compared to the one her husband led her to now.

The first thing that took Danielle's eye was the large brass tub sitting in a corner, and immediately she walked to it and let her hand rest upon the rim.

In only a few minutes Jamie brought up the trays of food, and before leaving Christopher asked him to see that the innkeeper had some hot water brought up for a bath.

Danielle smiled her thanks, but he did not seem to notice as he put his fork to his food.

Their dinner was eaten in silence; they did not seem able to talk or converse with each other. And as soon as Christopher had finished what was on his plate he stood up and told Danielle that he had business to which he must attend and that he would not be back until late.

Danielle did not answer, but sat with her hands folded in her lap and stared at her plate. She reminded herself that she had wanted this man as much as he had wanted her, and shame filled her heart, causing her face to turn red. What kind of marriage had she stepped into? She had thought to bring this man to his knees and to make him care for her but she had only succeeded in having someone share her bed and the thought of those nightly trysts added to her shame.

Christopher stood still for a moment and watched her pale features turn from creamy white to a bright red. "Dad blame," he murmured as he turned from her, grabbing his jacket and leaving the room.

Jamie Scott returned for the dishes and told Danielle that her water would be up shortly. At least she would have the pleasure of a warm bath, she told herself.

She lingered in the bubble bath until the water, which had been hot, turned tepid. She had pinned her blond curls atop her head and had leaned back against the rim, letting the heat and the soothing feel of the water work its wondrous effects upon her tired body.

She pulled herself out of the water with reluctance, but told herself that the water was now cold and tomorrow she would have another bath. After her long days at sea having only sponge baths, this was a luxury she hated to give up.

She was asleep instantly, after dressing in a sheer, yellow nightgown. She did not even hear her husband enter the room and light a small tallow candle, but slept through his silent perusal of the aftereffects of her toilet and of his beautiful wife peacefully sleeping upon the large fourposter bed.

Danielle did not find her life much changed from what it had been on the *Sea Wind*. After breakfast in the common room, Christopher once more escorted his young wife up the stairs to their room; and after seeing her safely within, he told her of his need to be on his way to tend to business.

Jamie Scott was left behind at the inn to watch over his captain's wife, but this did little to lift Danielle's spirits because she knew she was not allowed to leave her room until her husband told her that she could.

A few times she was tempted to try to outwit Jamie and to sneak out of the room, but quickly she realized that Jamie would be the one to take the blame if something happened to her and she also realized that she had changed in the last few weeks and some of her adventurous feelings had deserted her.

One evening Christopher announced that they would be leaving London the day after tomorrow.

Danielle hung her head as she finished the meal set before her. As on all the other evenings since arriving at the inn they dined alone in the confines of their room. Jamie Scott would at an appointed time bring up trays of food; and after eating his fill, Christopher would excuse himself, telling his wife not to expect him early.

Danielle felt absolutely deflated; she had sat day after day in this room. She had only been allowed to leave to have breakfast in the early hours of the morning with her husband. She would have had more freedom, she thought, if she had stayed on the *Sea Wind* and let Christopher conduct his business from his ship.

Christopher watched as his wife slowly ate her food. She seemed not to be hungry and even looked a bit peaked; he hoped she was not coming down with anything. That was all he needed—to be saddled with a sick female. "I was thinking, Danielle, perhaps you would care to go looking about the London streets tomorrow? You could do a bit of shopping if you wish."

Danielle was ecstatic and jumped to her feet, not able now to sit and finish another mouthful of her meal. "You are serious?" she asked as though she could not believe her ears.

"Why, yes, I am serious," he answered, smiling and leaning back in his chair and lighting up a cigar. "I would not play you falsely, Danielle," he added as he enjoyed her excitement.

Danielle hurried to her wardrobe to decide which gown she would wear on the following day. Her enthusiasm was obvious as she bustled about. "Have you asked Jamie if he will mind escorting me, my lord?" she asked over her shoulder, careful not to glance in her husband's direction.

A look of pain and jealousy passed over Christopher's features for the barest of moments. He had forgotten his words aboard the *Sea Wind* when he had told his bride that he would not have the time to be bothered with her and that she would have to be content to have Jamie Scott take her about town. Now, to his disappointment, she was ready and even willing to have the other man escort her. He rose to his feet, his good mood gone and replaced by a wish to hurt this woman whose last name he could not forget was Blackthorn. "Do not concern yourself with my first mate; he shall do as I tell him — as my wife had best not forget to do." He turned and started to the door, feeling Danielle's eyes now, not on her clothing but turned in his direction.

Danielle had turned upon his angry tone. What had she said to cause him to become so hardened toward her? she questioned herself.

As Christopher reached the door he also turned in her direction and his lions' eyes met and held her blue ones. For a moment his desire to reach out to her was almost overpowering, but since arriving at the inn he had made it a habit to stay out late until he was so tired he wished only to fall into bed and to sleep, so now pride stiffened his backbone and he turned about, slamming the door after him.

Walking away from the wardrobe, her gowns forgotten, Danielle went over and lay across the bed. How had things gotten so out of hand? she wept. She had hoped to show this man how much she cared for him so that he would succumb to her charms. Oh, she did not at first fool herself and she knew it would take some time for Christopher to trust her and to realize that she was not as he had at first thought; but the way things were now going he seemed to hate her more with each passing day. Her body did not even hold the power it had once held over him. She was sure that he would not long put up with her as his wife, but would more than likely deposit her either on Martinique or on some other island and be on his way as though she had never existed. Her tears ceased after a time and she fell into an exhausted sleep.

Christopher, after leaving his room, went down to the common room of the inn and ordered a goblet of brandy. He had pulled up a chair at a table near the hearth and now sat broodingly watching the flames as he sipped at the liquor.

Jamie Scott had looked on as his captain had come down to the large room of the inn, but not wishing to disturb Christopher, had stayed where he was, sitting in a far corner by himself. His captain looked rather out of sorts this evening, he thought. Him and the missy must have had another row. He shook his head, hating the thoughts that were rampant in his mind. His captain was wrong and was behaving like a spoiled young lad, who was not getting his own way. Why could he not see that he was in love with the girl and try to work out what was eating at him. Jamie knew that if something was not done soon, things would be too far gone to improve. He decided that perhaps he could talk a bit of sense into the younger man's head. Had he not been the one to tend to him as a lad and hadn't he taught him all he knew after Deke had been killed? At least he owed him his opinion.

As the first mate approached his captain, he noticed as he came closer that the man was indeed in an angry mood. He decided not to speak too soon, but instead took the opposite chair at the table and set his glass gently down.

Christopher looked up at this man whom he had found invaluable in the past and all he could think about was that his wife would rather have his first mate about her than her own husband. It never entered his mind how unreasonable he was being and that his wife had good reason to be close to Jamie Scott. His only comment as the other man took a seat was to grunt in his direction and then to bring his brandy back to his lips and turn his eyes in the direction of the fireplace.

"You be looking a might rugged this evening, lad; is it something you might be a-wishing to be getting off your shoulders? You used to be able to tell me all your troubles," Jamie ventured, not being able to stand the pain on the young man's face another minute.

"It is none of your concern."

"Perhaps if you talk about it, things will not be so hard."

Christopher slammed his goblet down upon the table and glared at the man in the opposite chair. "Leave me be, Jamie, before too much is said."

Jamie himself was beginning to get angry. Who did the lad think himself to be? He thought that he could treat the young woman up those stairs any way he wished, but this young whelp was not going to tell Jamie Scott what to leave be. "I have always loved you, lad, but I tell you this here and now. I be thinking that you are a bit addled. You have the finest woman I have ever known up those stairs and you treat her as though she were of no concern." Christopher held up his hand to silence the other man, but Jamie was not to be put off. "I'll not stand for it much longer, lad." He rose to his feet and was glaring down now at the younger man. "And if you think that you can start treating me in your foul manner you had best start looking for a new first mate. For I'll tell you this, no man or young whelp such as yourself is going to tell Jamie Scott what to be doing." His words spilled out without letup, and then when he was finally at an end he turned like a fierce warrior and stomped out of the inn, not giving Christopher a chance to have a say.

Christopher sat watching the coals burn down in the hearth until the early hours of the morning, Jamie Scott's words being replayed over and over in his mind. His anger had been apparent. His face had turned an angry shade of red before the first mate had finished, but when Jamie had left Christopher had had only one recourse — and that was to think of what he had said. Christopher was not a stupid man and he realized quickly that he had wronged Jamie Scott and he fully intended to make amends. But Jamie had been wrong about his wife; she was a Blackthorn and they were all alike. It was just taking Danielle longer than her mother to show her true colors. Jamie would realize in time that he had been right in his actions concerning Danielle Blackthorn. But as the night wore on other thoughts of his wife came to mind. He had taken some delight in her happiness at the prospect of an outing tomorrow. The happiness on her features had indeed lightened his heart. Then the thought of her lying asleep and peaceful each night on their bed up those stairs came to his mind. How long each night did he stand and just look at her beauty before disrobing and climbing in beside her, not daring to touch her for one gentle touch was enough to send his blood coursing through his veins? But his stubborn pride would not let him enjoy her; he wished to hurt her and he knew that their love-making brought her as much pleasure as it brought him.

The brandy lightly dulling his mind, Christopher went up the stairs, opened his door, and peered within. As he walked to the bed, he noticed that the dinner trays were still where they had been and that nothing had been straightened up. For a moment he tried to understand what was going on. Then he looked down and saw Danielle, still dressed in the gown she had worn earlier that day, her hair spread out upon the pillow and in one of her hands a small linen handkerchief. His heart caught for a moment as he imagined her lying and crying until she finally fell asleep. This woman was wreaking havoc upon his life, but still she seemed so innocent lying there in her sleep. Without thinking he gently reached down and started to unbutton her dress.

Danielle awoke when she felt someone tugging at her gown, but was pushed back down upon the bed as she tried to sit up.

"Lie still and let me get you out of these clothes."

"I can do that."

But her words went unheeded as Christopher pulled gown and petticoats from her body; he then removed corsets, and stockings, and shoes, and threw all into a heap at the foot of the bed.

As she lay naked to his gaze his yellow eyes softened, but quickly he turned to her wardrobe and pulled out a soft, satin nightgown and covered her body.

"Move over a bit." He tried to make his voice gruff so that she would not detect the softening of his mood.

Danielle, quick to obey, rolled over. With blanket pulled up to her chin, she tried to go back to sleep.

Lying upon the bed neither talked, but it was some time before sleep overtook either of them.

Chapter Fourteen

A loud knock awoke the sleeping pair the following morning. "Come in." Christopher sat up and tried to clear his head of the sleep befogging it.

Jamie Scott entered the room with a large grin upon his features for his captain and his wife.

"What is it, man?" Christopher bellowed, seeing who the intruder was. It seemed that he had just gotten to sleep and here was his first mate to awaken him.

"Most of the day's already gone. I thought that if the pair of you would be wishing to break the fast this day, you had better be quick about it or you may be hungry before dinner time." He smiled gently to Danielle. She in return smiled at him as she sat up in the bed with the covers pulled about her neck.

Christopher looked to the window, not believing that it was already past daybreak but he could see that the light was shining through the heavy, velvet drapes. "All right. Mr. Scott. Go down and order for my lady and myself. As soon as we dress we shall be downstairs."

As Jamie Scott reached the door, Christopher called to him. "Mr. Scott, if you have nothing else to do this day I would appreciate it if you would come along with Danielle and myself on a tour of the town."

Jamie smiled his delight that his captain was for once thinking about his young wife and he was doubly happy to see the pleasure revealed on Danielle's face. "Yes, sir, I would be more than happy to accompany you both. Will you be wanting a carriage, sir?"

"You had better order one to come to the inn in about an hour, Mr. Scott. It could be a long walk for the lady to the more respectable stores," Christopher said, rising from the bed, going to the pitcher of water, and splashing the contents over his face and head. "And, Mr. Scott, see if you can find something for this head of mine. Its throbbing is relentless."

Jamie nodded his head, though he felt no sympathy for his captain for his conduct of the night before. If not for the fact that the young man was doing something for his wife, Jamie would have left him to suffer, and laughed at the thought of his pain.

"You had best hurry and dress yourself, my pet." Christopher looked to the bed and noticed that Danielle was still in its midst. "Breakfast will be waiting."

Danielle jumped up and hurried to her wardrobe. Was this the same Christopher? She pulled a peach-colored walking gown out of the mass of clothing within. This would do nicely, she reflected, reaching down and gathering up matching chemise and petticoats.

Christopher stood for a moment and watched her rush to her wardrobe, feeling the same pleasure he had experienced last evening from her happiness. He also dressed, but his choice was more somber, a black jacket and pants. The only bit of color accenting this dark ensemble was his white, ruffled shirt. He looked back and went over his attire for the briefest of moments, usually not caring what he looked like; but this day for some reason he wanted to look his best.

And indeed, his wife's eyes reflected that he could not have chosen more aptly. The dark clothes gave him a daring and sinister look. Never had Danielle seen a man with ruffles down the front of his shirt and at his wrists look so dashing, the whiteness of his shirt contrasted drastically with his dark-tanned face and hands. For a moment she was reminded of a night months ago when she had met a strange man dressed all in white. Yes, Christopher Saxon, either as a sultan or a dashing rogue, was by far the most handsome man she had ever known.

"Are you ready, love? Jamie will be waiting breakfast for us." Christopher offered her his hand and Danielle, somewhat surprised by his gallant manners, reached out hesitatingly.

Christopher chuckled lightly, tucked the tiny hand in the crook of his arm, and escorted his wife downstairs and to the table laden with their food.

Breakfast was over quickly, for all seemed to want to be off to the adventures of the day. Jamie had ordered the carriage and it awaited outside the inn.

Christopher handed his young wife up into the seat and took the opposite one for himself; Jamie Scott rode above with the driver, since he felt as uncomfortable in a carriage making small talk as he had always felt in a lady's parlor.

Danielle sat quietly looking out her window and reflected on her husband's mood this morning. Never since knowing him had he treated her so kindly; perhaps this day would lead to something good for the two of them. Perhaps all that was needed was time for him to become used to her as his wife.

In only a short while Christopher was handing her down from the carriage and onto the sidewalks of London. Danielle looked about, amazed at all of the fine shops and sights that littered the streets.

This strange trio walked about the London streets until late in the afternoon. The dark, powerful man on one side of a petite blonde, who rushed from one shop window to another, her happiness plain for all to see on her laughing face. And Jamie Scott, lean and angular, stood like the beauty's bodyguard on her other side, warning off any who would dare to speak with the lady.

In one instance a young lad in his teens had seen this beautiful young woman walking down the street and had followed close behind, waiting for a chance to have just a single word or to be favored with one of her smiles. But the tall, larger man had noticed him from the corner of his eye. He had turned about and looked the youth full in the face. That look had told the boy more than mere words that this lady was not to be trifled with. Those lion's eyes held a look of murderous power in their depths that neither the youth nor any other would dare to dispute.

Jamie Scott was equally protective. When entering a store he would shake his head at any gentleman who started toward the young woman to warn him off. Indeed, the first mate was entranced by Danielle's enthusiasm and light-heartedness and smiled and laughed aloud with her on numerous occasions. And whenever her eyes would linger on a trinket or object that delighted her, Jamie Scott was the first to pull his coins from his pocket, but Christopher would scold his first mate and make him return his money, wanting no other to pay for what his wife desired.

It was late and toward evening when Christopher led a weary Danielle back to the carriage; and his arms as well as those of Jamie Scott were full of packages.

Danielle gladly gave up the day. Her feet were tired from walking and she herself, as she sat back against the soft interior of the vehicle, realized how tired she truly was.

"Do not go to sleep yet." Christopher laughed, viewing her from across the carriage. "We shall have dinner downstairs tonight and celebrate our last evening in London."

Danielle was pleased with his words and tried diligently to keep her eyes from closing. She occupied her mind with thoughts of her husband. What a strange man she had married. One minute he could be so harsh and unreasonable—and truly that was the only picture she had ever had of him, except for that one night before he had found out who she was. Carnival night. Yet today he had once again shown her how gentle, protective, and giving he could be. What were the causes of his moods? She was almost tempted to ask this question as she looked up through her long lashes at him lounging against the other seat. How at ease and kind he looked at that moment, she thought. But not willing to bring about a Christopher Saxon she did not wish to see, she kept her thoughts to herself. Perhaps, in time and if they could stay as comfortable with one another as they had been this day, he would open up and tell her what caused his anger with her.

After once more handing his wife down from the carriage and escorting her into the inn, Christopher placed her in a seat at a comfortable table so situated that it afforded them a little privacy. Then he sent Jamie Scott upstairs with the packages and told him to hurry back down to eat his dinner.

Christopher ordered the meal for both himself and Danielle when the young girl came to take their order. He also ordered a bottle of wine to top off the fine day that they had enjoyed.

After they had eaten, Christopher and Danielle sat sipping their wine and enjoying some small talk. During their exchange Christopher noticed a large man enter the inn and take a table near the front of the building. Turning his attention to his wife once more, he begged her forgiveness explaining that he had just seen a gentleman with whom he had had some business dealings enter the dining room and he would like to have a word with him. He rose seeing no reason not to let his wife finish her wine. He would be back quickly and if she were in need of anything Jamie Scott was at the bar. His first mate would be fast about fetching it for her.

Danielle did not object in the least to Christopher's leavetaking. In fact she welcomed the chance to have a minute to herself. Christopher was a bit overpowering in his courtship of her. Each time he looked at her she felt herself blushing and could barely catch her breath.

From out of nowhere, it seemed to Danielle later, a young man of medium build but with a handsome face and soft voice, appeared in front of her table, and of his own behest sat down at her husband's place.

"Ah, madam." He sighed. "I have been watching you from afar." He pointed to a table nearby that was now empty except for dinner dishes. "Never have I seen such beauty; do not send me from you."

Danielle giggled lightly behind her hand, enjoying this young man's banter. "I am afraid, sir, that to remain you would have to ask my husband." She nodded toward Christopher at the other end of the room. "And I am afraid that he has a vile temper at times." She smiled, seeing nothing wrong with enjoying a little flirtation.

The young man looked truly wounded. "I saw yon giant"—he indicated Christopher—"earlier, but little did it even pass through my mind that a damsel so fair as thee could be tied down with bonds of marriage."

Danielle's smile was radiant, and it was this look that Christopher saw her bestowing upon a strange gentleman as he turned to go back to his table. "I do not consider myself tied by bonds, sir, but more by, shall I say, a wish to be bound to a certain man."

"To be so beautiful and also faithful is almost more than one could hope to bear." The young man laughed, knowing now that there was no hope of conquest here. "I most humbly beg—"

He never finished his words of apology for he was grabbed from the back and lifted from the chair he had taken. "Get away from my wife, you young pup." The growl filled his ears with a deathly tone.

Danielle could not believe her eyes. What had possessed Christopher? What could he have thought was going on between her and the young man? She jumped to her feet, ran around the table, and grabbed hold of her husband's arm before he could do any further damage.

Christopher shook her off and shouted for Jamie Scott, at the same time sending the young man he held by the collar across the room. "Take my wife up to our room," he told Jamie, his eyes glaring a yellow loathing in Danielle's direction. "Do not expect me this evening, madam, and also do not expect, because I am not about, to have some cur such as yon pup take my place." He turned and stormed out of the inn.

Danielle could not believe her ears. Tears streaming down her cheeks, she looked at Jamie Scott. "What is the matter with him, Jamie?" She wept, wanting the man to tell her the answer to her questions.

"I think that the captain is a bit out of sorts from jealousy this evening, ma'am," he replied, taking her by the arm and leading her up the stairs.

"Jealousy? But most of the time he does not even know that I exist," Danielle reasoned aloud. "How could he be jealous—and of what? I did nothing wrong; I want no other man's attentions."

"I'm afraid the captain will have to reason all these

things out for himself. Give him time, lass; he's a good man." Jamie had been standing inside her room and now turned to go. "Good night," he added before shutting the door silently.

Danielle disrobed, wrapped a nightgown about herself, and then curled up in a chair and tried to read a book she had started. But her mind kept wandering back to thoughts of her husband. Where was he this minute? In another woman's arms, trying to find the peace that he desired, or was he off somewhere brooding over a glass of strong liquor?

Why had that young man come to her table and started talking to her? If only the thing had never happened.

The two of them had been getting along so well. Throwing her book down upon the chair, Danielle finally gave up and climbed into the empty bed.

It was daybreak when the door was thrown open and Christopher Saxon stepped through. "Get yourself up and be quick about it. I want to be leaving the inn early and get back to the *Sea Wind.*" He started gathering up papers and books that he had placed upon the table.

Danielle rose from the bed and went about washing her face. "Are you just getting in?" she asked in a small voice.

"Aye." Christopher had no wish to argue with her this morning. "I slept aboard my ship," he added and kept on with his packing. "Are you able to pack your belongings or will you need help?"

"No, I can take care of things myself." She was relieved that he had stayed aboard the *Sea Wind* and not with some lady of the street.

After a hurried packing and then a light breakfast Captain Saxon led his wife and first mate back to the

Sea Wind, anxious to be on board and to put out to sea.

Danielle once again was taken to the cabin she had a short week ago called her home. But Christopher, did not leave the room as soon as he had deposited her within as he had in the past. Instead, he went to his desk and sat, studying charts and ledgers that were scattered about the top.

Danielle, realizing that her husband was not going to leave the cabin, set about unpacking their bags, hanging clothes up, and setting objects back in their natural places.

They spent the rest of the day in this manner, Danielle trying find things to keep herself occupied and Christopher sitting at his desk. Even at lunch time, when Danielle expected her husband to leave, he had Jamie bring him a tray. He did leave, though, right before dark in order to give the order to hoist the anchor and to set course back to Martinique.

Danielle was not exactly thrilled at the prospect of returning to the island. When she had made up her mind to leave, she had meant to go back to New Orleans, and after searching her heart she knew now that the only place she would ever be able to call home would be Iva Rose. Martinique was nice, but her roots and her people were in New Orleans.

That evening after Danielle retired, Christopher, as though being on his own ship changed him and gave him the liberty to do as he pleased, blew out the candle, undressed himself, and gathered his wife up close to his body. He made passionate love to her and brought them both to peaks of ecstacy that they had never known existed.

But the next day Danielle found that his temper was worse than it had been. He had not mentioned the incident that had occurred the night before they left the inn, but at times Danielle could feel those lions' eyes upon her as though they were searching to find some hidden secret that was buried deep within her body. It was as though he were asking unknown questions and expected answers from just looking at her. She had hoped that the day after their night of love-making would perhaps resemble the one on which they had shopped the London streets. But Danielle was to find out differently. Christopher, as the day before, did not leave the cabin. But today he did not keep himself as busy. He still sat at his desk, but he watched Danielle's every move, and whenever she did something that did not meet with his approval he would make some unwonted remark.

On one instance, Danielle had all but burst into tears at dinner time. When Jamie Scott had brought in their trays and had smiled fondly at Danielle, a dark scowl had appeared on his captain's face. As he had at all other times, Jamie ignored Christopher's dark mood, setting down the plates in front of the two.

"There would have been fresh strawberries for dessert, Miss Danielle, but that lughead of a cook forgot to get them as I had ordered him."

Danielle smiled at the good man, knowing that he had ordered the fresh fruit for her welfare and that now he was fretting about her not getting it. "Oh, Jamie, they would have been delicious, but I can do without."

Christopher seemed to explode. "I imagine you shall do without; this is a ship, not a lady's fine restaurant. Now, Mr. Scott, if you would be good enough to leave us, I would like to eat."

Danielle felt the tears beginning to well up and she fought against them. How could he be so crude? Hurting her feelings was one thing, but to hurt this man who only wished to be kind was unthinkable.

As soon as Jamie left the cabin, she glared her hatred at her husband. "How could you?" she seethed. "How can you be so hurtful and especially to Jamie when he has nothing but good things to say to you?"

Christopher had only looked up from his plate, grunted some incoherent remark about loud-mouthed females, and gone back to eating his food.

Danielle's anger grew by the minute. How dare this man be so bullheaded. She had not done anything to offend him in any way and all he wished to do was to hurt her in some fashion or another. Her anger was beyond reason as she picked up her plate to throw it, but she was stopped, her hand brought up short by Christopher's icy yellow eyes.

"I suggest you put it down unless you enjoy cleaning up food off the floor. For the mess you make, you shall certainly be the one to straighten up." After this he resumed eating.

Danielle jumped to her feet, her temper now beyond mere words. She flounced about the room thinking of one vile name after the other to throw at him, but for some reason she knew that to say them aloud would bring more wrath down upon her head and also more embarrassment. So instead she quickly changed behind the dressing screen and went to bed, rolling her body into a tight ball and lying close to the wall, as though to protect herself.

Christopher did not act concerned in the least as his wife strutted about the room, he knew the things she would like to have said to him and he silently dared her to voice them. For some reason, he sort of relished the idea of laying hold of her in anger. But then as he watched she went behind the dressing screen and in a few minutes appeared in a nightgown. He chuckled to himself as she rolled over as far as she could away from his side of the bed. She could never get far enough away from him, he told himself. She belonged to him now and what was his he used as he wished.

He lingered over his dinner and then sat back in a chair and read from a book. His eyes kept rising though and going to the woman on the bed. He would make his rounds on the ship and then he would come back and show his wife that there was no place safe from him, he decided rising to his feet.

The next morning Danielle awoke to find the bed empty except for herself. As she rose she felt a bit shaky; the ship seemed to be a bit rocky and she had to hold on to objects to keep her balance. She had only taken a few steps when she turned back and fell upon the bed. She felt as though she were going to suffocate, and at the same time, as though she were in a hazy void. She had felt a little ill yesterday, but it had soon disappeared. She brought her hand across her forehead and felt the heat of her own body.

Christopher picked this moment to return to his cabin. His thoughts were of the night before and the pleasure he had had with his young wife. Though she had at first been reluctant as she was each time he took her in his arms, in short order he had her moaning softly and clinging to him in passion. But his daydreaming was brought up short as he opened the door and looked at the bed. Danielle lay in an awkward position across the foot of the mattress and to Christopher she looked as though she had fallen in that crazy position. He hurried across the room, his thoughts flying, not knowing what was happening. "Danielle," he called softly, kneeling down next to the bed.

Danielle heard a soft voice from a far distance, but thought it to be a stranger calling to her as she tried to

503

sleep. She shook her head from side to side. "No, no," she moaned.

Christopher reached down, felt his wife's brow, and caught his breath, she was burning alive with fever. He ran to the door and shouted for Mr. Scott, then he turned and quickly went back to Danielle, lifting her in his arms and cradling her to his chest.

"Do not touch me!" She fought him, her mind now delirious as she fought off the demons that seemed to be taking hold of her body.

Christopher cooed soothing words of comfort in her ears and tried to bring her to the top of the bed, though not daring to lay her down. His fear was overpowering; he could not let anything happen to this woman.

Jamie Scott found his captain in this position as he entered the room, holding his wife and gently whispering soft words in her ear as he held her tightly against him.

The first mate was shocked by what he saw and ran to his captain's side. "What is it, lad?" Before being told he knew by the look on Christopher's face that what the young lady had was serious.

"Let me have her, Captain," Jamie softly said, trying to take Danielle and lay her upon the pillows.

Christopher reluctantly turned her loose, sitting next to her as his first mate looked her over. She seemed to be in a deep, almost unconscious sleep and Jamie Scott shook his head sadly as he felt her head and then looked into her eyes.

"It don't look good, lad. She must have picked up some kind of fever during her stay in London. We'll have to pray that it ain't nothing too serious." But he was only saying this for his captain, for he held no doubt that what the girl had was indeed serious and more than likely they would not be able to save her.

"You stay with her, lad, while I go and get some medicine and water and compresses. Perhaps if we can keep the fever down she might have a chance." He saw the pain that was filling Christopher's face and he knew that the young man would be in a sorry state if the girl were not to make it. It was obvious that his captain loved his wife; he only wondered now if the captain realized it himself.

When the first mate had left the cabin, Christopher sat and stroked Danielle's hair. He did not know why he felt this knife-twisting pain in the center of his being, but he did know that he could not let his wife die; he would not let her leave him without a fight.

Jamie Scott was gone only a few minutes. He had rushed to the galley and then to the medical supply cabinet, and as he hurried back toward the captain's cabin a man stepped in front of him. The man was one of the new crew members whom Jamie had hired in England. Jamie laid his hand upon his arm and talked softly, not wishing for other ears to hear his words. When he had finished, the tall man's bearded face seemed twisted in pain and his blue eyes looked about desperately. Jamie patted his hand once more and left him, promising to return and talk to him later.

Danielle's fever raged the rest of that day and the next and next. Christopher stayed by her side night and day, only allowing Jamie to tend her when he spooned the required amount of medicine between her parched lips.

Christopher's hours at Danielle's side proved to be a living hell. When she opened her eyes to look about, he would hope that she would be lucid, but all too often she would scream and shout and trying to get away from him as though he were the one causing her

505

such pain.

The second day her body broke out in large red welts and Jamie assured his captain that this was brought about by the high fever. Christopher bathed her head constantly, trying to keep her temperature from becoming any higher than it was, but to him it seemed that he was fighting a losing battle, as hour after hour he could see no improvement.

On the third day Danielle awakened and for a moment Christopher thought she was her old self, but on closer inspection he saw that her eyes were glazed. She sat up in the bed and her voice for the first time since her decline sounded normal to his ears. But as he listened to her words, he knew otherwise.

"Mamma, why do you not act like the other girls' Mammas do?" Danielle was back in her childhood and she was upstairs in her mother's room at Iva Rose. "I want to go to the other children's houses and I want you to go with me, Mamma. Do you not think it would be fun, Mamma? I promise I will be good." Then as the little girl whom Danielle saw in her hazy mind was crying to her mother, one of the servants pulled at her to try to get her to leave her mamma's room. "Come along, child. Your mamma don't be knowing who you be. You mamma's sick and don't got no time for you. You just get downstairs and Sara will take time for you."

Danielle's shouts filled the cabin of the *Sea Wind* and Christopher felt his heart constrict as he saw her tears and heard great wrenching moans come out of her throat. "My mamma *does* love me. You should not say that she does not know who I am. You just wait. I shall have Sara make you say you're sorry," she cried, reliving her past.

"Now, I didn't mean anything. It's just that your mamma don't be knowing who anybody is anymore."

The black woman tried to reason with the little girl.

But Danielle was beyond caring. All she wanted was a mother who loved her. "No, no," she screamed and jumped from the bed, Christopher holding on to her and drawing her onto his lap.

"Sara, Sara," she cried and Christopher, seeing the agony written on her tear-drenched face, whispered over and over to soothe her, "I'm here love, I'm here."

His words seemed to settle her somewhat, but still she was in her own tormented dream world. "My mamma loves me, my mamma loves me." She wept, holding on to Christopher's shirtfront. "Sara, why does Mamma not act like all the other girls' mothers? Doesn't she love me?"

Christopher answered these heart-wrenching questions, hoping that he could soothe her. "She loves you, sweet, she cares."

These words seemed to have the desired effect, for Danielle shut her eyes and her body once more fell into a deep sleep.

Christopher sat and held his wife in his arms, her head pressed tightly against his chest and her arms wrapped about his neck. Though he knew that in her delirium she had mistaken him for a woman called Sara, still he felt relief that he was able to do something.

What kind of tormenting nightmare was she having? he wondered as she still gulped back sobs in her sleep. What kind of cruel woman was his wife's mother? What kind of woman bore a child and then did not express her love. Christopher knew that Danielle had reverted back to her childhood by the way she had sounded. To him she had spoken as a little girl begging for love and the only one who had cared was this woman called Sara. He had been right about Chastity Blackthorn and at this moment his hatred for the woman was beyond simple proportion.

Sometime later he lay Danielle back down upon the pillow and once more wiped her brow with a cool cloth. He had been unselfish in his care for her these past few days and now after what had happened this afternoon he knew that he wanted to protect her from any kind of further harm in her life. He would make it up to her, he promised himself. He would show her that he was sorry for the way he had treated her since the night of the Delmars' party when he had found out who she was. Could she help who her mother was? he questioned himself. She could help it no more than he could help who his mother had been. The woman who had given birth to him had been no more than a streetwalker, from whom he had fled as soon as he was of age.

His fingers gently caressed her silken cheek. If only she would get better, he would beg her to forgive him. The thought hit him like a ton of bricks dropped on a stone floor; he loved this small bit of a woman whom he had tried with all of his power to heal. He loved her with all of his heart and soul. Silently tears started to make a path down his dark face. He could not let her die, not when he now knew that what he felt for her was a desire to keep her at his side forever, to protect her, and to have children with her—children who would know love. He thought of Danielle as she must have been as a little girl, not receiving any love from her mother. Perhaps her father had loved her, he thought. What man would not love the girl she must have been? His thoughts seemed to be tearing him apart and when Jamie Scott stepped into the room and saw his captain sitting on the bed with tears on his face the other man also had to hold himself in check.

"Go lie down, lad," he ordered, not taking Christopher's shake of his head for an answer. "I shall stay by the lass and not let anything happen to her. You look terrible and will not be doing the girl any good if you collapse." Christopher still shook his head, but let the older man take him by the arm and lead him to the cot that had been set up.

"Only for an hour or so, Jamie," he said almost in a whisper and fell into an exhausted sleep.

Jamie looked down at his captain and sighed aloud. The man on the cot barely resembled the man he knew as Christopher Saxon. If the girl did not get better soon he was afraid that the captain also would be taken ill. He had not shaved since the morning the girl had taken to her bed and he had eaten hardly anything. He seemed to have shrunken in these past few days and his face seemed to have aged drastically. Jamie could see new lines that had not been on the young man's face before and his appearance was gray and haggard.

Christopher awoke and jumped to his feet; he looked about him frantically until he saw Jamie Scott sitting in a chair, pulling up to his wife's bedside. The older man was wiping her brow and talking softly to her. Christopher walked over and placed his hand upon Jamie's shoulder.

"You can leave now, Mr. Scott."

At Jamie's look of concern Christopher assured him that he was well rested.

"I'll run and fetch you a tray, lad. She seems to be getting a bit better. Her fever don't seem as high."

Christopher's face registered his hope at the other man's words, but to him his wife looked no different and when he reached down and touched her forehead he could feel no difference.

He sat in the chair Jamie had left and ate some of the dinner that the first mate brought to him, but his

509

every thought was of his wife. After having his own meal, he spooned a small amount of broth down Danielle's lips, washed her body, and changed her nightgown. Then he sat back upon the chair and watched over her, every once in a while wiping the cool cloth across her forehead.

Sometime during the night Christopher jerked upright in the chair because he heard his wife's voice. She seemed to be talking to someone in the room other than him and he reached down once more to feel her brow. It was as hot to the touch as it had previously been and he felt deflated as he watched her mumbling to someone unknown. He listened and could make out words every once in a while, and what she was saying burned deeply into his soul. She was talking about him, asking someone who he was and then telling someone else that she cared for no one else. He thought of the night in the inn and the unreasonable treatment he had dealt her. Was she thinking also of that night? he wondered.

For a moment she looked over at him and a radiant smile lit her features. Christopher knew that she was still ill, but for some reason he felt a weight lift from his shoulders. With a soft sigh she shut her eyes and slept and for the first time her sleep seemed peaceful.

The next morning Christopher was pulled from his sleep by the feeling of being watched. The first thing that greeted his eyes was his wife watching him intently.

"You look terrible; what has happened?" Her words sounded weak and feeble, but Christopher could tell that they were lucid and not the ramblings of fever.

He grinned down at her sheepishly. "You madam, are not quite the one to be speaking of appearances." He reached down as he had so many times in the past few days and felt her forehead. At his sigh of relief, Danielle looked deeply into his eyes.

"I have been sick?" When he nodded, she continued, "How long?"

"For about a week, a little more or less." Christopher sat down upon the bed but still caressed her forehead, not wishing to stop feeling her while her skin was cool and not raging with fever.

"Did you or Jamie take care of me?" She knew the answer before he replied by just looking at his appearance. She had never seen him looking so wrinkled and unkempt.

"No one else but I took care of you," he answered her, watching her face for her reaction.

She smiled lightly and shut her eyes for a moment.

"You are to rest now. I shall go and get you a tray, but you are not to get out of this bed." His voice was that of the old harsh Christopher and, noticing his tone, he softened it somewhat. "You were very ill and I thought that I was going to lose you a few times these past few days."

"Would that truly have bothered you that much?" Danielle asked and watched the pain twist across his face from her words. She scolded herself harshly for saying such a thing to the person who had brought her through such a sickness, but for some reason she felt herself waiting his answer.

Christopher rose from the bed and headed for the door and she thought for a moment that he was not going to answer her, but he turned and looked her full in the face. "Aye, I truly would have been sorrowed for you to leave me." His words filled her with a tender warmth and she shut her eyes and fell back to sleep.

For the next few days Christopher did not leave the cabin except to tend to his ship and most of this he put in Jamie's capable hands. He stayed by his wife's side, not letting her rise from the bed, reading to her and helping her to dress and making sure that she was comfortable.

Danielle told him time and again that he did not have to be so considerate of her condition. In fact, she told him that she felt fine and able to care for herself. But her husband had had a scare that he did not wish to repeat and he told her sternly that he would not let her rush into getting better and causing herself some harm or relapse.

Danielle did not argue, relishing as she did this personal attention given to her by a man she had almost despaired of ever getting to care for her.

They had not mentioned anything personal since that first morning when he had told her that he did care if she were ill or not. In fact, Christopher still slept on the cot that he had used during her illness, leaving her the big bed. He cared for her as though she was some fragile porcelain figurine but Danielle began to feel the bit of her confinement.

When she thought that she could bear no more of his tender treatment, she tried to tell her husband. He would still try to feed her, she thought, if she would allow him. Things would have to get back to normal and he had a ship to run. "Christopher," she said softly one evening as he sat next to her bed and read from a book of poetry. "You must realize that I am fine now. It has been a good week since I have gotten over my fever. I need some exercise and perhaps fresh air."

"But you are still weak," he tried to reason with her, the thought of her once more ill because he had rushed her recuperation, making him tremble with fear.

"I am only weak because I have been lying abed."

She smiled, sensing some of his fear. "I am fine."

"Are you sure?" He laid the book down and took up one of her fragile hands lying outside of the covers on the bed.

"I am sure; you do not have to worry. I have never been one to wish to be ill, so if I feel myself growing weary I shall be sure to rest." His tenderness filled her heart.

"All right then." He sighed. "Tomorrow will be soon enough for you to try your wings. But you must promise me that you will not do too much."

"I do promise," came her answer.

"Then I shall help you to bathe and you can get a good night's rest." He rose and fetched the bowl and pitcher of water and reached into the wardrobe and brought out a fresh gown.

This time of the evening was the most tormenting to Christopher. Helping to tend to his wife's personal needs made him break out in a cold sweat, but he had told himself that she must be fully recovered before he pressed himself upon her. He did not want to cause her anything but pleasure, and he wanted now for them to have something that was lasting and good. He would not treat her as he had in the past.

Danielle secretly relished this special care given by her husband. His hands were strong and cool upon her body and the way his tawny eyes lingered over special parts of her body gave her a deep, thrilling feeling deep within her soul.

The next day, she ate breakfast at the table with Christopher and Jamie Scott stood by, fussing at her as though he were a mother. When she had finished eating, Danielle asked if she would be allowed to walk about on the deck of the ship. She wished for sunshine and fresh air more than anything else.

Christopher agreed, but on the condition that she not walk. Jamie would take a chair and put it out of the way of the crew and she could sit for a time.

To Danielle, this sounded better than nothing. Christopher could be very hard when he wished and she knew that this would be the only way for her to leave the cabin. "That will be fine." She smiled at the pair of men.

Jamie was quick to do what was needed and took chair and lap robe out of the room.

Christopher smiled fondly at his first mate, glad that the man who had had such a large part in bringing him up cared so much for his wife.

"Are you ready, sweet?" he asked as Danielle rose from her chair.

Danielle did not at first understand his question, but when he lifted her off her feet she fully realized his intent. "Put me down now, Christopher." She pushed at his chest. "I will not leave this room being carried."

"Now, Danielle, I only wish for you not to tire yourself. Let me carry you out to the chair and then you can spend some time outside."

"No, Christopher, I'll not be carried." Danielle was adamant.

Christopher saw that to carry her would cause her to be angry, so he gently put her on her feet. "At least let me walk beside you in case you need my help."

Danielle's tinkling laughter filled his ears and a small smile came over his face. "I am fine, Christopher and I will show you." She reached over to the desk, took the book that she had been reading, and started to the door, Christopher having to hurry to keep up with her.

After seeing that Danielle was safe and comfortable, Christopher excused himself, explaining that he had let a lot of work go since she had gotten sick and now that she was better he could catch up on it.

Jamie had placed the chair close enough so that she could see over the rail, but far enough so that the sea spray would not shower her and cause her to get chilled. Danielle relaxed, drinking in the sun and breathing the fresh air. She shut her eyes and let a feeling of peacefulness settle over her. She could not remember ever having being so content with life as she felt at this moment.

When Danielle opened her eyes she was startled to see a man staring straight at her. He did not lower his eyes when her own made contact with his, but instead he smiled softly. She had never seen this man before and something about him was strangely disquieting. He stood, rolling a coil of rope in his hands, next to the rail, and he watched her.

The man was big and dangerous-looking, his gray-and-black beard covering his face, so that the only thing one could make out were his light-blue eyes.

When Jamie Scott approached Danielle to see if there was anything she needed she noticed that the strange man moved away out of sight. Jamie also brought her a cup of tea.

After her assurance that she was fine the, elderly man left her side to tend to his work and Danielle opened her book and started to read. But the man who had been watching her had unsettled her somewhat and she found that she could not concentrate on her book. Instead, her eyes kept rising every time she heard footsteps. She was not to see the man again, only other members of the crew, who would doff their hats and keep on with what they were about.

After an hour or so of sitting in the chair, Danielle found herself bored so she stood up and walked over to the rail. But she soon learned that she had picked the worst time to venture forth, for Christopher

515

stepped out of the companionway at the same instant she reached the rail and anyone within sight could see the angry tilt to his head.

"By all that's right, woman, what do you think you are about," he shouted and grabbed hold of his wife's arm.

But before he could say any more the strange man with the full beard was stepping between him and Danielle. Christopher's rage came to a full boil when one of his crew dared such an affront as to step between him and his wife.

The man did not talk, but stood and stared at Christopher eye for eye, both being about the same height and weight.

Danielle was flabbergasted. What was wrong with this man? Did he not care for his own hide? He must have thought that Christopher had meant her some sort of harm. "No, Christopher." She grabbed her husband's arm when he raised it as if to strike the strange man.

But Christopher was not going to strike the man. He had raised his hand to try to clear his head by wiping at his eyes. There was something familiar about this man and a part of Christopher's brain was screaming out that it was important for him to find out who he was. "Mr. Scott," he bellowed at the top of his voice. And when Jamie came up on deck and saw the trio, he rushed to his captain's side.

"Sir?" He looked from first one man to the other, trying to find out what had taken place.

"Who is this man?" Christopher left no out for the first mate.

"Now, lad, I think it best that we straighten this out in a few minutes. Let me take Miss Danielle to the cabin, Captain. She should not be standing out here in the heat." Jamie at least wanted Danielle to be spared what was about to happen.

But Christopher would not be put off; nor would he take his eyes off the man standing next to him. "She is fine." He pulled Danielle up next to him and put a protective arm about her. Feeling her trembling body, he knew that she was also being affected by this strange man and the play that was being unfolded before them.

"Perhaps we should go to your cabin before we start this, lad." Jamie Scott tried one last time.

"No," came his answer, and the first mate knew that both the captain and the man with the beard wanted the thing over with.

"We hired a few extra hands in London, Captain, and this here fellow was one of them," Jamie started. "Lad, there is no other way to say this. The man be Deke Saxon."

Christopher grabbed tighter to Danielle, as though she were his lifeline to sanity. "Deke Saxon is dead, killed years ago." His words were a mere whisper, for he had known upon first looking at the man that he was the same he had once loved.

Deke reached out a callused hand and touched Christopher on the arm. "I was not killed, but shang-haied. It was made to appear that it was I who was killed that day twenty years ago, but truly, lad, it was not."

"But all these years, where have you been?" The question was wrung from Christopher's depths.

"I have been aboard a slave ship belonging to a sultan. But that is a long story which can wait until another time." His light-blue eyes went from Christopher's drawn, white face to Danielle's.

Christopher had felt Danielle sag against him moments before when Jamie Scott had spoken this strange man's name, but he had been too overwhelmed to do much more than hold her upright. Now, though, after Deke looked down at his wife, Christopher remembered all too vividly that she had been ill and it looked as though she was having some form of relapse. "Love, love, are you all right?" He picked her up and held her tightly to him, one hand feeling for her forehead. "I must get her to our cabin." His words were for the man who stood next to him. "Would you care to come along?" He truly did not know what to do or to say.

"Aye, Christopher, I am afraid I have a great interest in this young woman."

Christopher did not understand what Deke meant, but he did not want to linger on the deck of the ship with Danielle half-faint in his arms. So he led the way to the cabin with Jamie Scott following behind the man he had just learned was Deke Saxon.

Danielle was laid upon the bed and as Christopher went to get the bowl of water and a rag to put to her head, Deke Saxon went to the bed and sat down, staring at the girl who now also looked up at him.

Christopher did not comprehend what was going on around him, things were moving too fast. And as he started to go to his wife, Jamie Scott took hold of his arm.

"Give them a minute, lad."

"Why should I give him a minute on my wife's bed?" Christopher had loved this stranger when he was a boy, but that did not give him leave now to be familiar with his wife.

"You do not know, lad?" Jamie asked and knew instantly that his captain did not have any idea who the man on the bed was to his wife. "Did you not wonder why this man would be concerned with your wife? Did it never occur to you that the woman he loved was your wife's mother?"

Something in his voice told Christopher that he was in for another surprise.

"Deke Saxon is her father, Christopher."

That simple statement was enough to widen Christopher's eyes and to keep him at a loss for words as he watched the couple upon the bed. He could hear his wife's soft sobs from where he stood near the door, and as he stepped closer he felt his own tears well up. The large man sat holding Danielle's hand, talking softly to his daughter.

"I have waited for over twenty years, daughter, with but one thought keeping me alive; and that was of your mother. And when my old friend, Jamie Scott, told me about you, I could not dare believe my good fortune. You are the image of your mother. I had no idea." He could not go on, but gathered his daughter up in his arms, their tears mingling.

Danielle herself could do nothing but cry; she had gone years without a father and now here he was telling her that he loved her and her mother.

It was some time before the pair upon the bed were calmed down enough to talk. Deke's first questions of his daughter concerned Chastity. How she was and what she was doing. He knew that it was impossible for him to hope that she had never married, but still he loved the woman and had to hear all about her. He had waited too many years without knowing how she was and he could wait no longer.

Danielle, after collecting herself, looked up and saw her husband near the bed. She reached out a hand to him and when he took it, she smiled. For some reason she knew that she would be needing Christopher's strength to tell her father about her mother.

Christopher pulled a chair up to the bed, not letting go of his wife's hand. The thought struck him that when she had been ill and delirious, she had talked about her mother. And Christopher almost wished for a moment to tell Deke Saxon the truth about the woman whom he had loved so dearly; but he decided quickly that it was not his place to kill the love that had kept the man alive for the past twenty years. He would let his daughter tell him of her mother.

To his surprise Danielle's words were not those he had expected to hear. She started out slowly, telling her father how when she was a child she had noticed that her mother had been different.

Deke had sat alert, "What do you mean, Danielle? Different in what way? Was she ill?" Deke's thoughts were frightening.

Danielle shook her head and started to continue. "Let me tell you, Father, in my own way and perhaps you will understand. I did not know until later in my years that my mother did not know anything that was happening about her. That is why I myself went to Martinique, to see if I could find some clue to her mental lapse. She still thinks herself to be on the island, Father, and she talks of no one but you."

Deke Saxon, imagining his love locked up in a

room all to herself and not fully knowing what was happening, went pale at these words.

"Her maid, Dabs, told me somewhat of what had happened on the island, and I gather that mother could not seriously believe that you were dead, so she set herself beyond any other person and lived in a world where you would one day come back to her." Danielle was weeping by the time she finished.

"I must go to her and help her," Deke Saxon said quickly, then he looked at Christopher. He had been told by Jamie Scott of Christopher's feelings toward the Blackthorns. That was why, on deck, he had thought of protecting his daughter. He truly thought that Christopher had intended to harm her in some way and he was not about to let him go through with it.

Christopher nodded his head, realizing that all of these years he had been wrong. "We shall set our course for New Orleans immediately.

"Thank you, lad," Deke said, rising from the bed. "I can see that I made no mistake in thinking that you would grow into a fine man. You have fulfilled my expectations. There is only one thing that I wish to discuss with you in private."

"Whenever you wish, sir," Christopher answered, not knowing what more could be said.

"Let us leave Danielle to get some rest now. I have heard that she has been quite ill and now that I have found myself a daughter, I fully intend to keep her." Deke started to the door and waited for Christopher to follow.

Once outside the cabin Deke turned to Christopher

with a grave look upon his face. "I do not want my daughter hurt, Christopher. I loved you as a boy and you gained all I owned. No, do not speak yet. Let me have my say," he said as Christopher tried to interrupt. "I have been told of your feelings for the Blackthorns and perhaps you were too young to know of the feelings that I harbored for that girl's mother, but let me tell you this one thing, lad. For twenty years there has been only one face in my mind night and day, one voice coming to my ears in my hours of trial, and those boy, belong to the woman I loved, Chastity Blackthorn. She never wronged me; she was always faithful and certainly was not the cause of my being shanghaied. It was the fault of some cruel men and if they are still on Martinique when I return I shall take care of them. But because of your hardness of heart toward Chastity Blackthorn, do not take out your spite on her daughter."

When Christopher was given a chance to speak, he smiled slowly. "You have no reason to worry over your daughter's safety, sir, or over my feelings toward her. I learned some time ago that I was deeply in love with her. And today I have learned something that I have needed to learn for some years, and my shame is deep. I should have realized it myself, but I guess a young boy losing the only person he ever loved took out on the closest person at hand all of his anger and impotence at not being able to change things."

Deke knew what it took for Christopher to say this and he reached out and hugged the young man closely to him. "Aye, boy, and I loved you. And I am proud that my daughter has you for her husband."

When Christopher went back to the cabin, he was greeted by the sight of Danielle scurrying about the room. She was straightening things up and cleaning, humming to herself all the while.

As Christopher entered the room, she flew into his arms. "Do not scold me for staying busy. I can not lie down now. Can you believe it, Christopher? My father is alive after all of these years." Her expression brought sheer happiness to Christopher and he took her in his arms and swung her about.

"I should truly be angry with you. Why did you not tell me that Deke was your father? And to think Jamie knew also. It seems that I was the only one left in the dark."

Danielle thought for a moment that perhaps he was truly angry with her and some of her gaiety left her. "I would have told you sooner, but I did not wish you to treat me differently than your own heart told you and I thought that knowing I was his daughter you would have been different. Though at times I was tempted to tell you, I must admit."

"So there were times when you had thought to tell me." He could well imagine those times being when he had been so bullheaded and harsh to her for no apparent reason. He carried her over to his chair and, sitting down, he pulled her onto his lap. "I do not blame you." He sat still for a moment, breathing in the sweet smell of her as she rested her head upon his chest. "You do know now the way of my heart?" he asked softly.

"I think so my lord." Danielle looked up into those warm lions' eyes that were watching her every move.

"Let me tell you then if the words must be said;

but mind you, never have I told another what I now tell you. You are everything to me; from that first night of carnival my heart belonged to you. I admit I tried to scorch you from my soul, but you stood fast, holding a place that no other before has ventured. I love you, Danielle." His large hand that was strong enough to steer a ship or gentle a wild horse, lightly caressed her cheek with a tenderness born of love. "I know your past experience as my wife has not been to your liking, but I promise you from this day forth I shall show you only joy. Bear with my love, for you are the woman whom I wish at my side through this lifetime and throughout all eternity."

Danielle's blue eyes held large droplets of tears, but her face was filled with radiance. She had waited a long time to hear such words from this man. She kissed him softly on the lips. "Aye, my lord, I shall bear forever with your love. I also knew that first night that you and I, our destinies, would be entwined and I have been praying that I would one day hear you say such things to me. I love you too, Christopher Saxon."

No more words were needed. Christopher's lips descended upon those below his own and without any further ado he stood up with Danielle still in his arms and carried her to the bed. "I think you are well recovered now, my lady," he murmured as he laid her down and then followed after her.

"Aye, my lord, well recovered," was her whispered reply as she unreservedly gave her lips to her husband. She would no longer regret her love or grudgingly give this man her body. He had finally admitted his love for her and come what may, she could wish for no more.

Now that Christopher had admitted the love that he held in the depths of his heart for his wife, he was completely at ease and willing to give all that he possessed.

The harsh and cruel treatment which he had without reason inflicted upon this woman came to his mind as his lips covered hers. He would spend the rest of his life making up to her for what he had done in the short span of time in which they had been married. He would treat her as she deserved to be treated, with only love and adoration, he swore to himself as with gentle fingers he slowly took her clothes and his own from their bodies. "I love you beyond all else, my heart," he whispered as he rose above her and filled her with his love.

Danielle was swept up into the sweet, delicious pleasures that her husband was evoking within her being; his tender words only added to her sensual delight. This man above her she had loved from the first night she had met him, that long-ago time when she had known him only as her sultan. He had captured her heart and had brought her to places where no other could tread. He was her heart also; he was all that mattered.

The large stone mansion of Iva Rose could be seen coming into view as the carriage pulled into the main lane leading to the plantation house. Danielle tightly grasped Christoher's hand. She experienced the same peaceful feeling that always had come over her in the past whenever she had seen this ivy-covered fortress. "There it is," she called excitedly.

With mixed emotions Christopher and Deke looked at her. Christopher wanted to view all of the place, for he and Danielle had decided that they would remain in New Orleans and Christopher would run the plantation and all the other Blackthorn dealings. Deke's thoughts were darker. He did not know what to expect of the place called Iva Rose. Would he find the Chastity whom he had loved over twenty years before? Would this woman who had for years lived in a world all to herself, locked up in her room, even remember who he was? Was he going to a place that was going to tear all of his hopes and dreams to pieces?

The carriage pulled up before the large stone steps leading up to the veranda. Before the people within the vehicle could climb out of their seats a large, black woman was running down the front steps and waving a white bandanna about in the air. "Miss Danielle, Miss Danielle. I can't be a-believing my own eyes," she yelled and grabbed Danielle around the neck and cried her happiness on her mistress' shoulder.

Christopher and Deke both looked on, smiles on their faces, glad that their reception was going to be a happy one.

Danielle herself was weeping as she hugged the woman to her. "Oh, Sara, I am so glad to be home. Is mother all right?"

"Yes, ma'am. She ain't no different," Sara said and then looked up at the gentlemen whom her young mistress had brought with her. "Come on in, child. I can see you still ain't learned your manners, leaving these fine-looking gentlemen out here in the heat."

Sara started fussing at Danielle as though she had never been gone.

"I want you to meet my husband first, Sara." Danielle laughed, pulling Christopher to her side. "Darling, this is Sara. She practically raised me."

Christopher smiled and told the woman that he was glad to meet her.

But Sara stood dumbfounded. "You say that this here is your husband, Miss Danielle?" And at Danielle's nod she burst into peals of happy laughter. "I never did think I would live to see the day."

"I also have a surprise for Mamma," Danielle said, looking toward her father. "Do you think she would be up to a visitor, Sara?"

"Why, Miss Danielle, I told you she ain't no different than when you be leaving. I doubt she even knows if she be having a visitor." The large black woman led the way into the house.

"Well, we shall try anyway, Sara. This gentleman has come quite some way to see her."

"Whatever you say, honey. You be knowing what's best. I still can't believe that you done got yourself a man."

Danielle smiled fondly at the woman and looked about her at all of the familiar things with which she had grown up. She would never have thought that she could have missed a house as much as she did this one. It was as though she had been gone for years. Even the smell of the interior of the old stone house was like perfume to her senses. "Well, Sara, we shall go on upstairs and see Mama. Perhaps you would like to fix us something to eat," Danielle said, realizing that Christopher and Deke were standing and waiting for her to make the first move.

"Yes, ma'am. It won't take me no time at all to have you-all something fixed right up," Sara stated and then turned and hurried off in the direction of the kitchen.

Now that it was time for Danielle to take her father upstairs to her mother, she found that she was reluctant. What good would it do for him to see her after all of these years considering the conditions in which they had both lived? Her father had talked of plans for returning to Martinique and though he had not said the words aloud, Danielle knew that his plans included her mother. Danielle remembered the quiet, dreaming woman whom she called mother. Would just the viewing of the man she had loved change her in the least? Though she had her doubts, she knew that this was the only chance—if there was a chance for her mother.

Deke had wandered into the parlor while Danielle had been deep in her own thoughts; he was having some frightening thoughts of his own. As he had entered that room his eyes had been drawn to the mantel. There hung a large painting of the girl he had loved. The beauty captured in that painting, was exactly that of the Chastity Blackthorn he remembered. She sat beneath a large oak, her gown and hat of white lace seeming to make her an innocent babe in a world into which she should not have been born. Her green eyes and her smile were the same as he remembered them to be.

Danielle and Christopher interrupted him at this point. Danielle took hold of his arm. "I never knew her like that, Father, though as a child I would stand or sit and look at this painting for hours. The woman up those stairs seemed sadder and even her eyes held a pain that seemed too great to bear. Perhaps you will be able to help her. I pray that you will."

Deke Saxon had tears in his eyes when he looked at his daughter. "Take me to her, Danielle. I can not bear this another moment."

The trio stood outside of Chastity Blackthorn's room and Danielle knocked lightly.

From within a soft voice could be heard talking aloud and Deke felt his heart lurch. It was the same sweet voice he had remembered in his dreams. He reached for the door and shook his head at Danielle. "I think it best if I go alone, child." He kissed his daughter on the forehead and entered the room, slowly shutting the door behind him.

Chastity had been sitting near the window and looking out, her thoughts miles away in another time and place. She had called absently to the door, expecting it to be Dabs. Usually she did not answer when the door was knocked upon and sometimes she would go for as long as a month without saying a word to another living being. Her thoughts were enough to keep her company.

Deke stood near the door and drank in the beauty of the woman sitting across the room. It was as though she had not changed. Her hair was long and shimmering; it still retained its copper color and the silkiness he had loved to feel between his fingers. She was dressed in a white dressing gown and, with her face turned to the window, she seemed still but twenty years old.

Without thinking, Deke quietly walked to her side and kneeled down. He reached out and took hold of her hand and as he did she jumped and looked to see who was disturbing her peace.

Chastity was surprised that the person in her room was not Dabs and she looked at Deke with questioning eyes.

Deke did not speak, but seemed to try to convey with his light-blue eyes all that he wanted to say.

As Chastity looked into the face of the man who was kneeling before her, she felt tears start to slip down her cheeks. "I knew you had not left me," she whispered.

Deke was beyond himself. "Oh, my love, my darling." He pulled her into his arms. She had known who he was, his mind screamed over and over.

Chastity's emerald eyes gleamed with a new vitality as she brought her hand up and caressed his bearded face. "You have changed. You should not have stayed away so long." Her world was normal once more. It was as though she had been having a long sleep and finally been awakened.

Deke kissed her lips and repeated over and over how much he loved her. "I shall never leave you again, my love. We shall not part."

"I should hope not. There has been too much time lost as it is," she said softly.

Once more, Deke kissed the lips that had stayed in his mind for the past twenty years. He could not believe this was truly happening to him. After all these years she still loved him, still wanted him.

Iva Rose

The ivy clinging to the large stone mansion was abundant, lush and green. Inside the towering structure all was quiet and dark, except for a lone tallow candle that sent its shadowed light about the recess of the master bedchamber on the second floor of the building.

Inside the room a man lay naked, his body tanned and muscular, stretched out on the soft down mattress. His lions' eyes watched expectantly for the woman who was his mate to come through the door.

Her soft gentle voice came to his ears from the adjoining nursery room. The soft cooing sounds she made for his child caused his chest to swell. He sighed with pleasure.

His mind's eye thought back for a moment to another time when he had tried to deny the feelings he had held for this woman, but quickly these thoughts flew. There was no denying now what he felt in his heart. She was his, belonging completely to him, heart and soul.

Her light footfalls brought his attention back to the doorway. The candlelight silhouetted her outline as she entered the room; the man's heart beat to a rapid tattoo. Her fleecy, translucent gown left little to his imagination, as his eyes boldly raked over her form.

She stood for a few seconds as though sensing his mood, but she was not one to stay still for long. Reaching up, she brought the gown over her head and let it fall in a soft wisp to the floor.

Slowly she glided over the small space from the door to the large, fourposter bed, all temptress and woman now that she was alone with her man. All thoughts of being a mother and mistress of a large plantation were gone from her mind as her blue eyes took in his power-ful body eager for her own.

Fire seemed to burn like molten liquid through his loins as her eyes went from his toes to his dark hair and then returned to his yellow eyes, staring, seeming to convey an open promise. "Come to me, wench." He reached out for her silken skin, his voice a husky vibration coming from deep within his chest and sending chills of anticipation over woman's body.

Her body had the feel and taste of the sweetest ambrosia to him and he marveled that after all of this time he still felt as though he could not get enough of this woman. It was each time, as it had been that first night so long ago on Martinique, the only difference now being that he could prolong his desires, knowing that she belonged fully to him.

A delicious contented purr sounded from her lips as she lay down in his waiting arms. "Aye, my lord, here I am and forever shall I stay. Love me."

"Forever and all time." His lips descended boldly.

Martinique

The man stood sober and reflective, one arm braced against the window siding, his light-blue eyes staring out of the pane of glass and slowly taking in the lush beauty that was displayed before him.

Before him the branches of a huge tree rose up to the roof of the two-story house. His mind, for a second, went back in time to another night when he had climbed those very branches in search of the woman who had touched his heart. That same night had been the beginning of his life.

He sighed softly, his features relaxed, his eyes now and then glanced about the room as though watching for a presence to enter the bedchamber.

As his senses were filled with the tropical, heady scents which were brought through the open window by the light stirring breeze, he thought of the times in past years when he had doubted that he would ever again see his island paradise.

It seemed as though only yesterday, instead of two years past, that he had stood on the deck of the *Sea Wind* with Chastity at his side and looked on as Martinique had appeared out of the ocean's blue depths. He could feel now inside his chest the feeling of elation he had felt at that time. He was once again coming home.

After almost twenty years of being a slave on a foreign ship and away from all he loved, he had stood in a quiet, breathless pose, holding tightly to Chastity's hand.

The first part of his everyday dreams aboard that cruel, slave ship had been fulfilled; he had found Chastity Blackthorn and, beyond belief, she had not changed in the slightest. It was as though she had awakened from a long, tormenting sleep. But on finding her, he had also changed her name from Blackthorn to Saxon as he had wished to do from the first time he had set eyes on her, years ago at the Blackthorn town house in New Orleans. He had learned, when he was in Europe, that his wife, Nicole, had died of a heart ailment so he had not waited long after finding Chastity before he made her his bride. On their wedding day they had sailed away from New Orleans, headed for Martinique.

A slight sound of movement brought the man back from the past and he glanced sharply around the room. The candlelight was dim, only one being lit, but with a quick eye he had seen the outline of a shapely leg being drawn in through the netting over the bed. On silent, pantherlike feet, he stood next to the bed and spied the outlined form of his wife.

He slowly sat down upon the side of the bed and began to pull his breeches down his legs.

"Are you not tired, my love?" Light, lingering fingers as soft as the sheerest wisp of Chantilly lace caressed his strong, bronzed back.

"Nay, Chastity." His voice was soft, but his hands were bold as they brought his wife up tightly in his embrace. As he inhaled deeply of this woman's hair, his senses now were filled with a sweeter fragrance than the flowers which abounded outside.

She herself seemed more than content to be held against that strong chest. To be content, she needed no more from life than to have this man by her side.

Theirs was not the fiery, consuming loving that it had been in their youth, but as Deke lowered his wife upon the soft mattress and his eyes looked deep into her own, he knew that this was where all of his dreams were held. In the very depths of her being she held all that he would ever need. "You are my heart, my desire, my life, and all that I have ever wished for, love," he softly breathed, his hand gently caressing her cheek.

Tears came easily to Chastity's emerald eyes, for these words so nearly expressed her own feelings. She clutched him tightly to her, pressing her body to his. "I also love you. There is no meaning without you."

Her voice touched something deep within Deke's heart. "Never again will you be without me. I promise you this, my love."

Chastity's smile filled his vision. She knew that he would never leave her again. She regarded the past as a bad nightmare. What she now kept in the front of her mind was their future. "Forever shall we stay together."

"Aye, forever, my love."

HISTORICAL ROMANCE AT ITS BEST!

EXCITING BESTSELLERS FROM ZEBRA

LEATHER AND LACE

#1: THE LAVENDER BLOSSOM (1029, $2.50)
by Dorothy Dixon
Lavender Younger galloped across the Wild West under the black banner of Quantrill. And as the outlaw beauty robbed men of their riches, she robbed them of their hearts!

#2: THE TREMBLING HEART (1035, $2.50)
by Dorothy Dixon
Wherever Jesse James rode, Zerelda rode at his side. And from the sleet of winter to the radiance of fall, she nursed his wounds—and risked her life to be loved by the most reckless outlaw of the west!

#3: THE BELLE OF THE RIO GRANDE (1059, $2.50)
by Dorothy Dixon
Belle Star blazed her way through the wild frontier with two ambitions: to win the heart of handsome Cole Younger, the only man who could satisfy her fiery passion—and to be known as the west's most luscious outlaw!

#4: FLAME OF THE WEST (1091, $2.50)
by Dorothy Dixon
She was the toast of the New York stage, a spy during the Civil War, and the belle of the Barbary Coast. And her passionate untamed spirit made her the unforgettable legend known as the FLAME OF THE WEST!

#5: CIMARRON ROSE (1106, $2.50)
by Dorothy Dixon
Cimarron Rose lost her heart on sight to the notoriously handsome outlaw "Bitter Creek" Newcombe. She rode with the infamous Billie Doolin gang, and if she had to lie, steal, cheat or kill, she would—to keep the only man she ever really loved!

#6: HONEYSUCKLE LOVE (1125, $2.50)
by Carolyn T. Armstrong
When Honeysuckle and Buck met, desire spread like wildfire. She left her home and family to ride the countryside—and risk her life—for the rapture of love!

#7: DIAMOND QUEEN (1138, $2.50)
by Dorothy Dixon
Alice was a seductive beauty whose gambler's intuition made her a frontier legend. And for Alice, the most arousing game of all was life—where the stakes were high and the winner took all!

Available wherever paperbacks are sold, or order direct from the Publisher. Send cover price plus 50¢ per copy for mailing and handling to Zebra Books, 475 Park Avenue South, New York, N.Y. 10016. DO NOT SEND CASH.